# The Ill-Made Mute

THE BITTERBYNDE TRILOGY:

BOOK 1: *The Ill-Made Mute*

BOOK 2: *The Lady of the Sorrows*

(available in 2002)

BOOK 3: *The Battle of Evernight*

(available in 2003)

The Bitterbynde · Book I

# The Ill-Made Mute

Cecilia Dart-Thornton

MACMILLAN

First published 2001 by Warner Books, Inc., New York

First published in Great Britian 2001 by Macmillan
an imprint of Pan Macmillan Ltd
Pan Macmillan, 20 New Wharf Road, London N1 9RR
Basingstoke and Oxford
Associated companies throughout the world
www.panmacmillan.com

ISBN 0 333 90753 1



1 3 5 7 9 8 6 4 2

A CIP catalogue record for this book is available from the British Library.

Printed and bound in Great Britain by
Mackays of Chatham plc, Chatham, Kent

For my beloved parents,
My wonderful husband, and my entire extended family,
For my friend, author Paul Witcover,
For Betsy Mitchell and Martha Millard,
And for Lizzie, who was the manuscript's first reader.

**Cecilia**
**Dart-Thornton**

# CONTENTS

# The Ill-Made Mute

# The Known Countries of Erith

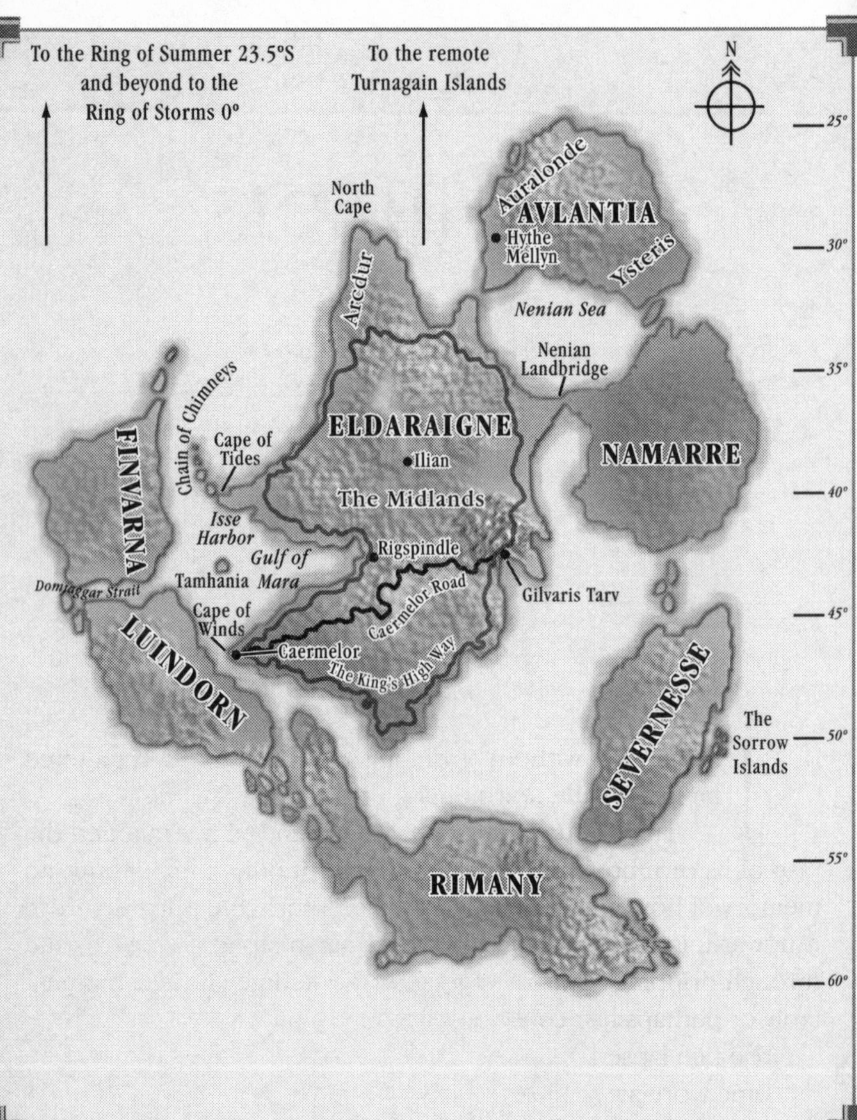

To the Ring of Summer 23.5°S and beyond to the Ring of Storms 0°
To the remote Turnagain Islands
N
25°
30°
35°
40°
45°
50°
55°
60°
North Cape
Auralonde
AVLANTIA
Hythe Mellyn
Ysteris
Arcedur
Nenian Sea
Nenian Landbridge
Chain of Chimneys
FINVARNA
Cape of Tides
ELDARAIGNE
Ilian
The Midlands
NAMARRE
Isse Harbor
Gulf of Mara
Rigspindle
Tamhania
Domjaggar Strait
Cape of Winds
Caermelor Road
Gilvaris Tarv
LUINDORN
Caermelor
The King's High Way
SEVERNESSE
The Sorrow Islands
RIMANY

# 1
# FOUNDING

*Speechless, castaway, and wry, a spellbound oddity am I.*
*My feet are planted in the clay, my gaze is locked upon the sky.*

FROM THE TALITH SONG "YEARNING FOR FLIGHT"

The rain was without beginning and without end. It pattered on incessantly, a drumming of impatient fingers.

The creature knew only the sound of the rain and the rasp of its own breathing. It had no concept of its own identity, no memory of how it had come to this place. Inchoate purpose drove it upward, in darkness. Over levels of harsh stone it crawled, and through dripping claws of vegetation. Sometimes it slept momentarily or perhaps lost consciousness.

The rain lapsed.

Time wore away.

With stiffening limbs the nameless creature moved on. Reaching level ground, it now rose onto trembling legs and walked. Thought-fragments whirled like dead leaves inside its skull.

The ground emptied from beneath its feet. It hurtled downward, to be brought up on a spear-point of agony. A band around its arm had snagged on a projection. The scrawny thing dangled against the cliff face, slowly swinging like bait on a hook.

Then slowly, with great effort, it lifted its other arm. Bird-boned fingers found the catch and released it. The band sprang open and the creature fell.

Had it landed on the rocks, it would have been killed—a kinder fate—but it finished, instead, facedown in a green thicket of *Hedera paradoxis.* Stealthily the juices of the poisonous leaves ate into its face while it lay there for hours, insensate. When it awoke it was too weak to scream. It used its last energies to crawl from the toxic bushes and lie frozen in the morning sunlight, its now ghastly face turned up to the sky.

A benison of warmth began to creep into the chilled flesh, seeping into the very marrow of the bones. Detached, as though it viewed itself from afar, the creature felt its jaws being forced open, inhaled the steamy aroma of warm broth, and sipped instinctively. The sweet, rich liquid coursed inward, spreading waves of flowing warmth. The creature sipped again, then fell back, exhausted.

As its body attempted to normalize, its thoughts briefly coalesced. It held tightly to the one idea that did not spin away: the awareness that for as long as it could remember, its eyelids had been shut. It tried to open them but could not. It tried again and, before being sucked back into unconsciousness, stared briefly into the face of an old woman whose wisps of white hair stuck out like spiders' legs from beneath a stained wimple.

There followed millennia or days or minutes of warm, foggy half-sleep interspersed with waking to drink, to stare again at that face bound in its net of wrinkles and to feel the first very faint glimmerings of strength returning to its wasted body. Recognition evolved, too, of walls, of rough blankets and a straw pallet on the stone-flagged floor beside the heat-source—the mighty, iron-mouthed furnace that combusted night and day. The creature's face felt numb and itchy. And as senses returned, it must endure the sour stench of the blankets.

Stokers entered the room, fed the hungering furnace with sweetmeats of wood, clanged the iron door shut, raised their voices accusingly at one another, then went away. Children with malt-brown hair came and stared, keeping their distance.

The white-haired crone fed some broth to her charge and spoke to it in incomprehensible syllables. It stared back at her, wincing as she lifted it, blankets and all, and carried it into a small room. Beneath the peelings of bedding the creature was clad in filthy rags. The old woman stripped it naked before lowering it into a bath of tepid water. Wonderingly, it looked down at its own skeletal frame, floating like some pale, elongated fish, and perceived a person, with arms and legs like the crone but much younger. The crone was doing something to its hair, which it couldn't see—washing it in a separate container behind the bath, lathering the hair thoroughly with scented soaps, rinsing again and again.

The woman dressed the rescuee in garments of a nondescript sepia hue—thick breeches, long-sleeved gipon, and thigh-length doublet corded at the waist. There was a heavy, pointed hood with a wide gorget that was allowed to hang down behind the shoulders, leaving the head bare. About the creature's neck, beneath the gorget, she strung a leather thong tied to a rowan-wood charm crudely carved in the shape of a rooster. The bathed one sat, obediently, cross-legged while gnarled hands combed the short hair dry.

Bewildered, feeble, it lifted its scrawny hand to its head and felt the short stubble there. Its spindly fingers wandered to its face, where there was no sensation other than slight irritation. They found there grotesque lumps and swellings: a knobbed, jutting forehead, thick lips, an asymmetrical cauliflower of a nose, cheeks like bags of acorns. Tears filled its eyes, but its benefactress, chattering gummily to herself, seemed oblivious of its agony of humiliation.

Time organized itself into days and nights.

The days organized themselves around eating, dozing, and the exhausting minutiae of existence.

The spider-haired woman jabbed a stubby thumb at herself.

"Grethet," she repeated. Apparently she had discovered her charge was not deaf.

Instantly grateful for this first attempt at communication, it opened its mouth to respond.

No sound came forth.

Its jaw hung slack, a crater of hollow disbelief—it had simply forgotten, or had never known, how to make speech. Frantically it searched its memories. It was then that the fist of despair slammed into the foundling.

There were *no memories*.

None at all.

The thing, pale and debilitated, stared into hot iron darkness for half the night. To its dismay, it could dredge up no recollection of a past and was unable to evoke its own name, if name it had ever possessed.

As days passed in bewilderment, meaningless sounds began to metamorphose into half-comprehended words—communications among other people. Although still confused, the newcomer compared their raiment with that which Grethet had put on him and concluded that its own sex was male. This was an identity, no matter how generalized, to be grasped and held secure, a solid fact in a morass of uncertainty.

He also discovered that he was unwelcome.

Despite his inability to guess or understand more than half of what they were saying, it was not difficult for the misshapen youth to recognize the despisal, contempt, and hatred of the people among whom he dwelled. He huddled into a smaller bony heap in the furnace room corner when children spat at him. They thought him too repulsive to be approached, or they would have pinched him, as indeed they slyly pinched one another. Men and women generally ignored him. When they noticed him, they ranted coldly at Grethet, who appeared unconcerned. Sometimes, as if in self-defense, she would point out the stranger's hair for their inspection. The apparent importance of his hair, he could not fathom. It seemed that she was tough, this old woman; they could not sway her. However, her frail patient had no illusions that she nurtured any love for him—she was kind, in a callous way, and he owed her his life, but all her actions were in the long term self-serving. To act selfishly, as the youth learned, was the way to survive in this place.

What *was* this place? The youth knew little of it beyond the windowless furnace room with its huge wood-stack, where translucent spiders concealed themselves with only their claw-tips showing in rows of four. The black walls of this chamber were rough-hewn blocks of rock; they sparkled with tiny silver points where they caught the firelight. One corner of the room held the hefty iron fire-tongs, pokers, and other implements with which Grethet poked the fire after the men stoked it, several times a day.

Men here wore the drab surcoat belted at the waist, the thick breeches stuffed into boots, and the oddly heavy hood that was left to hang down behind the shoulders. Their wood-brown hair was cut short. Some were bearded. They disregarded the stranger as they ignored the other crawling things scrambling out of the fuel or unwisely hiding in it, to be later incinerated, curling in silent agony like dried leaves in the flames.

The children would poke at the wood-heap, disturbing insects and arachnids that scuttled crazily across the floor. Curiously emotionless, the brats stamped in a frenzied dance—when they had finished, a random design of smashed cephalothoraxes and carapaces remained, like pressed orchids, scarcely visible on the black stone floor with its shining flecks.

Truly, the lesser creatures had little chance.

Most of the time, Grethet was elsewhere. She would appear briefly to tend the fire, sometimes bringing food, abruptly leaning close to her ward to whisper, so that he shrank from her stinking breath.

"Boy," she would always say, "you, boy. You do as I say. It is better."

The youth in his weakness was grateful to be left alone, to lie in the warmth, feeling the pounding of the ravening heart in his birdcage chest; drifting in and out of exhausted, dreamless sleep.

He had been discovered, like a babe, with eyes shuttered against the world; this finding was the foundation of his aliveness. But unlike a babe, he was gifted with more than raw, untutored instinct—his body remembered, if his mind did not. A wide, if basic, world-understanding was patterned there, so that he comprehended heat and cold, high and low, light and dark—if not the word-sounds that symbolized them—without having to experiment. He recognized that a frown or a sneer, a suddenly engorged vein at the temples, or a tautened jaw boded a forthcoming kick or blow; he could walk and work and feed himself as though he were normal, as though he were one of them. But he was not one of them. A huge piece was missing: the sum of a past.

Without memories he was merely an automated husk.

Some nights the youth half woke, with tingling sensations making a racetrack of his spine and standing his hair to attention. Some days that same surge charged the air, rousing the blood like strong liquor. These crispate experiences generally dissipated after an hour or so, and as time dragged on, he became accustomed to them and did not think on them any further. They were a phenomenon that issued from Outside, and Outside was, for now, beyond his reach.

But oh, it beckoned—and sounds came to his ears from Outside—voices, the distant silver fanfare of trumpets, shouting, the heavy tread of boots, the barking of dogs, and often, very often, the clatter of hooves on faceted planes of black stone that sparkled like a star-pricked sky.

One night, awakened by one such commotion, he crept on trembling legs into an adjoining storeroom. Through a thin slot of a window in the thick stone wall he glimpsed a round, red-gold moon. And for an instant he thought he saw an impossible silhouette flying across the bright face of it.

Soon—too soon for the nameless youth's liking or well-being—his benefactress decided he was fit enough to work at light tasks. She hustled him out of his pile of blankets and set him to sweeping floors, helping in the laundries, and cleaning the various ingenious instruments of lighting that had accumulated in this place over the years—brass candlesticks and chamber-sticks, candle-snuffers, wax-jacks, bougie boxes, wick-trimmers, douters, candle-boxes, and lamps.

His legs trembled constantly, and sometimes he nearly fainted with the effort. Fatigue and unfamiliarity made him slow—at whiles, Grethet lost patience and cuffed him. The first time it happened, he was greatly shocked and stared at her in horror, his thick lips wordlessly mouthing protestations. At this an expression of guilt flashed across her face, chased by a look of ruthlessness, and she cuffed him again, harder.

As day followed day like a queue of weary gray beggars, he became accustomed to her light, stinging blows and abusive tone, but alone at night he sometimes wept silently for want of love.

Nourished by food, sleep, and warmth, he began to gain strength as time passed. With strength came more understanding of the words employed by the other servants living and working within these dark walls. He "spoke" with the loveless Grethet, employing simple, universally obvious gestures.

"Hide yourself," she would nag. "Maimed boy, you are. Wrap yourself and they won't see."

*How did I come to this place?* he wanted to know, and, *Who am I?*

But he was unable to concoct a way of inquiring. Nonetheless, by keeping his eyes and ears keen he learned other things.

One law he learned first.

Miserable, stooped with weariness, he swept lint from the floors of the laundries. Steam imbued the air with breathless humidity. He pushed his taltry off his damp head for just a few moments of relief, but as he drew breath to sigh, a staff cracked down on his shoulder. He flinched but could not cry out.

"Taltry on . . . head!" screamed the chief laundress, her face empurpled as a ripe plum. "Never . . . off, understand?"

The wearing of the taltry hood was not merely a rule. To disobey it was a crime, punishable by beatings and deprivations. He must wear the heavy hood at all times, tied at the neck. It did not seem as important to wear it indoors, but outdoors was a different matter.

Later, Grethet took him aside and pointed to a slit of a window.

"Outside," she pronounced in the simplified language she used for him, "outside. When outside, wear hood. Always." She took him by the shoulders and shook him to emphasize the instructions. Working the drawstring of his hood, she compounded the ordeal by half strangling him. "Tie tightly," she hissed. "Like this."

The boy had examined his plain, mud-colored taltry closely, finding the reason for its peculiar heaviness. Between the outer cloth and the lining was a fine, metal chain mesh that could be felt through the cloth. Its purpose eluded him.

In the course of discharging his limited indoor employment, his toil in dark halls and cramped storerooms, the foundling came to understand in greater measure the vast and complex structure in whose understories he dwelt.

Grethet sent him to one of the kitchens to fetch bread. As he entered the fragrant, smoking cavern, one of the underbutlers spied him and emitted a yell of rage. By this time, the unnamed lad had become accustomed to loud vociferations of indignation accompanying his arrival anywhere. It had become part of his education.

"Get it out of here!" shouted the underbutler, brandishing a ladle. "It's not allowed in the kitchens!"

As the lad was being chased down the passageway, he overheard a couple of scullery maids attempting to stifle their giggles.

"Its ugliness might cause Cook to faint into the soup," said one.

"Such an accident might add flavor," her companion retorted.

His appearance might have prevented his entry into some areas, but there were plenty of other tasks to be undertaken indoors.

Simply polishing the brass door fittings consumed much effort. There were knobs and handles, lock-plates and chased escutcheon plates embellished with the zigzag lightning insignia, engraved lock-covers, door-hinges and beaten copper fingerplates and cast-iron doorstops in the shape of coats of arms. Sometimes, with a sinking heart, the polisher caught sight of a monstrous visage leering at him from the convex surfaces of the burnished doorknobs and recognized his own reflection.

When Grethet suspected him of possessing a few moments of idle time, she would rattle off lists of occupations with which he might amuse himself. Unfortunately, by this time he understood her well enough.

"Furbish the bronze wall-sconces!" she would cry. "Wax the aumbries! Scrub the flagstones! Clean the second-best silver, sweep soot and cinders out of the fireplaces, and black the grates!"

He fetched, carried, and scoured. He rubbed whiting on the moon-bright trays, salvers, and elegant handbells with which the higher-ranking servants were summoned.

Once, lost in the labyrinth of passageways and stairs, the nameless lad found himself intruding upon a hitherto unexplored level of his prison-home. He had ventured higher than usual, climbing an unfamiliar stair. To his astonishment he gained the last step to see before him a corridor hung with finery, lit by the rich, golden glow of filigree lamps.

Massive rectangles of fabric covered the stone walls from floor to ceiling. Across them blazed spectacular scenes of forests, mountains, battles, gardens—scenes the lad recognized with that primeval instinct, but which he could not recall ever having beheld. On closer inspection, he perceived that the landscapes were in fact composed of countless tiny stitches in colored threads.

A voice from farther along the corridor jolted him into a panic. He sensed he should not be here, guessed he would be punished severely if caught. There was no time to dash back to the stair-head. Softly he sidestepped behind the nearest tapestry, flattening himself against the cold stone of the wall.

Two men strolled leisurely into view. Their raiment was simple in design but sewn of sumptuous fabrics. The first, clad in black velvet edged with silver, was pontificating to the second, who wore brocade in the colors of a Summer sunset.

". . . lower third of the structure," he expounded, "which is occupied by the servants, was long ago hewn from a massive bulwark of living rock. Those levels are riddled with natural caves and tunnels extended by excavation, while the upper levels, reserved exclusively for us, are constructed of huge blocks of dominite mined out from those diggings. Internal and external stairways spiral their way between the multiple levels, but of course we of the House only travel in the lift-cages."

"What are the stairways for, then?" asked the second man, demonstrating remarkable obtuseness. Magnanimously, the first lord gushed on, gesturing with his pale hands, while the menial behind the tapestry trembled in his rags.

"The servants are arranged according to a complicated hierarchy. The lower ranks, being forbidden to ride up and down between levels in the busy lift-shafts, must needs use the stairways, which reach the ground at exits near the domestic goat caves. Forbidden to trespass in the higher regions of the Tower, they pursue their drudgeries out of sight of their betters. Only the higher echelons of servant are permitted to personally serve the lords and ladies of the Tower. They use the upper stairs or, on rare occasions, the lift-cages."

He cleared his throat.

"You, my dear peddler, who visit Isse Tower from regions rife with warm underground springs, will be interested to discover how our bathwater is heated for the Relayers and our scented ladies."

"Mmph," was the grunted response.

"All heating here on the upper floors is achieved by means of an ingenious furnace."

"Extraordinary," mumbled the orange guest.

"Extraordinary? But no," contradicted the black-and-silver lord. "Isse Tower is, after all, the chief stronghold of an ancient and powerful dynasty second only to royalty. We of the Seventh House of the Stormriders deserve only superlative service for our creature comforts!"

"Which no doubt is well earned, as compensation for being forced to dwell in such an island as this," said the visitor somewhat sourly, "surrounded as you are by wights and wilderness. No doubt you and your servants are rarely able to leave the Tower, or never, unless you go with a well-guarded caravan."

"On the contrary, we come and go on the sky-roads as we please," cried the other. "And what matter the servants? It does them good. They are safe here, and well fed—too well fed for the paltry amount of work they do, the lazy gluttons. What need have they to wander?"

Their voices had begun to fade, indicating to the cringing eavesdropper that they had turned around and were pacing away from him. As the conversation died to a whisper, he peeped around the fringed border of the tapestry. The aristocrat and the visiting merchant had indeed vacated the corridor. Instantly the lad darted from his haven and hurtled down the stairs.

But he was not to be so easily reoriented. Frantically, he searched through the lower level for some passageway or gallery he knew. He felt certain the first person he met would redirect him to Floor Five as ungently as possible, but he preferred to try finding his own way—which was why, when he heard an approaching voice for the second time, he concealed himself once more. This time he slid into a dim niche in the wall, between two stone ribs supporting arched vaults.

The figure that wandered into view was that of Mad Mullet, the compost-hauler. His job was to carry vegetable scraps from the kitchens down to the ground. There he blended them with animal dung to form a scrumptious medley for the use of the kitchen-gardeners.

His approach was usually heralded by his odor, and by the curious rambling monologue he voiced wherever he went—a monologue that was barely intelligible at the best of times. As he ranted, he drooled. He was, as his nickname suggested, mad. However, being proud of bearing and regular of feature, he was quite comely to look at, and thus rated higher in the servants' hierarchy than the deformed lad—not that Mad Mullet cared one whit.

Orating, chanting, and singing in a queer high-pitched tone, Mad Mullet passed quite close by the place where the lad crouched, endeavoring to resemble a grotesque carving decorating the wall. The lad noted that the eyes of Mad Mullet appeared unfocused, blank, as if fixed on some distant object that none but lunatics could discern.

On tiptoe, the lad followed him.

Mad Mullet was sometimes wont to frequent the furnace levels. He might lead the way back to Floor Five.

Through the worm-ways went the two, and Mad Mullet never looked back, nor did his step falter. He led the way, but not where the lad had hoped. Without warning, a gust of pure, cold air buffeted the two. Light broke on them like a blue crystal, and they emerged upon a stone-flagged balcony as vast and sheer as the floor of the ballroom.

For the first time, the lad was Outside.

In his awe, he momentarily forgot that he was trying to keep his presence hidden from Mad Mullet. Stumbling to the edge, he gazed out to the horizon, cramming his memory with the scene. When it was filled he looked down, then from left to right, and at last he turned his head and craned upward to discover what loomed above.

Built at the sea's edge, the dominite fortress, black and glistening, towered more than forty stories straight up above the canopy of the surrounding forest. A soaring pile crowned with turrets, battlements, chimneys, and slender watchtowers, the fortress was defined by walled demesnes flanked on one side by a harbor and on the other by a sea of trees.

Balconies randomly toothed the sheer outer walls. Footed by jutting platforms leading nowhere, several arched gateways, set at varying altitudes, faced the four points of the compass. High above ground level, at the seventh story, the circumference of the structure suddenly narrowed on the western side like a giant stair, creating a wide, flat shelf that ended in midair. No parapet or balustrade enclosed this space—instead, a row of iron-capped bollards, evenly spaced, lined the edge. Below, the outer walls of the Tower dropped precipitously—the lad reckoned it was more than a hundred feet—to the ground.

It was here, on this brink, that he was standing.

As he woke to that fact, he woke also to the proximity of the madman beside him. But in the next instant Mad Mullet was no longer at his side, for with a clear cry of "I can fly!" he had stepped joyously from the platform and plummeted to his death.

As the lad later overheard, such "flights" were no uncommon occurrence.

# 2
# THE HOUSE OF THE STORMRIDERS
## Tale and Travail

*Unremembered, yesterday is extinct.*
*Without yesterday, today has no meaning.*
*Who are you, if forgotten?*
*Who are you, but the sum of your memories?*

ERTISH SAYING

Despite being immured within the dark, airless, walled spaces of the Tower, despite the fact that he was badly informed and struggling to comprehend his plight, the foundling came to understand that in some way the existence of Stormrider Houses revolved around horses. The sound of horses echoed from unexpected directions in the dominite cavities, the warm scent of them wafted suddenly to the nostrils from Outside, along with a thicker, avian odor as of caged birds. Horses were hoisted up and down the towers in lift-cages, and horses were kept in stalls in the upper stories. When he began Outside work, the newest and most lowly menial of the House was able to divine their purpose.

One morning the foundling was sent Outside to a balcony, to trounce the dust from floor-rugs. Flat-based cumulus clouds floated tranquilly like latherings of soap bubbles on invisible water, their frayed rims gilded by the dawn. Viewed from high on the balcony, the clouds were almost at eye level. This was the first time the boy had ventured into the open air, and excitement made him shiver.

Leaning over the battlements and looking far down, he could see the demesnes laid out like a map—the kitchen gardens, the neglected flower gardens, the stables and training yards, the wizard's hall, and bits of the rutted road between the trees that overhung it. Horses roamed the meadows, hattocking tracks, training yards, and stables below. They all seemed to be burdened with pairs of panniers slung on either side of their flanks, but what those baskets contained, the watcher could not tell from a distance.

On the other side, a wide, flat expanse of water—Isse Harbor, shimmering like rose-and-gold silk in the morning. From the shore projected a pier on marble stanchions, reaching far out into the bay, with docks and wharves set at intervals along its length. Still standing firm after uncounted centuries, Isse Harbor's wharves had proved a marvel of engineering, a reminder of the lost skills of glorious days long past. Here anchored Waterships of the sea—splendid lily-winged birds of the deep, come from the outland runs to roost at this haven, if only for a while. They brought tidings and trade, their cargo was rich with barrels of pickled meats, fat flavescent cheeses, bales of cloth, sacks of flour and beans, casks of wines and spirits. There were stone jars brimming with honey, preserved and dried fruits, salt meat, sainfoin, stockfeed, leather, pots and porringers, pitchers and porcelain, fragrances, essences, spices, saffron, scrim, shabrack, musk, muslin, madder, purpurin, talmigold, tragacanth, wax, and all other manner of provisions.

The youth's goggling eyes traveled to the north and west. Here, wooded hills rolled gently away to a horizon wrapped in a niveous haze. Beneath the innocent roof of leaves, it was said, roamed all manner of eldritch wights both seelie and unseelie, but although the boy searched, he could see no sign of such incarnations. He had heard that a haunted crater-lake lay nearby to the northwest, and to the east, two miles from the sea, a puzzle most curious—the ancient remains of a Watership, its back broken, wedged in a cleft between two hills. Were such a legend true, the Empire of Erith must indeed be wondrous and perilous.

A satin scarf of a breeze floated up from the forest. In the south, gulls circumaviated Isse Harbor. Dust motes swarmed from the patterned rugs as the youth beat them, causing him paroxysms of sneezing. Reeling, he leaned against the parapet to recover. At that moment his watering eyes saw a sight that assured him he had sneezed his wits out through his nostrils.

At first it seemed to him that high and far off the dark shape of a large bird—an eagle or an albatross—was flying out of the sky in the southeast. Yet, as it approached, the silhouette resolved itself into the shape of a winged horse and rider galloping through powder-puff clouds toward the fortress. The youth blinked and shook his head. A second look cleared any doubt that the vision not only existed, but was closing in rapidly. The rider's head was the skull of a monster, or else he wore a winged helmet with a faceplate. Saddlebags bulged behind his thighs; his cloak billowed. The bird-horse moved fast, but with a strange and unnatural gait, placing its hooves with quick, mathematical precision just below the clouds' condensation level, simultaneously beating its wings in long, graceful arcs.

Sagging against the parapet, the foundling stared. Blood drained from his head. Almost, he fainted. Surely the world must be turned upside down if a horse possessed wings to fly! As he gaped, looking like some rooftop gargoyle, a fanfare issued from a silver trumpet on the ramparts, cleaving the morning air with long, ringing notes. The aerial cavalier reached an upper story of the fortress and entered in at a platform jutting from the outer wall. His heart jumping like a scared rabbit, the youth sank to his bony knees. Then, recalling his task and how he would be beaten more vigorously than the carpet if he were discovered idling, he hastily returned to pounding mats, invoking dust, and sneezing.

Now at last he could make sense of the term he had heard so often—"eotaur." The word referred to the mighty, horned Skyhorses, the pride of the Stormriders. And it was not the last marvel he was to discover.

Being shunned and ignored was not without its advantages. It meant that the lad was able to go about the mazy ways of the Tower largely unnoticed. He began to ascertain that insignificance was, in many ways, advantageous to his education.

In one instance, he had managed to elude Grethet and find an unobtrusive pantry-nook to doze in, when he was roused by a sound like the cooing of two doves. Within earshot a chambermaid was seated on a cider-barrel, her young child nestling on her lap. The two were conversing.

". . . brought news from Namarre," said the mother softly. "I heard one of the upper-level chambermaids say so."

"Where is Namarre?" asked the child, snuggling her downy head closer to her mother's shoulder.

"It is very far away."

"The eotaurs must be truly strong, to be able to gallop from very far away."

The mother shook her head. "Even the greatest among them has not the strength to come all the way from Namarre without resting. Letters and other air cargo must be relayed. Isse Tower is a Relay Station."

"What is a Relay Station?"

"One of the staging posts where inland and outland runs meet. At Relay Stations, incoming mounts and Relayers interchange with fresh couriers. Messages and payloads are transferred."

"Oh," said the child, sounding disappointed. "Are there many Stations? But I thought Isse Tower was important."

"Of course it is important. It is part of a network of Relay Stations and Interchange Turrets. They are the crossroads for communications networks spanning the countries of the world, far above the perils of land roads."

The child digested these facts in silence. Presently she said, "And Stormriders—they are the most important lords in all of Erith, are they not? Aside from the King-Emperor, I mean."

"They are aristocrats, yes," replied the mother, caressing the child's hair. "But there are other nobles at the court of the King-Emperor who are considered to be equally as important. Yet, hush now, for we must not talk so about our betters."

By now the foundling had learned that the Stormriders were indeed peers of the realm—an exclusive caste born and trained to become masters of their profession. Without them, messages could not be Relayed. Without them, valuable small cargoes could not be forwarded across the country, among cities, mining-towns, and larger villages. The Stormriders' trade was exacting, he knew, and it belonged exclusively to the twelve Houses.

However, the fact that his masters traversed the skies of Erith meant very little to the new servant-lad. Between the mortar of daily drudgery and the pestle of pain, life went grinding on. There was no shortage of provender in the Tower, but he did not receive a great deal of it. His ration, although insignificant, was often withheld or stolen. Emptiness always pinched at his insides, like tiny clockwork crabs.

Some of his fellow servitors shunned the nameless lad. Most ignored him. A few nursed a strong antipathy to him. No matter how obedient he showed himself, no matter how hard he tried to please, they discovered fault. These punished and bullied him continually; he feared them with every fiber of his being. When they came near, he shriveled and trembled to his bones. There was no appeal against their abuse and the pain they inflicted; it had to be endured, that was all. He became accustomed to the constant tenderness of flesh brought on by bruising and the cuts that occurred when he fell or was thrown against some unforgiving object.

Because it seemed obvious that the newcomer was a half-wit, no effort was made to communicate with him, let alone teach him. None offered kindness, save for the daughter of the Keeper of the Keys, who was powerless to help him substantially.

Her name was Caitri, and she was very young—perhaps twelve Summers old. She had encountered him once when he was at his work—waxing the aumbries and weeping, so that the wax mingled with his tears. She, like the rest, had at first recoiled from his ugliness—yet, after the shock of first sight, she looked upon him anew, and her gaze softened as though she viewed him not as a deformed idiot, but as an injured animal in need of succor.

"Why do you weep?" she asked. He could only shake his head. She perceived the way his belly hollowed beneath his tunic, and sometimes she brought him hunches of stale bread or withered apples. She was the only one who ever really talked to him. It was she who explained to him about Windships, the majestic vessels that sailed the skies and sometimes berthed at Isse Tower.

However, Caitri's duties kept her away from Floor Five most of the time, and he met her infrequently, only accidentally.

Over time, by way of eavesdropping and osmosis and rare acts of kindness, the youth learned more from those who lorded him. Most of it he gleaned in the evenings, for that was when the servants would often gather and tell stories. In this way the unworthiest among them began to discover the nature of the perilous and wondrous world beyond the Tower.

The servants' kitchen, Floor Five, was a spicery of sage and wood-smoke. Evening brought tranquillity to the bustling chamber. Fireplaces big enough to roast an ox glowed with the last of the day's incandescence. In the chimney corner leaned one of the battered straw targets that, when soaked with water, was used to shield the spit-boys from the fierce heat of the fires. Lamps flickered with a dandelion light, describing various implements: copper pans, stoneware jars—gray hens and gotches, skeins of thyme and lemongrass, garlic, hams, onions, turnips, and cheeses hanging like comestible jewelry from blackened roof beams. Beside a set of scales, an empty one-gallon blackjack stood on a wooden bench, its leather seams reinforced with brass mounts and studs. Brass mote-skimmers, basting ladles with handles over a yard long, ale-mullers, and skillets dangled against the walls. Someone had left a warming-pan sticking out of a copper-bound wooden bucket. Caudle cups, posset pots, and pipkins lined up on a shelf beside a gristmill and a meat mincer. Alongside brass chamber-sticks, their candles dripping yellow tallow in turgid formations, the table supported several pitted pewter tankards and a large brown spike-pot with a miniature spike-pot mounted in its domed lid.

Shadows distorted themselves into uncanny shapes. Dogs and small capuchin monkeys sprawled before the open hearth, scratching their fleas. Like restless bees, scullery maids, flunkeys, cooks, and a few children congregated in buzzing groups, drinking from wooden porringers of steaming spike-leaf and medlure. The thin figure that slipped in at the far door and huddled in the corner beside a food-hutch went unnoticed, being among grotesque shadow-shapes of its own ilk.

Softly, a sweet young voice was singing some kind of incomprehensible lullaby:

> Sweven, sweven, sooth and winly,
> Blithely sing I leoth, by rike.
> Hightly hast thou my este,
> Mere leofost.

The song ended. As the chief cellar-keeper cleared his throat and spat precursively into the fire, an expectant hush settled over those assembled. Brand Brinkworth held the respected and well-deserved position of oldest and best Storyteller at Isse Tower. As a jongleur, he had traveled Beyond; his own life and adventures had already passed into legend, and he still wore about his neck the copper torque shaped like a snake—his most prized possession, the sigil of a bard, a lore-master.

Many traditional gestes had been passed down through the generations, and newer ones had been imported to the Tower by sailors, aeronauts, and outland road-caravaners. Most had been relished many times without losing their savor and garnished a little more with each recounting.

Stories of Beyond were, more often than not, stories of eldritch wights. Yarns were told about wights of the seelie kind, who wished mortals well and even gave them supernatural help or who merely used them as targets for their harmless mischief. Then there were the tales of unseelie things—wicked, fell wights of eldritch, the protagonists of nightmares.

Those were dark tales.

"Speaking of unseelie wights," began Brinkworth, which he had not been doing, "did I ever give out about the time the Each Uisge happened by Lake Corrievreckan?"

The servants shuddered.

The stories described many different types of waterhorses haunting the lakes and rivers, the pools and oceans of Erith, but of all of them, the Each Uisge was the most ferocious and dangerous.

It was one of the most notorious of all the unseelie creatures that frequented the watery places, although the Glastyn was almost as bad. Sometimes the Each Uisge appeared as a handsome young man, but usually it took the form of a bonny, dapper horse that virtually invited mortals to ride it. Once on its back, no rider could tear himself off, for its skin was imbued with a supernatural stickiness. If anyone was so foolish as to mount, he was carried with a breakneck rush into the nearest lake and torn to pieces. Only some of his innards would be discarded, to wash up later on the shore.

The occupants of the kitchen waited. They had heard the tale of Corrievreckan before but never tired of it. Besides, Brinkworth with his succinct style had a way of refreshing it so that it came to his audience like news each time.

"'Tis a very old story—I cannot say how old, maybe a thousand years—but true nonetheless," said the old man, scratching his knee where one of the hounds' fleas had bitten him. "Young Iainh and Caelinh Maghrain, twin sons of the Chieftain of the Western Isles of Finvarna at that time, were hunting with their comrades when they saw a magnificent horse grazing near Lake Corrievreckan."

"Where is that?" interrupted a grizzled stoker.

"In the Western Isles, cloth-ears, in Finvarna," hissed a butterymaid. "Do you not listen?"

"I thought the Each Uisge dwelled in Eldaraigne."

"It roams anywhere it pleases," said Brand Brinkworth. "Who shall gainsay such a wicked lord of eldritch? Now if you don't mind, I'll be on with the tale."

The other servants shot black looks at the stoker from beneath lowered brows. The stoker nodded nonchalantly, and the Storyteller continued.

"They saw a magnificent horse grazing near Lake Corrievreckan," he repeated, and as his pleasant old voice lilted on, there unfolded in the minds of the listeners a place far off in time and space, a landscape they would never see.

A white pearl shone like an eye in a hazy sky. The sun was past its zenith, sinking toward a wintry horizon. It cast a pale gleam over the waters of the lake. The entire surface was lightly striated with long ripples, shimmering in silken shades of gray. Through a frayed rent in the clouds, a crescent moon rode like a ghostly canoe, translucent. A flock of birds crossed the sky in a long, trailing V-formation. Their cries threaded down the wind—wild ducks returning home.

Dead trees reached their black and twisted limbs out of the waters, and near the shore, long water-grasses bowed before the breeze, their tips bending to touch their own trembling reflections. Tiny glitters winked in and out across the wavelets. The play of light and shadow masked the realm that lay beneath the lake. Nothing could be seen of the swaying weeds, the landscapes of sand and stone, the dark crevasses, any shapes that might, or might not, move deep beneath the water.

As the wild ducks passed into the distance, the tranquillity of the lake was interrupted. Faint at first, then louder, yells and laughter could be heard from the eastern shore. A band of Ertishmen was approaching.

Eight of them came striding along, and their long, tangled hair was as red as sunset. They were accompanied by dogs, retrievers wagging feathery tails. Baldrics were slung across the shoulders of the men, quivers were on their backs and longbows in their hands. At the belts of some swung a brace of fowl, tied by the feet. Already they had had a successful day's hunting. Buoyed by success, they were in high spirits. This last foray to the eastern shores of the lake was considered no more than a jaunt—they did not intend to hunt seriously, as was evidenced by the noise they were raising. They chaffed and bantered, teasing one another, sparring as they went along. All of them were young men, hale and strong—indeed, the youngest was only a boy.

"*Sciobtha,* Padraigh," laughed the two eldest, slapping him on the back as he ran to keep up, *"ta ocras orm! Tu faighim moran bia!"* The looks of the two Maghrain brothers were striking—tall, copper-haired twins in the leather kilts and heavy gold torcs of Finvarnan aristocracy. Their grins were wide and frequent, a flash of white across their brown faces.

*"Ambarcaim! Ambarcaim!"* Padraigh shouted suddenly, pointing to the black and leafless alders leaning at the lake's edge. The men halted and turned their heads.

A shadow moved there. Or was it a shadow?

Gracefully, with arched neck, the stallion came walking out from among the trees. Clean were his lines, and well molded; long and lean his legs, finely tapered his frame. He had the build of a champion racehorse in its prime. His coat was sleek and glossy as the water of the lake, oil-black but highlighted with silver gray where the sun's diffuse glow caught the sliding of the muscles. Clearly, here was a horse to outrace the wind.

The men stood, watching in silent awe. The creature tossed his beautiful head, sending his mane flying like spume. He too stood still for a moment, then demurely, almost coquettishly, began to walk toward the huntsmen. The stallion seemed unconcerned by their presence, not frightened at all, but friendly and tame. They were able to go right up to him—he did not shy away but allowed them to stroke the midnight mane and marvel at the grand height of him, the sheer perfection of his contours and the power implicit therein.

Then, in their own Ertish language, Iainh Maghrain spoke huskily, from the back of his throat.

"That is the finest steed in Aia," he said, "and I shall ride him."

His brother threw him a swift, hard glance. "I, too," he said immediately, not to be bettered.

Fearless, these two—and competitive. It did not enter their heads that appearances might be deceptive.

"Easy now, easy, *alainn capall dubh,*" said Iainh, caressing the elegant arch of the neck. The stallion stood as steady as a cornerstone, almost as though he were *encouraging* a rider to mount. His eyes were limpid pools, fringed with lashes as a pool is fringed with reeds.

But young Padraigh was wary.

"Don't do it, Iainh," he said. "See how the hounds droop their tails and slink away? They are afraid of him, for all that he is so fine." Indeed, the retrievers were cowering in the shelter of a clump of tall rocks at the lake's edge, a hundred yards away.

The brothers paid no heed to the youngster's warning. In a trice, Iainh had vaulted up on the horse's back, and in the next instant Caelinh was up behind him. Still, the stallion appeared unperturbed. At the touch of Iainh's boot-heel he trotted amicably in a circle.

"The fine one is as quiet as a lamb!" cried their comrades. "Hey, make room for us—why should you two be having all the fun?"

One by one the other youths mounted. Like all Ertishmen, they were proficient horsemen and had been able to ride bareback since they could walk. They sprang with ease onto the stallion's back. Meanwhile Padraigh hung back cautiously—prompted by some inner caution, he had decided to be last.

It seemed apparent, as he watched each man jump up, that no space would be left for the next. Yet each time a new rider took his place, there was still enough room for another. Padraigh's eyes strayed to the horse's croup. Something unusual about it disturbed him. He thought that under the satin hide, the bones of the skeleton were shifting in an odd way, and the sinews were—the only way to describe it was *lengthening*.

The last of his comrades leaped onto the horse. Now seven were seated there, laughing, jesting, and beckoning to him from atop the friendly steed.

"Come on, Padraigh *mo reigh,*" they cried. "Get up and let's see how he gallops!"

A flash of understanding scorched the boy's brain.

In horror, Padraigh realized that the horse had grown longer to fit all its riders. Utter terror seized him, and his voice choked in his own gullet. Too frightened to scream a warning, he ran to the lofty boulders that stood at the lake's edge and concealed himself among them, with the cringing dogs.

Black against the silver-gray ripples of the lake, the horse turned its long head. It looked toward the rocks. Dark lips curled back from teeth as square as tombstones. An utterance issued like fumes from that aperture.

"Come along, snotty-nose, do not be left behind!" A voice to corrode iron—cold, unforgiving, appalling.

The boy did not move.

The seven mounted men abruptly fell silent.

Then the horse came after Padraigh among the boulders, dodging this way and that, flinging the riders from side to side, and all the while they were screaming, unable to tear their hands off its back. Back and forth they ducked about among the monoliths, and the hounds fled, howling, and Padraigh's stricken gasps tore at his chest like claws, and the pounding of his heart thundered in his skull as if his brain would burst; but the boy in his desperation proved too nimble for the Each Uisge. At last it gave up and tossed its stormy mane, and with a snort like laughter it dived into the lake and under the waters.

The last echo of their screams hung over the place where the men had vanished. Padraigh stared at the ripples spreading slowly from that center. He was shaking so violently that he could scarcely stand. Sweat dripped from his brow, but his flesh was cold as a fish's.

He listened.

Nothing reached his ears but the fading staccato plaint of plovers on the wing, the sough of the wind bending the long water-grasses until their tips kissed their own reflections, and the *lap, lap* of wavelets licking the shore.

When the white sun sank into the mists on the edge of the world, he was there still, his face bloodless; listening, unmoving.

"The seven youths were never seen again," concluded the Storyteller, leaning back.

"Let storms blow hard and wolves for flesh howl on!" a porter expleted fervently. Similar sentiments gripped the entire kitchen.

"What about the next morning?" persisted a wide-eyed pot-boy, perversely fascinated with the tale's usual grisly ending.

"The clan went down to the lake at *uhta,*" said Brinkworth, "the hour before dawn. They found the boy, living but unable to speak. Some dark shapes were washing to and fro in the shallow margins of the shingle. When they went near to see what they were, they found human livers, five of them, torn and bloody."

"What became of the other two?"

"Nobody kens."

This narrative having been discussed and gravely pronounced upon by all, another took his turn to speak; a belligerent kitchen-gardener with a clever tongue who was always vying for a position in the storytelling echelons.

"Well, I heard of a lass what escaped the Each Uisge," he argued. "In the south of Luindorn there was a farmer what had a large herd of cattle."

"Luindorn now," commented the stoker obstinately.

"Yes, Luindorn," the kitchen-gardener confirmed, glaring. "And one day a round-eared calf was born amongst them. Well, he did not know what this meant, so he asked a woman what dwelled nearby—she was a carlin—and she said that it were a calf of a *water-bull*. It were lucky to have such a calf, she said, but it must be kept apart from the other cattle for seven years and fed with the milk from three different cows, each day. This farmer did as how she had told him.

"Some years later, one of his servant-lasses was down by the lake, keeping an eye on the cattle as they grazed. A young man came up to her, a tall, handsome lad with long dark hair and a winsome smile. She had never seen him before, but she was struck by his good looks."

The gardener's listeners nodded wisely.

"'Fair damsel,' says he, 'will you do a favor for me?' She, very much flattered by his attention, says that she will. 'My hair is so matted and tangled,' says he, 'I thought a charming maid like you might have clever fingers enough to straighten it for me, for surely I am at a loss.'

"'Of course, good sir,' says the lass, and she seats herself on the grass with the young man's head on her lap and proceeds to part and comb his hair with her fingers. But suddenly she freezes with fear, for what does she spy growing amongst his hair but green waterweed! Then she knew that he was no man of Erith but the terrible Each Uisge himself!"

On cue, the audience gasped.

"Woe the while!" they murmured. "O strange day and night!"

"She came to her senses at last and did not jump or cry out, but sat very still so as not to disturb him and lulled him to sleep with her combings, all the while craving deliverance. When she saw that he was indeed sleeping, she carefully untied her apron strings and worked her way out from under the head, then swiftly and silently she ran for home as fast as she could go.

"But before she reached the gate she heard, hard at her heels, a thundering sound of hooves. The Each Uisge was coming for her, and his rage was dreadful!"

The servants shuddered.

"'Loose the water-bull!' cried the carlin, and the farmer, seeing what was about, did so. Just as the Each Uisge was about to seize the maiden and take her under the lake to be devoured, the water-bull came bellowing and charging between them. The two creatures fought each other all the way back to the lake and under the waters. The Each Uisge was never seen again at that lake, but the mauled body of the faithful water-bull was washed ashore next morning."

A sigh swept the servants' kitchen, like the passing of a Summer breeze.

"Water-bulls be good wights," boldly squeaked a junior page. "My nuncle said there were water-cattle blood in his herd, and there were always milk a-plenty."

"Aye," said a cellarman knowingly. "'Tis true that seelie wights such as water-bulls do not wantonly injure folk the way unseelie wights do, and they reward anyone who does them a kindness. Some of them be helpful and some be just pranksters, but mark you, they too will readily revenge any insult or injury and can cause great destruction."

"Them duergars is some of the worst and most malicious order of unseelie things," said a scullion.

"Aye," echoed old Brand Brinkworth, "a sailor who came here last year on the *Pride of Severnesse* has a cousin who lives in the hills of northern Severnesse, and he knows of a fellow on his way to Riothbury what lost himself on the hills when the night came on."

The servants pricked up their ears. They huddled closer together as the old man conjured a vision of a place far beyond the black-beamed kitchen and the cold stone walls of the Tower. The old man's voice softly filled the night.

"O viper vile!" cried the scullery maids when the tale was ended, clutching each other in delicious horror.

At this display of sensibility Rennet Thighbone, a greasy-haired cook, snarled, "Fie, wenches!" and blew his nose on his sleeve. Old Brinkworth stretched his arms until they cracked and downed a draft of medlure, but he was not to be left in peace.

"Tell us more tales of the King-Emperor in Caermelor, and of his wizard, Sargoth the Cowled!"

"No, tell us a story of the Greayte Cities in the glorious days of old."

"Tonight," intoned Brand, unruffled, unswayed, "I will tell one more tale—the tale of the beautiful maiden who slept for a hundred years under an enchantment, until she was woken by a prince's kiss."

"Beauty, always beauty," whined a peevish skivvy.

"By cock and pie! Nobody wishes to hear a tale about an ugly maiden," her companion retorted.

"That's why they've never made a story about you," another added. He was thanked with a shove.

The Storyteller wove the words and embroidered the tale's fabric according to his way, casting his own wizardly enchantment over his audience. And when the story was finished it made a mantle that covered them all and held them together for a time. The Keeper of the Keys sawed mournfully on her fiddle, and her daughter, Caitri, sang an old song of Eldaraigne, a ballad from days of yore when the Icemen used to sail from Rimany to raid the southern villages of the Feorhkind and the great wizard Lammath had overthrown the enemy at Saralainn Vale:

Oh, the fountains were frozen in Saralainn Vale
And the mountains of Sarn were on fire,
And the leaves blew like streaks down the dusty old streets
And the wind in the valley rose higher,
When down to the glen came four hundred men
While the rest of the village was sleeping,
And the light from their blades glittered bright through the glades
And the cruel kiss of ice was their greeting.
Behold the grim Icemen so pale and so bold!
Beware of their frostblades that glitter with cold!
But I saw them come and right swift did I run

Till I came to where Lammath was lying
"The Icemen are here!" I cried out in fear,
"And the folk of the village are dying!"
Then Lammath he rose and he put on his clothes
And he kindled a torch from the embers,
Saying, "I have a plan that I learned from a man
With such wisdom as no one remembers."
Behind him I strode as through darkness he rode,
And the Icemen he met in the dawning
As the sun's first flare turned to gold in their hair.
I cried out to Lammath in warning,
But the torch he held high drew the light from the sky
Flaring out with a terrible power,
And it turned them to stone and to ash and cold bone
All in that cold morning hour,
As the morning sun started to flower,
All around Saralainn Tower.
"Oh, Lammath," I said, "what price have you paid
For the power of light against shadow?"
But he smiled with his eyes and they held no surprise
As he walked with me down to the meadow.
And I thought it might seem it had all been a dream,
Except for the ice on the fountains,
And the leaves in the street and the dust on my feet,
And the fires that burned on the mountains.

Singing along drowsily, the servants fell asleep, and a disharmony of snores jarred the kitchen.

There would be other nights, other songs and tales. . . .

The lad was intrigued: What powered the Tower's lifts? How was water pumped up hundreds of feet of internal conduits to make possible life in the tall fortress? How could eotaurs lift themselves into the skies? Indeed, they were fine-boned horses, lean and sharp as swords, but surely even such powerful wings would not suffice to raise them. More puzzling yet—what was it that elevated the huge bulk of Windships?

Eventually he discovered the truth.

Their reputations among their peers being neither trifling nor illustrious, the newcomer ought to have guessed that the serving-lads Spatchwort and Sheepshorn would gift him with trouble—and perhaps he did, but as the saying went, When the ship's a wreck, what's one more storm? Yet when he chanced to overhear them whispering together, his curiosity mastered him.

"Ustorix will bribe the treasury guards tonight."

"How many and of what purity?"

"Two, of alt four hundred. He says there is no activity scheduled for Gate South Four Hundred at moonrise. We meet there."

At night, nothing much lit the winding internal stairways except moon and stars slicing pale light-blades through slits in the thick dominite walls. The servants all lived below Floor Fourteen, but for someone who was used to effacing himself, melting into shadows and doorways at the first hint of approaching torchlight, it was not difficult to reach Floor Twenty-six unnoticed.

Gate South Four Hundred stood open, its portcullis upraised. The floor of the gatehall formed a road that went out to the edge of the jutting doorsill and ended abruptly there, hard against the night sky. Far below, beneath a wispy cloud-layer at two hundred feet, pocket-handkerchief horse-yards and orchards gave on to a carpet of forest.

On each squadron level, alcoves and vestibules led off the gate-halls to either side, filled with an array of equipment for Stormrider Relayers and their steeds. These entrance rooms opened onto wide corridors that circumnavigated the fortress's walls and rejoined themselves. The floor of these circuits was strewn with straw, for this was where the strappers walked the Skyhorses to cool them down after a long, hot ride.

Hidden among racks of saddles and tack beside a lift-shaft, the eavesdropper was able to glimpse a pattern of silver constellations on an ebony backdrop, dominated by a pale ship of a moon surfing cloud breakers. Somewhere in the dank and secret courses of the walls, water hammered in the pipes, or perhaps something else was pounding in there.

The festoons of lead-ropes, saddles, saddlebags, stirrups,

surcingles and girths, reins, bits and bridles, martingales, cruppers, and breastplates about his ears were disturbed only by a scuttling of serpiginous rock-lizards that were in the habit of basking daily on the outer walls. Cool air brushed the back of his hand like lily-petals.

Three youths entered the gatehalls silently, two of them pulling their taltries up over their heads and tightening the draw-strings. They carried a horn lantern. The third was clad richly in black velvet edged with silver braid, colors denoting a Son of the Seventh House, for he was the heir of the Storm Chieftain. The noble youth wore a high-collared doublet, belted at the middle; full sleeves were slashed to show a lining of gleaming jet satin beneath a cloak that swung to meet turned-down boots just below the knees. Relayer uniform besported a V-shaped embroidery from shoulder to waist to shoulder in the colors of the House, and epaulets starred to indicate squadron status. The belt buckle was cast in the form of the zigzag Stormrider device, which, with its motto, *"Arnath Lan Seren"*—some relic of a dead language—was also emblazoned on the left side of the chest, over the heart. Two daggers were slung from his belt, in ornamented sheaths, black leather embossed with silver. The young lord's long, walnut-brown hair was combed smoothly back and bound tightly into a club with cords of black and silver. His taltry, thrown back daringly, was edged with tiny diadems like the glints in dominite rock and sported a sable plume. Shining boots rang on stone as he approached the gate and carefully unwrapped a heavy package he carried, a blue metal box whose lid he opened. Two lustrous ingots gleamed dully in moonlight.

Grod Sheepshorn, a lanky servant-lad with a receding chin, laughed nervously in his throat.

"Go on, Spatchwort," he said to his friend, "you be first since you are the clever one."

"It matters not who is first."

So saying, Lord Ustorix tossed the silvery bars over the edge of the platform, out into the chasm of night.

From behind distant mountains the moon continued to rise,

the stars slid imperceptibly across black glass. To the south, ink-dark waters stretched to the head of the bay. The sound of waves on the shore far below was carried upward on a salt wind. Horses nickered faintly, and hooves drummed in the meadows. The two silvery bars hung motionless, four hundred feet off the ground, level with the doorsill's rock shelving.

"Pure alt four hundred sildron ingots, I see," said Grod Sheepshorn with an exaggerated bow to his superior. "Enough to forge hoof-crescents for half a squadron! Worth a gold piece or two to the guards for the borrowing, eh, my lord?"

"Worth none of your business," the aristocrat said coldly. "Let's see you boys perform, now."

"First the wager," demanded Tren Spatchwort. He stood half a head shorter than Sheepshorn, wiry and lithe.

"One gold eagle each if you do it. Nothing if you don't. Maybe a broken neck."

"Wha— one eagle?" stammered Spatchwort. "But my lord said three!"

Ustorix rounded on the menial, teetering on the edge of civility.

"Well do I recall the agreement. One for the first attempt, two for the second."

"But there was nothing said about a second—" Sheepshorn broke off and turned away. When he turned back, he was grinning. The grin did not reach his eyes. He bowed stiffly.

"Is my life worth twenty shillings?" He laughed. "Hey for two sovereigns! My lord knows that we can do the trick once, twice, countless times! For us it is easy! True, Spatchwort?"

The smaller youth nodded uneasily.

Sheepshorn flung off his cloak. Measured strides brought him to the back wall of the gatehall. With a lunge, he broke into a run, straight toward the gate, where the sildron bars hung side by side several feet from the edge. His soft boots made no noise on the dominite floor. There would be no noise as his body hurtled down through four hundred feet of space—perhaps a slight disturbance when it encountered the ground below. The nameless watcher seized a martingale and gripped it fiercely. Having reached the platform, the servant-boy flung himself out and up. His leap brought him to the hovering bars. His feet planted firmly, one on each bar, the boy skated through the air, leaning back slightly, carried by his own momentum. It was a daring act, an act of great skill—for a second, as he slowed, he teetered on the brink of losing balance and life, caught it again, and stopped.

His friend Spatchwort whistled nervously through his teeth. Ustorix said nothing.

Squatting on his precarious perch, Sheepshorn tied the sildron bars to his boots. When he stood, he grinned again with his eyes—posed, poised like a dancer.

"Now look at me!" he crowed softly, so softly, on the breeze. Noise would bring discovery. "I can walk on the air, like a wizard."

A rush of exhilaration had accompanied success. His confidence rose. Lifting a boot, he took a careful step, then another, almost swaggering. Lightly he bobbed in nothingness as he returned to the doorsill and simply stumped back inside.

Blandly, Lord Ustorix handed over the gold coin to the erstwhile performer, who, suddenly conscious of finishing an entertaining display in style, swept him a deep and ingratiating bow. Perhaps his cynicism was lost on the noble youth; perhaps not. Ustorix showed no sign.

The sildron ingots having been untied and returned to their gravity-defying position in space, it was Spatchwort's turn. Moonlight accentuated the two gray wells of eyes in his pale face as he made his run. He stumbled before reaching the platform but recovered well to make the leap, and like Sheepshorn before him, he gained foothold and glided away as if on some invisible cushion. Triumphant, he slowed to a halt and fished a rope out of his pocket to tie on the bars so that he could walk. Then he looked down.

Presently the young lord called in a low tone, "Playing statues is not part of the game. This bores me." He drew out a dagger and started cleaning his fingernails with it.

"Tie them on, Tren, just tie them on," came Sheepshorn's urgent whisper.

After a minute, the boy in the air moved. He moved as if he were made of crystal and the dark were a tightening vise.

He moved, and he fell.

* * *

The hidden watcher caught his breath. A dislodged stirrup clattered to the floor near his shoulder, but the noble and the servant made no response. Spatchwort had caught hold of a sildron bar as he fell and now hung there by one hand. He simply hung, as if he had no strength or will left. An image of his own recent past formed in the watcher's mind. Sheepshorn pulled a coil of rope from a wall-hook, unwinding it rapidly.

"Catch hold when I throw to you," he called. As he prepared to throw, Ustorix took the rope out of his hands and tossed the entire coil out the gate.

"What are you doing?" Sheepshorn's face blazed with anger and disbelief.

"Let him hang there awhile longer. Give him a chance to prove himself by pulling himself up on top of the bar."

"No one could do that. It is not possible. The ingot is too small."

"Imagine if the unstorm came now and blew off his taltry." Ustorix smiled. "What a joke! They wouldn't want to use this gate for a thousand years!"

Sheepshorn grabbed a second rope and held firmly to it, tossing one end out toward the dangling figure. Spatchwort reached for it but missed. At the second try he caught it, and Sheepshorn reeled him in like a fish. Ustorix was laughing silently. Spatchwort collapsed, trembling, on the floor. Sheepshorn lassoed the hovering ingot and drew it in.

"You didn't succeed," said the Son of the House, regaining his customary coolness, "so you haven't earned your reward. This time. However, you have another chance."

"How gracious of you, my lord," replied Sheepshorn with eyes of flint.

Lord Ustorix drew two rectangular plates of a dull blue metal from his cloak and clipped them onto the upper surfaces of the sildron ingots. The container for sildron had been made from the same stuff.

"Andalum!" cried Sheepshorn. "Not andalum!"

"Hush—do you desire discovery? This will be easy for you, as you boasted. It is no more difficult than what you have just done, and it will earn you two more gold eagles each. I want to see it."

"But if we should somersault, if the andalum should come between the sildron and the ground, we should fall." Sheepshorn opened his hands palms up in a gesture of honest astonishment.

"Of course you would, but it shall not happen—why should it?"

"My lord, we have never practiced with real sildron before, as you know." An edge of real fear had crept into the servant's voice. "We have only practiced with wheelboards, and with ice in Winter. What we have done is no mean feat. But to do it with an andalum surface could be suicide. We never agreed to this."

Ustorix shrugged. "I will leave now."

"No, wait." Sheepshorn licked his lips nervously. His eyes were very bright, as bright as coins.

"Cur, you do not honor me sufficiently," hissed Ustorix, now irritable.

"I am sorry, my lord—prithee wait, my lord. I will do this."

Ustorix threw the ingots into the air. One came down and settled at its usual height, about two inches above the floor. The other crashed on the floor, the blue side facing down. He flipped it over casually and pushed them both out of the gate. They hovered. Sheepshorn walked to the back wall. He prepared to run, to build up speed for that final leap off the ledge.

To fall four hundred feet would take four and a half heartbeats, but it would seem longer until, accelerating to meet the cobblestones at 980 miles per hour, the descending note of a scream was cut off. This realization apparently illuminated Sheepshorn. He softly swore an oath and propped, shuddering, against the wall.

Ustorix shrugged.

Cramp seized the eavesdropper's leg, and he shifted minimally. The forgotten stirrup, by his foot, rang against stone. Heads turned.

"Methinks I heard a sound there before."

Crouched, heart pounding, the nameless one saw them draw back the curtains of harness and tack, peering down at him.

"What is this?" Ustorix's tone dripped with the acid of disgust.

Spatchwort uneasily choked out, "It's an ill-made thing that goes about with one of the menials, my lord. A half-wit and a mute."

"From whence?"

"They say he's a peddler's son who was caught in a cave-in near Huntingtowers during that tremor in Autumn, or else some servant's get, abandoned on the road."

"What's it doing here, spying on us? Hey, Poxface, what do you think you're doing? Come out of there."

As the discovered youth scrambled to obey, the lift-shaft rattled. In its remote depths, a cage began to ascend shakily. But before it hove into view, a deep voice boomed through the gatehall. Breathing hard, two men stood at the top of the stairwell—the dun-robed Chief Steward of the Household and the Master at Swords, cloaked in scarlet.

"Damn my eyes," uttered the former quizzically.

"What brings *you* here, my lord Ustorix?" inquired Mortier, Master at Swords. "Do these louts trouble you? Something fell to the courtyard below this gate, and voices were heard up here. Others follow now, to investigate."

Ustorix paused a moment before replying. He eyed the spy reflectively.

"My dear teacher, this creature here has stolen sildron from the treasury. Two of my servants discovered him, but instead of returning the sildron, they decided to play games with it. I was about to put a stop to all that when one of the common, blood-beggared scoundrels elected to try and kill himself."

"Commendable action on your part, my lord, I'm certain your father will be proud to hear it."

The Master at Swords bowed graciously. The lift-cage rose up in the shaft and bumped to a stop. The lift-keeper pulled back the folding iron grid, and several men strode forth. Mortier peered more closely at the disfigured youth.

"Most interesting," he murmured nasally. "I was not aware of this boy. Take him away. Assuredly he shall be well punished."

And he was.

He had known what Grethet, his keeper, would say:

"Who beat you? Did they see you? Did they see it is not only your face that is so repulsive?"

Early, she had informed him of the loathliness of his flesh. He had gone to great pains to conceal the skinny frame from which he himself now always averted his gaze, but in the end they had not bothered to uncover more than his back and shoulders for the whipping. A severe lashing, it cut deep and bloodily. The wounds began to weep and brought on a fever.

For weeks he lay ill in the darkness of the candle-store, with only the spiders to hear his moans of agony. Grethet would come in to wash his wounds with herbal decoctions and impatiently pour water into the parched and choking well of his mouth. In his delirium he thought himself trapped in the stories he had heard in the servants' kitchens, his liver being torn out over and over beneath some lonely mere, drowning in his own blood.

Eventually he recovered, but the scars remained.

When a Windship was due in before dawn, he used to creep out of a crumbling window and seat himself upon a narrow roof-gutter, buffeted by the breeze. In that hour, the ground and trees were black. The eastern horizon, between dark gray shoals of clouds, was singed brownish orange like burnt toast, fading to the palest lemon farther up the sky, blending to dilute, ethereal blue, which in turn shaded gradually to the deep, rich hue of the night sky overhead, still dark, still hung with stars.

Beyond Isse Harbor, along the world's edge, the auburn singe deepened.

Birds uttered uneasy, sporadic sounds from the trees and the duck-pond far below. Their quacks and trills increased in proportion to the strength of the iron glow in the east, whose warm facade was smudged by cloud floatlets as a smith's ruddy countenance is smirched by soot and ash. Above, the profound blue drained from the sky and the stars dissolved.

Burnt orange transmuted to pastel gold. A surprising ribbon of rose pink unrolled. Against the horizon, lacy foliage was pricked by unbearable motes of gold. The sea turned from black to gray green. A line of fire ran along the world's rim, and the sun rose, to slide away from the ground, a silver coin through the wolf-gray clouds. Out of the south, half on fire, a sailing ship would come dipping and gliding through the air.

The world depended on the properties of sildron for many purposes.

Eotaurs' beautiful swanlike wings were used mainly for maneuvering, the species having been bred, over hundreds of years, from the original tiny bird-horses to a ridable size. However, their greater bulk now required sildron to become airborne. Sildron, like magnetized iron, possessed invisible properties so strange and powerful that it seemed almost eldritch.

Diverse cargoes were brought from the outlands by Waterships. Some were destined for the Tower, others must travel farther inland. At Isse Harbor, freightage that was too large or inexpensive or heavy for thoroughbred Skyhorses was offloaded to heavily guarded road-cart caravans or hauled up on ropes to the Windship Dock 112 feet above ground level, at the seventh story. There it was loaded onto the mighty sildron-raised vessels. Eotaurs and carrier pigeons were not the only sky-travelers to come and go at the Tower, although they were the swiftest. The grandest of all, the Windships had the capacity to carry passengers and large cargoes.

The wind bellied their sails as it did for any Watership, but swaying treetops were their waves, birds their fish, mountains their reefs, the diurnal pulse of light and dark their tide, and clouds their foam. Sildron gave them lift, sildron pushed against the ground to power their small, unstable propellers.

This silvery metal shod and girded the eotaurs, it lifted and propelled the vessels of the sky. All the wealth of the Windship lines and the status of the twelve Stormrider Houses, the glory, the power, the skills, passed from generation to generation in traditions going back many centuries, all depended upon that most costly and rare of metals, even though it exerted no force against water and could not cross the sea.

It was so precious that it was the property only of kings and nobles. Watching the Windships go by in the skies, the most lowly of servants at Isse Tower often wondered what it would be like to go voyaging in them, up there where the clouds drifted like pillowy featherbeds, their scalloped borders gilded by sunshine, where it seemed that a voyager might sail on without a care, without pain, and the past would not matter.

* * *

His entire history was forgotten, gone without a trace. What took its place, always, was an aching sense of loss. Sometimes, when not too weary to ponder at all, he wondered who it was that peered out from his eyes and listened with his ears. Sometimes he conjectured about who his parents had been and where they might be now, and whether they had abandoned him because he was mute and malformed. Brand Brinkworth had once told of a legendary prince who had longed for the perfect wife and whose wizard had fashioned a maiden for him out of a mass of beautiful flowers. Later, the servants had speculated on one another's origins had they been created from some fleshless material, mostly guessing "weeds" or "dung," and the foundling wondered, in the cold recesses of his reverie, whether such a misfit as he had never been born but had been shaped or raised up out of starless depths by some raving and witless magician.

Often he tried to convey to Grethet the many questions about his beginnings. She seemed unable or unwilling to understand, slapping him away impatiently. He knew only that he was imprisoned here by his need to survive and that in this fantastic Tower he had come among a proud people who scorned excessive displays of joy or sorrow, excitement or fear, but who, beneath the iron bands they imposed, seethed with hidden turmoils.

Taunts and blows made life painful. Loneliness was his only companion. But certain things made it bearable—the sound of the wind crooning in the battlements, the days when vapors blanketed the world far below and he stood on an island in the clouds, the nights when rain pattered on the outer walls, the songs of birds on the morning breeze, the *tok-tok-tok* of the moss-frog whose call was reputed to improve the flavor of cellared wine, the salt sea-breeze tasting of far-off adventures, the sight of the Greayte Southern Star like a green firework burning low in the night sky, the warm, friendly noses of goats, hounds, and capuchins, glimpses of eotaurs and the mighty Windships that crossed the airs, stories told by the kitchen fire.

The stories, too, marked the passing of days and provided vicarious journeys from the sequestered Tower. They were the only way of finding out what it was like in Aia, the world, beyond the demesnes—lifelines to something Beyond.

He wondered: *Will I escape someday, or are the demesnes of the Tower to be my graveyard?*

All the talk was of the wedding to be held at the Tower in Teinemis, the Firemonth. The Lady Persefonae, daughter of Lord Voltasus and Lady Artemisia, was to be married to the young heir of the Fifth House, and the ceremony was to take place only forty-two days after Greatsun Day. The word on the floors below the dock was that the wedding cake was to be decorated with real Sugar shipped from the Turnagain Islands and that a Confectioner was to be flown from Caermelor, the Royal City, specially for the job.

In response to the servants' complaints about the burden of extra work imposed by the forthcoming celebrations, Brand Brinkworth increased the quality and quantity of his evening tales.

He related a cheery account of the lucky and extremely virtuous farmer's wife who would rise up in the morning and find that all her work had been completed for her overnight, finished to perfection—the cows already milked, the hens fed, the butter churned, the house cleaned from top to bottom, and a fire twinkling brightly in the hearth, with a pot of porridge bubbling merrily over it.

"Life went on like this for some time," said the Storyteller, "but then the goodwife became curious to see who was being so kind and helpful. One night she rose from her bed, opened the kitchen door a crack, and peeped through. You can imagine her astonishment when she saw a crowd of busy little bruneys with green caps, sweeping and polishing, making everything spick-and-span. But she noticed that their clothes were rather plain and ragged, and she felt sorry for them, so she spent the next week sewing until she had made splendid new outfits for them all. These she laid out in the kitchen one evening, and that night she rose again from her bed and peeped through the door. Well, those little bruneys were delighted with their new clothes. They put them on at once and danced about with glee, but then with a shout they vanished clean away and the farmer's wife never saw them again."

"Addle-pated woman!" exclaimed a scullery maid. "The first

thing any fool knows about seelie wights is that they mislike being thanked for their good turns. Thanking them with gifts or compliments is taken by them as an insult!"

"Not so," another disagreed. "I'll warrant they vanished because they thought they were too fine, in their new clothes, to do lowly work anymore."

"Now there," said Brinkworth, stroking his beard, "is a matter about which many folk disagree. A bone, one might say, of contention. To thank or not to thank. My own opinion is that by the thanking-gifts, the bruneys knew they had been spied upon. They detest spying as much as any eldritch wight, seelie or otherwise, and that is why they went away."

"Body o' me! If any of them helping-wights ever come here to the Tower, I'll thrash anyone what spies on them or thanks them," declared Rennet Thighbone. "I never get no thanks, and I don't see why tricksy wights should. Anyway, I never seen one in me life, and I reckon it's all just cock-and-bull."

"So ringed is the Tower with rowan, iron, and wizardry," commented Brand Brinkworth, "there's never a minor wight of seelie or unseelie could invade us. That is why you have never seen one, Rennet."

"What I say be no cock-and-bull," said Teron Hoad the ostler, licking his lips. "This be truth."

The kitchen's occupants nervously gathered closer together. Hoad's accounts were famed for their gruesomeness, and they did not want to miss a word. It seemed he felt it his duty to darken the mood if it chanced to become too cheery; for this he had unwittingly acquired the name "Hoad the Toad." Two of his fingers were, inexplicably, missing. He kept them pickled, in a jar—a foible that added to his sinister reputation.

"I speak of the Beulach Beast what used to haunt the Ailagh Pass in Finvarna," the aforesaid ostler began with relish.

"Used to haunt it?"

"Aye. It went away after its blood-search was successful. Only during the night hours it used to be heard, uttering shrieks and howls that chilled the blood of those who heard and made them flee in horror and set them to locking their doors and shutters."

"How was it formed?"

"Sometimes like a man with one leg, sometimes like an ordinary man, sometimes like a greyhound or a fell beast of foul description. Folk dared not venture out after dark in these parts, for the Beast would be always on the prowl. Finally it got what it was after."

He paused for dramatic effect.

"What, Hoad? What?" bleated the listeners. Hoad deliberately looked over his shoulder and lowered his tone confidentially.

"One morning," he said, "a traveler was found dead by the side of the road—pierced by two deep wounds, one in his side and one in his leg. He had a hand pressed to each hurt. It was said that these injuries were too frightful and strange to have been made by a man, and indeed the Beulach Beast must have done it, for it was not seen or heard again at the Ailagh Pass."

"They might have got rid of it, but it will just go somewhere else," commented Thighbone, scraping his callused fingers with a paring-knife. "They'll never get rid of the Buggane what haunts that Great Waterfall near Glyn Rushen."

"That is a water-bull, is it not?" the stoker interjected dubiously.

"Aye. Not a seelie one, my friend, not at all, but a water-bull just the same. It is particularly dangerous and vicious. It lives in the pool right under where the Waterfall drops. Sometimes it is a man, but usually it takes the form of a big black calf what crosses the road and jumps down into the pool with a sound like the rattling of chains."

A lackey shook the chains of the cast-iron stew-pot, and everyone jumped.

"I'll box yer ears for yer, ribald clown!" Thighbone yelled indignantly.

The servants soothed the cook, and eventually he went on with his contribution.

"I heard a story of the Buggane not long ago, from a peddler in the last road-caravan. Seems a girl was working outside her house in Glyn Rushen, which is not far from the Great Waterfall—she was cutting up turnips for the pot, when the Buggane came roaring along in a man's shape, picked her up, slung her over its back, and made off with her towards its home under the pool before anyone had time to save her. But the lass was lucky—she still held in her hand the knife what she had been slicing turnips with. Just as they reached the pool she cut through her apron strings and was able to get free and run home like the wind, all the while in terror thinking the thing was coming behind her."

"That be not unlike one of the tales of the Each Uisge," mused an understeward. "Seems a good idea to wear an apron around the haunts of these water wights."

"You'd look a right gowk in a pinafore," snorted the buttery-maid.

A half-deaf cellarman with crow's-feet engraved at the corners of his eyes now roused himself.

"What about the old Trathley Kow what haunts the village of Trathley, in middle Eldaraigne?" he shouted. "He's a bogie more mischievous than bad, but they'll never see *him* leave."

"On my troth! I hope he never does go," said the understeward. "He's always good for a fine story, the prankster that he is. Always he finishes his jokes with a laugh like a horse's whinny, at the expense of his dupes!"

"I heard a good tale of the Trathley Kow," offered a dimpled chambermaid, "which happened to two young men from a village near Trathley. It being a holiday, they had arranged to meet their sweethearts one afternoon at a stile by Cowslip Lane, but lo and behold, when the lads arrived there they saw their sweethearts across the meadow, walking away. They called out, but the lasses seemed not to hear, so the lads ran after them. On they went, for two or three miles, but although they went as fast as they could the young men could not catch up! They were so mindful of watching their quarry, they did not much look where they were going, and to their dismay they found themselves up to their knees in a muddy bog. At that moment their sweethearts vanished with a loud 'Ha ha!' and there was the Trathley Kow instead. Well, as you can imagine, the lads got themselves free of the muck in a trice and took to their heels at once. That waggish wight pursued them over hill and dale, hooting and mocking them. They had to cross the Shillingswater to get back home, but in their fright they both fell in! They came up covered with weeds and mud, and of course, each took a look at the other and immediately mistook him for the Trathley Kow!"

The chambermaid's audience fought to contain its merriment.

"Go on, go on," begged the stoker, red in the face, his eyes watering.

"Bawling with terror, they fought each other off and ran to their separate homes, each telling a story of having been chased by the Trathley Kow and almost drowned in the Shillingswater!"

The listeners stuffed their fists in their mouths, from whence burst sounds like escaping steam.

"Well," Hoad the Toad interjected darkly, "those foolish lads are fortunate they did not live closer to the mountains."

The mood dampened.

"Why?" piped up a spit-boy dutifully.

"Well, if they went out a-walking like that, the Gwithlion would have had them for sure."

"Ah, the Gwithlion," said Brinkworth, nodding. "Wicked wights they are."

"What do they do, Master Hoad?" inquired the spit-boy.

"Hideous hags they are," said the ostler, "hideouser than old biddy Grethet, if your brain can invent such. They mislead and waylay travelers by night on the mountain roads. Sometimes they take the form of goats. Not content with roaming about in the dark, they even visit the houses of the mountain people, especially in stormy weather, and when the Gwithlion knock at the door, the folk within know they must be greeted hospitably for fear of the harm they might do."

"Yea, but draw a knife against them and they are defeated," observed the wrinkled cellarman loudly. "They do hate the power of cold iron."

"In truth," acknowledged the Toad. "But cold iron and other charms are no help against the greater ones."

At this grim and accurate observation, the kitchen fell silent for a time, until the spit-boy spoke up.

"Now, Master Brinkworth, sir, I have a request for you."

"Ask away."

"Pray tell us of the time the wizard Sargoth sliced the King-

Emperor's jester in two halves and put him back together again and he living still!"

Well aware of the man's skill with a whip, the foundling tried to avoid the Master at Swords. Burial among the servants' catacombs allowed little chance of encountering him: However, if he thought never to see his adversary again, he was mistaken.

Grethet said, "You can go down to help in the stables. You are very lucky. Do you understand? They are short of a stablehand down there. They need a boy to work. You do as you are told. You do not touch the horses unless you are told. The horses are precious. More precious than you. Mind your ways."

So her ward minded his ways and went, for the first time, down to the stables and the eotaur training yards.

It seemed a long age since he had first come to live with the Seventh House of the Stormriders. He did not know how long, although his hair had grown a hand's length until it touched his shoulders. When it fell across his eyes one day, he was astonished to see that its color was gold and hated it at once for being utterly different from the shades of brown around him. From that time onward he always wore the taltry pulled up to cover his head, whether indoors or out.

At mealtimes the fruits and berries of Autumn had given way to the dried-bean pottages of Winter. The Tower had celebrated the Midwinter Imbrol Festival on Littlesun Day, first day of the New Year and of Dorchamis, the Darkmonth. The New Year 1090 had been ushered in with feasts and garlands of holly, bonfires in midnight meadows, and hulking great plum puddings blazing like little suns, little of which the lower menials tasted. The preserved fare of Winter had in turn been replaced by green worts and herbs as the seasons revolved. During all that time, the nameless one had been within walls, above the ground, able to glimpse very little through the attenuated windows of the servants' levels. Now, at last, he was to venture into the demesnes.

The dominite stables adjoining the northern flank of the Tower harbored almost a hundred winged horses. Grooms, trainers, and strappers lived with them, slept with them, watched and tended them at every hour. Capacious storerooms, harness rooms, loose-boxes, exercise tracks, hattocking tracks, and lunging yards bustled daily with their noise. There was a smithy where the farrier plied his trade and workshops for the lorimer and saddler. The pungency of stables was tinged with the odor of a mews. Passing an open door, the youth glimpsed the rumps and tails of a dozen aviquine creatures standing in their stalls. Their well-groomed coats and feathers shone in shades of bay, chestnut, roan, and gray.

That fantastic plumage surely belonged to something beaked, tendril-tongued, and hollow-boned that had hatched out of an egg: an avian creature with a cold round eye, scaled claws, and quick, sharp movements. Instead it stroked the flanks of a round-haunched, hot-breathed mammal, feathered of fetlock and streamlined, certainly, to the utmost degree, but apparently as far removed from a bird as the moon from a loaf of bread.

The sound of steady munching was punctuated occasionally by the stamp of a hoof or the clatter of a rope. On the floor, wisps of straw mingled with horse-feathers. At the far end, a fledgling colt paced restlessly around a loose-box.

To the southwest, the stables overlooked Isse Harbor; to the north lay the green, fenced fields where eotaurs and landhorses grazed. Westward, the orchards. Beyond the acres of fruit-trees stretched the forest, apparently without end.

"You'll be the lad they sent!" called a gruff voice. Keat Featherstone, the second groom, looked him over, nodding his closely shaven head. Light stubble dusted the jawline of a bluff face.

"You be a sorry sight, as they told me. Still, I suppose it be not your fault, and horses don't take fright at ugly faces, thank the Star, or I'd be out of a job by now. They said you don't talk, neither, but that makes you all right by me so long as I don't have to look at you overmuch. I suppose you can polish tack?"

The youth nodded eagerly, willing to please any person who offered a way out of the servants' quarters if only for a few hours, but particularly willing to please the first man who had not spontaneously displayed active hostility toward him.

"Aye. Well, here's the tack room, so go to it. And keep your taltry tied on tight." The second groom rolled his eyes.

* * *

The tack room walls bore an interesting clutter of saddles, bridles, rope halters, and baffling contraptions of leather and iron. Benches were strewn with tools, leather skins, bits of metal, rusty horseshoes, and nails. Horse-brasses cast in the shapes of roosters, daisies, loaves, rowan-berries, and hypericum leaves hung on tanned boars'-hide strips alongside strings of little bells. Canisters and bottles of simple equine physic stood arrayed along a shelf on one wall. Crude labels had been stuck on. Pictures were drawn on them, since most of the stablehands were illiterate, but there was also painstaking lettering that proclaimed the contents to be castor oyl, tarre, magneesya, malanders-oyntmente, jinnjer, and spyryts of wyne. A couple of horn dark-lanterns swung from iron hooks.

In these comfortable surroundings the lad worked hard all morning to please Keat Featherstone, rubbing in the mellow oils and pungent polishes until leather glowed; setting aside whatever needed stitching or replacing; creating order out of chaos caused by strappers who had thrown down tack and other equipment anywhere in their careless haste; picking up, hanging up, arranging, storing, always blending with shadows in case attention should bring the usual vilification. But there were unshuttered windows and an open door through which blew the sound of voices, barking dogs, hooves on the cobbles, metal on metal, seagulls on the wing.

Stableboys hurried in and out and past the windows. Through the doorway, the new polish-boy could see the smithy, its stone floor raised three feet above the andalum lining that spread between the building and the ground—an essential foundation for any place where sildron was worked freely. The high-chimneyed workshop, its windows barred against theft, was roofed with gray slate and shaded by antique chestnut trees, over a hundred feet high, dropping their alabaster flowers like snow. A roan eotaur mare, bronze-winged, was being ushered, unshod, up the ramp—a champion by the sleek, fine-muscled look of her.

A brass horn blared a signal; the fanfare, the lad had learned, that heralded the arrival of a Windship and a cause for excitement.

It was silver for Relayers, bold brass for Windships, the Greayte Conch for Waterships, and the drum tattoo for land approaches.

External hubbub increased. The temporary stablehand craned his neck to get a better view out of the window and up toward the Tower.

She came in over the treetops, her masts, yards, and rigging appearing first. Festooned with a brave display of heraldry, she flew a pennoncel at the masthead, the standard of Eldaraigne at the forecastle, four other banners aft, including the yellow ensign of the Merchant Service, and streamers, thirty yards long, charged with yellow dragons, blue lozenges, and white birds. Her gittons, the small swallow-tailed flags, waved various devices of tyraxes, dragons, and lynxes' heads.

A three-masted barque of the Rhyll-Desson Line, two hundred feet from bowsprit to stern, thirty feet across the beam; her mainmast rose 140 feet above deck. Her figurehead was a flowing-haired woman: the North Wind personified. Four aileroned wings jutted, two on each side of the keel. Wooden propellers whirled on their leading edges. As she neared the wharf on Floor Seven of the House, all sail was rapidly clewed up and furled, for to miscalculate velocity and hit the fortress, even though it was well buttressed, would bring a disaster beyond imagining. A Yeoman Stormrider circled, tossing mooring-lines to deckhands. Anchors were let go overboard to bite into the mooring-yard below the wharf; the tower's dockers leaned out with pikestaffs and grapplers to push her off and pull her in, and with long springy baffles, hooked at either end, that would attach ship to wharf at a safe distance.

Whistles shrilled. The master and mates yelled commands. Aeronauts frantically cranked the onhebbing winch-handles, adjusting chains of andalum plate that slid back and forth between the sildron lining and the outer hull, to negotiate altitude so that ramps could be stretched across the gap for the exchange of cargo; for this was a supply ship from Gilvaris Tarv on her way to Rigspindle. A name was painted on her bows in flowing script—*Dragonfly*. She bobbed lightly, as a ship would in calm waters—shifting weights on board lent her this movement. Small mosses and lichens bedizened her wooden outer hull, where barnacles would have clung on a Watership, and she cast a stupendous shadow over the kitchen gardens.

"She's passing fair, the *Dragonfly,* ain't she!" An uncouth voice shattered the youth's reverie and he started guiltily.

Dain Pennyrigg, a stablehand who ofttimes frequented the servants' kitchen on Floor Five, walked into the harness room. His lively eyes missed nothing. Freckles foxtrotted across a face with a turned-up nose and a wide mouth.

"No need to cower, lad, anyone with half an eye could see you're no shirker."

He paused, a corner of his mouth quirked.

"Don't go bragging that I said so, but you may have done a better job than any lad since I worked in here. Here's a packet of bread and cheese for your meal—Keat Featherstone sent it. The well's around the corner if you're wanting a drink."

The youth knew he would have to go thirsty; others invariably complained of pollution if he drank from a common source.

"You've not been here before, eh, lad?" The eyebrow Dain Pennyrigg cocked was not unkind. The youth shook his head.

"You be always stuck in that dungeon with old mother Grethet. 'Mind your ways now, mind your ways,'" he mimicked, cackling. "Silly old crone. I only go up there to hear the stories. Brinkworth's the best Storyteller hereabouts—better than Hoad the Toad, at any rate. The Toad relishes gloom and darkness—makes it all up—invents characters just so's he can kill 'em off in nasty ways. Lucky if anyone's alive at the end. Now stop your chattering, lad, you're distracting me from my work—Featherstone sent me to take you to your next job. Put away your polishes and follow me."

Tucking the bread and cheese into his wallet, the youth followed, glancing up intensely at the moored Windship floating beside the Tower, now linked to it by wide boarding ramps, mooring-lines, flying foxes, and baffles and swarming with sailors and cargo-handlers. Down in the yards, horses and stablehands trotted to and fro. Shouts mingled with the hammering of iron, the blowing of bellows, the clanking of metal, boots ringing on stone. Gaps between buildings revealed glimpses of long meadows fringed by dark forest whence a westerly breeze brought green perfume and the "tink" of bellbirds. An andalum-lined horse-float clattered past, taking a sildron-shod eotaur to the Tower. Overhead, a whirlpool of Skyhorses cantered in training circuits, and the sun was a goldfish in a blue bowl.

As the two servants crossed the cobbles in front of the smithy, three riders almost mowed them down. They jumped to one side as landhorses squalled past.

"Curse him," growled Pennyrigg, recovering equipoise, "Mortier the arrogant, the sly. Cares nothing. Does anything he pleases—how does he get away with wearing colors instead of trainer's gray?"

The crimson-cloaked Master at Swords with his two attendants cantered around a corner of the stables and out of sight. Ivory chestnut-blossoms swirled in their wake. Pennyrigg was about to speak again when a commotion by the smithy door cut him short.

A gray Skyhorse reared and plunged, wild-eyed, snorting, out of control. Its huge wings thundered at full span with the noise of ten thousand feathers; dust billowed. At the eotaur's hooves crouched a capuchin, one of the small, apelike creatures that were kept as pets. Someone had covered the urchin's hairy, half-armored hide in a decaying leather jerkin. Shrieking stridently, the animal waved its hands, then ran off on all fours toward the nearest chestnut tree, a party of stableboys hard on its heels.

"Cock's passion! How came that vermin here?" bellowed the blacksmith, scarlet-faced, appearing at the doorway brandishing red-hot tongs. Eotaurs were notoriously spooked by capuchins—the smith's enraged blustering exacerbated the situation. The stallion screamed, backing into the wall. Two strappers hung from its rope, but it was too strong for them in its distraction, flinging them aside and breaking loose. Feathers flew.

Hooded men came running from every direction. An eotaur was far too valuable to be allowed to injure itself. The mighty gray pounded blindly down the smithy ramp, heading straight toward Pennyrigg and his obedient follower. Pennyrigg bawled a curse and flung himself aside for the second time in five minutes—his companion reacted from instinct. As the gray passed, he snatched its halter and hung on, was dragged several yards, and slid to a sudden stop.

Steam rising from its trembling flanks, the stallion stood motionless in a dust-haze, snorting like a dragon, its nostrils the color of flame. The great wings remained outstretched, the sun shining through the radiating pinions, frost white.

The youth never took his eyes off the horse. Holding its gaze, he reached up, still holding the halter in one hand, and stroked its girder neck. His fingers combed the coarse mane, traced the small silvery horns protruding from the brow ridges. His breath mingled with its burning exhalations, and he saw one of these amazing creatures closely, for the first time. Avian and equine, the two forms of life fused perfectly. The wings simply grew out of the hide at the withers, a velveted swelling musculature budding into the long arc of bone, down-wrapped, from which blossomed the primaries, the secondaries of flight in a sweeping fan, feather overlapping feather in perfect tessellation down to the pointed tip. The eotaur regarded the boy, and the boy held its liquid gaze. The crowd made a horseshoe of itself.

After a time, dust settled. The great animal breathed evenly and folded the powerful wings.

"Sods and little fishes!" Keat Featherstone strode forward to take the halter easily. Without turning to the new polish-boy, sweat-stained and streaked with dirt, he said quietly:

"That was well done, lad. Well done indeed."

As the second groom began to lead the stallion away, three riders burst the bubbling crowd apart. Casually they reined in.

"What's the fuss here?" a nasal voice demanded.

Master Mortier's crimson taltry, brocade-edged, rested heavily on his head. Although the drawstring was tied under the chin, strands of long, lank hair showed, pulled back from a face that might have been handsome had the chin not been so weak and the pouting lips so soft and shapeless. A slight paunch betrayed his propensity for sampling new and different flavors. Gloved hands held the reins lightly. At one side he was flanked by Galliard, Master at Aerial Navigation, and on the other by his valet.

The blacksmith, rotund and rubicund, panted down the ramp from his forge.

"Sir Masters," he announced imperatively, "I never seen no 'puchin loose in these grounds that I can remember of, lately, at any rate!" Then he added as an afterthought, "And I never seen nothing like that there, neither."

He pointed at the uncomely youth who followed Keat Featherstone. Here was a likely scapegoat.

"That there distempered wretch is what caused all this mischief, I'll be certain—upsetting Storm Prince's nerves like that, getting him all of a pother so's he can't be shod."

The Master at Swords gazed down upon the accused from the height of his horse's back. The youth stopped in his tracks, flushed. The crowd of stablehands loitered uncertainly.

"How now! 'Tis himself," cried the fencing-tutor, adjusting his riding-gloves, "a known troublemaker. Have our lessons taught you nothing, young paragon? Alas, we shall have to teach them again."

The valet giggled—short, sharp, high-pitched. Mortier pointed his riding crop at the youth.

"He shall accompany me now."

A stocky figure pushed through the crowd.

"Good sir," Dain Pennyrigg rasped grimly, "the lad is not at fault."

"Hold your tongue, lackey, this is not your business."

Keat Featherstone paused in his stride, turning on his heel impatiently.

"Nor is it yours, sir. These are stable-yards, not fencing-halls. The lad saved the gray from certain injury. The 'puchin which frightened the horse belongs not to the lad, nor did it accompany him. I know not how it came here, but it is being removed by my lads, as you can see."

The lads in question, having been unable to entice the little ape out of the tree, had taken to hurling stones at it. Hissing and insulted, it bared its yellow teeth, leaped from a branch, and fled away across the rooftops.

His expression subtly transformed, Mortier turned his gaze back to the object of his previous discourse. His beady eyes raked the youth from head to foot. Then his lip curled.

Without deigning to reply, the Master at Swords and his companions jabbed their spurs into their landhorses' ribs and galloped away, scattering the crowd.

"A bad enemy," said Keat Featherstone later in the harness room. "I cannot guess how you've crossed his path and come to his attention, but it is the worse for you." Abstractedly he picked up a currycomb that had been left on a shelf and turned it around and around in his hands. "If you're as good with horses as it seems, I would have you work here, from time to time. Keep out of his way, lad. I don't want to see you end up in the same straits as poor club-footed Pod, the little half-fey lad Mortier keeps as a page. The Master . . . er"—Featherstone scratched his nose, and his gaze slipped sideways for an instant—"studies the Nine Arts. He prefers def—I mean, weak sort of folks to perform errands for him. 'Tis said he has dealings with unseelie wights. The Lord Stormriders are unaware or seem to be unaware of all such matters as do not interfere with their own doings. Mortier is a master swordsman, there's no doubt, and an excellent teacher for the young riders, who ought rightly to be skilled in such ways. His services are valued." He sighed. "You'll be safe, just as long as you stay out of his way."

Having replaced the currycomb, he headed for the door. "Come, lad—it be nigh on dusk. You'd better be getting on up the Tower."

There were things he would have liked to say; questions he would have liked to ask. They hammered at his skull from the inside, demanding to be freed, but they were locked in, as he was locked within this Tower and its demesnes. There was no password, no key, not even a hairline crack to suggest the door might be ajar.

And the raging trees, the raging trees did roar,
And the stormy winds did blow,
While we jolly sailor lads were skipping up aloft
And the landlubbers lying down below, below, below,
And the landlubbers lying down below.

Tren Spatchwort sang out of tune, in the servants' kitchen on Floor Five.

"Hold your noise, Spatchwort," said Dain Pennyrigg. He yawned. "I'd rather hear a capuchin squalling."

"That's an old sea-shanty, is it not?" said the Keeper of the Keys. "But you've changed the words to suit Windships. Got a mind to sail on Windships, have you?"

"Aye. One day I'll crew my way out of this place," Tren Spatchwort answered.

"Why? It's not so bad. Besides, what would you do to earn a crust? Not sing for your supper?" Pennyrigg took a draft from a cracked mazer of hot medlure and propped his boots on a table. Wooden paddles leaned against the still-warm bread-ovens. Lamplight danced off belt buckles wrought like various animals' heads, reflected in eyes, and softened the faces of the gathering. Lounging on benches and stools around the tables, they gambled at cards and dice, drank, conversed, whittled. Children played Mouse and Stringtangle.

"I would assay for the Dainnan, just as you would, Pennyrigg, just as any of us would. Unlike you blunderheads, I would pass the trials and become a member of the Brotherhood. I would travel, then, and see the world, and fight, and be part of great ventures, and the Royal Bard would make songs about me. How can anyone do anything in this place? 'Tis like an island, here. We're trapped, surrounded by a sea of forest filled with evil wights, gray malkins, and bruigas and—" Tren Spatchwort bit off his words. "Other things. And ships sail on it. If the forest has become the sea, shall the sea become the forest?"

Pennyrigg punched his friend lightly on the arm. "You've been drinking too much spike-leaf. You're in danger of becoming a philosopher."

"And my friend Sheepshorn is in danger of becoming worm's meat."

"In trouble again?"

"Aye, and locked in the cellars for punishment."

"The cellar-keeper had better beware. Grod will drink the barrels dry by tomorrow morn!"

Spatchwort's proclamation of discontent touched a chord

within the nameless one. He yearned to leave this place of no answers, to journey until he found answers, and if there were none, to travel on. He knew that strange dangers and untame things lurked in the forest—such things were often spoken of among the Household. To him, as strength developed, the prospect of the forest's eldritch perils seemed no worse than spending the rest of his life cringing in humiliation and servitude.

Curled in the lap of the Keeper of the Keys was a capuchin clothed in a perished velvet jerkin. It whimpered.

"Inch grieves for Punch," the woman said softly. "He got into the stables today, and they chased him off into the forest."

"Indeed, and 'puchins are supposed to be trained not to go to the stables, so who's at fault?" commented a scullion offhandedly.

"I heard it had something to do with Poxface over there," said a footman. He indicated a figure crouched in a corner that drew even further into itself, toward the spark of anger within.

To most of the other household servants, the only thing that made amends for the presence of the spindle-shanked lad was that they were now the second-lowest-ranked group. This warmed their spirits somewhat, although not toward him. In fact, most of them were torn between bullying him to prove their rank and ignoring him out of laziness or because it pained their sense of the aesthetic to look at him. This conundrum proved too much for their intellects to resolve, and to avoid further mental suffering they ended up alternating between the two approaches.

"Why is it always creeping around here with real people?" interjected a drudge. "Why doesn't it stay in the furnace room with batty Grethet?"

"Grethet's sheep, it is," gibed another. "Grows its yellow wool for her. Says she'll sell it off for a pretty penny, and why should she get the benefit? Why not us?"

"Things like that oughtn't to be allowed in places where people eat," muttered another.

A bowl thrown by one of the older children found its mark on the youth's shoulder.

"Leave off—he's harmless enough," snapped the Keeper of the Keys.

Attention drifted from the youth. The servant Grech began to hold forth about the hideous monster known as Nuckelavee, which came out of the sea spreading evil wherever he went, blighting crops, destroying livestock, and killing every mortal he encountered.

"His head is ten times the size of a man's." Grech grinned, accidentally spitting as he spoke, "and his mouth juts forth like a pig's snout, yet 'tis wide enough to drive a wheelbarrow in. His home is the sea. He blights crops with mildew and sea-gales, he throws livestock over the rocky cliffs along the coast, he brings plague amongst all mortalkind. Poisonous is the foul blast from his nostrils, withering plants and causing animals to sicken. Never does he visit the land when rain is falling, and 'tis known he brings long droughts."

"Droughts?" someone questioned. "Has he then some earnest disapprobation of fresh water?"

"That he does, and no mistake," replied Grech wisely.

"You'll be giving us nightmares! It's naught but a sour-natured and pestilent fat-guts you are, Grech!" the other servants exclaimed. "You polled bachelor!"

"Pray tell us a kinder story, Brand," implored Rennet Thighbone. The old man obliged, and the evening passed quickly with the telling of tales.

As the nameless youth pursued his task of polishing the door fittings, a man came to him.

"You have been summoned, Lickspittle. The Master of Swords summons you to his presence *now!*"

Mortier's chamber was dark. Velvet curtains muffled the slits of windows. No fire shed its cheery glow; the only light emanated from a quincunx of blue flames on a long table of polished oak. A broken orrery stood before a tall and tarnished mirror; also a tellurion, slightly damaged. Dirty retorts and vials disarrayed a wooden trestle. A similar edifice opposite supported rusted iron cogs, toothed wheels, springs, an astrolabe, a headless automaton, and several other half-gutted clockwork apparati of whose purpose the visitor had no idea. Over the whole chamber hung a heaviness, a shroud of lethargy. Things dismantled had never been reassembled; nothing stood complete—all projects abandoned, half-done.

The Master at Swords had melded with a high-backed chair.

"Come here."

Accustomed to obedience, the lad obeyed, fighting for breath. Rising terror threatened to suffocate him. Even twilight could not hide the unsavoriness of the master's helminthic features. For bleak moments the cold, watery eyes scanned the lad from head to foot, as if measuring him, while the youth trembled, wondering when the blow would fall. Mortier was not one to prolong suspense. Abruptly, wordlessly, he leaned forward and struck, suddenly and hard. The lad reeled and on finding his balance retreated a step or two.

"That is for your impertinence at the smithy yesterday."

With surprising swiftness, the man rose out of his chair, lunging forward. A second blow landed like thunder on the side of the lad's head. He felt blood trickle.

"And that for daring to turn folk against me to save your own hide. And that"—the third blow felled his victim—"for paining my sight with your ugliness." The lad scrambled to evade the booted foot now, but it was useless. When the Master at Swords had kicked him to the other side of the room he rolled under a table, finding shelter behind its thick, carved legs. There he knelt, his ears ringing, his thin ribs rising and falling.

"Come forth. You shall kneel before my chair and beg pardon for your offenses. Come forth at once, I say, or you shall be further punished for your wanton disobedience, vile and ugly boy!"

Across the room a door opened. Distracted, Mortier turned. A servant's head peered through the doorway.

"Master Mortier, sir—oh!"

The unfortunate intruder jumped back. Something fled past him, out the door, and down the dark corridor, away.

The lift-keeper slid the double sets of doors shut and locked them with a sonorous clang. Inside the lift-cage the boy without a name stared at the walls and ceiling.

The sildron-powered horse-lift was roomy. At that moment it carried an eotaur and five servants: the foundling, Keat Featherstone, Dain Pennyrigg, Teron Hoad the old ostler, and the lift-keeper, all dressed monotonously in tawny doublets, breeches, and boots, taltries pulled up to cover their heads. Lord Isterium's bay mare, West Wind, was returning to work after a field-spell, to embark on a run that very evening.

Featherstone had called upon the young servant to accompany the mare. Famous for her hatred of lift-cages, she had in the past damaged her handlers and the cage in her display of contempt for such confines. After the last performance, there had been doubt as to whether she could continue her role as a Skyhorse.

Now she stood docile, nibbling at the youth's hand, nuzzling his tunic as the lift rose. Featherstone and Pennyrigg looked on, bemused. They had not queried the bruised eye, the swollen lip.

Fresh straw heaped the dented andalum floor, padded corduroy lined the walls. An ornate box projected from each wall, seven feet up. The lift-keeper now opened one of these to reveal a row of ten andalum keys with elaborate filigree handles, each in its own recess, set well into the wall. He pulled out the first one almost as far as it would go—a long, narrow plate that had been shielding the slender sildron hoister attached to the lift's outer wall. He did not withdraw it entirely but stopped it when it reached a certain notched position. By this simple and direct mechanism, the lift rose.

All the sildron hoisters in the main lifts were grade alt 640. Only the turret lifts went higher. But the exiguous dimensions of a single alt 640 hoister bar could lift only the weight of the cage, a horse, and six adults to a height of one story. Two hoisters, unshielded, could lift to twice that height. When the payload was lighter, the andalum keys for each floor were only partially extracted, to a pre-reckoned calibration.

The lift-keeper watched through an open slot in the wall as descending marks passed by to indicate levels. As they neared the top of the first story he pulled the second key out smoothly, and so they ascended, evenly, barely altering in speed. He moved around the walls opening one key compartment after another until all four had been opened and thirty-one keys pulled out. leaving nine untouched. Deftly he made some final adjustments. The lift stopped at Floor Thirty-two, the level of the Noblesse Squadron.

The part-time stableboy led the compliant eotaur out into the circuit corridor. Other Skyhorses hung their long heads over the half-doors of loose-boxes, watching.

A black-and-silver horse-rug covered West Wind's back; on it, her name and the Stormriders' zigzag lightning device were embroidered in frosted capitals. Her coat glistened as if oiled, every muscle delineated. Her horns were polished marble. She was iron-shod—only when a Skyhorse had been brought up to the height of its run would the sildron hoof-crescents be clipped on and the flying-girth added.

"This way," said the second groom, tightening his taltry strings from sheer habit.

The three stablehands worked together quietly in the saddling rooms while the youth, his job finished, looked on. When the girth had been tightened and checked, when sildron hoof-casings had been attached and the mare had taken her fill from the water-trough, Hoad walked with her around and around the circuit corridor to warm her sinews. She floated slightly, placing her feet with calculated exactness as she had been trained, flexing her wings.

Two other saddled eotaurs joined in. Their strappers chatted to Hoad as they strolled.

"Bad uncomber yesterday," said the old ostler gloomily. "Couple of our boys were caught, out past the far meadow. Came in and got drunk, after. Bad tableau down in the forest near the boundary. You know the one?"

His companions nodded.

"Reckon unstorms are worse these days than when I was a lad. Much worse."

The others somberly grunted agreement.

"Pirates, too," Hoad the Toad continued savoringly, "sailors on the *Dragonfly* said there's some about. Windship was plundered up northwest in the high country. Vicious, they were. Showed no mercy."

A gatekeeper hurried in, extricating a timepiece on a fob from the folds of his tunic. He opened its gilt-metal lid, revealing a single hand on an unglazed face. After consulting it briefly, he raised the portcullis of Gate West Five Hundred.

The wind was warm. It was the beginning of Summer: Uianemis, the Greenmonth. Already the new season had provoked those downstairs into preparations for the Lugnais Festival and Greatsun Day.

A passenger lift descended and opened into the mounting rooms. The lift-keeper bowed deeply as three Relayers and their attendants swept out of the doors. Within the open cage, lamplight shone on pale buttoned-satin walls and intricately carved rosewood seats strewn with beaded cushions.

The Relayers of the Noblesse Squadron, in short cloaks and leather riding boots, clipped sildron flying-belts to their waists and paced restlessly. Beneath belted doublets of soft black leather they wore black linen shirts, the full sleeves gathered at seams just below the shoulders. Three silver stars glinted on each epaulet, echoing the gleam of the Stormrider *V* across the chest and the insignia over the heart. Thick black breeches completed the riding outfit. Two Relayers were silent; one badgered the equerries with questions and demands, obviously impatient to be off.

Pages, footmen, and stewards busied themselves. The gatekeeper stood watch, staring westward over the forest toward the mountain range. Mellifluous colors surged in and lay in pools of honey on the floor. Unable to restrain his curiosity, the flawed youth peered from around a corner.

"They come," announced the gatekeeper, stepping precariously out on the doorsill. As he finished speaking, a single, silver note sounded from the watchmen on the parapets, whose spyglass saw farthest. Three dark specks came out of the sunset, forming themselves into horses and riders, wings double-arched, cloaks flying.

"Wind's still from the west," said the gatekeeper, eyeing a windsock, "about ten knots."

Equerries helped their masters to pull on flying helmets and gauntlets. The Lord Relayers swung themselves up into the saddles, their silver and black matching the caparisons of the eotaurs who danced sideways and tossed their heads, held back within the mounting rooms by the practiced hands of their riders.

"They're late," someone muttered.

The dark shapes grew and slowed. Suddenly, with a blast of wind and a jingling, sweating clangor, they were in, alighting with a rush in the high-vaulted gatehall and adeptly drawing in their wings as they continued with a decelerating ride along its length.

Equerries and grooms ran to catch hold of bridles as the incoming Relayers dismounted. Stewards started unbuckling the saddlebags.

All the newcomers were clothed in Stormrider black, but the uniform of one man was trimmed with magenta where the others displayed silver, magenta being the color of the Ninth House. After pulling off his flying helmet, he shook the sweat from his eyes. The three outgoing riders entered the gatehalls for the exchange of saddlebags and the latest weather report.

"Isterium," called the Son of the Ninth House, "I know thee beneath thy helm; I offer thee greetings from myself and my lady."

"And to thee, Sartores. Rest well in our House this night," responded the other. "What news?"

"Rumors, only rumors. Unrest in Namarre. I can say no more here, but all shall be known in due course."

"Good morrow, Sartores."

"Wind be with you, Isterium."

West Wind burst forth, leading the others in an explosion of energy down the middle of the gatehall to gain momentum, leaping out from the doorsill onto the powerful updrafts at the most dangerous moment of a Relayer's journey, when horse and rider could be blown back and smashed against the tower by the capricious gusts called windhooks. But they were away, all three, out over the forest and turning to the south. As they dwindled, so did the fires of the sky.

From a balcony below, Mortier, Master at Swords, craned his neck to watch them go. He stood awhile there, in accumulating darkness, as if waiting: a lone hooded figure on the Tower's black wall. Shadows coagulated. An echoing howl grew from the forest and broke off; voices drifted up from the yards in snatches; a sickle moon swung up over the world's edge. The wind abated.

With a sigh, another wind rippled over the tops of the trees. Leaf-edges glistened as if brushed with rime. A stronger sigh seemed to bring dim lights to life beneath the canopy and a faint echo, as of chiming glass. Mortier did not move, but he trembled. Beneath his fingernails, blood trickled from the palms of his hands. A low moan started in the depths of him and erupted suddenly in a short cry—he spun around and fled into his quarters, slamming shut the outer doors. Through more doors and into another room filled with fantastic apparatuses, then deeper still into the Tower he fled, until he reached a corner among woven hangings, where he pressed himself, face turned to the wall. Presently a smaller door opened hesitantly, admitting a limping boy.

"Master?" a thin voice quavered. "Master, I have come as you bid. I beg you, forgive Pod if he is late. Are you here?"

There was no reply.

Outside the tack room a light rain was falling, backlit by pale sunlight—a shaking of sharp, silver powders.

"Yan, tan, tethera," instructed Keat Featherstone. "D'ye get it, lads? Yan, tan, tethera."

He was teaching numeracy to some of the younger stableboys and the ugly menial. Featherstone had learned from his father, who knew only the shepherd's procedure, used for tallying their flocks. He would count up to three, one for each finger-joint, then count the number of fingers. By this method, the counter could reach a total of thirty.

Laboriously, the impromptu school had reached this landmark.

"But what about if you want to count more than all your fingers times tethera?" an enterprising boy wanted to know.

"You get a wooden stick," explained Featherstone, "and notch it with your knife, like so. One notch for every fingers times tethera."

The eyes of his students bulged.

"Why," they said, "you could count all the stars in the sky by that there stick!"

They went quiet for a moment, until one, reaching the end of a fruitless cogitation, said, "No, you couldn't."

Another added, "What if some of your fingers got chopped off, like the Toad's?"

Featherstone glared at them. "What d'ye want to be counting up stars for?" He frowned. "How many hoof-crescents, how many apples and bales of hay, that's what you'd be counting."

"Yan tan tethera," said the enterprising boy. "That ain't right. Sailors count by their fingers, that's tethera times tethera and one more for luck."

"Sailors count by tens," said Featherstone.

"That ain't right, neither," said the boy who had commented on Teron Hoad's fingers. "I know more than that. There's twelve inches in a foot and twelve pence in a shilling. We ought to be counting by twelves."

"Sheepshorn can count all the Floors of the Tower," complained another, "right up to the topmost, where the battlements are."

"Look," Keat Featherstone said exasperatedly, "if you want to be learning, then sit and listen. Don't be arguing. 'Yan tan tethera,' that's how it goes. That's how I do tallying, and it's been working for me all my life."

Noting the second groom's deepening grimace, the lads opened their eyes wide and developed expressions of innocence. As their tutor continued the lesson, they nodded, to all appearances drinking in every word.

It was a pity, as the servants usually said when they talked of the King-Emperor in Caermelor, it was a pity about the dreadful loss of the Queen, taken by wights of unseelie, and Prince Edward only a lad at the time. It was a blessing that the Prince and his father, King James, had survived, but a shame that the lad had to grow up motherless. Many whispered that the wickedness of unseelie wights was growing, their numbers multiplying. The world outside the Tower was reputedly becoming a darker and more dangerous place.

It was rumored, too, that some kind of trouble was brewing in the northeast, in Namarre. What it was, no one could be certain. Speculation was rife. Several of the servants lived in terror.

"Barbarians and unseelie wights shall come sweeping out of Namarre and slay us in our beds!" they said. Others scoffed at their fears.

"The King-Emperor's warriors will overcome. The Dainnan Brotherhood shall water the turf with the blood of his enemies, and so shall the Royal Attriod and the Legions."

In the kitchens at nights, these rumors revived talk of battles past and of a legend that was largely unrecalled.

"In time of great need, the Sleeping Warriors who lie beneath the Raven's Howe," proclaimed Brinkworth, "can be awakened. When their strength is most needed, a champion must find the entrance under the Hill, which is covered with briars and rubble—he must make his way in, down a long passage until he comes to the vault where they lie. Beside their King he will find a horn, a garter, and a stone sword. He must cut the garter with the sword and then blow the horn."

"Has no one ever found the entrance?"

"Many have tried. It has been found, but only once. And the Sleepers were almost roused. It was poor Cobie Will that discovered the entrance by accident—a shepherd he was, sitting on the Hill winding a ball of wool while he minded his sheep. The ball slipped out of his hands and rolled down a deep and narrow hole. Cobie Will thought he must have found the entrance—all spirited up, he cleared away the brambles and rocks until he had uncovered a tunnel into which he could go. He followed his track of wool down under the ground, along a dark, vaulted passageway, until he saw a distant light. He pushed on towards it and found himself in the mighty chamber where the Sleeping Warriors lie, lit by a fire that burned without fuel. On a hundred rich couches round the room lay the sleeping bodies of caparisoned knights; in the dim light behind the fire, sixty couple of noble hounds lay sleeping, and on a table in front of it he saw a gold-clasped horn, a curiously wrought stone sword, and an embroidered silk garter.

"Foolish boy, he touched the stone sword, half lifting it, and at once the knights stirred and sat up on their couches. In fright, Will let go of the weapon and they lay down again and went to sleep. He must have breathed a sigh of relief then, looking around the chamber once again as still and silent as a tomb. But instead of leaving well alone and tiptoeing hence, he thought to interfere one more time. You see, he was an inquisitive lad and like to try things out to see what would happen. Many a lad has come to grief in this way, Master Pennyrigg. So he picked up the horn and blew it. A clear ringing sound like the purest silver, loud enough to reach the farthest valleys, came out of that instrument, and all the knights rose up, drew their swords, and leaped towards him. A great voice cried out:

> Woe to the coward, that ever he was born,
> That did not draw the sword before he blew the horn!

"A howling wind sprang up and whirled him out of the cave and down a precipice. There he lay broken until some shepherds found him—to them he told his story and then died. The Warriors remain there to this day," concluded Brand, stroking his beard, "under Raven's Howe, or some say Eagle's Howe, all in their fine armor, with their shining swords and jeweled scabbards and their shields at their sides. Time has not corrupted their flesh. Their faces, it is said, are as noble and handsome as ever they were. And they sleep, and they wait. But every Midsuntide Eve, it is told, they come out of the mound and ride around it on horses shod with silver."

As he finished speaking, an uneasy silence fell.

"Some say," said Grech the cooper, "that Cobie Will did waken some of them, and they have stalked the secret ways of Erith ever since."

"That's just a story to frighten gullible idiots," said the seamstress, "like tales of the—you know—"

"What do the Sleeping Warriors wait for—the kiss of a Prince?" interrupted a coarser voice. As tension broke, laughter bubbled but was suppressed. Dain Pennyrigg, the speaker, climbed onto a table and lay there on his back, his hands crossed upon his chest and his eyes closed, snoring stentoriously. Stifled giggles sprinkled themselves among the skivvies, becoming shrieks as the burly lad sat up abruptly, flinging out his arms.

"Oh, my Prince," he falsettoed, "how my heart flutters!" Puckering his lips, he emitted slurping squeaks.

Smiling benevolently at the general merriment, Brand Brinkworth said:

"Laugh—be jolly. There are those who think it lordly to be cold as a stone, but feelings are like wolves. When caged they become more ferocious, and at the end, they always escape."

He took up a poker and stirred the fire. At his feet, the capuchin Inch yawned and stretched.

A dispute that had arisen, between those who believed the Gooseberry Wife was just a nursery tale to frighten children and those who thought otherwise, was halted by the entrance of a large, dough-faced woman.

"There will be no more storytelling this eve in any of the kitchens—no, nor any eve until the day of the weddin' and the days of feastin' thereafter."

Dolvach Trenchwhistle, the Head Housekeeper, banged an oak-root of a fist on the wooden tabletop for emphasis. In the ensuing silence, her small black eyes darted like flies around the kitchen, scrutinizing the faces of all those present. Satisfied that all due heed had been taken, she stood up, hands on hips.

"Larks' tongues in aspic, pheasant under crystal, quails' eggs, pigeon pies, venison, truffles, oysters, hulkin' great puddin's, syrups and spices, seedcakes, honest-to-goodness Sugar sweets and jellies from the Confect'ry House in the city, salmon and big blue squid and trout, not to mention wine, stout, mead, and cider by the barrelful, smoked eels, pickled tongue, fresh forest fruits and foods flown in specially, yellow and red cheeses, and pitchers of cream. Not in that order."

She paused for effect.

"And that's only the start of it."

"And a snoutfish in a pear-tree," shouted Dain Pennyrigg.

Conversations buzzed. Dolvach Trenchwhistle held up a meaty, work-chafed hand and received silence in the palm of it.

"We all have work to do, and there be no mistake. Every spare room must be cleaned and aired for the 'portant guests. And fresh bed-linen, perfumed, and towels and oils provided. There must not be a speck o' dust to blacken my name. And decorations. The Great Hall is to be decked out in the colors of the two joinin' Houses and weddin' white. White satin everywhere, and silver lace by the yard, and bows of pale blue silk."

"Fig's end! Sounds like a weaver's market. Will there be any room for the guests?" Pennyrigg inquired.

"Flowers everywhere, gathered fresh on the day," Trenchwhistle continued, "and the road from the sea-docks to the main gate strewn with petals, all bedorned with silver and sky-blue and white buntin', and every courtyard like a flower garden. No guest will have any reason to criticize. It will be done proper, and it will be done on time. Else heads will roll. You will all have a job to do—many jobs. And you will do them as best you can. Better."

The servants nodded, mumbling tired assent.

"Porter and metheglin for us all, at the end. And odds bods, we're goin' to enjoy them leftovers," muttered the Head Housekeeper, grimly hitching up her apron and departing in majesty.

"Shan't be real larks' tongues," said the spit-boy. "Ain't got no hawk-mews; ain't got no merlins to catch larks."

"Prob'ly be the nasty bits off billy-goats or somethin'," his friend rejoined luridly. "No tellin' what Rennet Thighbone puts in when 'e's cooking."

Eyes gleamed in the stuffy darkness beneath the benches. The unnoticed listener there tried to work out how he could escape the forthcoming extra workload. Soon he was to hear words that would make him fervent for a greater escape.

The roan gelding cantered through the air, mane and tail streaming, wings pumping, muscles flexing and stretching beneath a glossy hide. Its young rider shook the stirrups from his boots, leaned forward, and then with a shout launched himself sideways off his steed, beneath the pinions.

By means of a rope attached at one end to his sildron flying-belt and at the other to the saddle, he was dragged along, rotating rapidly and flopping like a fish on a hook, half-strangled by his own taltry. It soon became obvious that he could neither pull himself toward the horse nor free himself from the safety-rope. Gasping, he bellowed a command.

The eotaur halted.

"Most elegant, my lord," commented the Master at Riding, who was standing on a circular wooden platform six feet above the sawdust floor of a lunging yard, on a level with the eotaur and the student trying to drag himself onto its back. His assistant held the training horse on a long lunge-rein.

"One can perceive," he continued, "that if your steed threw you, startled by some bird of prey or jolted by some unexpectedly rough terrain, you would have no trouble in regaining your seat."

"The rope was twisted. It spun me."

"You coiled it yourself. You checked your own equipment, did you not, as part of your routine before riding? One of the first rules. And mark you—riders who cling with their knees are wont to pop off, like a peg on an apple. Enough of this for now. Come, let us to the hattocking circuits."

The assistant, whose crippled face belied the agility of his body, leaped lightly down from the platform as the rider remounted.

"I will not be led like a child, six feet above the ground!" the trainee Relayer said brusquely, "and I in my second year. Throw me the lead-rope."

The Master at Riding nodded to the helper, who did so; the student, a heavy-jawed husky fellow, jabbed his heels and galloped dangerously over the helper's head and out of the yard.

"And may fate preserve us from young idiot hotheads who know it all," muttered the Master at Riding, glancing at the skies. He spoke to himself—not to the awkward figure who stood waiting on the sawdust floor, whose aid had been thrust upon him by Keat Featherstone and accepted with reluctant martyrdom.

Greatsun Day and the Lugnais Festival were well past, giving way to Grianmis, the second month of Summer, warm and welcoming. A brass cup of a sun poured golden benevolence over the red-roofed stables and the training yards. The foundling followed the Master, becoming part of the dance that was the daily running of the busy demesne. The greensward was smooth. Sildron-shod hooves could not scar the ground.

The concentric hattocking tracks were graded in order of difficulty; piled and stepped with rocks, boulders, and monoliths in imitation of shrunken mountains. The wings of eotaurs had once been vestigial. Breeding had developed them, but sildron flying-girths and sildron hoof-crescents were necessary to compensate for the weight of the horses. Without sildron they could not fly.

Sildron repelled the ground only when directly opposed to it. Rough, rock-strewn landscape was no obstacle if the ground was relatively flat and the rocks relatively small. Moreover, the higher the altitude, the less the flight was affected by terrain. However, an eotaur, traveling above a plain and arriving at a sheer cliff face whose top was higher than the traveling altitude, would not be able to scale the cliff and would have to skirt it. Sudden upthrusts of landscape disrupted an eotaur's progress; steep-graded ground-slopes rising at an angle of more than twenty-nine degrees were unridable. For these reasons, hattocking circuits were designed to allow practice. The Skyroads were plotted to fit the land's contours—although jagged patches and unforeseen deviations were inevitable and had to be taken into account.

The student Relayer, who had not yet earned his first star, wore the usual black. His linen riding shirt, open at the neck, was belted and tucked into jodhpurs, which in turn were stuffed into boots. Beads of perspiration stood out on his forehead. A taltry flapped loosely down his back, revealing long brown hair tied fashionably in a club. The lunge-rein had been removed from the Skyhorse, and the Son of the House guided it with the reins, picking a way above the dirty jumble of rocks on the intermediate circuit to find the most even and scalable path.

"Of course, Star King would know these circuits in his sleep," the Master at Riding remarked to the Second Master at Riding, who had just joined him. "He could hattock them unridden, blindfold, after all these years. The real test comes on training-forays in the field."

Something shaped like a miniature dinghy with a rapidly revolving apparatus on the back suddenly shot past alongside the fence, two feet off the ground, raising a cumulus cloud of dirt. It was silent, save for a slight squeak and grating sounds at various pitches. Its driver was a white-robed, stripe-bearded man wearing gloves.

"Zimmuth and his evil engines," muttered the Master at Riding, spitting dust.

The highly unstable sildron-powered skimboat grated to a stop, barely missing a lopsided outbuilding that was used to house the wizard's experiments. While a henchman chained the vehicle to a post, the wizard disappeared indoors.

The Master at Riding and his companion turned their attention back to their protégé, who was negotiating the terrain circuit with surprising prowess, and regarded him critically, bestowing advice occasionally. Meanwhile, nine landhorses wearing curiously fashioned saddles were led into fenced yards beside the circuits. Sunlight slivers danced off buckles and stirrups. Their riders, eager young stablehands, urged them into a fast and furious gallop around the arena. They vaulted, somersaulted, and jumped on and off the horses' backs—sometimes riding backward or standing up, or balancing on their hands, or riding three-tiered on one another's shoulders.

"How fare the other entertainments for the wedding celebrations?" inquired the Master at Riding of his second, who gazed in open delight.

"Well enough, sir. The performing capuchins will be a great success, I am told."

"Ho there, our young Lord Ariades has finished the circuit."

As the two Masters, followed by the assistant, strode toward the circuit-exit to meet him, a ball of flame erupted from one of the grilled fenestrations of the wizard-hall, accompanied by a thunderous roar.

Shouting, two men came running from the arched doorway, trailing smoke. They threw themselves to the ground and beat at their clothes with their hands. Others ran to their aid. Acrid vapors belched from orifices in the outbuilding, veiling the scene.

"Another of the wizard's failed experiments," Ariades observed blandly from his saddle high above. "I believe he is working on a more sophisticated mechanism for the operation of the lifts, amongst other things. Behold!"

He pointed to where some dark specks of escaped sildron hung high above a gaping hole in the wizard-hall roof.

"He accidentally shot down a whole flock of wood-pigeons once," remarked the Master at Riding. "I'm told they made a delicious pie."

"I trust his wizardly achievements are good enough to redeem the skins of his roasted henchmen," mused his second. "The House needs every servant fit to work during the forthcoming nuptial celebrations."

The mention of servants reminded the Master at Riding of the flunkey waiting in the shadows. He eyed him distastefully.

"Good my lord Ariades, your circuit work has improved. Go now to the dismounting platform and then we shall take refreshment before the afternoon's onhebbing lessons. You—servant—follow and tend the eotaur."

"And what manner of servant is this?" asked the Second Master at Riding, noticing the youth for the first time.

Lord Ariades, his eyes straying to the appalling aftermath of the wizard's fiasco, interjected:

"Even those of us who dwell in the higher regions have heard of the Beauteous One. Indeed, its face is worse than had been described—quite a monstrosity. I think it ought to be exhibited as a curiosity, as part of the wedding entertainments."

"Nay, 'twould disgust the guests from their feasting," protested the Master at Riding. "'Tis a shameful eyesore. I have never seen such a bad case of paradox ivy poisoning. Can it not be cured?"

"I have heard that it can," said the second, scratching a stubbled chin.

The youth froze.

"A fingertip poisoned yesterday, perhaps," said Ariades. "But an entire face poisoned for—how long? Years?" He shook his head.

"They say," persisted the second, creasing his brow, "that there is something the city wizards know of—is it drinking toadwater? Or is it piercing with hot needles to open the boils, followed by the application of a certain herbal paste? . . . I don't rightly recall."

"In any case, cures would be too expensive to waste on a fly-struck scoundrel of a servant," Lord Ariades said, kicking Star King into motion.

The youth stared at the trainee Relayer's retreating back for several moments, before a similar kick from the Second Master broke his reverie and sent him hurrying.

The shadows in the goat-caves could play tricks, especially when outside daylight was so bright. The mute one moved uncertainly. No goats jostled therein; they were grazing at the forest's fringe, under the herd-boys' care. Their smell was there, patiently waiting for their return; some old straw and dung kept it company. Farther into the hollow places there was a hole in the wall, smaller and darker than the rest. It was toward this that the lad moved. He held a brass bougie-box by its handle, a wax taper coiled inside its drum-shaped interior like a pale, parasitic worm. The lighted end projected through the lid, breathing a weak flame, transparent.

"You! You followed me. Don't tell anyone . . . don't show anyone this place. What do you want?" wheezed a voice.

Clubfoot Pod's pale face leaned out of the gloom. The intruder stood immobile. He put down the taper-box and slowly lowered the burden he had carried on his shoulder. Pod stared suspiciously.

"Don't tell anyone that this is where I hide, will you? You won't, will you? You cannot?"

The youth shook his head and held his hand out in a gesture of friendship, from which Pod shrank back.

"Go away, go away. Someone might have seen you come here."

The youth shook his head again, pointed to Pod, and put a hand behind one ear as if listening. Pod nodded, watching the signals.

"Aye, but only if you make it quick."

The nameless one pointed again to Pod, then to himself, then to the cavern's entrance. He made flapping movements with his arms and shaded his eyes as if staring into the distance, then unwrapped the bundle to display a small pile of food: dried fruit, cheese, and hard bread.

"Go from here? You must be addled—don't you understand? Nobody can live in the forest unprotected, and the forest's all around. It stretches for miles and miles. I don't know how many miles. Thousands."

Pod's eyes were white in their sockets, and his voice rose to a strangled squeak.

The youth made a shape with his hands.

"Windship? You mean, stow away on board? Kill yourself without my company. Don't you know what happens to stowaways? Go! Go! Take your nightmares and stolen food. Don't come near me! I'll not have anything to do with it. You shall be discovered. You shall be punished."

The mute one gazed at him for a moment, then nodded, folded his bundle, picked up the bougie-box, and moved out into the sunlight.

*There is a cure for me out there. I shall go, one day,* he said in his heart, *I shall go Beyond the Tower and make a journey, a quest to find three things—a face to show the world without shame, my name, my past. I will not rest until I find them.*

But without company, he was afraid to leave, so for now he endured.

"Wake up, wake up. Sunrise soon. Wake up, Lazy, you are strong now—hard work has made you grow strong, so now you must work harder."

The partnership of Grethet's parrot-squawk and her boot in his ribs dissolved the mists of slumber in an instant.

The crone's ward no longer slept in the furnace room—she had made him move his bedding because she said the room was too bright, what with the constant opening of the furnace's maw to feed the fires; and he must hide himself away in shadow. He now slept, washed, and dressed in a small windowless cell used to store candles, laundry soap, and beeswax—a cupboard shared with optimistic spiders that, when their roommate sat upright on his heap of rags, would spin their way down from the ceiling on their long threads to hang level with his eyes, staring, before reeling themselves up again.

"Undress in the dark," Grethet reminded him constantly. "Don't let them see you. No one must see you. You are deformed. They would have you thrown out. You understand?"

He understood. He obeyed.

Accustomed to darkness, he poured water from the ewer into the bowl and washed, as she had taught him, and dressed, tying the taltry over thick lustrous thatch, now the length of his fingers. He completed his first duties before eating the scrag of bread euphemistically known as "breakfast," disposing of waste, sweeping the furnace room floor, drawing water for washing garments, setting fires under the laundry tubs, and vigorously rubbing a glass mushroom with a knopped handle across linen sheets to smooth them out.

His shoulders and arms ached always. Later he would be set to checking the stores. Featherstone had taught him to count. Now the mathematical equal of most of the other servants, he would repeat, over and over in his head, *Yan, tan, tethera; yan, tan, tethera,* after each trio, cutting a notch on a short green stick as evidence.

It was the twelfth of Teinemis, the Firemonth. From within the dominite walls came the screeching and thumping of sildron pumps assisting the flow of rainwater from the great roof-cisterns and drawing water from wells beneath the lowest dungeons. The sounds, as of a screaming, beating heart walled up behind stone, testified to the large number of guests occupying the upper levels on this important day, the wedding day.

A Stormrider wedding at the Relay Tower at Isse in Eldaraigne—a momentous event. Marriages customarily took place only between and within the twelve Houses. The eldest daughter of the House, the Lady Persefonae, was to be joined with her cousin Valerix from the Fifth House, whose chief stronghold was in Finvarna. The betrothal had been pledged on the day Persefonae was born. It was a *bitterbynde,* the lower servants whispered at the time—a geas laid upon someone despite their own will. This was a babe too young to know the light of day, let alone whom she would choose to wed, were she of marriageable age. It was a shame, they agreed—but these alliances must be made if the glory of the Houses was to continue to wax strong. Fortunately, the pairing of these two had proved to be to the liking of both, and when the time came there was no reluctance on either part.

From realms scattered over Erith came representatives of all

Stormrider Houses and several noble and royal Houses. They came by Windship or Watership, riding sky or in guarded cavalcades along the King's High Way, the great road that ringed Eldaraigne, to the Tower's gate. Three or four Windships rode at anchor against a mackerel sky, above the far meadow; another waited at the dock on the seventh story, their sails furled and propellers motionless. Lord Valerix remained aboard his Watership anchored among his fleet and the other visiting ships in Isse Harbor, where he made his preparations. He would not set foot on land until the morrow.

Above the Tower fluttered a forest of pennants and standards. The Stormrider device, a white lightning bolt zigzagged on a black background, had been raised for the twelve united Houses. The flag of the Seventh House was identical, but black on silver, while the Fifth House displayed black on sky blue. *"Arnath Lan Seren,"* the motto, translated as "Whatever It Takes"—whatever it takes to fulfill duty and preserve honor; whatever it takes to serve the King-Emperor, uphold the strength of the twelve Houses, and rule the Skyroads.

A high stone wall, topped with shards of flint, embraced the demesnes of Isse Tower. A second fence of sturdy rowan-trees grew all along the wall's outer perimeter. Set in archways at wide intervals, the half-dozen posterns of oak and iron opened on little-used roads, scarcely more than cart-tracks, leading into the forest or the dunes. To the southeast, the main gate opened to the King's High Way running along the coast.

The time had come for the servants to go gathering fruit and flowers in the forest.

In the oblique, insipid light of dawn a convoy jingled along the path by the walled kitchen gardens and the low-roofed dairy with its underground cellars. Led by armed riders, it comprised a wooden cart drawn by two old draft-horses and a straggle of assorted domestic servants, some sitting in the cart, looking out through the trellised sides, and others walking. Capuchins and children clung to the cart like barnacles or chased each other.

Every measure for protection against unseelie wights had been employed. Many folk wore their clothes turned inside out for the expedition, discarding comfort for added security; some were crowned and garlanded with daisy-chains. The cart was hung with bells, as were the headstalls and bridles of all the horses; horse-shoes were nailed around it. The servants carried empty sacks, baskets, and rowan-wood staffs topped with bells and festoons of fraying red ribbon. Mumbling, Grethet clutched at the wooden rooster dangling around her scrawny chicken neck. Of all places, the charms known as tilhals were needed most in the wight-haunted forest. Tintinnabulating gaily, at odds with the somber visages of its members, the procession reached the Owl Postern and proceeded through it into the forest, at which point those with the sourest expressions began to whistle, a practice said to repel unseelie wights for miles around. Judging by the tuneless discord of their symphony, this was not surprising.

The fern-embroidered Owl's Way twisted through overhanging trees forming a leafy tunnel. Tiny opalescent flies threaded themselves on gold needles of sunlight pricking the canopy. Sphagnum moss and skull fungus covered fallen logs. Wrens darted, and a gray shrike-thrush trilled. The convoy followed the track until it reached a clearing, at whose edge it halted. The horses dropped their heads to graze. A guard shouted orders: Hooded gatherers spread out in groups and disappeared among the trees, shaking the bell-tipped staffs and whistling. Some boys with capuchins who remained climbed the cart's sides to pull vines of purple coral-pea from overhanging boughs. In the center of the clearing, in the full light of the warm morning sun, women and children knee-deep in grass gathered armfuls of yellow everlasting daisies, perfumed boronia, and rosy heath-myrtle, pushing the stems deep into the damp moss with which they had lined their baskets.

Grethet's stooped figure pushed through nettles and undergrowth.

"This way, this way," she panted. "Berries here, too, maybe. But beware of paradox ivy."

She was one of a group of two that, although ostracized, reaped a good harvest during that morning: trails of fireweed, satiny snow-blossom, and a small bag of early berries, whose livid juices prevented premature consumption by promising to advertise it. Tree trunks like pillars of a palace soared to a filigree ceiling. Grethet's helper sucked greedily on sweet airs and feasted on the million green shades of wilderness, the thousand subtle songs of it.

The shouting of guards beckoned the gatherers back to a cart now overflowing with flowers; some folk began tying their baskets to the outside to avoid bruising the petals.

The certainty that it was about to happen had been with the nameless one since he and Grethet first pushed their way into the forest. He looked forward to it with excitement, light of step, eager, the blood already leaping in his veins. It was that same sensation he sometimes felt when inside the Tower—only now he was Outside. Now he would see what caused it.

The prickling wind came first, soft as a child's breath, strengthening. A clamoring of birds. Clouds suddenly clustered over the sun, day turned to night, and gusts sprang up, bringing with them a racing exhilaration. Laughing soundlessly, the youth could not restrain himself from breaking into a run—at the same moment cries and violent oaths broke out on all sides:

"The unstorm! Cover your heads!"

Men and women clutched their taltries even closer to their scalps, hurrying toward the rocking cart. Some children laughed, some cried—capuchins shrieked, swarming like startled beetles. Soft lights then shone unexpectedly from darknesses among the trees, and as the wind gained power it seemed to awaken other lights and deepen other shadows. The dark forest sparkled. It *changed.*

Colored jewels of flowers glowed fiery against velvet; the edges and veins of leaves were dusted with tiny spangles of silver and gold along their skeletal networks; pinprick stars along each blade of grass brightened and faded with each gust and ebb of the wind. Branches tossed and bucked like restless horses, leaves dancing like seaweed in a shifting current, a current that eddied and swirled all around, satin smooth and cool, alive with movement. Behind the haunted sighs of the wind, soft glassy chimes. Bells on bridles winked with silver glitter and rang with a different, purer note, somehow poignant.

The driver's whip cracked blue stars along its length, and the draft-horses sprang into motion, striking red sparks from their hooves. The cavalcade moved through the unstorm like swimmers underwater. As the wind's voice rose to a moan, the strange fires brightened and weaker ones began to appear.

The youth longed to leap up and ride away on the wind's back, far from contumely and contusion, but he must run with the tattried crowd who followed the cart with eyes downcast. They did not look to left or right, but he did, and he saw under an archway of trees halfway down Owl's Way a flickering scene, half-transparent, made of light. Two men, unhooded, dressed outlandishly, dueled with swords. Weapons clashed but made no sound. A tree grew in the center of the scene, unheeded by the combatants, who passed through it as though it were not there—or perhaps it passed through them.

They parried and thrust, intent on their silent game. One stumbled, wounded in the arm, and fell back before a fresh onslaught, his mouth open in a wordless shout. Yet then there was an instant like the blink of an eye, and the scene jumped; he was on his feet, whole again, and they thrust and parried as before, fading as the wind drew breath and shimmering brighter as it blasted. This, then, this subsidiary impression left over from physical energy, was what the inhabitants of the Tower called a tableau.

By the time the troupe reached the Owl Postern the unstorm had passed. Lights dimmed and winked out, the skies cleared, and leaves hung stagnant. The flower-laden cart and its followers passed through from the forest into the demesnes.

Later that day, Lord Valerix of the Fifth House in Finvarna and Lady Persefonae of the Seventh House in Eldaraigne were married. And after the long, formal rites, the celebrations began.

At his master's command the Chief Steward beat a smart tattoo on the traditional stump-drum to command silence in the Greayte Banqueting Hall, and silence obeyed. Five hundred and eighteen nobles and almost as many servants turned to face the dais.

The long table running from one side of the hall to the other was lavishly slathered with fabric; silver and eggshell-blue. Laden with rich and decorative viands, it offered as centerpiece a cake like a cloud of frosted rosebuds bursting with Sugar doves. This glittering white affair was a symbol of the affluence of the House; brought from the highly renowned Confectionery House in Caermelor, it had been created with real Sugar from the perilous canefields of the Turnagain Islands in the far north of Erith. The price of the rare white crystals was exorbitant, for survival was difficult in the Turnagains. Not only were the islands the haunts of the unseelie—the surrounding oceans matched them for treachery.

Thirty-four lords and ladies were seated along one side of the high table, facing down into the hall. The bride wore a satin-lined cloth-of-silver surcoat, bordered with gushes of lace. It was embroidered richly, with a thousand white silk forget-me-nots and four thousand tiny rock crystals. The long, tight sleeves of the kirtle worn beneath ended in long, hanging cuffs worked with wide bands of silver needlework. Her girdle, enameled with intricate designs of silver swans on a pale blue sky and set with sapphires, matched her necklace and the bracelets she wore on her slender wrists, a gift to her from her husband. On her fingers, wedding rings; on her head, a simple circlet and veil adorned shining chestnut braids bound in a silver net.

Like snow to coal she contrasted with her lord. His Stormrider black was broken only by Fifth House blue. Worn over the silk shirt, his surcoat, which reached to midthigh, was cut from tapestry richly patterned with black on black threads—the many different textures caught the light and showed the heraldic design. At the back, it was pleated down to the waist; the high collar, long sleeves, and hem were edged with sable. From his shoulders hung a cloak of azure and black brocade. His sword-belt was slung at his waist, the ornate scabbard embossed four times with the heraldic shield of the Fifth House. Tight-fitting hose were tucked into black thigh boots whose turned-back tops displayed contrasting azure. Topped by a winged helm, his long brown hair, unbound for the occasion, flowed down his back. Lord Valerix regarded the Lady Persefonae with proprietary satisfaction; she kept her eyes modestly downcast.

They had been married by the wizard Zimmuth in the Upper

Hall of Ceremony, a chamber reserved for solemn occasions; then the whole party had proceeded down the wide stairway lit by candelabra, carpeted with tapestries, and garlanded with flowers, to the Greayte Banqueting Hall, where they were now seated at twenty-eight long tables set at right angles to the high table and snowed with white linen, frosted with silverware. The first six courses of twelve had been served and cleared. After the third course Lord Voltasus, the Storm Chieftain of the Seventh House, had made his speech of welcome and insincere praise for the Fifth House, and Lord Oscenis had replied in kind. Eloquent panegyrics had poured from both sides, and all formalities had been seen to be performed with grave decorum. Tradition dictated that it was now time for the bard of the host's House to speak.

The announcement was made; Carlan Fable, the lean, weathered bard of Isse Tower, rose. He bowed deeply toward the high table and surveyed the scene.

The Greayte Banqueting Hall spread almost as wide as the Tower itself, its ceiling supported by slim dominite columns and sildron strategically embedded within the structure. Wall tapestries depicted historic battles in which Stormriders had overwhelmed their enemies. Beyond the lanceolate windows a flowered sunset flaunted poppy and marigold hues.

Two Storm Chieftains sat at the high table. Turnip-nosed and slab-cheeked, Lord Voltasus of Isse was a massive boar of a man in a black velvet cloak bordered with embroidery in silver thread and lined with the pelt of a silver-white bear from the ice-mountains of Rimany. His dour countenance was framed by a coarse mane of gray hair, which in turn was edged by a high ermine collar. His lady, Artemisia, was dressed in a sleeveless surcoat made from cloth-of silver and stitched with seed-pearls, showing her long-sleeved black velvet kirtle at the armholes and hem. Silver bracelets jangled at her wrists: Necklaces of pearl and jet swung on thin silver chains about her neck, and her fingers glittered with multiple rings. Beside Lord Oscenis sat the Lady Lilaceae of the Fifth House in figured blue rylet lined with sable. Over the gilt fretwork covering her hair, she wore a fillet overflowing with dyed osprey plumes that infuriatingly tickled the noses of all those seated nearby. Lady Heligea of Isse, sister to Ustorix and Persefonae, sulked in moonlight samite, her eyes forever drawn to the windows and the skies forbidden to the Daughters.

All around the hall the same colors were repeated in the limited designs demanded by current Stormrider fashion, which, here in the far reaches of Eldaraigne, may have lagged behind city trends. Servants moved quietly among the guests, topping up goblets with wine. Judging his moment, Carlan Fable began.

"At this time, when there is news of a dangerous situation developing in the northeast, we must pause and look back upon other times of trouble. For it was then that we of the Stormrider Houses lived our golden days."

His gaze raked the hall: the faces, the wall hangings.

"During the Three Hundred Years' Strife, Stormriders were the greatest warriors of all the lands on Erith, and every King and lordling sought their strength and feared their swords. On the wings of the storm they rode, like avenging eagles."

Fable took up his harp and sang the lengthy "Song of the Storm Warriors." Outside, the skies faded to lavender and violet over the flawed glass of Isse Harbor. Distant, metallic screeches drifted in from the forest, and a light Summer breeze lifted the festively unbound locks of the guests seated near the windows. Candlelight starred crystal goblets. The song completed, Fable took a deep draft of wine during the listless applause and continued:

"But the lands of Erith were given peace at last, when arose King Edward the Conqueror of the ancient lineage of D'Armancourt—a man of formidable wisdom and enduring strength. The Houses and the lands were united as Empire under one ruler again to live at peace. Thus returned the D'Armancourt Dynasty, whose line had been broken for two centuries."

The rather more rousing "Deeds of Edward the Conqueror" followed, accompanied by the trumpets and harmonies of Fable's students. Some of the guests joined in heartily at the chorus.

"Yet what is lost can never be completely regained." This statement, delivered in tones of thunder, killed the mood of triumph, Hoad-like. A hush fell.

"Much knowledge passed out of man's keeping, and the Cities

were never rebuilt. Yet the Relay Towers and Interchange Turrets remained as sentinels and ports of call in the civilized lands, and the Windships began again to ply; trade prospered, and our strong line of Kings continues to this very day." He concluded his speech with a song in praise of James the Sixteenth, King-Emperor of Erith, and a toast to his health. Then the seventh course was served.

Two more courses followed. The hall hummed with genteel exchange and soft music provided by a quintet on tambors, lutes, and flutes who stumbled apologetically among the tables. Smiles crossed the faces of the guests, but there was no unseemly laughter.

"My Lord Chieftains, lords and ladies: Zimmuth the Gloved, mighty Wizard of the Nine Arts and Master of Gramarye, begs your indulgence to humbly demonstrate his skills for your amusement."

The portly steward finished his announcement with an unsteady bow supported by a tucket-sonance—a flourish on trumpets. A display of wizardry at any meeting of Stormriders was not performed merely for the sake of entertainment—it was important for the host House to show its strength in many ways. Although now peace reigned and there was intermarriage among the clans, old rivalries remained and there were those who would not let the memory of past feuds rest.

The wizardry began.

Magnolia colors had faded from the west, leaving the high-vaulted hall of the sky where now stars sang of unimaginable distances. Treading softly, servants snuffed out many of the waxen candles in their silver branches. From the corners of the hall came the smooth lament of violins, and on a dais, blue lanterns began to glow. Five masked figures swayed there in the cerulean light; they formed a circle and moved anticlockwise, then stepped back before a loud explosion of yellow smoke that flared within the circle, clearing to show the figure of Zimmuth standing, staff in hand. His bird-like face was heavily creased and slightly scarred. Black eyes sparkled from beneath beetling brows.

"My lords, my ladies, what you shall see here tonight is true wizardry. Many are the imitators, the makers of cheap illusions, the deceivers. Few are those who have mastered the Nine Arts of Gramarye. I, Zimmuth the Gloved of the Seventh House, am numbered amongst those few and have pledged my powers in the service of the Seventh House to ward against unseelie forces and destroy all enemies."

His demonstrations were truly spectacular. Aided by his five masked henchmen and with many roaring flashes of flame and smoke, he caused a variety of animals and birds to Appear and Disappear or become Invisible. To display the Art of Healing he guillotined a hand from an arm and with a spell restored the bleeding, severed limb to its former status. The Arts of Binding and Levitation were combined with the Art of Disappearance when a prone, silk-covered figure was levitated to a point above his head. When Zimmuth snatched away the covering, only naked air was to be seen. He made iron rings pass through each other, Motivated a wand to dance by itself, Shifted a capuchin into the shape of a mouse and the mouse to a dog and the dog to a dove, and, last, locked one of the masked henchmen into a box and stuck swords into him. By another spell, the man emerged unscathed! After Zimmuth had Disappeared in an explosion of red smoke, the last three courses were served and the dancing began.

While guests in rich raiment arrayed themselves along the dance floor in rows, bowing to each other before beginning a stately gavotte, a contrasting performance was being given many floors below in the sculleries, where stacks of soiled dishes teetered against walls, greasy serving implements filled wooden pails, dogs fought over scraps, and bag-eyed minions danced attendance on Dolvach Trenchwhistle.

The ugliest servant, who had slaved ceaselessly for twenty hours to the tune of conflicting commands, brayed scolding, dinnerware ringing like gongs, and occasionally the crash of porcelain dropped on flagstones, went missing. Among the bustle, nobody noticed.

He ached for peace and sleep, but first he would catch a glimpse of those Above the Dock, so that if perchance he dreamed, which he never did, he would dream of perfumed beauty and sweet music. Torches sputtered in sconces, shedding fitful splodges of light in the stairwell. With taltry pulled well forward to overshadow his face, it was simple to slip from darkness to darkness up the stairs and surprisingly easy to climb swiftly without gasping for breath.

On reaching an outer chamber of the Greayte Banqueting Hall, the would-be spy awaited his moment, then walked quickly through the open door as if on an errand, sidestepping behind an arras.

Under a vaulted ceiling of intersecting arches, long lines of dancers met and parted, crossed and separated again, in a solemn elegance of black and silver and pale blue. Spilled wine and gravy stained white linen tablecloths. Candles burned low, dripping their milky wax onto the silverware. Servants pulled the shutters closed against the cool airs of after midnight and the forest's weird noises. The lilt of violins and pipes swirled.

He watched, a delighted smile twisting his swollen lips.

Noticing him, a seated visitor gestured blearily for more wine. His glance alighted on a full pitcher; he brought it and was thus drawn into service among the tables until by mischance he found himself at a trestle occupied by several Master teachers of the Seventh House, who recognized him.

He sighed, then faced them squarely, even pushing the taltry back a little. He did not cower. His bold stance was intended to say:

"I have worked my bones to the marrow while you took your leisure. I am tired to my heart, and I am tired of cringing like your cur. Do your worst now—I die with dignity."

But, intoxicated, they only waved him away, except for Master Mortier.

"Come here to me."

Mortier put down the pointed knife with which he had been picking at the carcass of a small woodland bird. He beckoned. His surcoat and sleeves were splashed with food, his forehead flushed and beaded with fine droplets. Again he beckoned. The lad stepped closer, defiance in every line of his attitude. The man leaned forward confidentially, unsteadily. His breath stank, and with his soft, pouting lips he reminded the boy of the slimy creatures he had discovered under wet stones in the lower stories of the Tower, where the water-pipes had been leaking for years.

"Lad, fear not, for I mean you no harm. A coin for you if you answer me truly, yea or nay." The tutor's eyes narrowed. "Do you fear the shang unstorm?"

The youth began to shake his head, spied a glint in the man's eyes, and changed to a nod, but too late. Mortier smiled.

"Do not lie to me, lad. You have no fear of it."

He leaned back.

"Most people are nobody, and you are even more of a nobody than most. Be my errand-boy and rise above your station. You are the lad I need. Pod waxes obstinate. From this night, you shall be my page. Go now and wait in my chambers."

The new page paid him a deep and exaggerated bow, turning his face away lest his rage should be read thereon. His lips shaped the words *Mortier, thou slug.* To his ears, the music of the wedding feast had turned to a jangling of rusty iron, a clanking of chains, and a screech of hunting owls in the night.

Out of the hall he fled and down the stairs. From the wide flights he passed as he descended, into the narrow spirals where the treads were worn down in the middle. Down and down he hastened, stopping only once, at Floor Five, to collect a small parcel from a niche.

"How do you always find me?" croaked Pod from a hole in the cellar wall where he rolled, inebriated. "I go deeper and deeper, but you always find me. I don't like you. Mayhap it is you I am hiding from, eh? Something stole your voice, something stole your face and your past. I think some curse shadows you. How do I know that?" he rambled. "I am Pod the Henker, and I know. You know nothing of this place, this"—he spread out his thin arms in the watery glow of a rush-light—"this world. Hearken, I will tell you." He leaned forward, somewhat incoherent.

"The Windships they sail the tree-heads, the eotaurs they tread the skies for the twelve Houses, the Towers they rise up over the known lands of Erith, and the lands of Erith be the lands of men, but also of unseelie wights you cannot even dream of, that harm and haunt us. The King-Emperor rules in Caermelor Palace and courtiers all around, and he the sovereign of all Erith, possessing riches beyond telling. The world's wind blows through the empty courts of ruined cities. The shang wind blows through our heads and makes nightmares for us to look at. But I don't fear the shang, not I."

He leaned back, staring at the wall's utter blackness.

"Some fear it, some don't. It be like spiders." He paused. "And some spiders be poisonous, and some be not." He paused again. The whites of his eyes gleamed. The listener hearkened, trying to make sense of these ramblings.

"My lord Pouchguts fears it. Fears it to the death. And so he tries to rule it, to get power over the shang and over unseelie wights. With his books of lore and black candles and blood. He was to become a wizard, one time, but they threw him out of the College of the Nine Arts. He was caught treatying with unseelie things, trying to buy the power he lacked. He tries to bind me to serve him." Pod shuddered. "And serve him I do, sometimes, but still his fear grows. Now he prepares me to go down into the Forest. To bargain with them. But no, I shall not go, when the time comes. And you, you are no better! You also would make me go there! The shang I do not fear. But the things in the forest, in the dark of night—ah! 'Twould be better to jump from the topmost turret than face them, oh yes indeed."

Without warning he sat bolt upright. His face sharpened with urgent horror, his eyes clouded like muddy pools.

"Terrible things happen out there! A person could get lost, could pass right out of knowledge. Beware of footsteps in the night and dark wings that beat against the windows. Beware of the Hunt! Beware of water, wind, and stone! I warn you." His voice cracked and subsided into a kind of droning hum.

Mortier's potential page made hand-signs. Pod looked vapid. The mute one slapped his hand to his head in a gesture of frustration and flung his sack to the floor. Wrapped food and a leather bottle spilled out.

"Run away? No!" squeaked Pod, abruptly lucid—and then, rapidly, "Well, yes, then. You will never give up. You want to save me, eh? Then follow me. No doubt you mean to try the merchant ship hanging off the dock. 'Twould be a fine night to stow away on board, would it not? And sail away above this accursed forest. Now, while the wedding feast draws to a close and most are sleeping or too busy or too drunk to notice us. Let us go."

Too weary and grateful to wonder at the other's sudden sobriety and change of heart, the youth slung the sack across his back and followed Pod up dank and winding backstairs from twenty feet belowground to the wide dock 112 feet above.

It was well past midnight—almost dawn. Strains of melodies still drifted from above. The Tower stood silhouetted against an ice-crystal moon on lavender gauze. Land and sea lay sprawled below, a relief cast in pewter. The Windship *City of Gilvaris Tarv* bobbed at anchor over the mooring-yard, yellow lamps swinging from her rigging. Baffle bows, mooring-lines, and two gangplanks joined her to the dock. Barrels and crates stood piled beside bollards, but no guards or crew were to be seen. The surplus viands and liquors from the Stormrider feast had proved too strong a temptation.

Pod limped painfully up a swaying gangplank, dragging his foot. Despite his disability he moved quietly. His companion pressed close behind, darting glances into the shadows on all sides. Moonlight behind the masts and yards made intricate cobwebs of the shrouds and stays.

They reached the deck with a minimum of noise and cast about for a suitable hiding place. From an open hatch, a companionway led down toward a lower deck from which a second ladder led farther down to the dark well of the hold.

"You go first," urged Pod.

The mute youth descended both ladders and waited, looking up. Presently Pod's voice whispered down through the gloom:

"I am going back. I will not do it. Go into peril without Pod."

The lad in the hold dropped the sack and began to climb, furiously. Pod's uneven footsteps thudded on the lower deck, then the upper ladder. Hands grasped his ankles.

"Let me go," he croaked. "I was drunk—I did not—"

"Hoy, what's amiss?" a deep voice queried. "Who's there?"

Pod yelped, felt his ankles freed. He reached the top of the companionway, crawled from the hatch, and made for the boarding ramp at high speed. A commotion ensued, out of which a sailor brought a lantern, holding it high.

"By thunder, there be something unseelie on the gangplank!"

"Catch it! Kill it!"

"Search the ship for others. Check the hold!"

Burly aeronauts began to swarm over the Windship and the dock. But Pod was gone—gone to some secret hole in the Tower wall.

And no intruders were found anywhere else on the ship.

In the morning, the *City of Gilvaris Tarv* sailed with the wind's change.

# 3
# THE WINDSHIPS
## Sail and Swordplay

*The pine grows high, the holly low, the Windships sail where eagles go.*
*A hundred feet above the ground ship's timbers make the only sound.*
*Our roads have never felt the wheel, the tallest treetops brush the keel.*
*Amongst the spruce and fir we go, while birch and yew lie far below.*
*Like ocean's reefs the mountains rise, where birds are fishes of the skies.*
*Like foaming billows, clouds roll by, and currents wrack the windy sky.*
*On tides of light we chart our run and ride the highways of the sun—*
*To aeronauts of mist and air, 'tis only fools who live down there.*

SKYFARERS' SHANTY

Out of the pale predawn light emerged the rim of the world, painted with the hasty brushstrokes of clouds. It was suddenly split by the rearing bowsprit before sinking out of sight altogether. A moment later it soared up once more as the Windship struck an air pocket and dropped suddenly. Blinking away sleepiness, able aeronaut Ared Sandover felt his innards rise with the familiar thrill of falling, as if the deck left him momentarily suspended, and the surging lift that followed when it scooped him up again. The sun's first rays gilded a vast and endless view of undulating greenery, of tossing treetops.

Bells clanged to signal the half hour. Sandover took the wheel, pulling back slightly to tilt the elevator and lift the prow. Beside the wheel the aileron levers were locked into position. The sails cracked taut, bellied full of wind, and to the steersman it felt as if the spoked wheel beneath his hands were the heart of some spirited thoroughbred. Elated, he stood firm at his task despite the bucking timbers beneath his feet, keeping one eye on the compass, glancing at the rise and fall of the terrain and the approaching line of cumulonimbus building up along the nearby coast. The *City of Gilvaris Tarv* lifted gracefully over the surging foliage, elegant as a white swan. The taller trees rose so high alongside that Sandover could look straight in among their branches. On the bow the forest canopy fanned out, while overhead on top of the masts the ensigns of Eldaraigne and the Cresny-Beaulais Line fluttered in the morning light.

At seven bells the relieving watch came out of the fo'c'sle and a savory tang drifted from the galley. Scanning the approaching weather, the captain gave orders to reduce sail, and the first mate cried, "Haul away on the clews!" Sailors clewed and bunted up the sails from the deck.

"Main upper topsail it is, lads," shouted the first mate. "Aloft and stow!"

Oblivious of the fickle gulfs of air below, Sandover climbed the ratlines. After reaching the futtock shrouds, he swung out and over, stepping on up the topmast. There was no chance to look down; the boots of the man in front of him were disappearing quickly, and the man below was wasting no time, either.

As he stepped carefully from shrouds to yard, the sail boiled and bounced around his face; he and the other hands leaned over and lugged it up in great folds. Embracing it with both arms, they shoved it under their bellies and sprawled across it to hold it there until it was lashed. Over the curve of the yardarm Sandover caught a giddy glimpse of a forest lake far below. The ship's reflection was trapped in it.

Belowdecks, among the bulk of stacked cargo, the stowaway adjusted the bale-cloth he had rigged to hold him in the angle of a massive wooden rib curving around the hold. A couple of loose casks rolled; wine gulped in them. Stone jars knocked and rattled inside crates. Footsteps drummed on the deck overhead; beams creaked, rope slapped. His bundle of belongings sculled about. He dozed in snatches, ready to take evasive action should he hear the sound of boots descending the companionway.

His body ached from the tension of the hours of search, when he had wedged himself up under the hold's ceiling, arms and legs braced against the supports. They had searched the deck area thoroughly but, as he had hoped, had not thought to look up to where he sweated and strained right above their heads. To relax, even for an instant, would have been to drop down on top of them, and now his sinews felt the aftermath of the effort. Stowaways were not looked upon kindly. If he were to be discovered, the punishment would likely be severe. Thirst troubled him, but he dared not drink more than a few sips from his leather bottle, not knowing where to find more water or how long the voyage would take to wherever the ship was bound. Not even scummy bilge moistened these decks; no waves slapped the hull, no spray rattled into the sails—the only waters that would caress this ship were the rain, the mist, and the cloud-vapor that condensed in her moisture-scoops, collecting in the ballast-tanks.

A dragon figureheaded this three-masted clipper, full-rigged with square sails on all masts. Four stubby wooden wings projected from her hull. Mounted in their cases below them, small but strong sildron-powered propellers whirred. Ailerons occasionally tilted along the following edge of each wing as the helmsman made small adjustments to the ship's course. The ailerons were not the main source of stability, since sildron remained at a constant height above the ground and the ship would not roll unless driven above a steep incline; but they were required, along with the rudder, to make changes of direction.

A Windship could sail swiftly in the same direction as the wind or steadily across the wind. But like its cousins on the water, it could not sail directly into the wind's eye and had to tack. As powerful as the propellers were, they could not fight against the wind; their role was to impart maneuverability and added speed under the right conditions. Iron being anathema to sildron, these engines were held together with cordage and glue; they were incapable of undergoing the strain of high speeds or large loads without bursting apart.

Her rig was what harnessed the wind's power to drive the vessel forward, and the working of it through the changes of wind and weather required skill, hard work, and constant attention, for the wind was always changing course, and higher up the masts, it blew from different directions.

She sailed a predetermined course at an altitude of 150 feet, this height having been set by the amount of andalum shielding rolled back from the sildron inside the double hull. As cargo was unloaded or loaded at various ports of call, the shipmaster would ensure that the shields were rolled in or out to compensate for the changes in the ship's weight. It was every shipmaster's desire to sail as close to the designated altitude as possible and to reach each destination as fast as possible, without deviating, at least officially, from the legal trade routes. Windship routes and altitudes were carefully chosen by the Sky Moot to enable vessels to voyage with maximum efficiency and safety. Many mountain peaks jutted up well over four thousand feet. Around them the *Tarv* would have to navigate; to travel at lower altitude would mean more and wider obstacles, but she could not rise much higher without the purer-grade sildron used by swifter and more expensive Windships. There was also the Law of Quadrants, which dictated that Windships of her class bound in a certain direction must maintain a particular altitude to minimize the risk of collision. So, at 150 feet she sped along with a bonnetful of wind, sometimes brushed by the tops of pine, alder, and spruce as she crossed the Greayte Western Forest on her voyage southeast, bound for the city, her namesake.

The winds of the cold front escaped into the northeast without much hampering the Windship's progress, and by sunset she soared out over the edge of the Forest and began to pass over the meathenlands, a prosperous region of farmed countryside and small villages. Sheep scattered like thistledown before her shadow. A thick layer of altocumulus tesselated the skies like acres of teasel-tufts, reflecting hues of peach and amber.

These lands were patch-counterpanes of meadows and tilled fields edged with the green brocade of hedgerows and winding ribbons of lanes. The ship sailed through the night and docked next morning for half a day at Stockton Wood Interchange Turret for fresh water and cargo to be brought on board—grain, cheese, wool, salt beef, and beans. At that time the stowaway had to hide again, wedged among the supporting beams of the overhead deck.

Naught saw he of the Turret with its few inhabitants—little more than a slender column with landing platforms set at each level and each direction. Naught saw he of the village of Stockton Wood or of the green fields and patterned red soil that passed below. He knew only the restless twilight of the Windship's distended belly. From time to time, aeronauts would be sent below to check that the cargo was shipshape and had not come loose from its lashings, and that was what led, inevitably, to his discovery.

Able aeronaut Sandover dragged him up the companionways past several faces screwed up in astonishment. He stumbled, blinking, onto the quarterdeck and stood transfixed, looking up at the monumental wooden trees that rose forever above his head, tapering into a dazzling sky and decorated by the cordage of sailing; fathoms of standing and running rigging; halliards, sheets, foot-ropes, ratlines, tackles, shrouds, stays and braces, buntlines, clewlines, and downhauls. Sails bellied from the yards, and the flags of the Cresny-Beaulais Line fluttered from the mastheads.

With a contrary wind, she was close-hauled. The yards were pulled in as far as possible against the shrouds, and she was sailing at some sixty degrees to the wind with the propellers halted.

"Captain, sir . . ." Sandover saluted the stiff-backed, lean man who stood with feet braced against the rocking deck, flanked by the bosun and the cabin boy. Captain Chauvond waved him away impatiently without taking his eyes off the tossing treetops below. There was a ship to be sailed—discomfited stowaways must bide. Chauvond spoke to the bosun from the side of his mouth.

"Wind's veering now. Prepare to tack."

Orders were shouted: "Ready about!" Sailors in yellow uniforms rushed to their stations, threw the coiled lines off the pins, and checked that they were clear to pay out. Lee braces were flaked out on deck, free to run.

"Foremast manned and ready!"

The ship was eased off the wind to build up enough speed to help her turn through the wind's eye. The propellers sprang to life, groaning and rattling as they woke to the full force of the wind. Then, as the wheel was slowly put hard over, the 'tween mast staysails were dropped. The yards on the main- and mizzenmasts spun around as the orders were given, and now came the critical moment. Headsails clattered as they went aback. She was turning, with the jibs, staysails, and sails on the foremast aback to help push the bows around, and the decks a web of ropes. For a long moment she slowed, with the sails flapping backward.

"Mainsail haul!"

Sails on the main- and foremasts were braced around as soon as they began to fill. Then the mizzenmast was braced around, jibs and staysails sheeted home, 'tween mast staysails reset, course steadied, and the spanker eased off. Aeronauts busied themselves recoiling lines and hanging them neatly on their pins. Now the captain directed his attention to the business at hand.

"Stowaway, Cap'n, sir," Sandover announced unnecessarily, still gripping the lad by the elbow. Captain Chauvond grimaced. He was not an unkind man, but he ran a tight ship, in complete accordance with the rules and regulations of the Sky Moot, and had no time for those who broke them.

"Shall I clap 'im in leg-irons, sir, or give 'im six of the best?"

"In truth, Mr. Sandover, I have half a mind to have you throw him overboard," the captain said testily. "What say you to that, lad?"

The lad shook his head miserably. The cabin boy scrutinized him with intense curiosity.

"Think 'e 'as a wooden tongue, sir," said Sandover.

The captain turned away, hands clasped behind his back.

"Aye, well, we shall have to put him off at the next port of call, that's the correct procedure—hand him over to the local authorities. Until then he is to be adequately fed and put to scrubbing the decks and whatever else he can do to work for his ticket. And make sure he keeps his taltry tied on!"

"Aye-aye, sir."

For the rest of that day and all of the next, the lad was set to polishing the brass binnacle and the fife-rail around the mainmast, scrubbing the mess deck, and scouring pots and pans in the galley, where the cook was preparing a pungent stew. The aeronauts, at first uncertain as to whether he might be some eldritch wight about to curse the ship, were too busy to take much notice of him. More widely traveled than the parochial inhabitants of the Tower, they were accustomed to strange sights and thus more tolerant. The lad pondered bleakly on what might happen to him in Gilvaris Tarv and whether he would be sent back to the House of the Stormriders. Until now his only ambition had been to leave the Tower, as if somehow simply roving out in the wide world would give him the answers he craved. He dreaded being sent back to the Tower even more than he dreaded a beating for stealing illegal passage on the Windship, but if he were allowed to remain in the city, would he not merely end up as a drudge, toiling in sunless chambers for the rest of his life, polishing aumbries, bleeding, broken? Yet at least in a city, through which strangers passed, he might meet someone who could help him find out his name. . . .

Topside, the ship was a bee's nest of activity—yellow-jacketed men spliced and coiled ropes, mended and trimmed sails, and ascended and descended the rigging; orders were shouted and bells were rung; canvas strained against rope and every eyelet was a slit pierced by the red needles of the sinking sun as the Windship sliced through the sky with her sails heaped up like storm clouds.

They dropped anchor on the third evening at Saddleback Pass. The sheer and purple walls of the Lofty Mountains loomed up far above the masthead on each side. Below, wooded clefts lay in deep shadow. The next part of the voyage, through the steep, uninhabited ranges, would be difficult and dangerous, but it was the last leg, and the captain expected to reach Gilvaris Tarv on the following afternoon.

The lad took his meal with the aeronauts but was unable to stomach the stew, making do with hard bread and water and small, sweet apples. They sent him to the cargo hold to sleep and closed the hatch lest he escape and walk among them like a night-fright, disturbing their dreams.

During his watch, Ared Sandover could see far away a tiny glow shining through the darkness—a Lightship that was moored, eternally, at Cold Crow Peak.

Through the night, a sound reverberated through the mountains from some indiscernible point—now near, now far—the weeping of a heartbroken woman.

From time to time, an anguished keening gathered into a long, rising wail before breaking again into wrenching sobs. Indescribable sorrow communicated itself in those wordless cries. None of the crew slept. The skin crawled on their backs. They stayed silent in their discomfiture, tense as stretched shrouds; a strange, cold heaviness weighed them down, slowing every movement, even breathing. For it was the cry of a weeper, a harbinger of doom to mortal men. Three times it echoed forth, and then in the night fell an almost unnatural silence.

Someone, soon, would die.

First light was cool and blue, like the sea. High-level cirrus wisped in soft curls like swan's down. It was the hour to call all hands to man the capstan and raise the iron anchor from its bed somewhere in the mold of the Forest floor 150 feet below. White fog lay low in the deep vales, and cloud wreathed the mountains' heads. Bringing up the massive chain was a lengthy task; the shantyman's tune echoed among the hills as the great iron flukes rose in time to the tramp of the men marching around the foredeck with the capstan bars before them.

A light wind was breathing down their necks, and conditions were fair for climbing the rigging as the men went aloft to cast off the gaskets that lashed the sails to the yards. Soon ropes were flaked out neatly on deck, and buntlines and clewlines were ready to be eased out. The hands aloft by the mast at the upper staysails stood on the cranlines. Looking up at the yards, Sandover could see the loops of folded cloth, sails not yet set, as all around the decks aeronauts checked the layout. Orders were awaited. Not much canvas would be unfurled today—the *Tarv* must cruise slowly in this precipitous region.

Whistle blasts signaled commands along the length of the ship. Propellers spun into action, and they began to make headway. Gradually, as more sail area was displayed, speed increased.

The sun was not yet visible behind the peaks, and great swaths of lavender shadow fell from steaming crags into blind depths. Skillful navigation was crucial here. Uneven ground exerted unequal pressures on the sildron in the hull, which caused pitching and yawing. The steeply rising landforms forced the air currents to break up into strong turbulence; a run through this part of the country was always bumpy.

The Windship floated between giant castles of escarpments like a fragile moth, lit once or twice by stray shafts of light spearing between the eastern tors. Toward the middle of the morning, the lad's skin prickled. Fine, pale hairs on his arms stood on end, and excitement drilled through him like a silver auger. He shivered with expectancy—an unstorm was approaching.

The day-star climbed beyond the Lofty Mountains at last, and it seemed that the ship was making fair headway, when a minor solar eclipse occurred. Startled, the crew looked up to see, silhouetted against the morning sky, a brig, her two-masted rig laden with sails, floating across the fiery path of the sun.

The *Tarv*'s bell clanged fiercely.

"Sail ahoy! Black sail! Black brig fifty degrees high to starboard! All hands on deck!"

"Plague and madness! Where did that evil hulk spring from?" bellowed the first mate, letting fly a stream of curses. Confusion ensued, escalated. Men raced to load the mangonels and arm themselves. A black sail meant a pirate vessel—here in the mountains they could not outrun her; nor could they outmaneuver her. The black brig was smaller, leaner, built for speed. Their only chance was to fight.

But the brig, long and sharp as a knife, had the ally of surprise. Preceded by her iron-shod ram, she had glided silently from behind a high rocky wall where she had lain in ambush, and now, from her position overhead, a deadly hail of arrows and stones came clattering onto the merchant's decks. Two or three men fell, wounded.

"Captain, sir, I suggest flaming arrows," the bosun panted.

"And would you have burning debris rain upon us? Order the mangonels to prepare to fire."

The bosun's shouts were drowned in the broadside that exploded from the black ship's own mangonels, expertly aimed. She was so close that her shotmen could not miss, and with a splintering roar the mainmast crashed down onto the deck, bringing the foremast with it. Sailors who had been clinging aloft were hurled overboard. Their cries tapered off into deep mountain gullies, lost in the booming echoes of destruction. The stern wing on the starboard side was smashed off and tumbled down to vanish in the abyss while bits of sildron from the propeller floated away. With one blast, the *City of Gilvaris Tarv* had been disabled.

Her decks erupted into scenes of chaos, rolling and bucketing as the ship wallowed. Broken spars and yards rolled, sliding within a tangle of ropes. Orders were shouted in a desperate attempt to salvage the situation, but Ared Sandover, hanging on to the railing to stop himself from sliding, could see the brig swinging close alongside and knew they were doomed. The long arm of one of the *Tarv*'s mangonels, released from torsion, was flung up against its transom to hurl forth its heavy missile. The ship recoiled, slewing around like a dying thing, and the ball went wide of its target, slamming into the mountain wall, where it blasted a hole.

The nameless youth stood, unheeded, by the bridge, feeling the unstorm coming closer. There was no fear, only numbness; he felt detached from the scene, as though watching a play. Besides, there seemed nothing he could do; he had no training in bowmanship or working catapults or sailing. He gripped a tangle of ropes and watched the rugged horizon seesawing. In the next instant he regretted his lack of voice more than ever he had before; *oh, to be able to scream a warning!* Now his heart burst into pounding life at what he saw. Iron grappling hooks erupted over the railing, cast up from below, and thudded into wood. He flung himself down the canting slope to where able aeronaut Sandover struggled for balance.

"What? Leave hold of me!" They scuffled briefly, then the man turned his head and saw, too, the row of heads appearing up over the poop rail; the dark shapes of men swarming over, leaping down to the deck, knives glittering. More and still more came up the ropes from the longboats that had slid silently in under the hull while all attention had been diverted to the brig.

With shrill cries and bull-bellows the reivers swarmed over the clipper, wielding their long, curved blades with expertise. The fighting was fierce; the merchant sailors had been trained to defend themselves and their ship, but there had been few pirate attacks on record in recent years, and they were ill prepared. Standing side on with feet braced apart and knees bent, duelists fought desperately up and down decks that soon ran slippery with blood.

A battle-hardened, scar-faced pirate advanced within a sword and arm's length of his adversary. Grinning, the cutthroat swung his scimitar from right to left in front of his chest. The aeronaut extended, trying desperately to deceive, knowing he was outmatched. Scar-face repeated his playful action several times, advancing and retreating. All at once their weapons engaged, Scar-face's scimitar deflecting the other and coming in over the top to scoop up the blade and fling it aside. A ring of metal on metal, a rainbow in the air. With a thud, the aeronaut's severed hand hit the deck, followed a moment later by his torso.

Another pirate, a stringy fellow with no teeth who had been attacking, parrying, and riposting in a rapid rhythm, suddenly rapped sharply on the boards with his forward foot. His adversary, distracted from the scimitar, let down his guard. It was only for a fraction of an instant, but that was all the time necessary for the point of Toothless's cutlass to slash the aeronaut's forearm, slicing through the sinews. The sword fell from the impotent hand, and with a swift forward thrust Toothless skewered him to the heart.

One brave sailor crept up behind a roaring brigand who had bodily lifted one of his shipmates and was hurling him overboard. As he finished his business with a grand yell, the canny pirate positioned his scimitar along the underside of his left forearm. In a lightning movement he stepped back with his left foot, thrusting the scimitar straight out behind him and twisting his body to the left. The sailor, advancing with upraised weapon, was taken unawares and fell, cut almost in two. With a vengeful cry, one of his fellow aeronauts attacked, lunging with sword outstretched. The still-bellowing pirate retreated out of range. As he had hoped, the aeronaut shifted his weight backward to recover. In that moment of vulnerability, Roarer jumped forward and cut him down.

A bald, one-eared reiver hacked his way through the fray, naming his cuts and thrusts as he gave them: "The Hedger! The Reaper! The Thresher!" His blade clove the air with a rushing, hissing sound; it clove flesh with the succulent smack of an ax through cabbage.

When the shang wind came on them it seemed to increase the ferocity of the fighting, as if it got into the blood of the men. Smoking clouds boiled across the sky. Twilight glinted with strange, rainbow fires like ice, like jewels, like frosted stars. The brig's rigging was a dew-beaded cobweb giving off stabs of diamond light.

"Make her a ghost-ship!" cried a dying aeronaut, his last breath bubbling away in the crucible of his breast. The combatants, their heads bare of taltries in the heat of battle, danced to the rhythm of life and death in a soft radiance that burned their images on the air. Where they had been, a moment ago, their shapes remained—translucent, shimmer-edged, and slowly fading. A sailor swung a knife, and a fan of ghost-knives hung dissolving. A man fell, and his numberless ghosts fell again, many times. Phantoms and men leaped from deck to deck, their cries and the clash of weapons underpinned by a faint chiming of crystal bells.

The clipper, still staggering with the momentum of her dismasting and the counterthrust of the mangonel's firing, lurched sideways into the mountain wall. There, tall, dark pines clung, deep-rooted, glittering, growing straight up out of land that fell almost straight down. A wild-eyed pirate jumped back as his adversary moved forward and lunged with a cruel upward cut that opened his belly; the man fell forward with a gurgling cry. Another invader chopped at a sailor, missed—his scimitar sliced through rope. Sandover, who had been pulling hard at the other end of the rope for leverage while fending off blows, shot down the deck and out over the side. He crashed through the branches of a tree that gave way forgivingly and brought him up, scratched but living, against the trunk. The Windship spun away and left him. Foreseeing the ship's doom, many aeronauts slashed through ropes depending from the yards and swung themselves over the side in long arcs to throw themselves on the mercy of the trees and take their chances with whatever beasts and wights roamed the pathless slopes below; but not all were as lucky as Sandover.

When it was over, the pirates took some prisoners and threw the rest of the crew overboard. They plundered the *Tarv,* loading chests of precious things into the longboats to be ferried to the brig. Little of the less valuable cargo they stole—there was too much to take all;

it would have weighed down their ship and slowed them. Then they scuttled the white bird of a clipper, driving her into the mountainside and wrecking her on the rocks, raping her of as much of her sildron as they could get. She hung broken there, her lacerated timbers red-stained. The ghost-tableau faded out as the shang storm passed away over the mountains to the north and the sun shone, croceate, in the late afternoon.

When the next unstorm blew, the *Tarv*'s ghost-image would fly again, in memoriam.

In the wake of the unstorm the black Windship fled among the peaks. Patrol ships would come looking for the *Tarv* when she missed her rendezvous at the docks of Gilvaris Tarv, and the captain wanted to be far away by then. His ship was fast and maneuverable and had been drastically modified to enable her to change altitudes quickly, gaining or losing height ear-burstingly as the slatted andalum linings shielding the sildron were rolled back and forth inside her double hull.

The merchant sailors taken prisoner had been selected from among the unwounded for their size, strength, or nimbleness. Now they were shackled and manacled with iron, lest rope-chafe damage their appeal to prospective buyers. They were given food and limited room to move. Hale workers fetched worthwhile prices in this illegal trade. One of these captives was the stowaway.

The pirate's crew were thieves and cutthroats recruited from the dregs of cities, or simple country lads who had been seduced to piracy by tavern talk and could not now go back, or disillusioned soldiers; men who looked for rich rewards preying upon the Merchant Lines or who sailed in the sky for their own reasons. One of these stood now before the prisoners, his feet braced apart on the planks, his brawny left arm roughly bandaged where he had sustained a wound from a poniard. The lad squinted up at the head outlined against the sails. Tangled red hair like stiff wire had been randomly knotted with thin braids; in the thickets of it, a gold disk winked from his left ear. Blue eyes squinted over a ginger mustache that, although bushy, was clipped short. A copper torc clasped his bull-neck, from which also hung a tilhal of amber with two coupling flies trapped inside. A stained taltry hung from his shoulders. His barrel chest was swathed in a torn shirt that had once been white, overtopped with a rabbit-skin jerkin, and he wore olive-green breeches belted with gold-worked, purple leather with a wicked-looking skian scabbarded at his side. His feet, ginger-tufted and with dirty nails like goats' horns, were bare and tattooed with scorpions. The nameless youth had a good view of these feet because he was lying in front of them. To his left lay Captain Chauvond and the cabin boy. To his right reclined half a dozen merchant aeronauts, also bound with ropes.

"Deformed!" proclaimed the red pirate. "Twisted, ugly, and deformed!" He leaned closer to the youth and said confidentially, breathing garlic, "Hogger has one eye, Kneecap's got a wooden leg, Black Tom is missing three fingers, Fenris be earless, and Gums ain't got a tooth in his head. A man has to be ruined to sail on the *Windwitch*. Fires of Tapthar! You'll fit in well here, *mo reigh,* you'll fit like an egg in its shell!"

He laughed, revealing gaps in his dentition that seemed to go through to the back of his head.

"Me, I'm physically perfect. See that?" He flexed bulging sinews in his right arm, which was tattooed with ravening birds, their toothed beaks gaping, looking faintly ridiculous.

"I wouldn't like to meet *me* in battle, *mo reigh*. It's the brain—the brain that's twisted. I'm mad, see?" His jutting eyebrows shot up and down rapidly. "Sianadh the Bear, unconquerable in battle!"

He roared, a wide grin splitting his weather-lined face. The cabin boy whimpered.

"What is the matter, *tien eun?* See, I unbind you and your *reigh* friend." Squatting, he did so. "You two are to join us! You shall be buccaneers on the upper drafts. Every now and then, such as today, we lose a few hearty hands. Captain Winch needs to replace 'em with young 'uns nimble in the rigging. Don't look so sad! 'Tis better than being sold as slaves in Namarre like these *shera sethge* shipmates of yours here. And you, Captain, are to be ransomed to your Cresny-Beaulais Line."

Captain Chauvond groaned, licking blood from his lips.

"Now, don't bleed all over the clean deck. You lads, see that keg over there? Go and fetch water for yourselves and your shipmates. Make yourselves useful or Winch will notice you and you'll taste the lash. We sink anchor at dusk, then we eat and suffer. 'Tis a shame we left your cook in a tree—ours is a sadist and poisoner—'twould have been kinder to our aching bellies to have swapped one for t'other. Look lively there!"

The two youths hurried to obey.

The brig was a lean, streamlined ship, but run on more slovenly lines than the merchant clipper. The crew, less disciplined, were more careless and prone to unprovoked outbursts of violence. Captain Winch, however, ruled with a steely hand.

Having risen, the wind was blowing hard.

"Aloft and stow the top-gallants!" Winch's stridor, with all the power of a gale behind it, burst over the decks like a hailstorm. "You new lads, get aloft before I kick yers aloft."

The cabin boy looked frightened and opened his mouth to protest, then thought better of it. He and the deformed youth followed some of the hands up the thrumming ratlines on the weather side of the rigging, not having the least idea of how they would do the job demanded of them. Although the ship moved in relative harmony with the wind, its speed and direction deviated somewhat. The wind beat the lads down against the shrouds and banged at them. Climbing over the overhanging futtock shrouds was not for the fainthearted; their feet and legs disappeared from sight, and all their arm power was needed for the last heave onto the tiny platform. Once over that hurdle, the climb to the second platform with its smaller overhang was easier. The black top-gallant sails leaped and slatted among the clouds. Ropes and rigging tautened on all sides. Far below, perhaps a hundred feet down, they could see the men working on the decks. The massive yards slanted perilously over wild tors and scarps, crevasses and clefts, stretching in every direction like crushed lime velvet tossed over a table setting. Trees raced by below, each leaf sharply delineated in every shade of green and gold.

They must step resolutely from the ratlines to the thin foot-rope festooned beneath the spar. It shuddered as the draperies of flogging canvas cracked the wind like whips. The foot-rope sagged under the first man's weight so he sank almost below the yard, but it lifted as more men stepped on it and, finally, the two lads. There were now about four sailors on either side of the yard. The sail hit the lads in the face and knocked off their taltries. The brig rocked in its passage along a rocky crevasse, the masts swung in long, graceful arcs. They were clinging to an erratically swiveling pole a dozen stories above the deck. The cabin boy's face was pale, and his teeth clenched. The nameless lad did not look down again. Panic ebbed and was replaced, gradually, by exultation. Up here, he felt like a King. Had he possessed a voice, he would have shouted.

The sail had already been partly gathered in from the deck, the clewlines drawn to raise its corners and the buntlines pulling in the bulk of it up to the spar. The men leaned over the yard, seeming to hang on with their own belly-muscles so as to leave two hands free. They reached far down to grasp a ruck of wind-shaken canvas. It beat back at them and blew from their hands. The wind pinned them flat against the yard, tearing at their clothes.

"Heave, you laggards!" an angry voice brayed.

The lads copied the men. After pulling the sail up, they jammed a pile of it under their bellies, then grasped some more. When all the sail had been bunched up, they flattened it along the crosstree, then rolled and lashed it. Then they must descend, climb the foremast, and do it all again. There was no tuition for new crewmen on this vessel; it was "learn or die." Most of the buccaneers had learned that way and were prepared to give as much quarter as they themselves had received: namely, none.

At sunset, the *Windwitch* anchored in a deep and narrow ravine. Lurid light speared between almond-shaped clouds standing in the lee waves of the land formations, reddening a mountain peak shaped like three old men standing in a row. When the Windship was snugged down for the night, sails furled and lines coiled, the crew partook of their meal on the mess deck, so aptly named, slopping it into their mouths, wiping their greasy hands on their hair or clothing or any other surface that tended in any way toward absorbency.

The two lads drooped, almost too exhausted to eat. After a few bites they huddled together where some of the wounded pirates lay at the side. There they dozed, oblivious of the gibes halfheartedly hurled their way. Adversity had created a kind of comradeship, despite the fact that neither knew the other's name and never a word had passed between them.

Hawking, swaggering, elated by their recent victory, the hale crew-members argued about the division of the spoils.

"Let's have it now, I say. We've worked hard for it. Let's see the color of the gold in them chests."

Cheers and the banging of pewter tankards greeted this oratory.

"If we divvy it up now," said a horse-faced rascal, "where should we stow it on this bucket? In our hammocks? In our ship-bags? To have them made lighter by some sneak-thief such as Spargo as soon as we turn our backs and go aloft?"

Spargo, who had just then buried his nose in a jar to take a deep draft, thumped the jar down, spluttering. Rum splashed out of it. Also, carelessly, he had *thwack*ed it right in the middle of his dish. Grayish gravy flew up, splashing his face and nearby diners, who snarled aggrievedly.

"Did I hear you aright, Nails?"

Nails leaned closer to him, lips curled back to show the remains of his teeth. Spargo did not flinch.

"Blow me down," Nails invited, thrusting forward a stubbled jaw like a fist.

Spargo's eyes slid from side to side in his frozen face. Most of the crew had stopped eating and were watching.

He pushed Nails's shoulder.

Laughing, Nails playfully shoved him back, harder. Spargo's face turned purple. He thrust against Nails with all his strength; Nails barely kept his balance, then returned to land a blow squarely on Spargo's jaw. They rolled together across dinner plates loaded with boiled cabbage, charred mutton, and flour dumplings in gravy, to the chagrin of their shipmates, who instantly joined the melee in revenge for the ruining of their dinners, no matter whether the fault had been the brawlers' or the cook's. The lads from the *Tarv* prudently removed themselves as far as possible from this storm of flailing fists, cabbage, and pewter.

A sharp crack split the air along a black seam, and silence gushed out. Winch stood, whip trailing negligently from his paw. Beneath his horsehide jerkin he was shirtless. His bare chest sported a pattern of snakes and the usual tilhal, dangling on a thong. Wide leather bands studded with iron adorned his wrists and tree trunk waist. His brown hair was shaved to stubble on one half of his head and hung in long greasy braids on the other. He wore a necklace of sharks' teeth, and gold rings flashed in his earlobe and one nostril.

"Reef it, you puke-stocking rabble of misbegotten dung-eaters."

Growling, sullen, the crew scraped dumplings and gravy off themselves and began to eat the larger chunks. Still standing, the captain surveyed them with a surly visage, adding for good measure:

"Anyone care to have a conversation with Lady Lash?" He grinned then, bulge-eyed as a lunatic, but received no reply.

As the men settled back into order, or a semblance of it, red-haired Sianadh said conversationally:

"Dung-eaters? Now why should he call us dung-eaters? What does Winch know about Poison's secret recipes?"

"Poison don't use no recipes, 'e makes it all out of 'is own 'ead."

"That explains the texture"—Sianadh nodded wisely—"but don't be concerned, Croker—you ought to be used to eating things other people would scrape off their boots."

Croker, an irascible giant with an enormous blue-veined nose, jumped up and pulled a knife out of the cutting laughter. In answer, Sianadh sprang to his feet facing him, one hand gripping the top of his scabbard.

"I'll slice out your foul tongue, stinking Ertishman."

"Don't be so certain, *mo gaidair*. I have a long, wicked weapon to trounce ye with." Tension mounted again, so soon. Winch devoured mutton noisily, seemingly unperturbed.

"Do not be so quick to provoke me. All my foes run when they see me coming!" the giant thundered.

"Really, Croker? Even before they smell you?"

Veins stood out on Croker's brow. "Toad-spotted scum! I have never been defeated."

"Well, ye must run swifter than we gave you credit for."

"You think you're so clever. I've seen donkeys with more wit than you."

"Aye, someday I'll meet your brothers."

"I'll kill you!"

Sianadh rolled his eyes upward. "Ye'd be doing me a favor, me bucko."

"Draw yer weapon!"

Croker sliced runes on shadow parchment with the flash of his knife's blade. Responding with one fluid movement, Sianadh whipped a large sausage out of his pocket and flourished it triumphantly. Guffaws galed back and forth over the mess deck. Pressure released like the spring of a fired mangonel as Croker caught the sausage tossed to him, dropped his knife, and clapped a meaty hand on Sianadh's back.

"Ah, you be not such a bad jack for an Ertishman, Bear."

"And I've always loved ye, Croker. The rain shall never fall on me while ye are my shipmate. There is always ample shelter beneath your nose."

Croker joined in the laughter, his cheeks swollen with sausage. A moment later he looked puzzled, then shot a frowning glare at Sianadh, but it was too late. The red-haired man was by then seated in the middle of a circle, clutching a tankard in one hand, telling a story.

"This be a tale from Finvarna, my home in the west. The hero, Callanan, when he was a youth was trained by Ceileinh, the famous warrior-woman."

"Ha! Only the Erts of Finvarna would have women warriors!"

"That is because the least of our women is mightier than most Feorhkind men," was the seamless reply. "Do ye want to hear the tale or don't ye?"

"Aye! Aye!"

"To continue—Ceileinh held a stronghold in the mountainous country, wild and lonely. It was built atop a high plain surrounded on most sides by a sheer drop hundreds of feet down. From up there ye could look out across the heights and deeps to distant mountain peaks. Those who ventured there had to be stalwart and stouthearted. Ceileinh's fastness was renowned far and wide. All youths who wished to learn fighting skills went there for their training, which was arduous but made the best warriors of them, in the end—the best with spear and sword and bow, the best at horsemanship.

"One day as Callanan's training was nearly finished, sentries came riding in at a gallop, shouting that an invading army was pounding up the mountain path. It was headed by the infamous she-warrior Rhubhlinn, Ceileinh's fiercest rival, in her winged chariot. They swept away all who stood in their path, until they reached the cliff-top plain where Ceileinh and her company waited, forewarned, armed and ready, some on foot, others on horseback or in their chariots. Then a battle began. Rhubhlinn's mightiest heroes were slain single-handed by Callanan, but there were heavy losses also on Ceileinh's side. Both armies drew back for a breather, with neither side having gained the upper hand, and the leaders, despising this waste of their best champions, challenged one another to decide the outcome in single combat.

"But young Callanan demanded to take the place of his instructress. Knowing the measure of his keenness and valor, she agreed but warned him of Rhubhlinn's renowned ferocity. He only said, 'Tell me what Rhubhlinn cherishes most.'

"'She loves above all things her chariot, her horses, and her charioteer. Such a team they are, skilled, experienced, and peerless, her pride in war.'

"'I shall not fail you, my Chieftain,' said Callanan. He saluted and went forth to battle.

"The watching warriors kept vigil in a wide circle on the dusty, gore-spattered plain while those two combatants met like thunder-giants in the middle. First they fought with spears, but they were closely matched, and the spears shattered without doing harm. Their swords were brought forth, then. But Rhubhlinn was the more seasoned in this play, and soon she disarmed Callanan, breaking off his sword at the hilt. A great cry arose from the throats of the watchers. Rhubhlinn bared her teeth, seeing victory within her grasp, and drew back her arm for the fatal blow. But Callanan was no fool and had prepared himself.

"'Your chariot and horses have stumbled at the top of the cliff and are in peril of slipping over!' cried he.

"Rhubhlinn, tricked by this hoax, turned her gaze for one instant. In that instant, Callanan seized her in his arms. His grip was like steel—he threw Rhubhlinn down and pressed his skian to her neck, demanding surrender or death.

"Then she yielded to him and promised that she would never again fight Ceileinh. See, this tale goes to show that it is not strength alone that wins battles."

"This tale goes to show that Ertishmen tell improbable stories," commented Black Tom, who was immediately gifted with an eye to match his name.

The night wore on; the fights wore off; the tankards were refilled. This was a celebration of the day that had been. Talk turned to the day's battle, then to other ships, the ships of the sea. The legend of the Abandoned Seaship was told, and tales of the terrible shang unstorms and waterspouts in the northern seas, past which no ship could sail. Nothing lay beyond the Ringstorm—it was a barrier around the rim of Aia to stop ships from falling over the edge into nothingness. They spoke of the lands of the south: cold Rimany, where the Icemen dwelled with their milk hair, snow skin, and magnolia eyes, and of the known lands of Erith, where warriors slept for centuries deep beneath the hills while eldritch wights stalked the green turf above their heads. And, in whispers, these ruthless cutthroats mentioned, shuddering, the Nightmare Princes of the Unseelie Attriod.

They spoke, too, of strange tableaux they had seen in various parts of the world, left by the shang winds to repeat for centuries, gradually fading over time. They talked of the sailor who, among these very mountains, had been ordered to climb down the outside of the hull to effect repairs on a moving Windship but had been so terrified that he had stolen sildron to put in his belt. Strong winds had snapped his safety-rope, and he was cast adrift, helpless in the air and blown into tall gullies where ships could not go. Aeronauts claimed to have seen his decomposing body flying past at twilight, even when his bones must have dropped to the ground long since. A scoop net was kept ready by the helm in case that sildron belt was ever spied.

"Stormriders have flying-belts," said one of the crew, "but you never hear of that happenin' to them!"

"Of course not," said another, "they are not so stupid as to put high-grade around their middles. Their flying-belts are personally made to their weight, see, so that if'n they fell, they would be brought to a halt ten feet up from the ground. Then they unbuckle and drop down."

"Aye, but that do not 'elp them much if a tree gets in their way!" someone chuckled.

"Pig on a spit!" the first offered wittily.

Once, Red-Hair heaved himself to his feet, swaying out of synchronization with the ship. Gravely he called for attention, raising his tankard high; his audience responded with an expectant hush.

"I would just like to say, me buckos," he slurred, "that at no time in my life have I ever"—a pause for emphasis—"ever"—another ripe pause, during which the crew focused on him with difficulty and enormous expectation—"had any idea . . ." The red-haired man looked up with a confused air as he trailed off. "what I was talking about!" he finished, thumping himself down and smiling benignly all around. The crew cheered weakly.

At the last, one of them sang a song—not a bawdy song, for once, but a ballad about a maid who dressed herself as a boy in order to follow her true love into battle. The pirates listened, hiccuping and belching. Soon, sentimental tears salted the rum.

At various times during these tales, the deformed youth floated in and out of uneasy sleep. Snippets of stories concerning unseelie wights, monsters, and legendary warriors mingled with the whistling breath of the cabin boy, adrift in slack-jawed slumber on his shoulder.

He woke fully, later, to find that most of the lanterns had gone out or been extinguished. Men reclined or slumped, snoring, in a variety of positions about the patchy dimness of the sweltering deck, which was redolent with the reek of their bodies and rancid fat. The cradle of the ship rocked gently, incessantly, in crosscurrents.

The big, red-haired sailor called Sianadh was sitting opposite, his back to the hull's timbers. A lantern spilled a rose petal of light on a paper he held in his hand. He was gazing at it intently. The youth did not move a muscle. He studied the sailor's face, alert to any twitch that might indicate the man was turning his head. Could pirates read? This one must have that ability. Or was it a map he was holding so carefully? At last the man folded the paper and slipped it inside an inner pocket of his rabbit-skin jerkin. The crinkle-edged blue eyes slid sideways and pinned the lad. He started, jolting the somnolent cabin boy's head, which slumped down onto his knee.

"Oho, so ye be awake, be ye, *mo reigh?* Ye did not see that," the pirate said softly, soberly. "Foolish of me to bring it out here. But it is gone now, and ye saw nothing."

The lad shook his head vigorously. The blue gaze did not leave him. It studied him as intently as it had studied the map. "Ye be mute, be ye not?"

A nod for reply.

"I had wondered. I never heard ye cry out, even when we came in over the rail—even when your shipmates were slain. I thought ye were too tough, too tough to cry like a babe. And I still believe that, now. There's more to ye than meets the eye, *mo reigh.* Ye do not wear the uniform of the lemonlegs. Ye be not one of theirs, are ye? Ye did not belong on that benighted clipper. And that straw-thatch I saw when your taltry blew off, aloft—ye be Talith, be ye not? Color like that, so bright, right to the scalp, cannot be false. Talith—that be rare. Where be your people?"

The lad shrugged.

"Ye wear the brown of a drudge. Topsy-turvy are ye—brown garments, lemon hair! Topsy-turvy in more ways than one. Ye be not what ye seem, eh? I knew that as soon as I clapped eyes on ye."

The youth gazed back helplessly. Aside from the young servant Caitri, nobody had ever spoken to him like this before—not that he could remember—not even Keat Featherstone, so *personally,* as though he were worthy, worthy of notice and opinion. It was stirring and frightening. What did this bull of a man see when he looked at him? What in Aia was he talking about? Suddenly he wanted to reach out and clutch that knotty shoulder, to shake him, shake answers out of him. *What is Talith? What do you see? What am I? Who am I?* But he restrained himself, staying as rigid as canvas in a stiff wind.

And that did not go unnoticed, either, but was misinterpreted.

"Do not distress yourself. I shall not give away your secrets if ye do not give away mine. Shake on it."

The red-haired man held out a calloused palm, and they shook hands.

"Good." But Sianadh looked troubled.

"As thick as most of this *sgorrama* crew is, this be a Windship, *mo reigh,* and quarters are cramped. . . . You should get away, if you have a chance."

Spargo rolled over in a hammock and fell out on top of Hogger. The ensuing racket distracted the lad's attention, and when he looked again, Sianadh was nowhere to be seen.

* * *

The crew of the *Windwitch* woke like thirty soreheaded bears to a breakfast of lukewarm spike, ship's bread, and half-cooked, stolen bacon doled out by Poison—himself not in the best of moods from having had to get up earlier than the rest. Captain Winch and the first mate, the purple-veined Cleaver, shouted orders. The two new lads were sent aloft, where they were kept busy.

In the stillness of predawn, the mountains rang with the liquid warblings of magpies, heralds of morning in the wilderness.

As the sun's first ray edged between the three pinnacles to the east, a tremendous noise of crunching reverberated through the ravine, as of massive grindstones grating against one another. On a nearby crag towered a pile of gigantic, flat rocks. The topmost rock was turning around by itself. Three times it wheeled laboriously around its own axis, and then it ceased and gave no other sign but seemed an ordinary stone, unbudging. The lad from Isse Tower glanced at his companion for confirmation that his eyes had not deceived him. The cabin boy, however, with his eyes tightly shut, was engaged in vomiting over the yardarm.

Down on the decks a large party unwittingly mimicked the action of the queer stones, toiling around the capstan to raise the anchor. Soon the Windship was under way. Morning came on still and hot—it was Grianmis, the Sunmonth, and almost Meathensun. Clotted-cream clouds sailed past, level with the ship. Higher up, puffy pillows floated. Sometimes the ship would pass under a cloud archway or between two towers; sometimes she would sail into them, and then cold, clammy mist would fold in closely, blanketing out sunlight and bringing the world to an end at the taffrail. There seemed not a breath of wind, and all the power of the propellers was needed. As soon as the brig was under way, the two boys were sent to attend the prisoners and clean the fetid mess deck.

The first mate sauntered by.

"No talking to the prisoners," he rasped, spying the cabin boy handing tankards to the men from the *Tarv*. His piggy eyes snapped wide as he seemed to notice the other lad for the first time.

"By my pizzle! What manner of beast is this? Poison, do not let it near the galley again. It is not only ugly, it is filthy."

The lad looked down at himself. His clothes and arms were stiff with dried blood and gravy. It was the blood of the *Tarv*'s crew. Captain Chauvond and the others were in the same state, but Cleaver ignored them. He sneered, spat at the lad's feet.

"You insult the eyes of Captain Winch with your ugliness and dirtiness. At least wash! There is a pail in your hand. Use it!"

The lad blinked. It was a pail of lukewarm spike, but he did not feel inclined to argue. Then he froze, the pail still in his hands. Formless dread gripped his heart like a black hand. He dared not turn his head but hunched himself imperceptibly farther into the thick, baggy folds of his tunic, as if he could curl himself up inside it and disappear. Grethet's voice in the back of his head said:

*Don't let them see you. You are deformed. There's no knowing what might happen. Do not let them see you.*

"I said wash! Are yer deaf as well as dumb and ugly?"

Behind the lad's back, the cabin boy coughed nervously. Captain Chauvond, straining against his chains, shouted his fury. They were all behind the lad's back, the crew of the *Tarv*. Only Cleaver stood before him. The lad set down the pail, undid his belt. Slowly he began to raise the hem of his tunic over his head. Cleaver's sudden intake of breath hissed in the silence like a flaming arrow plunged into water. The lad could not see his face through the brown fabric.

"Stop! Cover yourself!"

Obeying, the lad could not fathom the strange look in Cleaver's eyes. It might have been shock or horror. It might have been the look of a wolf entering its den to find a rabbit waiting there. It might have been delight. He walked around the lad in a circle, viewing him from all sides as a buyer might view a slave in the market.

"Back straight! Shoulders back!" The first mate gave a bark of laughter. "Get topside, you!"

Avoiding the poorly aimed kick, the lad dropped the pail and fled up the companionway. Cleaver followed, crowing.

The air was pure up there—like pale blue wine, its crystal cup made to ring with bird-chorus from all sides. Majestic folds clothed in dark green fell toward mist-filled hollows. The *Windwitch* sailed, straight and level, on a white thistledown ocean among island mountains, but the lad could not see their beauty now. He saw only scarred and bearded faces gathering around, staring dourly at him without an ounce of compassion. Searching frenziedly for Sianadh, he saw him standing by the taffrail, curiously idle. And what could one man do against twenty-nine, even if he had taken pity on a peculiar waif?

"What have we here, me buckos?" the first mate crowed triumphantly.

"We know not, Cleaver. What *have* we here?"

The crew, unenthusiastically diverted from their soreheadedness, peered at the lad.

"I seen worse sights than that in the city," said one.

"I seen worse sights than that when Fenris gets up for first watch," said another.

There was a clear line of sight to Sianadh at the taffrail. He was taking something out of a knapsack and buttoning it in a back pocket of his belt. He wore a long leather tunic over his shirt.

"You ain't seen *this* at first watch," said Cleaver, gleefully savoring the suspense. "Haul up your tunic, dogface."

All at once the past two days of terror and humiliation culminated. Hot, white hatred gushed through the lad. He struck Cleaver a blow across the face and darted through the wavering crowd to the side of the deck away from Sianadh, climbing up to perch on the rail and gripping a rope for balance.

Two hundred and fifty feet below, the rumpled forest swayed dizzily and white birds flew. Mauve whales of mountains swam on the horizon. It would be so good, when he flew. He would spread his wings and soar to greet those whales. But no—to breathe the air of such freedom brought breathlessness. Losing all could not be worth that fleeting moment and never would be.

The passing moments seemed to slacken speed. Cleaver opened his mouth in a long, enraged bellow, crimson snakes streaming from his nose. A man had climbed up on the opposite rail. Another laughed that this was good sport. The crowd, fleering and braying like farmyard animals, surged forward. The lad prepared to jump. At the same moment, something huge out of the sky smacked into him and knocked him overboard, and he was not flying. He was falling.

# 4
# THE FOREST
## Tree and Trickery

*A bitter gust howled through the night. It shook the tall Watchtower*
*That stood upon the barren height and braved the Winter's power.*
*Three wildcats prowled on fellsides dim where freezing winds went clamoring,*
*When from the valley's icy rim the sound of hooves came hammering.*
*All o'er the moon-drench'd countryside the storm clouds were encroaching,*
*"Now bar the gates!" the Watchmen cried. "Two riders are approaching!"*

FROM THE FEORHKIND SONG "THE WATCHTOWER"

Like the waters of a narrow channel gushing out into a broad river, time slowed. Falling seemed to take a long while and evoked imperative, primeval responses; his limbs flailed in a vain quest for a hold on solidity; his blood surged in a dark tide, and the bellows of his lungs worked to suck in the air stolen by the vertical gale that tried, too, to steal flesh from bone.

The thing from out of the sky that had knocked him overboard was falling with him. It had somehow hooked itself around him and was bawling in his ear, but the sounds soared out of reach as soon as they left its mouth and were lost in the scream of air. The lad grabbed hold of it. It was solid. He kept his eyes tightly shut lest they should be blown from their sockets or lashed by the hair whipping around his face. He abandoned himself to utter terror.

A pressure began to evolve in answer to the pull of the

ground—a gradual, inexorable push, strengthening. The deafening rush of air softened. Its thrust from below slackened off. The descent was slowing. The lad opened his eyes just in time to see a mass of foliage rushing up, the forest-sea, to drown in.

"Take hold! Take hold!"

And then there were cold leaf-needles and stinging twigs giving way, snapping and cracking, but the sky-divers were slowing yet and bouncing down through the higher branches. The lad clung to the red-haired man with his left hand and reached out with his right, grasped a bough, and felt it wrenched up from his hand, grasped another, let go of Sianadh, and dangled there, then fell sprawled on top of a third bough and hung on grimly to its corrugated rind.

Having lost ballast, Sianadh, cursing, was now lifting skyward, towed by his belt. Crashing up through arboreal galleries he shouted and thrashed; every spray or sprig he grabbed broke off, for he was too far from the trunk and too near the top to reach durable sprouts. Needles tumbled in a green rain.

The lad's perch swayed gently, rocking him comfortingly. Gazing up, he saw the Ertishman come to a halt six feet above the topmost fronds of the tree. There was no sign of the pirate vessel.

"Spikes and spurs! I cannot reach the knapsack on my back. I stowed a rope in there, for all the good it will do me."

Sianadh kicked like a drowning swimmer and drifted slightly to the right.

"This belt will cut me in half. I'm hung like a carcass on a *doch* butcher's hook!"

A soft updraft, rich with the clean tang of resin, brought a traveling cloud of fluffy white seeds. It blew the struggling man yet farther away, out into an airy lacuna where no trees reached. From the bluest of skies, sunshine prickled in gold pins. Birds warbled and chirruped. Rocked in a perfumed bower, sheltered within bearded curtains of green far above the ground, the lad felt rinsed through by waves of relief and tranquillity, the legacy of aftershock, marred only by his concern for the man to whom he owed his freedom.

"Bide where ye be!" Sianadh's voice called. The upper airs had pushed him toward the cupola of a towering fir. He waited until he was directly above it, then unfastened his buckle and dropped, hanging by one hand from the belt. His boots flicked greenery.

"Curse Cleaver and his sudden fad for cleanliness. I won this wormhide belt at Crowns-and-Anchors, in Luindorn, and I've never owned a better. The buckle's a dragon, real silver—only one I've ever seen like it. If I could save it, I would, not to mention the moonslag stowed in it, but—"

He interrupted himself with a mighty roar as he released his grip and hurtled down. After a few splintering crashes, silence came down like a steel weight. The purple belt, having bobbed higher, pirouetted away.

A volley of murmured oaths issued from the direction of the fir. Then, louder, "Climb down as far as you can go without setting foot on the ground. Danger lurks below. Wait for me."

The mumblings resumed, emanating from farther and farther down.

The lad sighed, gave up his perch, and began to negotiate a way to descend, aware for the first time of the stinging scratches and bruises donated by his introduction to the spruce. His clothes hung in tatters. The tree whispered and swayed. Its boughs sprouted at arithmetical intervals from the stem—regularly spaced, if a little too far apart for comfort. The climber passed an empty bird's nest. Farther down, a second nest cradled three young rosellas who watched him quietly with round, enigmatic lenses. Squirrels scampered.

So this was freedom.

But, being free of overseers and sharp tongues, should he now place himself within the power of this stranger who kept company with cutthroats and was likely one himself? The lad hesitated, looking down. The ground was too far away to be seen. What a giant of a tree! Surely it would reach a third of the height of the Tower. His hands were sticky—here and there resin had exuded from the bark and solidified into dripping chunks of honeyed amber. He began again to descend.

This Sianadh, whoever he was, had risked his life and deserted his ship, for obscure reasons. It would be well to reach the forest floor early and elude him, vanishing into the understory. But then, the understory was probably monopolized by creatures with their own ways of making things vanish. Be the man trustworthy or not, throwing in his lot with Sianadh seemed the safer plan, if he stayed wary. Perhaps this was not freedom after all. Perchance that vision was only a vanity.

Butter-yellow bundles of feathers darted after clouds of tiny flies. The presence of insects perhaps meant that he was nearing the ground. It was harder, here, to keep from falling; the lower boughs were so much fatter, impossible to grip, wider than the yardarms of the *Windwitch*. And twenty feet from the forest floor, the stair of horizontal boughs came to an end. Cascades of perfumed lilacs grew all around, flowering pale mauve, white, and dusky pink. The lad crawled along a great arm of the spruce until its tapered point dipped politely beneath his weight, lowering him until he was able to jump down into the lilac-sea, whereupon it sprang up out of reach and waved farewell. Beneath his feet, the ground sloped steeply and seemed to pendulate like the deck of a ship.

"Where be ye, *chehrna?*"

It was not difficult to judge the man's direction from the sounds of snapping twigs as he pushed through long, fragrant clusters of starry mauve flowers.

"Lilacs blossoming in Summer," he said worriedly when the lad found him, "'Tis not *lorraly.* Something of eldritch taints here. Are ye hale, *chehrna?*" The blue eyes squinted under bushy brows. His skin and clothing had not been gently treated by his descent, and he looked to be a wild ruffian just emerged from a tavern brawl. Remarkably, the knapsack remained intact.

The lad nodded. Sianadh took the rope from his knapsack and, using the skian, cut a length of it to use as a belt. The lad's own pathetic bundle of belongings had been confiscated upon his discovery on the *Tarv,* and he had never seen it again.

"I took a good look at the lie of the land whilst I dangled above like a great gawping fish on a hook. We must strike out northeast, keeping the high ground to our left. Come, let us not linger here. Already we will have attracted too much attention."

He stepped out decisively; the youth followed. Sweat dripped from beneath his taltry, irritating his scratched face.

There were no paths. Or, if there were, they were false—narrow and winding, backtracking, leading nowhere, petering out. Insects droned in the humidity. Green light filtered through multilayered leaf screens, shutting out the sky.

Once they had left the lilac thickets the undergrowth became sparser and the straight columns of trees crowded closer together, their tops soaring out of sight. A curious twilight reigned. Sianadh consulted a compass often and muttered to himself, his eyes darting from right to left. Bushes rattled. Sometimes small animal shapes started up nearby and fled, squeaking. Orange toadstools squatted. Tiny, bright-eyed birds squabbled among low shrubs, and a spiny echidna dug among the fibrous roots of an ancient mountain ash. Painted honeyeaters upside down in mistletoe said, "George-ee," and, "Kow-kow-kow."

But there were other sounds and other sights.

Presently, from away to the right, there came the sound of something running. Nothing could be seen, but the footsteps sounded like the feet of a deer. The sound came up and passed them, but still they could see nothing, only hear the sound of drumming hooves, fading.

"Never show fear," Sianadh said in a low voice, "no matter what happens."

Farther on, an ululation of hundreds of voices came out of the trees—some crying and the others laughing—but the travelers passed them by without looking to right or left, although their skin crawled. Later, a wooden tub rolled along ahead of them for a time. Sporadically, pinecones dropped from the upper tiers like scaly fruit, too green to have detached themselves yet.

Here and there tiny streamlets threaded their way downhill. Underfoot, cushion plants, damp mosses, and dwarf brackens jostled against clutters of fallen logs, which made walking difficult. After plodding for a long time, a despairing anger overcame the lad, that he must have been so stupid as to have donned iron boots that morning. He tried to think back to his last sip of water, but the world, already on a queer angle, inconsiderately turned upside down and fell on him.

"Flay me for a *cova donni,* what was I thinking of? Drink this."

Supporting the youth's head, the man brought a leather bottle to his lips. He drank and fell back, watching as the man took a swig.

"Rest now. Aye, I need the rest, too, and some tucker. But we have not much longer before what's left of the light fades. I think we will not walk farther this day—I shall look for a place to spend the dark hours out of reach of night-stalkers."

Gazing upward, he walked away and the forest quickly closed in to swallow his bulky form. Alone, the lad fought panic. He could still hear the faint, regular crashes that marked Sianadh's progress.

The drone of insects seemed louder now and the trilling of birds shriller. So innocuous the forest seemed. Then, piercing through the natural babble, a strangely beautiful music; the dim skirl of distant bagpipes and the thud of drums rising from below the ground, filtering up like an invisible, audible mist. Indeed, its cadences evoked a land of mist; vaporous cobwebs through which tall and glittering ferns could be glimpsed; a land of mountain and cloud and of somber lakes lying close under dark skies. Closer these sounds traveled, until the wild melody rose up all around, blocking out all else, it having halted right beneath the lad's feet. As if carved from stone, the listener stood, at a loss. His fingernails bit into his palms. The vibration of the drumbeats rattled the ground. Stately, the music moved away, evaporated.

Sianadh came racketing back, oblivious and triumphant.

"I have found just what I was looking for, *chehrna*—a tyrax's nest, halfway up a weather beech. They are easy to climb, those weather beeches."

A sobbing wail sounded, like a lament, far off. Almost human. The music's spell dissipated.

"There is no time to lose. Come quick."

The weather beech's lower branches were within easy reach. Sianadh coiled his rope around one shoulder and swung up, then dropped an end of rope down. His companion tied it to his own belt and ascended, half-hoisted.

The tyrax's nest was a huge, messy weaving of sticks, twigs, mud, and dead leaves, more than roomy enough for two people. It was lined with dry grasses; there was no sign of feathers.

"Their reek has gone," said Sianadh, sniffing, "The big fliers have not occupied this for a long time."

He took food from his knapsack, ship's bread, cold mutton, some dried figs and raisins. They ate in silence as daylight drained through an unseen rent in the western sky and the oppressive heat faded to balminess. Great flocks of dinning birds came in to roost, bringing uproar to the forest, but none settled in the weather beech.

Sianadh's hair gleamed copper in a last blink of light. He put away the few remnants of food and busied himself with changing the makeshift dressing on his wounded arm.

"Give me a hand with this, would ye, *chebrna?*" he said between clenched teeth that held one end of a strip of clean cloth. His companion obliged, tying on the fresh bandage carefully. The man stowed the bloodied cloth in the knapsack.

"'Twouldn't do to drop that overboard hereabouts. The whiff of blood, even dried blood, attracts many things fell and foul. Here, wet this cloth and wash those scrapes. 'Tis not wise to leave wounds uncleaned in the wilderness."

Sianadh tossed him a linen square and a hip-flask of some potent spirit that stung when applied. After tending his hurts, the lad lay back with his head on the woven rim, eager for sleep in the aftermath of terror and exhaustion.

"What be your name?" the man asked, settling himself comfortably. "Can ye tell me in the speech of signs, the handspeak? . . . No? Then it must be that your tongue has but lately been tied, for none could live long in company without parlance. My sister learned the handspeak when she was no more than ten Winters old and taught it to the rest of the family. She became mute on Littlesun Day in the year she turned sixteen. If ye like, I shall teach you something of this, maybe tomorrow, in daylight."

Delight leaped in the lad. He nodded, smiling.

"But ye must have a name, *chebrna,* mute or not," continued the man. He was answered with a shrug.

"Do ye mean that ye have forgotten it? That I cannot believe!"

The lad shook his head. He pointed to himself and shrugged again. The man stared suspiciously.

"Ye're not having me on, I can tell that. And ye be a bright one as I took ye for, not some half-wit. And I do not think ye be *scothy,* that is mad, although I could be wrong. Well then. If ye've lost your name, ye'll be needing another, until ye find it. I cannot go on calling ye *chehrna* forever, and we may have a long road to go together. Have ye a preference in names?"

That word, *chehrna*. It seemed significant. Before that night on the *Windwitch,* the Ertishman had called him by a different kenning—what was it—something sarcastic? *Mo reigh.* Why had Sianadh changed his form of address and his manner? An irritant scrabbled at the lad's thoughts. Something was very wrong—he had known it for a long time. He had known it in the Tower. He pushed the scrabbling thing away again.

"No? I have many spare names that folk have given me over the years, but none fit for the likes of ye. I usually save them to hurl at my enemies. Nay. I have it! When I saw them flitting in the forest they brought me to mind of something . . . an Ertish name it shall be for ye, until ye have your own one again, and a fair name and honorable it is. Imrhien. Shall ye be pleased with your new name, Imrhien?"

Sianadh cocked an interrogative eyebrow.

*Imrhien.* As a name it had a good ring to it, a sound of lightness and color. The lad showed his lack of objection to it with a smile. Sianadh nodded. "Imrhien," he repeated, as though hanging the name on the walls of the world and stepping back to admire it. The lad began to drowse—content, named, promised, protected.

Sianadh cleared his throat loudly and spoke again, hesitatingly, fidgeting. The words he uttered thrust a lance of ice down the listener's spine and jolted his eyes open.

"Ye need not fear," said the man, his features barely visible in the dregs of twilight, "I shall not take advantage. I have never harmed so much as a hairstrand of a maid or woman yet, and nor do I intend to. Besides, I've a sister who'd box my ears if I did."

The youth sat bolt upright.

"What—hey!" Sianadh lunged forward to seize the slender form scrambling out over the side of the twiggy platform. Hauling in the struggling figure, the man took one look at the dismay-filled eyes and cried, "*Oghi ban Callanan,* what have I said now?"

The figure pinned between his hands quivered, aghast. *Sianadh must be crazy—mad in the worst possible way, seeming sane on the surface but dangerously unbalanced at the core and not to be accompanied a moment longer.*

"Peace, *chehrna,* peace! Knock me down with a belaying pin, what have I done to deserve this? Think ye that I would allow ye to throw your life away down there after all the trouble ye've given me saving it?"

The newly named Imrhien became as still as a block of glint-flecked dominite. That which had been plucking and wearing away at the edges of thought was knocking more loudly now. It was bashing deafeningly, threatening to splinter the doors. For the moment there was no escape from the madman's clutches. Perhaps, after a false lull, he would sleep, then the one called Imrhien could slide away quietly and the doors would remain intact. . . .

Sianadh's grip loosened slightly. His brow knit.

"'Tis turnabout now, I see. This time ye think I am *scothy*." He shook his head. "Ye have me foxed. I cannot fathom it. I do not know what is eating at ye, but I can guess what would be eating ye should ye go down to the ground at this hour. I mean ye no harm, I swear it. Can ye not see that, lass?"

His companion jerked violently away, almost eluding him. Sianadh's grasp tightened again. His visage cleared, and a look of amazed enlightenment dawned on his blunt features.

"Ah. Can it be? I have heard tell of this. Mind-rinsing, they call it, or thought-training or some such. Can it be that ye yourself do not know? There was a tale in Finvarna of a baby whose parents were lost at sea, shipwrecked. He was given to his grandmother in a distant village, to be raised, but she had no fondness for boys and she got him up as a girl. He went about in skirts with his hair in ribbons. Not having any other way of knowing, he grew up believing what the cracked old biddy told him. The truth found him out at last, but I do not know what happened to him in after days.

"And ye with your forgetting—it makes sense . . . if ye had forgotten what a girl is like, ye wouldn't know of your being one. Stranger things than that I have seen and heard, yet . . . it is strange. Someone has made ye believe what is not true. I heard it has best effect on folk in a weakened and sick condition. Ye, so wasted and gaunt, a slight shape not obvious beneath those rags—what have ye suffered? Starvation? Is that how ye were weakened? And aye, that answers another question. I heard it said by my sister that maids who starve lose the moon's blessing; some call it the curse. My sister, the mute, she is a carlin. She knows these things. Someone has drawn ye into a lie, *cheh*—Imrhien, I do not know why. Mayhap to protect ye. It protected ye on the pirate vessel, indeed, for a time. Nay! Do not weep!"

But his protests were in vain. The doors had fallen in with a roar, and light had burst through. Great, silent sobs racked the *girl's* body with uncontrollable spasms.

Oh yes, it was true. It was all plain, now, looking back. The songs told of such things. There was the maiden who could not be parted from her lover and had dressed herself as a soldier and gone to battle, to be by his side. And in truth, there had been a scullion in the Tower who had pined for a sailor-lad from a Windship, and would not take food, and had worn to a shadow and lost the moon's blessing before she died. There was a young girl who had once been fair but had grown old knowing misuse at the hands of men, and her name was Grethet. And there was another maid who had forgotten and been tricked, to spare her just that.

To be a maiden, a lass, a wench. To be born in second place in the world's favor—from what he—*she* had seen at the Tower, she *knew.* To be subjugated, idolized, preyed upon, used, and pampered. To be judged on appearance by all men, and in her case to be judged and found wanting, worthless, guilty; to be condemned. To have one's essence dismissed and overlooked because of the vessel that contained it. To be forbidden the opportunity to ride sky. To be forbidden the rights of the heirs of Erith. That was to be a maiden, she understood.

But she did not weep for that. She did not weep for the sorrow of losing that one fragile status, that illusion. She wept for joy; for joy, because at last, here was a Truth.

A cat of a wind sprang up during the night, playing with the forest giants as if they were skeins of yarn. It battered them this way and snatched them that, now gentle, now suddenly cruel. The sturdy beams of the weather beech did not flail in panic, they merely rocked the tyrax's nest: a mother lulling her babe.

It might have been the fading of the wind's deep-throated choir or the easing of the branches' protesting creaks or the cessation of the lullaby swaying that roused the transformed refugee. It might have been any of these things, but it was not. Uneasiness had pervaded his/her restless half-sleep. The erstwhile lad opened her/his eyes to see that Sianadh, who had volunteered to keep the first watch, was asleep, twitching and snoring intermittently. Some inner prompting caused her to remain motionless—only her eyes slid laterally, like oiled buttons. Sloughing the last shreds of drowsiness and redundant self-image, she became aware of the effect that had woken her—a high-pitched whine, thin and unbroken like a wire stretched taut against the darkness, an ill-boding humming, dreary and remorseless, that set the teeth on edge.

What it was she could not guess, that narrow, winged form flying very slowly, as if searching, into the rift in the leaves. Sidereal light illuminated the diaphanous membranes, devoid of color, the delicate antennae, the feminine waist and long, improbably spindly legs and arms that shone as if covered with tiny scales, the face with its bulging, faceted eyes, and the attenuated tongue, still searching. The whine's volume increased. The creature could not turn her head much from side to side, and indeed, it seemed as though she hardly needed her eyes to hunt. The antennae flicked responsively. Elegant, fragile, she drifted closer.

A slight movement told the girl that her companion was awake. He, too, had seen it.

"Culicida," he breathed. "They travel the path of living breath and target the warmth and sweat of flesh. Burrow into the leaves."

Cold leaves abounded, shredded drifts of stained and twisted parchment in the deserted nest. In their depths, infinitesimal spores bedded, each mycelium a gangling hair, a frail, inexorable agent of decomposition. In this mold the cuckoo's nestlings dug themselves in until they were completely covered, not daring to breathe the fungous atmosphere. The monotonous song of the hunting Culicida came and hung right over them, piercing their ears, drilling into the marrow of their bones. A long time she hung there, sensing, while those she sought, with burning lungs, endured the scarlet flashes of oxygen depletion vivid against their eyelids.

The predator moved away, droning off into the night. Her would-be prey exploded from the heap of leaves and melancholy yeasts like corks from ale-jars, gulping fresh air. Panting like a hunted fox, the Ertishman scanned their surroundings.

"I'll warrant she's foretasted something she liked better. Ha! Here are dry leaves of pennyfoil and elder, which the tyrax used to line its bower, praise be! Those herbs and some others may drive away her kind. For the moment, we are out of peril. I never thought to see Culicidae here—their clans dwell mainly in Mirrinor, where they lay their egg-rafts among the bulrushes in the long lakes and the swamps. They can only fly short distances and that only in still airs. But winds can blow them hundreds of miles. You do not know of them . . . Imrhien? Mosquito-folk, they be, cousins to the insect swarms. Their prettiness belies their strength. They be not eldritch wights, aye, but they be deadly evil. Vectors, like the one we saw, be the worst among them. Their pricking tongues bring diseases and plagues the like of which have wiped out countless numbers of mortalkind, and they know that. Yet they have no conscience, none at all." He fell silent for a time, craning his neck up at the nets of white stars framed by the trees.

"There, ye see? That is the Swan—the constellation of the Swan. Nine stars. Ye can see them at this time of year, here and at home in Finvarna." He traced out the bird's shape with a stubby finger, then began to pick leaves and a small caterpillar out of his mustache.

"Sleep now. I will watch."

Shaking her head, his companion jabbed a thumb at her own chest. Sianadh shrugged.

"As ye wish, then, *chehrna,* if you be so set on it. But first let me teach ye to say that in handspeak."

He pointed to himself, then held out his left hand, curled in a fist.

"This be the *slegorn* rune, the dragon, that hisses like a snake.

With the right hand ye make the *vahle* rune, that is the valley, with the index and middle fingers extended. These fingers be the two eyes watching. Rest the heel of the right hand on the back of the downturned left hand. This be the sign for watching with the eyes, the dragon watching under the valley. Now ye have had your first lesson in the handspeak."

He yawned and then fell asleep almost immediately.

She could not sleep. She walked on the edge of oblivion but could not have let herself drop into it, even had she tried. For danger she watched, all the while the salt of self-doubt rubbing on the raw graze of confusion. All the hidden embers of defiance had been doused now. How had she prevented herself from knowing that Truth? When Grethet had pulled tight the straps confining her chest and hissed warnings in her ear, how had she snapped spontaneously into apathetic acceptance?

*Because,* she told herself, *Grethet was all and only. And you were new, bruised, needing guidance. The crone had seen too many wenches suffer. It may be supposed she herself had been violated. Ill-tempered and selfish, she was, but she saved you. She gulled the rest, too. Do not condemn her for gulling you.*

But she condemned herself. To be gullible was to be adrift on the world's sea at the mercy of tide and current.

*Search your heart, fool. You knew in there, all along. Plunder your heart for the Truths therein and cleave to what you find.*

An owl "boo-booked" across the scufflings of Summer night, and the quenched firedrake's eyes kept watch under the valley.

The quicksilver notes of a magpie struck the bleaching air like a bell-hammer. Dawn's alchemy transmuted the canopy's edges from blue gray to green gold. Sianadh snorted awake.

"Time to go, *chehrna.* 'Tis not wise to stay in one place for too long."

They climbed down the whispering weather beech. Not far away, a freshet sprang from spaghnum. There they drank and bathed discreetly, tending their various hurts. The Ertishman rummaged in his pack and produced food.

"Pah! This mutton's rotten. The heat has sent it off. I took it but yesterday morning from the ship's galley, even before Poison had tampered with it—this other provender, the dry stuff, I have had stowed in readiness since before I boarded the *Witch*. No matter, there be plenty."

After eating, Sianadh brought out a battered compass.

"Needle's swinging all over the place. These things be never reliable when eldritch creatures be close by. Never mind, I can find the way. We continue to follow the line of this ridge. Wights and wild beasts may be about, but we both wear tilhals, and what's better, I have the skian. I never miss when I throw a knife. Still, 'twere prudent to go quietlike."

He bounded ahead like a firecracker, twigs snapping and bending before his broad shoulders and flailing back in the face of his follower. After they had walked for a time, a white hare started up and ran beside them. When it bounded ahead they saw a woman in white before them among the trees, but when they came up to her, she was gone, having been no true woman.

"*Doch* shape-shifters," grumbled Sianadh. "Not a mortal man or woman for miles about, yet with these shifters I feel crowded!"

Here, the forest canopy was thinner and the travelers could look out through the parallel stripes of tree-boles, through a tapestry of nodding foliage and long cascades of leaves, a green-gold cochineal flickering embroidery; across steep-walled valleys to where layer upon layer of ridges marched into the distance in ever-deepening shades of blue. The long folds of the mountains' mantles rolled against a sky scratched by the wind's fingernails—a blue sky paling to silver at the horizon.

It was hard going, but in the middle of the morning they came upon a faint trail of sorts, leading in the right direction. Now that they could proceed more easily, Sianadh began to talk.

"And now ye most likely want to ask me some questions. Why did I jump overboard with ye, and where are we going? Truth be known, I b'ain't no pirate. I be a trader, see, a traveler and a trader. I have turned my hand to many things—crewed on merchant ships, sold wares in city stalls, labored in the fields and byres—but I be my own man. There's some as envied me my successes, some with power who brought it against me. I have been hounded and harried across most countries for one thing or another, never my fault. I've had a wife. Two children I have in Finvarna, but I cannot go back there now. They be grown and flown anyhow, older than I reckon ye to be.

"I never lifted steel against your shipmates, believe me or not, as ye will. I b'ain't never been a pirate, never killed a man, though I could do it easy, and I have fought enough fights and beat them all within an inch of their lives. See, *chehrna* . . . Imrhien, there was this guardhouse, and I was inside it. Locked me up they did, the black-hearted *skeerdas,* and I was in there with a man who was dying. I did what I could to ease him. I be not a heartless man. Gave him part of my water ration and covered him with my jacket . . . he gave me this here map before he faded."

From an inner pocket he drew out the crumpled parchment he had been looking at on the mess deck of the *Windwitch.*

"Do not laugh." He smoothed it out. "In tales, pirates always have these. 'Tis a map to find buried treasure. He said it was the location of a sildron mine." He looked sideways at her, and she merely nodded.

"Funny thing about ye, Imrhien. Ye do not seem surprised by that. Most folks would have stopped in their tracks and swooned. A sildron mine! Do ye ken what untold wealth would be buried there? A man could be a King. A man could be many Kings."

She repeated the nod. He refolded the parchment and replaced it meticulously.

"A long-abandoned, sealed, and forgotten mine, he said, still loaded with ore. Loded! Ha ha! Anyhow, I suppose the stuff must be layered with andalum or else stashed high in a mountainside. Else it would not be a mine at all but a *doch* great chunk of ore blundering about the sky. I wanted to search for it alone—there are few who can be trusted these days, and those who can are too precious to be risked on a venture that might prove worthless. So I paid the last of me savings to a wizard to put extra wards of protection on my tilhal so that I could go alone. How to reach it was a riddle, for it was stuck in the wildness of these inaccessible Lofties.

"There be a river running out of these parts to Gilvaris Tarv, but

I could not get aboard a boat, could not afford passage, and besides, there be not one river-boat captain trapping in and out of Tarv I would trust as far as he could toss me, which be not an inch. Even if I got a boat, the map was not clear on which tributary to follow—there be many unnamed and unmapped streams in those parts.

"So I found out through means too twisted and tangled to describe that the outlaw Winch planned for to sail these remote areas in the Summer, and by further devious means I got aboard as crew. I sailed with 'em and put up with 'em and their foul methods, all the while waiting until the ship should come over the right spot. A few words in the captain's shell-like ear about the best course to take did not go astray, I might add. We were almost there, lass, almost there, when ye were discovered. I had some king's-biscuit, that is, sildron—the stuff has many names—which I had managed to get. A small piece. I had planned to go overboard in the night, quietlike, but when I saw ye trapped by the rail I just upped on the mainsheet and swung over like a capuchin on a vine. Chariots o' fire! Ye clawed me like a gray malkin as we fell! So here we be, a day or two's journey from the mine. I can see ye be brimming with asks. Let me teach ye the hand-signs what, why, how, who, when, and where. Also yes and no for good measure."

He taught her. She had to be shown only once. She signed, <<Why me?>>

"Why do I bring ye? Ye can help me carry the treasure, of course, strawgirl!" He chuckled.

A bolt of excitement went through her—not because of this supposed wealth waiting around the corner, but because she had spoken with her hands and made herself understood! The greater treasure apparently lay already in her hands, waiting to be brought to light.

<<How? How?>> she signed urgently, flapping hands.

"How what? How shall we find it, carry it? . . . No? Peace, *chehrna,* I cannot read your thoughts. How to handspeak? Aye. I will show ye more as we go along. Ye learn quick. Wait—where has our talk taken us?"

He halted. The trail had led them under ancient trees clasping oddly dark places between them, shuffling with their ropy roots in the mosses. Beneath, silent rainpools lay in the wide angles of their toes. Their boughs spread wide, rich with scalloped leaves. Young saplings had sprung from the trunks of felled trees, and the coppice floor was misted with hooded flowers, blue as sapphires.

"A bluebell wood! Imrhien, we must away from here at once!"

Leaving the path, he plunged down the slope to the left, the trees hemming them in. Roots tripped them up; branches billowed around their ears. Seeing the Ertishman begin to run, the girl did likewise, seized by unreasoning panic.

Suddenly Sianadh's boots left the ground. His eyes bulged. An intermittent snorting left his mouth, followed by no sound at all. His tongue lolled out, purple, like the protruding head of some internal worm.

A branch of holly had whipped around his neck, and he was being hanged. As he dangled, strangling, hacking at the branch with his skian, another prickly bough swung lazily out at the girl's neck; she ducked under it and danced away. Sianadh's blade sliced through. He fell heavily to the ground. The girl seized the skian from his limp hand and slashed at the wicked branches. Thorny leaves sewed her skin with fine red embroideries. With a shuddering gasp, the Ertishman heaved himself up and rolled out of reach of the holly-tree.

Laughter rose on one side, then another. Queer voices called out mockingly in words that could not be understood. Unseen things came on behind them on silent feet, only their squalling and guffaws indicating their proximity. Sianadh staggered to his feet and stumbled on, clearing a path for his companion, but as fast as they sped, they could not shake off these pursuers. At last the Ertishman balked before a thicket of interlocking thorns. He flung the knapsack into the girl's arms and snatched the skian out of her hand.

"Imrhien, delve out the salt—'tis in a wooden box. And the bells, Imrhien—rattle them!"

She obeyed. The brace of bells jingled, a jarring sound here. Other sounds ceased.

"Ahoy!" Sianadh bellowed hoarsely, his flaming auburn mane plastered to his sweating brow. "We have cold iron. And salt! Hypericum, salt, and bread, iron cold and berries red, by the power of rowan-wood—harm us, and we'll burn ye good! A plague on ye *skeerdas*. If ye come near us, we will make ye suffer!"

With a jerk of his head he indicated that his companion should follow him. Warily they walked along the edge of the thorn thicket, she ringing the festive-sounding bells, he with a clump of salt in one hand, the dagger in the other. He was whistling. Something small and gnarled hooted, grabbing for his boot—he dashed salt on it, and it fled, shrieking. Sudden spears of hoots and howls stabbed out from every direction. Once, she thought she glimpsed a grinning face, a grotesque caricature of humanity.

She clutched the heavy knapsack, hoping the charms would prove ward enough. The prickly bushes thinned and dwindled on one hand, the oaks on the other. After what seemed a year, the wights' quarry burst out from the coppice's precincts to find themselves amid stands of beech. The sounds of pursuit could no longer be heard. Stilling the bells, the girl cocked her head and stood listening. Silence ruled, heavy and thick as paste.

"Make haste," Sianadh said grimly. Like the juice of ripe plums, blood ran from deep scratches on his neck and arms. He sheathed the skian and shouldered the knapsack, striding forward with a determined look. As they marched beneath the beeches, birds began again their arias.

When a safe distance stretched between themselves and the oaks, Sianadh stopped.

"Time to rest." Soberly he began to shrug off his burden. "The Barren Holly," he said. "A murderous tree. Yet when hollies grow in pairs they bring good luck! What were the wights that hunted us, I wonder? Not oakmen—they be guardians of wild animals. I haven't killed any beasts lately. Spriggans, maybe. Ach, it matters not. Imrhien, we must both watch out for fey places."

<<What? Which? How?>> Her hands, speaking.

Exasperatedly he hurled the pack to the ground.

"Eldritch sites! *Obban tesh,* girl. Fey places, I said. What be the matter with ye? Do ye do this to harass me, or do ye not know anything?"

<<No!>> The pinch-beak hand-sign and the shake of the head together, vehemently, repeatedly.

He grasped her by the shoulders. She returned his stare unfailingly.

"What mean ye?"

His puzzled gaze flicked over the ruined face, trying to read something from its lumpish landscape.

"No? Ye do not know anything? Ye be new to Eldaraigne, then, a foreigner?"

<<Yes, no, yes, no.>> Hands fluttering. Like a bird in a cage, the meaning could not free itself.

*"Obban tesh,"* he exclaimed again. "I wish to the Stars that ye could parley the handspeak. It is impossible that nobody taught ye signing—how did ye get along? Ye learn so quicklike, how could ye have . . . forgotten?"

<<Yes. Yes, yes, and yes.>>

His eyes widened in realization. He released her.

"Forgotten, eh? Forgotten, is it? Ceileinh's spear!" He groaned, sat down, covered his face with his bloody hands. "No voice, no *doch* memory. I have saddled myself with a right *mor scathach* here." He continued to curse, softly, in Ertish.

She stood watching him. Here was her rescuer—large, grimy, and bedraggled, his left boot torn. Many things he had risked—his life, a treasure—many things he had given: freedom of sorts, a name, language. And somehow she had let him down. Sinking to her knees, she held out her hands, palms up. She waited, motionless. Eventually he raised his shaggy head and sighed.

"No, it is this." He made a fist, the thumb sticking out, and rubbed his hand over his heart in a circular motion, "*Atka,* the thorn, pierces the heart with sorrow. Meaning, ye be sorry. And," he added feelingly, "if ye be sorry, how d'ye think I feel?"

Later he said, "There be benefits in your loss. Many try to lose it at the bottom of a winecup or by other means. Memory be the mother of grief."

They drank some water, there under the pale green-haired dancers of beeches, and made a frugal repast supplemented with creamy, frill-petticoated fungi discovered by Sianadh. He examined his boot, thanking the hand of fate that the thing that had clutched him had not pierced his skin with some fungoid poison. He then reminisced about the way his grandmother used to cook black-ear fungus, smothered in lard with a pinch of salt and pepper, as a sauce over a juicy slab of tripe and bacon with a rind of fat *this thick*. And there were the fried onions, the crispy chicken's feet, the sheep's eyeballs in batter, the gravy. . . .

"She be still living, my grandmother. A century old. Goes to watch the chariot races twice a month. Now if I am not mistaken, I believe we have somewhat lost our way by courtesy of those cursed spriggans or whatever they were."

He consulted his map, squinted up to where the leaves hid any suggestion of the sun's location, and after much muttering and casting about decided on a direction and set off again.

For the remainder of the day they tramped upward through open forest, crossing steep, fern-fringed gullies stitched with water-threads, ascending rocky inclines. The lands of Erith had always been sparsely peopled—this was one of many places as yet never trod by mortal feet. Treetops on the opposite slopes caught flecks of sunlight here and there. A breeze sprang up. When it got caught in the blowing hair of the trees, it roared like the ocean. Once, they saw smoke coming out of the ground—doubtless an eldritch phenomenon.

In wary murmurs Sianadh informed the girl about fey places—bluebell woods, mushroom rings, especially under moonlight, rings of standing stones, mushroom-circuses known as "gallitraps" and the grassy circles folk called "Faêran Dances"; the turf-covered hills known as raths or knowes or sitheans; oak woods, wells, especially those overhung by trees; rings of hawthorn and certain trees such as holly, elder, willow, apple, birch, hazel, and ash; bushes of broom and thorn.

"Eldritch wights, both seelie and otherwise, gather in these places."

He taught her more of the handspeak. "For my own safety," he said.

They had climbed high among the mountains, leaving the forest-lands below. Trees were sparse here and stunted by lofty winds.

As evening drew in, without warning the weather turned. A gray, chill wind sharpened itself on the rocks, and the travelers tied their taltries on tightly to keep it from snipping at their ears.

"Unseasonable weather," Sianadh grumbled suspiciously.

The ground steadily became treacherous. Quagmires and bogs appeared suddenly in hollow places between the rocks. Darkness made it impossible to see these traps until the travelers were almost upon them.

"This country be not safe for those what are not familiar with the territory," muttered the Ertishman. "If I was not an outdoorsman, I'd be afraid of losing our way or perishing in the cold. Best look for somewhere to shelter until the morning."

The night became bitter, but all that they could find was a rock to crawl under—until they spied a faint light in the distance. Cautiously they moved toward it and found, much to their joy, a small hut such as foresters used when traveling. A fire was burning brightly inside, with a large gray stone on each side of it.

"Flay me! A woodmen's hut of all things!" Sianadh said enthusiastically. "If this be what it seems, we shall be spared the discomfort and peril of a night in the cold. The axemen build these huts from rowan-wood. Not a wight will go near them." Yet he examined the place warily before he set foot inside.

"Nobody's here, but surely the bloke what made this fire cannot begrudge us a little warmth. Come in, *chehrna*. We'll toast ourselves while we wait for him to return."

Trusting her mentor's good judgment, the girl sat beside him on the stone to the right of the fire to warm herself. Both travelers rubbed their chilled arms, stamped their feet, and kept their taltries tied on. In front of their feet was a pile of kindling, and on the other side of the fire lay two big logs. Sianadh added a little of the kindling to the fire, and as the warmth began to creep into their bones they became drowsy, sitting there on the stone. They woke with a start when the door burst open and a strange figure came stamping into the room. He was a swart dwarf, no higher than the travelers' knees, but broad and strong. A coat of lambskin covered his back, and he wore breeches and shoes of moleskin. Upon his head he wore a hat fashioned from ferns and peat moss, adorned with the plume of a ptarmigan.

"A duergar!" Sianadh hissed as the door slammed shut noisily. The Ertishman spoke not another word, and silence clamped down like a metal claw. The manifestation glowered at the visitors but did not speak, either, and sat himself down on the other stone.

The girl knew that duergars were of the race of black dwarves. They hated Men. In the Tower, stories of their bitter cruelties had been rife. She trembled but was determined to brave it out alongside Sianadh. To show fear or run would be to invite attack—the Ertishman had assured her that was one of the rules with wights.

So there they sat, staring at one another. After a time the flames began to die and an unbearable chill came back into the room, so, greatly daring, Sianadh leaned over and put the last of the kindling on the fire. Then the duergar, in his turn, bent and picked up one of the two huge logs lying to the left of the fire. It was twice as long as the dwarf was high and thicker than his waist, but he broke it over his knee as if it had been a twig and cast it on the fire. The duergar looked at the man scornfully and tilted his head with a sneer as if to challenge him to do the same with the other log. Sianadh steadily returned the look but did not budge—the girl knew that he suspected some trick. The fire flamed up again and gave out great heat for a while, but again it began to dwindle. The duergar's face mocked the Ertishman, inviting him to pick up the last log, but Sianadh would not be tempted, even when the glowing fire ebbed so low that the bones of the two mortals felt turned to ice and darkness pressed in. So they sat on in silence, like three statues in the gloom.

At last came the first vague light of dawn and the far-off warble of a magpie's salute to sunrise. At this sound the duergar vanished, and so did the hut and the fire. The travelers were left sitting on the stone, but first light showed that the stone was in fact perched at the top of a precipitous crag. On their left was a deep ravine—if Sianadh had taken up the duergar's challenge and leaned over to pick up the last log, he would have tumbled over the cliff and ended up a heap of broken bones at the bottom.

"As soon as that *uraguhne* walked into the place I kenned we were in no ordinary hut but some conjuration of glamour," the

Ertishman muttered. "No wight can pass over a true threshold uninvited."

They hastened from that place as soon as there was enough light to show their way. After turning downhill, they walked throughout the day with little conversation, tired and uneasy, jumping at every sudden sound. On the lower slopes the trees began again to crowd closely. As they descended from the heights, the chill of duergar country gave way to Summer's balm once more, and the travelers found themselves back in the forest.

Toward evening the trees thinned. A light appeared, moving about over the treetops. Other lights materialized among the branches. The forest was full of twitterings and mutterings.

The hair stood up on the girl's head. Dread seized her. Something walked beside her, but it was not to be seen. She dared not turn her head to look; her pupils sidled, looking through an emptiness to the trees on the other side. After a time she and Sianadh forded a little stream; then the fear left her, along with the sense of a nearby presence.

"Me granny used to say, 'Put fear aside, for only then will ye see your way clearly,'" Sianadh murmured.

The lights vanished, the ground leveled out, and a clearing opened out between the trees ahead. Here, forest giants had been felled years ago and taken away but new growth had begun and proliferated. In the center stood a rusting four-legged tower of iron struts and girders, stretching up to the sky, so tall that it overtopped the trees by far.

"An abandoned Interchange Turret." Sianadh grinned in relief, wiping his sweaty forehead. "Fortune has shown favor. Plenty of iron here. No duergars."

Then his face fell.

"Although," he added, "no Interchange Turret be marked on this here map."

He brightened again.

"'Tis a crudely drawn thing and smudged somewhat. Mayhap this mast was left out in error or blotted out by the greasy stains on it. It don't make no matter. We shall roost up on its heights this night."

The wooden top half of the Interchange Turret was missing, having been dismantled for the retrieval of the sildron cunningly embedded and concealed in the upper timbers. Mooring Masts and Interchange Turrets had to reach so high that an impracticably wide-spreading base would have been necessary to support the weight, were they entirely made from iron. Sildron lifted the weight off the base and was redeemed by the builders when the operation of the mast was no longer necessary. Massive lengths of timber lay at the tower's foot where they had crashed, some leaning against the structure. Sianadh tied one end of his rope around a stone and flung it high among the girders. It fell back. He tried again, and this time it hooked around. The weighted end came down, pulling the rope behind it as Sianadh paid it out. Triumphant, he made it fast.

"Now, Imrhien, ye tie this to your belt, hold this part in both hands, and use it to help ye walk up these here slanting supports to the body of the mast. When you reach them struts where the rope is looped around, make yerself secure and throw the rope's end down to me."

The ascent was not easy, particularly since a hot, gusting wind had arisen, punching through the trees to shove the climbers off balance.

The mast's ribs sloughed eroded scales of rust in their hands. The wind and the tremor of their climbing caused orange decay to rain in their hair, their eyes, the taltries hanging from their shoulders.

A rotting encrustation gave way beneath the girl's boot; she slipped, was brought up by Sianadh's hand on her arm with an iron grip of its own.

"Hold on there, *chehrna.* This be harder to climb than a tree, but safer when we get there!"

A ladder began halfway up the remains of the mast, leading the climbers to a wooden platform higher up. It was partly sheltered by jagged pylons. Here they rested, shaking oxidized particles from their hair. The sky flared above from horizon to horizon, overcast and darkling.

"Wind's got up again." Sianadh took a swig from the leather bottle, wiped his mouth with his sleeve. "Could be rain coming, I reckon." Then a thought struck him. "If it be thunder and lightning, we must get down from here quicklike, Imrhien. I have seen these masts attract sky-bolts."

Night came on swiftly. The wind pushed and shoved. Below, the sea of foliage tossed this way and that, churning, boiling. They roped themselves to the platform and ate some dried fruit. It was impossible to sleep or converse with the wild airs humming and haunting through the rusty cavities of the mast.

There was no thunder, but the wind kept up all night. Near dawn it ceased, and in the stillness the sky lowered its soft gray blanket down onto the top of the mast and a warm, drizzling rain began. Their taltries, pulled over their heads, were scant protection. Soon the travelers were wet through. Rust particles worked their way under clothing, abrading skin. Grumbling and cursing, the Ertishman led the way down as soon as there was light enough to see by, and they continued their journey under the frondescence of the mountain forests.

Water chuckled in rivulets, rolled its glass beads along glossy leaves, strung necklaces on spiderwebs and silver chains down from the drooping ends of branches, pattered rhythmically on little feet, whispered soothingly in soft voices. In the rain, the verdure of the forest appeared richer, deeper, stronger, leaping out vividly. Through the drizzle, Imrhien fancied she heard, high and far off, a quaint little piping ditty:

*I bring quenching and drenching,*
*I bring peace and increase,*
*Filling the veins that net the hills*
*The silver blood of everything,*
*I bring. I sing.*

Despite the discomfort, Imrhien felt happy and refreshed. Rain was the lifeblood of Aia, after all, as the tides were the world's pulse. Water was the life-giver, the welcome assuager of terrible, burning thirst. She listened to the rain's music, splashing along in her wet boots.

A brown-skinned figure about three feet high started up out of the undergrowth and went on ahead of them for a few score paces before disappearing. Later, they saw a little wizened man coming toward them, growing bigger as he went. By the time he passed them he looked like a giant; then he reached a rock and shrank down into it, and there was nothing left of him.

"'Tis all glamour," Sianadh muttered in her ear, "illusion."

Farther on, the girl saw a black dog about the size of a calf, standing in the shadows of some blackthorns and watching them go by. His eyes seemed huge and terribly bright. The travelers, grim-faced, strove to show no fear—they did not alter their course, passing closely by the thing. It made no move to attack them or follow.

There were no shadows, no signs of the sun's progress. Sianadh did not bring out the map for fear the weather might further damage it. After several hours he stopped and threw down the waterlogged knapsack.

"No use going on until I can get a direction. We might be walking in circles. We shall start a fire and dry out, at least."

By now the rain had diminished. Squirrels alighting on boughs tipped sudden wet avalanches on the travelers' heads as they searched for kindling.

Sianadh gave a shout.

"What luck! A hefty heap of sticks, nice and dry in the hollow of this here fallen log." He trussed up the pile with a piece of rope and heaved it onto his back, lugging it around while he searched for some dry moss to start the first flame. His companion had gathered a bundle of wetter twigs under one arm.

*"Obban tesh,"* groaned the man, "but these here sticks be getting heavy. My back is breaking." Stooping, he staggered over to where the knapsack lay. "We shall have to make the fire here. I can carry this no longer. Aagh! It weighs like a stone!" He straightened, letting the burden slide from his back.

*"Doch!"* he shouted suddenly. The bundle of sticks, to his surprise, had risen up and started to shuffle away. Sianadh made a grab for it, but it neatly avoided him and shuffled farther.

"Get around the other side of it, Imrhien. Round it up!"

The two of them chased the dodging bundle around the trees

until finally it vanished right before their eyes with a shout and a laugh.

"Cursed tricksy wights!" shouted the man into the spaces between the trees. "A murrain on ye!" There was no reply. He rubbed his aching back. "What be ye a-smirking at?" He glared at the girl.

They lit their smoky little fire with the help of Sianadh's tinderbox. The rain stopped. Sunlight filtered down and made shadows. Their clothes steamed. Sianadh mixed water with grains and raisins in a small pan and cooked porridge, after which he seemed to be in better spirits and waxed informative.

"Eldritch wights be divided into two kinds—seelie and unseelie. Nay, I should say three kinds, for those that ye might call *tricksy* are partway between and might be benevolent or nasty, depending on many particulars. Seelie things at best be helpful, at worst be jokers, but the evil things of unseelie b'ain't capable of affection. They hate mortals. There be nowt anyone can do to make unseelie wights love mortalkind.

"Seelie wights must be treated with care, else they can turn against us, too. Both kinds be often dangerous and deceptive, sometimes helpful, but they have their rules that they must abide by. If ye know these rules, it helps ye survive. Like, if ye see an unseelie one and ye don't show fear, ye get a degree of immunity. If ye meet their gaze, they get power over ye, but with some of them, like trows, as long as ye keep looking at them without meeting their eyes they cannot vanish. Or if ye tell it your true name, ye're instantly in its power. It be an unwritten law never to speak the true name of a man aloud in eldritch places—unless he be a foe!

"But if ye can find out a wight's name, seelie, tricksy, or otherwise, ye can have some governance over it. They have other rules, too, strange ones that betimes ye can only guess at. But one thing's for certain—they never lie. Aye, they never can tell an outright, spoken untruth of words—'tis not possible for any of them. Mind, but they be not above equivocating and may twist the truth, mislead, and deceive in all other ways if they can, with their shape-shifting and false sounds and twisted meanings. They use the glamour, too, which in Finvarna we call the *pishogue,* but it be only an illusion, not true shape-shifting."

He paused for breath, then plunged on loquaciously. Words were wine to him, and here was a steady two-eared jug in which to pour them.

"There be trooping wights with their green coats and solitaries with their red. There be wild ones and domestic. Some be small, some be large, and others be shape-shifters. They dwell on the land and under it, in the sea and in fresh water. Some be nocturnal, and be blasted by the light of the sun, but others not.

"Some wights be clever, some be stupid, same as men. Stupid ones, ye can trick. 'Tis even possible to catch the smaller ones as long as ye keep your eye on them without blinking and never loosen your grip, rough or smooth. They have to give ye a wish, then, or tell ye where their gold is hid. The lesser of the unseelie kind can be warded off with salt and charms and such. Or, if ye have skill with words and rhyming, like the bards, ye can beat them by getting in the Last Word. They do not love the sound of bells, although some say that seelie wights used to ride with the Fair Folk who had bells on their bridles. Truly, as the old rhymes say:

*Hypericum, salt, and bread,*
*Iron cold and berries red,*
*Self-bored stone and daisy bright,*
*Save me from unseelie wight.*

*Red verbena, amber, bell,*
*Turned-out raiment, ash as well,*
*Whistle-tunes and rowan-tree,*
*Running water, succor me.*

*Rooster with your cock-a-doo,*
*Banish wights and darkness, too.*

"But the greater of the evil wights cannot be put off with simple talismans and jingle-bells. Nay, that needs a greater gramarye, which is why we have wizards. But even wizards would hold small sway against such as the Unseelie Attriod."

The Ertishman finished his porridge.

"Be not fashed—we shall find our way through these wild places. Why, not even a stray sod can lose me. What? You have not heard of the *Foidin Seachrain?* Ha! Those who step on one of those eldritch turves lose their way, even if they have traveled that very path a hundred times before. But a canny man can protect himself against it by whistling. A woman, too," he added as an afterthought.

The girl clutched at Sianadh's sleeve, pointing urgently up to where the sky showed through the leaves. A horse and rider galloped overhead and were gone in an instant.

"Stormrider! Well, I'll be flayed for boots. I guess that was an outrider or scout come looking for the missing merchant ship that never reached her dock at Gilvaris Tarv. The main Stormrider runs do not pass over these remote places . . . unless we have been puck-ledden farther astray from our course than I reckoned. Aye, lass, we are a little off course—not lost—ye will never be lost with Sianadh the Bear, *chehrna*. I have my bearings now, and northeast we must go."

If his companion harbored misgivings, she did not show it.

They stamped out the fire, despite their clothes being still damp, and went on their way, putting fatigue aside, straining all their senses to detect approaching danger. Presently Imrhien heard distant music ahead. Sianadh cocked his head and listened.

"Harpstring trees—a rare find. They be not perilous in themselves." The music became louder as they neared the groves of harpstrings—melodious notes of liquid gold, as of a million tuneful harps plucked by gentle fingers.

Rows of thin rootlets or tendrils grew down from each leafy branch to fasten themselves to the branch directly beneath. Glittering insects flew among these stretched cords, alighting momentarily, to leap off, leaving the string twanging. The man ran his fingers along a set of filaments, causing a cascade of notes like bubbles: a flurry of sequined insects.

"Pretty, ain't it. I always wanted to play a musical instrument."

<<Look!>> signed the girl. Sianadh followed her gaze. The trees a little farther away gave on to a path—not a faint trail like that which had led to the oak coppice, but a fair, broad way paved with stone. The travelers approached it with caution. Around them the air rang, tinkled, thrummed.

Sianadh's brow furrowed in thought.

"If this means what I suppose, then we be on the right track. Aye. We shall follow this road. This b'ain't made by no wightish paws, though they may likely tread it."

Together they stepped out along the path.

It took them higher and higher up the slope but remained smooth and unbroken. No weeds poked their fingers up through the seamless joins in the pavement. Late primroses bloomed by the wayside. The lilting harpstrings dropped behind, and larches crowded close. It began to get dark, oppressively gloomy.

As the travelers passed a big tree, slowly the hairs rose on the girl's neck. Presently a man and a woman—or what seemed to be a man and a woman—came out and walked along with them. The strangers did not speak but walked along on each side of them, she dressed in a gown of gray and wearing a filmy white veil over her head, he garbed also in the color of stones. The cold sweat of horror prickled the girl, but she followed the Ertishman's lead and continued to march on as if nothing had happened. The tense line of his shoulders showed the strain. From the corner of her eye, she saw that the woman's face was comely, but her ears were long and pointed like those of a horse. The man was ugly, with a cow's tail that he switched back and forth as though swatting flies. Eventually the woman-simulacrum went away, and the man-thing seemed to go, too, but his footsteps remained with them until they crossed a footbridge over a stream.

Sianadh sighed like a deflated bellows. He fingered the faintly obscene amber tilhal at his neck. "Praise be to Ceileinh's blue eyes—the protection holds. This trinket may well have been worth the wizard's price. Still, the sooner we be out of here the better."

The shadows lengthened. The path topped a low rise, and they found themselves looking out over a shallow valley. The girl stared, amazed.

"Flaming chariots!" exclaimed Sianadh. "'Tis that old city of the map, after all!"

Rising up on the valley's other wall, tier upon tier, were the crumbling ruins of a once great citadel built of pale stone. The travelers followed the path down to a bridge over a willow-lined stream, crossed it, and zigzagged their way up to the outlying buildings and into the city.

Broken towers and caved-in roofs caught the last rays of afternoon sun. Windows stared, sightless, at dry fountains filled with soil and weeds. Ivy-covered walls surrounded vacant courts and overgrown gardens. Mossy facades peeled, overlooking empty streets whose choked gutters bespoke ages of neglect. The intruders walked delicately, as if the city slept and they feared to wake it.

"We must find a stronghold in which to spend the night," whispered the Ertishman, looking over his shoulder, "somewhere with a roof in case it rains again."

Even the small sound of their boots on the cobbles seemed to bounce too loudly off disintegrating architecture as they tramped the streets. Every abandoned mansion, every collapsed bothy and gaping hall, seemed to be roofless, dank, still puddled with the morning's rain.

"There be no choice," Sianadh said reluctantly. "We shall have to retrace our steps. Near where we came in, not far from that bridge, I saw a building with a roof, beside a pond. It looked to be an old mill. 'Twere too near the stream for my liking, right on it, in fact." He shrugged. "Anyhow, ye need not fear with me by your side."

His hand strayed again to the amber tilhal.

Chipped gargoyles watched the travelers return through the echoing streets, now dim in the graying light. The structure beside the green glass pond turned out to be an old mill indeed; the great wheel in the race below the dam had mortified countless years ago. Slime dripped from its flanges. The front door of the mill had long since rotted to dust. Sianadh looked up at a weathered inscription over the gaping doorway.

"*Faerwyrd,* the key; *idrel,* the sword; *nente,* the stitch; *ciedre,* the moon . . ." Painstakingly he deciphered the runes. "The thorn, *atka;* the dragon, *slegorn;* F, I, N—Fincastle's Mill. Well then, Fincastle must needs welcome visitors this night."

Inside, the mill was cool but dry. There were several chambers, but the travelers settled on a small one that boasted a large stone table in the center, as well as a fireplace. Sianadh gave a shout of laughter when he saw this, and it was not long before they had gathered enough wood from a nearby garden, rampantly overgrown—which also yielded onions and ripe passionfruit—to have a fire going and fuel to spare.

"This will keep away wild beasts and cook our supper as well!" the man said gleefully, rubbing his hands. "And we can eat like Kings at our own table. I have strips of dried beef to make an onion stew, thickened with a bit o' oat flour. That'll stick to your ribs!"

His companion fetched water from the stream, whose waters in the evening were now colorless. Willows trailed long withies onto its surface. Sickly stems of paradox ivy twined about the feet of a collapsed bridge.

Their supper was comparatively lavish, but despite Sianadh's urgings the girl could not touch the meat. The passionfruit tasted delicious. Afterward the Ertishman leaned contentedly back against the knapsack with his hands behind his head and wistfully reflected, in the glow of the fire, on the delights of a drop of whiskey after a meal. The girl, however, wanted to ask questions.

<<What?>>—indicating their surroundings.

"The city? There be many such as this throughout Erith. The Ancient Cities, some call them. They were built many centuries ago at the beginning of the Era of Glory, now long gone. Some gramarye be in them, they say, for the walls of the Ancient Cities still stand and have not been buried beneath layers of dust and silt blown in by the winds of centuries, or cracked apart by heat and cold and living roots. Cities so fair and wondrous have never been made since. But they were abandoned, because they were not built from dominite. Dominite be full of talium trihexide, that metal what the mesh in taltries is made of. The power of the shang wind can pass through all other stone and all other metal, and so it did. The folk in those days were careless about wearing taltries. Nowadays there be severe laws governing that. So ye see, the Ancient Cities became cities of ghosts whenever the unstorms came. Too many ghosts, as time went by, until few had the heart to live amongst them.

"See, the images be the imprints of real folk, stamped forever on the places where they have suffered or had great joy. When we feel strongly and passionately, we make a force. The shang wind stains the air with that force—also it whips up those feelings in us. Some people are afraid of the shang, and others revel in it. They say the name comes from some old speech, 'sh' meaning wind and 'ang' meaning the Greayte Star of the south, so it be the Star's Wind.

"I have heard of another old, forsaken city in the far north, in Avlantia where the Talith used to dwell—but the architecture of that place is different. And there are no ghosts. They say the folk all left that city in a time before the Era of Glory and never returned. It is not known why or where they went, but the most common story is that a sickness or a plague drove them away. Now the ruins of the old city steep alone in the mull of their splendor, I guess, and only the great gold lions of Avlantia roam there."

A glister of sparks arced from the fire as he tossed on an extra piece of wood.

<<What? Why?>> She drew her taltry away, pointed to her hair.

"Your yellow locks. Aye, the Talith were a yellow-haired race. Not many of them left now. Still, a few of them do dwell scattered about in different countries. Avlantia was their native home. They say it is a fair country, full of red-leaved trees in the west and overflowing with flowers in the east. The climate be warm and pleasant. But that does not suit the other races, I suppose, else Avlantia would now be overrun with Feorhkind, Erts, and Icemen. But it be not. Few folk visit those northern lands, and fewer dwell there, if any."

He tilted a red, bristling eyebrow at her. "How far back in your own past do ye recall?"

She conveyed to him as much as she could, drawing in the dust with her finger and using gestures. He showed her more hand-speak, which she absorbed greedily. Then he shook his head wonderingly.

"I do not know what to make of ye, Imrhien. Ye wear a poor excuse for a tilhal that looks to be not worth the wood it's chewed out of—and what be that scar on your throat?"

Her hand went to her throat. She had not been aware of a mark there, being in the habit of avoiding looking at reflective surfaces. Indeed, a raised weal of hard tissue striped the front of her neck. It had nothing to do with the beatings she had received in the Tower—those had always been directed at her back and shoulders. She shrugged, frowning.

"Ye have no memory of it? 'Tis like a whiplash. My cousin had a mark like that on his arm he got when he was cracking whips with some of the feckless lads on the farm." Thoughtfully he chewed on a twig. "I was born and bred on a farm, see, in Finvarna. 'Twas a good life. We had a bauchan to help us in them days. He and me dad often fought, but the bauchan helped us when we needed it."

He pushed his toes closer to the fire and stared reflectively at the cracked ceiling.

"One day, for instance, as me dad was coming back from the market, the bauchan pounced out on him and they ended up in a brawl. Then when me dad got home he found out he had lost his best handkerchief, the one he prized because a wizard had put charms in it and me ma had embroidered his name on't when they were courting. He was certain the bauchan had it, and he went back to look for it. Sure enough, he found the bauchan rubbing the handkerchief on a rough stone. 'It's well you've come, Declan,' says the bauchan. 'It'd have been your death if I'd rubbed a hole in this. As it is, ye'll have to fight me for it.' So they fought, and me dad won back his handkerchief. But it was not long after, when we had run out of firewood and the mud was feet deep and me dad's bad leg stopped him from fetching a birch he had felled, we heard a great thud at our house door and there was the tree, lugged through the mud by the bauchan."

Sianadh scratched his beard abstractedly. "He was a good thresher, too—I do not know how we would have managed without him at harvest time. But I had no mind to be a farmer, when I grew up. I was too restless. This sildron mine will be the making of me, for sure. Mind, I have told no one else of the map, not even my nephew Liam in Gilvaris Tarv. See, I knew I had to come alone, just to find out if the map was valid or merely a jest."

He fell silent. Drowsily the girl poked the fire with a stick. It blazed up.

"Time to sleep now." The Ertishman stretched his arms and settled down with his head on the knapsack. His companion folded the small blanket under her own head and soon fell fast asleep.

She did not know how long she had been asleep when she struggled awake, feeling a great weight pinning her feet down. The fire's light showed the mountain that was Sianadh snoring nearby. Something very heavy was moving up on her body, breathing heavily. With all her strength she shoved it off and sprang to her feet. Sianadh awoke with a start, and there was a sound of something rolling out the door.

The Ertishman half crouched, drawing his skian.

"What was that? Did ye see it?"

She shook her head, picked up a stout stick of firewood, and went to the door. Beneath her ribs a rabbit jumped.

Looking out, she could see nothing but starlight on water and the dark outlines of trees, hear nothing but frogs gurruping in the millpond. Sianadh stoked the fire. They sat with their backs to the flames, staring into the shadows. The fire leaped and crunched. The girl's blood thumped in her temples.

Knockings and scrapings began in the next room, but when the man put his head around the door to look, they ceased. Then came the sound of objects being thrown around, behind the walls, and ringing blows as of hammers on anvils.

"Pah! 'Tis a pack of foliots. They be only trying to scare us," said Sianadh.

*They are succeeding,* thought his protégée.

A pitiful howling cranked itself up and abruptly turned into laughter. From various places in the floor and through holes in the walls, flame *whoosh*ed high, dazzlingly bright, and was as inexplicably extinguished. Strange lights came and went, stones were flung, chains rattled, doors ostensibly opened and shut, although no doors existed within the premises.

The frightful manifestations continued into the night. Neither of the travelers slept.

Silence had descended and the fire had burned low when a fuath came in through the mill door. Fuathan as a malignant, water-dwelling genus comprised many species—this particular fuath appeared like a small, ill-favored man, about three feet in height, very raggedly dressed in gray-green clothes that were dripping wet.

"Who are you?" it said. "And what do they call ye?"

At that, Sianadh spoke up.

"Who are ye yourself? And what do they call ye?"

"My Self," said the fuath slyly.

"And I am called My Own Self," the man replied casually. "And my friend be called Me."

The travelers kept sitting by the fire, and the fuath sat down with them, closest to the flames. Its clothes could not seem to dry; they were still sopping wet, although a puddle formed around it. Behind the walls the noises abated. The girl sat very still. Deep-cored shadows came creeping in from the open door. Undaunted, Sianadh vigorously stirred up the fire. But in the next instant his companion wished he had never done so. Sparks and cinders blew out and burned the fuath, who jumped up and went whirling about fiercely, shrieking and bellowing in a voice quite disproportionate to its size.

"I am burnt! I am burnt!"

And from under the hearthstone a dreadful voice answered.

"Who has burnt ye?"

"Get out of sight!" Sianadh cried, diving under the stone table. The lass slid in behind him, and not a moment too soon. They huddled there in the darkness, shivering, and heard the awful voice ask again, "Who burnt ye?"

"My Own Self and Me," yelled the fuath.

"If it had been any mortal man," said the voice, "I would have been revenged, but if it was ye yourself, I can do nothing."

The fuath rushed out, lamenting. A pressing silence folded around, thick and gelatinous.

All night the girl stayed with Sianadh under the table in suspense, hoping to be saved, scarcely daring to breathe. Toward dawn, when the stirring song of magpies beckoned the sun, there came the presentiment of an unstorm.

Then morning gleamed, and with the sun's first light they were free.

They gathered up the precious knapsack and left Fincastle's Mill as quickly as possible, heading back into the city. When they had put several streets between themselves and the mill, they halted. The sky was clear and hard, like blue enamel, and the morning was already warm.

"My breath and blood! The nights here be more tiring than the days," groaned Sianadh. "If I don't get some sleep soon, I shall be starting to look like Domnhaill's old bloodhound. *Doch,* my mouth tastes as if I've *eaten* Domnhaill's old bloodhound."

He rinsed his mouth and spat on the ground.

"Pah! This drink's not much better. For mountain stream water, it smacks of slime. Slimy fuathan, no doubt. 'Tis plain the one that so cannily calls itself My Self be half-witted, which be fortunate for us. It has a mighty protector somewhere under the hearthstone. If things like that be about, 'tis time to take stronger measures. Ah! for a few wizard's spells and a good broadsword . . . "

He bade Imrhien go behind a dilapidated wall for modesty, to turn all her clothes inside out and put them back on, while he did likewise. Then he broke two stout, straight branches from a mighty ash tree that overhung the street—"to bash their heads in with"—and trimmed them. With staffs in hand they marched along the wide lanes and byways that crossed one corner of the sprawling municipality.

A sweet, clear ringing started up as if all the bluebells in a wood had tiny silver clappers and trembled in a breeze.

"Uncomber's on the way," said the Ertishman, reflexively touching the hood hanging back from his shoulders. "Ha. No matter if we leave off our taltries. What be two more ghosts among many? Besides, I cannot speak for ye, but I be too weary to drum up any excitement, unless a big featherbed appears in front of me."

Imrhien glanced at him and smiled. With bloodshot, red-rimmed eyes sagging above smutty pouches, he did indeed look like a mournful hound. She wondered what bale-eyed monster she herself resembled.

He took a bite of a piece of hard ship's bread and handed her another.

"No need to be so cheerful."

But she felt happy, and the unstorm's approach amplified that. There were wild herbs thrusting up vital shoots in the creviced shoulders of marble statues and warm breezes sweeping unhindered through necrotic palaces. There were reasons for cheerfulness.

All the leaves in the weed-choked gutters rose up as one; the air swirled thickly with them in the first onrush of the shang, and the blue-black clouds it brought covered the sun's face. Her hair stood up yet again in justification of one of the wind's many nicknames.

"Not afraid, *chebrna?*"

<<No.>>

"Well then, we shall keep on walking and see what we shall see."

Day became night and sunshine, moonshine. The lights began, and so did the silent tableaux, faint because of age.

In a casement window overhanging the street, two slender lovers wept and parted, each richly dressed in brocade and jewels of an old-fashioned style. His coach and matching four waited below at the door; the horses arched their frosted necks and tossed sparks from foaming manes. Carriage lanterns flickered. The young man turned and looked up for one last glance before he boarded, and she waved with a lace handkerchief. The burnished coach, with escutcheons painted on each door, bowled silently away, suddenly vanishing, and the lovers were back again in the window, the carriage waiting below.

In a wilderness garden a child on a swing flew endlessly back and forth, laughing; the golden ropes stretched up to nothing, for the tree had fallen centuries before.

A funeral procession came up the street, lavishly ornate, the hearse drawn by six shining blacks in silver harness and tall midnight plumes. A chatoyance of flowers covered the bannerol over the coffin. Six tall men in black top hats walked ahead; behind came hundreds of mourners: mounted knights, veiled women, and men in black outfits of a mode long past, their pale faces sagging with grief. They passed so close that Imrhien fancied she could hear the rustle of silk.

Parks and civic gardens must once have existed here, for the travelers saw tangled places where no jagged towers or smashed porticos reigned. Here, two gallants dueled, as in the forest near Isse Tower, dying over and over. There, people with flowers in their hair danced around a bonfire. A translucent youth and maiden stepped from the boles of horse chestnut saplings, to twine arms and kiss, her girdle a lattice of misty emeralds.

A castle had stood on the higher ground. Its many turrets now were crumbled, but a lone piper yet paced far above, where the battlements had been, where now was emptiness. With his bag beneath his elbow, the pipes slung over his shoulder, their tassels swinging as he strode, he played a dirge for some dead and long-forgotten prince. All these passionate joys and sorrows, which had meant so much to those who had lived, which had been the world to them, now were only flickers staining the airs. As dry leaves before the wind, their reasons, their thoughts, their cherished plans, had been long swept away; those who viewed these brief afterimages could never know their story.

The city lived its glory days again, poignant memories pulsating brighter and dimmer with each fluctuation of the shang wind that spangled with metallic fires the overgrown shrubberies and arboreta, that limned with thin streams of molten argentum the fallen capitals, ruined spandrels, decomposing parapets and balustrades: the stairs leading nowhere.

Imrhien had pulled on her taltry, but Sianadh, uncovered, turned and flung up his hands as they walked through a square lined with stone dragons and cried in a flare of exultation:

"I be My Own Self, and I be here, so look ye, I have *gilfed* this town with my mark."

Looking back from a tangential boulevard, Imrhien saw the imprint of him standing triumphant. The wind fled, chiming away to the distance. They crossed the farther outskirts of the city and reentered the forest just as the sun came out.

* * *

Sianadh squinted at the map.

"Now we have been led out of our way somewhat, but we be back on the right track now." He tapped the compass, whose needle spun wildly.

"Reaper's Pike should be off to our left, and Skylifter rises over there." His hand waved vaguely. "We be walking on the flanks of Gloomy Jack. These mountains be snow-capped in Winter, but not now, not when Midsummer's almost here. And well for ye, Imrhien, I might add. If 'twere Winter, ye should have to catch a wolf and skin it to clothe ye in the cold. Look for round stones as we go. With my slingshot I might go hunting later for something smaller for our supper."

The flanks of Gloomy Jack were dominated by stringybarks and peppermint gums. Brittle twigs and sloughed strips of bark crunched beneath the wayfarers' boots. There was a sameness about the tall, pale trunks that made the girl feel as though they were getting nowhere. Even in the shade the air shimmered with heat, and from somewhere ahead came the piercing shrill of cicadas.

He could plainly be seen, the lissom brown youth who walked for a time under the leaves a few yards to the left, for he made no effort to conceal himself. He did not look toward the travelers, but Imrhien studied him until he left them. His features were elfin: a turned-up nose, high cheekbones, a sharp chin, and pointed ears jutting from long dark hair that tumbled past his shoulders. His feet were bare and his sylvan raiment gorgeous; a collar of yellow, scarlet-veined leaves of the flowering cherry, ovate and serrated; a long russet-brown tunic of five-pointed plane tree leaves stitched with green thread and trimmed with lace of oak, moss-lined, belted with braided rushes; dagged bell-sleeves of wine-crimson Autumnal foliage that hung to his calves; breeches of velvet moss tied with ivy at the knee; and two folded lily leaves for a cocked hat with a feathery fern frond for a plume. He carried a staff of goldenrod, and at his feet trotted a small white animal with scarlet slippers of ears and crimson garnets of eyes.

"I have heard him spoke of back in Tarv," whispered Sianadh. "They say he took care of a little girl, Katherine, who was lost in the forest; she was later found unharmed and grew to be a fine woman, and she always did say how kind he had been to her, the Gailledu. I know it be he, for he has black hair and is dressed all in moss and leaves like they say. And if I b'ain't mistaken, that there little red-eared pig with him be a beast of good fortune."

At midday they came to a steamy gully overhung by tree-ferns and refilled the leather bottle from a sweet-tasting, tan-colored streamlet. Two ladies in long black dresses had been sitting under the trees, their long dark hair crowned with circlets of bloodred garnets. They stood up and went on to a little pool in a hollow. A powerful rush of wind roared up from the dell, and with a cry, two black swans rose away through the air.

"We shall rest where we are," said Sianadh, "and not disturb a pool favored by swanmaidens." He opened the pack. "This dried stuff be dull to the palate, and I could wish for nobler fare. Plenty of it left, however. Ye do not eat much."

His companion was by now getting used to thinking of herself as a girl and being thought of as such by this educated gentleman of a rough peasant who treated lads and lasses the same except for an extra degree of mannerliness to the latter and a degree less of badinage and freedom with his language, both of which slipped when he forgot about them. She watched him picking round pebbles out of the stream, pocketing the slingshot he had taken out of his knapsack.

"Bide here, *chehrna*. I saw turkeyfowl in the brushwood, and I've a mind to catch one."

<<No.>> In panic she pulled on his coat, <<I will not see you.>>

"Have no fear." Gently he disengaged her hands. "The Bear always comes back. 'Twould take a pretty big turkey to best me. Mind the knapsack, and do not stir from this spot. The ashen staff has power in itself—keep it by."

Then he was gone, not noiselessly, but the sounds of him were soon swallowed up in the forest and overridden by the pitiless, maddening cicada thrum arising now on all sides.

Listlessly she lay for a time on the cool, scratchy grass of the stream's bank. Bubbles formed and danced on the water. The insects' buzzing made her head ache. A small white pig with poppy-petal ears snuffled in the herbage by the water's edge. It lifted its head and looked at the girl with a pair of holly-berry eyes, then trotted away and stood as if waiting. When she did not move, it advanced a few steps, then moved away again and put its head down in a patch of long grass. Her curiosity aroused, she picked up the knapsack and went to look. Instantly the pig kicked up its heels and scampered off. Where it had stood, not a blade of grass was broken. She knelt and picked a handful of grass. It was full of four-leafed clover. Tucking some in her pocket for luck, she returned to the stream.

It was difficult not to doze; heat and lack of sleep pressed on her eyelids, and Sianadh seemed to be taking a long time. She splashed her face with water to stay awake and stuck her fingers in her ears to shut out the cicadas.

Sianadh burst out of the trees, turkeyless.

"Imrhien, there be a market going on over that rise! Ye should see! A fair green, full of little folk buying and selling just like any town fair. They be dressed in red and yellow and green like proper little lords and ladies—their pretty painted booths have all sorts of commodities for sale. There be pewterers, shoemakers, peddlers with all kinds of trinkets—everything we usually see at fairs be there, including the food stalls. Roasted quails! Raspberries and cream! To my mind, if we step up politelike, we might be so bold as to barter for some of their cakes and pies and glazed hams and custards and ale. . . . Come!"

He grabbed the knapsack and led the way. When they came almost to the top of the rise, they dropped to their bellies and crawled to peer over the edge.

What Imrhien saw differed vastly from what Sianadh had described. She shot a puzzled glance at him, but his eyes were aglow, and a wide, vacuous grin split his stubbled jaw.

There was indeed a smooth, close-cropped sward and a milling crowd of little folk at their market fair, but the booths were shaky affairs of peeling bark, the garments of the participants were tattered and dirty, the dishes and ornaments they hawked were crudely carved from wood, and the dainty foods of which the Ertishman had spoken were nothing but fuzzballs, weeds, live and dead insects, cuckoo's spittle and acorns, piled up on leaf plates.

The girl tried to stop him, but ineffectually, as Sianadh rose and went down among them, opening the knapsack to show what he brought to barter. The men and women, no higher than his knee, crowded around, laughing shrilly and talking in some foreign tongue, picking over the oatmeal, the dried figs, the raisins, hazelnuts, bread, and salt beef. Overjoyed at the bargains he struck, Sianadh reached out to take the ghastly victuals they offered him, cramming them into his mouth straight away. At this the girl jumped out of hiding and ran to him, knocking the rubbish aside.

"Hue and cry, girl! There be plenty for both of us," he growled through a mouthful. She grabbed his wrists; he pushed her away, and then a pricking of a hundred pins stung her calves; the little folk flocked around armed with thorn-weapons to drive her away. It was no use persisting. She hopped out of their hostile reach and waited for Sianadh. Presently he appeared, wiping his mouth on his sleeve. The knapsack bulged.

"Full of goodies." He patted it contentedly. "Ah, what a feast. Did ye try some?"

She frowned. <<Not food.>>

"Ye be too choosy, lass. Come now, we must be off."

<<Not food. I watch, I see.>>

Sianadh flinched. He took a moment to consider this.

"Ye see?" he repeated carefully. "What did ye see, Imrhien?"

Unable to explain, she flung up her hands in frustration.

"Come back to the fair with me. Put your hand on your hip and crook your arm so that I may look through it."

To the rise they returned. It seemed the fair was over, for the last of the little folk were hurriedly abandoning the stalls, not packing them up but leaving them as they stood.

Sianadh bent to look through the crook of Imrhien's arm.

A torrent of oaths and expletives in at least three languages followed. He ran down the slope, shouting and kicking the stalls to pieces. Weed, seedpods, and bits of bark went flying.

"*Doch pishogue! Doch, doch skeerda, sgorrama* wights with their glamour! *Obban tesh,* what have I eaten?" He charged into some bushes and was violently ill. Between spasms of choking he raged, "Sun's teeth, did I eat that? Blast me beardless, I ain't never seen nothing green like that . . . plagues of rot, but those look like slugs . . ."

When he finally emerged he shambled off to the swanmaidens' pool and jumped straight in. Meanwhile Imrhien emptied the detritus out of the knapsack and watched parts of it crawl away.

"Have ye the Sight, then?" Sianadh: hunched, sour, and dripping.

She shrugged.

"Ye might have warned me."

She stamped her foot.

"All right, ye did warn me. The worst of it be, those weevilly siofra have taken the best part of our provisions. And I have lost the stomach for hunting—I think it bailed out with them slugs."

Despondent, she made no reply. In silence they resumed their journey.

Birds came clamoring to their evening roosts. Darkness was already gathering, and they had found no safe nook in which to spend the night, when the Gailledu reappeared with the white pig and beckoned. The travelers hesitated, undecided.

"They say he be seelie, but . . ."

Imrhien pointed to the pig, jabbed a thumb at herself, and showed the Ertishman the wilted clover from her pocket.

"The pig gave ye what? Four-leafed clover? Ach! So that be what peeled the glamour from your bonny green eyes and not the Sight, after all." He took some for his own pocket.

"When these dry I shall tuck them inside the lining. The little maggots shall never put the *pishogue* on me again, and if I ever see 'em, I'll do more than box their pointy ears. Yon leaf-boy looks the same to me now as he did before I took the clover. I believe he means us well. Shall we follow?"

Imrhien nodded. The Gailledu and his pig seemed different from the other wights they had encountered. Nevertheless they followed warily through the gloaming, Sianadh's hand resting on the skian. The warm and darkening forest was teeming with presences. Their guide urged them to hurry forward. A sound of galloping horses came behind; the travelers broke into a run, but there seemed only trees and more trees and the Gailledu's half-glimpsed form and the pig, flitting ahead—then Sianadh stumbled against a great, smooth bole, gasping, and the unseen riders thundered past and away.

"Rowans."

The girl caught her breath, looked up. The Gailledu had indeed led them into a wood of rowan-trees, the trees of protection, before he and the pig had left them.

Soft mosses made a comfortable resting place. Imrhien's legs ached. After they had eaten from their depleted rations, she took off her boots. In the safety of the rowans, the man and the girl slept the profound sleep of absolute weariness, sprawled as if dead in the deep leaf-mold.

In the morning they left the rowan-grove and struck out north-east on their journey.

They had not gone more than a few yards when the Gailledu barred their way. Without speaking, he shook his dark head and pointed to the west. Sianadh stopped, planting his staff firmly in the ground.

"Good morrow to ye. Ye led us to good rest last night, sir—now we be at your service. But if it be another way ye're wanting us to go, that we cannot do."

With a sharp, chopping movement the leaf-clad youth brought the side of one open hand down into the upturned palm of the other. The gesture could mean only one thing.

Sianadh shifted uneasily.

"He wants us to stop going this way and go around, Imrhien."

She nodded, feinting a step to the left.

"So ye think he be right, eh? Nay. It cannot be. We must take the direct route. We have already lost too much time, and our supplies be short. Our goal cannot be more than a day away if we keep on. Who knows how many extra leagues we may walk, how many days we may lose by changing our course? Good sir, your advice be gratefully received, but with respect, we cannot follow it."

Sianadh began to walk around the Gailledu, but there he was, barring their way again. His brown eyes flashed in anger. One last time he shook his head and made the "stop" signal. Then he stepped aside. Uncomfortably Sianadh met Imrhien's eyes.

"Do as ye wish. I b'ain't changing."

From her hair the girl took a blue wildflower she had plucked that morning, not knowing its name. She stretched her hand out to the Gailledu. After a few moments he took the flower from her fingers, turned, and went into the forest. She stared after him, then followed the Ertishman.

There was little communication between them, many an anxious glance over their shoulders and many a jump at wind-tossed shadows. After an hour or two they came under dark pines growing among granite boulders. Roots gripped the rocks like arteries caging hearts. Malice brooded beneath heavy boughs. Queer sights and sounds troubled their passage as before, but this time the travelers knew that they were not being deceived, that what they saw was real. While they carried the four-leafed clover, their eyes penetrated glamour's masquerades.

The Summer heat thickened, grew stifling. Glad they were to find, in the afternoon, a black forest pool. Although they bathed their feet and splashed their faces, some inner cognition warned them not to drink. The pines had snared a patch of flawless lavender sky between them, high above, but it was not permitted to reflect in the inky water.

Branches swished aside, and a shaggy little horse came to drink. It cocked a friendly eye, shaking droplets from the soft muzzle, snorting softly.

The allurement of waterhorses was such that when they were near, they seemed in no way to be eldritch or perilous—a certainty drew over those who beheld them that here was but an innocent and playful steed, as *lorraly* as themselves, and that it would be ridiculous to suspect otherwise. Only gramarye or a determined stubbornness could save mortals from this enchantment.

"Put your boots back on quicklike and let's get out of here," hissed Sianadh.

The horse trotted over to them, its hooves almost soundless on the pine-needle carpet. Imrhien's hands were shaking so much that she could not lace her boots. Sianadh's lips moved silently. The horse nuzzled his shoulder, pranced and frolicked in the most joyous manner, curving its neck enticingly to be caressed.

The more they avoided the pretty thing, the more it played. As they moved away it bounded in front of them, bending its foreleg in a seductive invitation to mount and ride. In and out of the trees it gamboled, the long tail flouncing high—everywhere they turned the horse frisked in their way, its spell drawing its net over them, until in desperation Imrhien brandished her ashen staff in both hands, right before its eyes. The creature reared on its hind legs, neighing, then Sianadh was there, the skian's leaf-shaped blade glittering cold in one fist, a scoop of salt glittering cold in the other.

"Avaunt!"

Shrilly squealed the horse. It rolled its eyes and pig-rooted. The travelers advanced. It backed off, wheeled, and galloped straight for the pool. In it jumped, smoothly, with hardly a splash. Only ripples were left behind, spreading slowly across the dark face of the water.

A tear stood in Sianadh's eye. He stared at the pool's secret waters, shaking his head.

"Ah, but 'tis a *tambalai* thing, and a rare, or I'm no judge of horseflesh. It went hard with me to repel it. A pity."

Without waiting to see more, the two companions hastened on their way.

The needle-carpet deadening their footfalls, they pushed through curtains of shadow. There seemed no end to the pine forest. Imrhien's scalp prickled with the certainty of being followed. Dread of some terrible stalker swallowed her heart.

Light emptied out of the afternoon. Tree trunks loomed like prison bars, and growing darkness made it difficult to see where they were going.

A grayish glimmer ahead, more a decrease of darkness than an increase of light, showed where the trees thinned. In a few more yards the travelers stepped out from the forest under a starry sky. A half-moon was ascending. The Greayte Southern Star lit the landscape palely. To either hand, the forest rows stretched out in an endless picket fence. They stood at the top of a slope covered with low bushes: gorse, melaleuca, and broom. The long hillside slanted down to a narrow gorge running from north to south, along the floor of which flowed a swift river. To the north, an escarpment rose to a mountain peak. Faintly discernible on the ravine's far side there rolled undulating grasslands scattered with trees.

"The river!" Sianadh's eyes glittered. "At last, the river that runs from Bellsteeple to the south. Ah, but I cannot tell at which point we have arrived at these reaches. We must follow this tributary of the Rysingspill, but whether upstream or down is not clear."

Undecided, he stood in thought, surveying the scene until frenetic laughter from the forest startled them both into action and they hastened down the slope.

Riddled with holes, Imrhien's boots were giving way; they were not as stout as Sianadh's, not being made to withstand journeys in the wild. Now the sole of the right boot came adrift, flapping. She had to stop and take it off.

"Do not throw it away, lass. Do not leave behind any things ye have used. Fires of Tapthar! What can that be?"

A groove was gouged into the hillside to the right, running straight down from the forest to the ravine. No vegetation grew on its worn and slippery surface.

"This queer slide be too treacherous to cross. We must turn upriver," said the Ertishman when they had reached the lip of the channel. "And may the Star grant us safe haven this night."

A pearlescent cloud layer roofed the gorge. Halfway up its slopes, wispy shreds of cloud clung. The river's cleft was narrow and very steep, the sides plunging straight down from the cliff edge perhaps sixty feet to the water below. Massive boulders humped out of the gushing waters like gray leviathans. The current raced and boiled, churning furiously among them with a sound of torrential rain. The loud voice of the river filled their ears with its hissing roar, threaded with limpid notes like bubbling silver.

The travelers marched along the cleft's rim. Tiny white moths flitted. Something came hurtling down the hill on the muddy slide, shrieking with laughter, and shot out over the river, leaving only echoes of its madness.

*"Obban tesh,"* swore Sianadh, quickening his pace, "I could not tell for sure, but it looked as if that sliding thing were headless and carrying its noggin under its arm."

Imrhien limped after him, lugging her ruined boot in one hand, her ashen staff in the other. The moon rose a little higher. Far below, the river gushed. Then the terrible sound began.

*Thud, thud*. A rhythmic pounding shook the ground like a giant hammer, then stopped, giving way to an empty silence. From somewhere behind, in the darkness, it had come. Abruptly it started up again: *thud, thud,* getting nearer. Again the sound ceased.

A strange lisping sound was emanating from Sianadh's mouth. He was trying to whistle, but his lips were too dry. Beads of sweat stood out on his brow. Nausea gripped the pit of the girl's belly like a squeezing fist. *Thud, thud;* it came again, remorselessly, the vibrations running up through the travelers' feet. The Ertishman began to run, the girl hard on his heels.

The moon vanished behind a cloud, and Sianadh stumbled; a cry escaped his lips, and his head jerked up toward the greenish light that appeared, bobbing, several yards away. An obscure figure held up a lantern. Long, dagged sleeves draped from its arm.

"Follow me, quickly!" Low and pleasant, the voice was slightly cracked, like that of a youth entering manhood. "Come! There is no time to lose."

"Who are ye?"

"Have you forgotten so soon your friend and guide of the rowan-wood? Hasten. If you do not, the Direath will get you. The lantern shows the path."

*Thud, thud.*

Sianadh opened his mouth to speak, but the lantern bobbed away. He grabbed Imrhien's hand and scrambled after the light, his breath grating in great shredded gasps, but she pulled her hand free; something was wrong. She wanted to scream out a warning but could only tug at the receding knapsack. The left shoulder-strap broke and hung trailing. She could hear nothing but the voice calling, see nothing but the lantern dancing away, away, and out over where the cliff edge must surely lie, and Sianadh being lured to it, like a moth to his doom, heedless of her tuggings. She flung herself at his back, managing to catch the trailing strap in the same moment that he lunged forward and, with a shout, dropped out of sight. The sickening crunch of sliding gravel came to her ears and the brief clatter of Sianadh's staff spinning into the void.

He was gone.

The light went out.

Flat on her belly the girl lay blindly in the dark somewhere on the rim of nothing. Blood walloped in her ears. A small wind soughed in the gorse, and the Greayte Star's light struck through thin altostratus cloud. Peering over the precipice, the girl saw Sianadh's brown, stubby fingers clinging to clumps of clay, his shaggy head pressed hard against the rock face. Immediately she twisted the trailing packstrap around the nearest firm-rooted bush, for the knapsack still hung from his shoulder.

Sianadh looked up, blinking dirt from his eyes.

"The ledge beneath my toes be crumbling. I do not want to die. O Ceileinh, Mother of Warriors, save me!"

His companion leaned over, pulled on the knapsack from above. At that moment, Sianadh's footing gave way. He reached for the strap and with a jerk was brought up short, his full weight depending from it. The little bush bent sharply. Faithfully, it did not break. Screwing up his face, Sianadh heaved himself up with the strength of his knotty arms—his head, then shoulders appeared over the edge. The girl helped him up by his sleeves and hair. The leather strap snapped apart as he grabbed the little bush. Thus anchored, the man paused for breath, still halfway over the cliff, before levering the rest of his bulk up to safety. The battered pack dropped from his shoulder. Unable to stand, he crawled away from the edge. Something small and wicked shot out of nowhere, kicked the knapsack over the cliff, and fled, repeating, "Tear, tear," as it went.

Imrhien wiped the filth from the man's face. He was very pale beneath the grime.

*Thud, thud, thud.*

The thumping thing was coming after them yet.

Sianadh struggled to his feet.

"Ye be the leader," he gasped. "I am a fool—he only speaks to children, the Gailledu. I should have known that light-man was but a hobby-lanthorn. 'Tis too late—we have already shown fear. Give me your staff. I shall take on whatever comes thumping at our backs."

It was midnight. The fishing-boat moon with its one sail rode a fathomless sea, casting star-nets to catch comets. In the vast landscape below, two tiny figures ran along a cliff top pursued by the footstep of some fierce and gloomy specter from a madman's dream. The land fell sharply, the river's walls diminishing and the roar of the water becoming louder, until the hunted ones found themselves beside a sluicing torrent in a channel not ten feet below. Loud as it was, it could not dull the approach of the predator, a hunter that seemed to sport with its quarry, now speeding up, now dropping back, driving them on to the limit of endurance.

"If ye can swim, we should try to get over the water. They cannot cross it, especially southward-running. But I fear ye should be swept away."

It was then that they saw the bridge.

Massive river redgums lined the opposite banks. One had fallen across the river. Half its roots were still buried, and it lived, its green branches spilled in a cluster on the ground on the near side. Spurred on by the sight, the companions raced for this thicket, but too late. The heavy pounding increased its pace, and with a roar, the Direath was upon them. They turned, at bay.

A monstrosity.

It loomed over them, taller by at least two feet, clad in a close-fitting mantle of dark blue feathers. A single hard and hairy hand grew out of its breastbone, and a single veiny, thick-soled leg grew from its haunch. Its one eye glared from the center of the forehead. In its bony hand it held a thick club. It poised motionless, as if waiting.

Without taking his eyes off the apparition, Sianadh drew out his knife and dropped it behind him.

"Take the skian, lass, it is not much use with this one. I need both hands to wield the staff, and if I get close enough to use the blade, that will be close enough for Lord Handsome to grab me by the throat. Take the knife and get over the water, quicklike."

She shook her head, although he could not see her. She would not leave now, would not desert her friend.

Then with a bellow, the man lunged forward. Mortal and wight joined in battle.

The Ertishman was quick on his feet, ducking under the swinging club or spinning away from it. The staff's six-foot length was an advantage, and the monster seemed to hate the touch of the ash wood. But there was no doubt that it was the stronger adversary. On its single foot corded with sinews and bulging veins, it hopped forward, forcing the man to give ground. The eye above the cavernous nose and thick lips rolled from side to side, fixed on Sianadh. Curiously, or it may have been a trick of the moonlight, the monster seemed to move not by swinging through space in the normal manner, but rather by metamorphosing rapidly from one position to the next—a confusing trick that hampered anticipation of its actions.

Giving it a wide berth, the girl dodged around its back and darted in, striking with the skian. With a scream of outrage it turned on her, and Sianadh was able to *thwack* it a mighty blow across the ear while its attention was diverted.

The heavy club narrowly missed her, but she had drawn blood—black blood; the knife-blade smoked with it. Never could she get close enough to wound it with the knife after that, for it was wary of her. But she did not stop hounding and harrying it, and each time it came morphing after her, Sianadh would attack it and it would turn to assail him afresh.

On into the long hours of night they fought, until the ground was bare dust all around. The river dashed past inexorably; the fishing-boat in the sky sailed away. Now the Ertishman moved more slowly. His adversary carelessly allowed him leeway, as if savoring the drawn-out conflict. Sianadh's aim had deteriorated. The next time he struck, his staff hit the ground and broke in two.

"I be done for. Run!" he grunted, staggering.

The Direath came thumping at him. In a flash of inspiration Imrhien hurled her boot at its eye—it lurched off balance.

In that same instant a light wind ruffled the leaves of the fallen tree, and somewhere in the distance a magpie warbled.

The Direath froze.

The magpie called again, exultantly heralding the dawn. The eastern sky paled to a dishwater taupe; the Direath let its club slump. At the third crow it took one last eldritch swipe at Sianadh, who had lowered his guard; the blow caught him in the ribs. Then it bounded away, *thump, thump,* toward the forest.

The Ertishman collapsed, clutching his side. Crouching, Imrhien supported his head, helped him to his feet; together they half crawled to the fallen tree and picked a way among the branches to the broad trunk.

Bent double, arms pressed to his flanks, Sianadh edged across the river in front of her. When they had gained the opposite bank he lurched forward a pace or two, crumpled beneath a river redgum, and did not rise. She cradled his unconscious head in her lap, keeping watch while the first light of dawn opened the world's doors anew.

On reviving, Sianadh propped himself on an elbow and drank greedily of the riverwater Imrhien had brought. He fell back with a sigh and a wince.

"That were like wine to me, even though it tasted of old boots."

It was, in fact, his own boot in which she had fetched the water, there being no other container available. Her remaining piece of footwear had gone to pieces like its mate, and she had flung it in the river. No boots, no ashen staff, no knapsack with its supplies and tinderbox, no leather bottle.

"The map, the map!" The man fumbled in his pockets. "Aagh, a red-hot knife works between my ribs. The *uragubne* has bruised them mightily, or cracked them."

She drew out the map to show him, then replaced it in his pocket. Reassured, he slept again, and she went to the river to bathe.

* * *

On this side, the banks were lower and more gently inclined. After rinsing her ragged garments, the girl spread them on the grass to dry. It swirled fast, the current—too fast to risk immersion. Holding on to a branch that leaned out, she scooped up water in Sianadh's boot and poured it over herself, gasping at its cold touch. Grethet had told her she was disfigured, but that had been part of the lie. There was no fault, no stigma. White and slender, her limbs, like the smooth-barked boughs of the river trees, clean and hard. Like them, she was tall and elegant, cool to the touch. How lovely were the trees . . .

She dressed in damp clothes and returned to keep watch over the sleeper.

Sianadh twitched and groaned in his sleep, waking in pain when the sun had scaled its ladder halfway. With difficulty he stood up, rubbed his eyes, and looked around.

"A fair land, this side of the river. It looks to be *cuinocco* country. May as well be walking, even if my foot be drowned in this soggy boot."

Equipped with redgum staffs, they set off along the riverbank, still heading upstream, toward the escarpment that bulked ever nearer, rearing its blunt bank against the clouds.

The skyscape, as if under the hand of a dissatisfied sculptor, kept re-creating its cauliflower fields, snowy mountains, foamy forests, and lakes of mist. The free airs of open country, rich and invigorating as green-apple cider, rippled across acres of short-cropped grasses dotted with stands of peppercorns, bay trees, and flowering jacarandas whose piercingly blue blooms mocked the sky.

They rested often. Sianadh spoke rarely and did not complain of pain or hunger, but it was clear that he was suffering. At every halt Imrhien brought him water, her brow creased with concern, and made him as comfortable as possible.

That night they rested under a tree. What would happen in the dark hours the girl could not guess. She tried to stay awake to keep watch but could not prevent herself from dozing in snatches. Nothing assailed the travelers but a dream of a silver-white horse in the trees, impaled on a shaft of moonlight. Then again, the girl never dreamed.

The next day and the one after it were much the same. Tormented with hunger and the desire for sleep, ridden with anxiety for Sianadh, the girl trudged on beside him with bleeding feet, hardly noticing their surroundings. There seemed no hope and no choice but to go on until they fell at last, or were felled.

Jacarandas crowded close in the shade near the base of the escarpment, their petals carpeting the ground with luminous azure. The travelers followed the river's twistings and turnings; here it ran under overhanging banks dripping with flowers and into clear pools and backwaters; here it chuckled over shallow ledges; there it glided like polished pewter into dark leaf-tunnels.

Dense and secret became the woodlands. The sky was obscured behind foliage. All around, they could see nothing but trees, straight-boled, narrow, or stout, crowding close or scattered thinly. Beyond the trees, more trees, on and on into a gray subfusc. Half-asleep, Imrhien stumbled onward, lending support to her companion's arm. As dusk approached, a thunder, which had been rumbling far off, grew louder. It was a sound that had been audible now for a long time, yet in her dulled state of awareness the girl had ignored it.

By now they had come right under the shadow of the mountain wall. As they rounded a bend in the river, the trees drew back. Pale sunlight poured down from open sky, a hissing roar assaulted their ears, and an awesome sight greeted them.

Filled with rainbows, its millions of droplets appearing to float slowly down from such a great height, a waterfall hung like a silver curtain. Its hem was lost in spray over a rocky pool. Sianadh leaned on his staff and laughed weakly.

"We have found it, *chehrna,* the sildron mine. We are come to Waterstair."

# 5
# WATERSTAIR
## Candlebutter and Spiderweb

*Soft intaglio of light, glinting like a frosty morn;*
*Armèd with a stalactite—silver white the single horn.*
*Mirror'd in a forest mere, strangely fleeting, ever wild,*
*Seen by night when skies are clear, never near, fancy's child.*
*Legend that the minstrels spun, sorrow never touched your kind—*
*Free as air, elusive one. Lightly run—outrace the wind.*
*Strange and rare, to mankind lost; fairer than the moon above;*
*Diamonds from your mane are toss'd. Beast of frost, yet warm as love—*
*unicorn.*

MADE BY LLEWELL, SONGMAKER OF AURALONDE

Sheets of jade water plunged, hurtling from the heights in a torrent of raw energy. Rainbows bridged its quivering mists. A haze of droplets hung in the air, pearling every leaf and grass blade that fringed the pool, beading hair and eyelashes, collecting in miniature crystals on the skin. The continuous roar pressed around Imrhien's head, drummed and threshed in her ears like the sound of battle.

The rocky basin receiving the waterfall was cradled in the heart of a dell whose gently sloping sides were clothed with tall, spindly trees. There was no sign of a mine-shaft—no broken ground, no weedy tumescences indicating overgrown mullock heaps. Beyond the basin's granite lip the grasses grew smooth and green among the trees, dappled with the tiniest flowers.

*Hunger must have curdled Sianadh's brain,* thought the girl—

until he led her into the core of the water's tumult, around a slippery path of stone, behind the powerful curve of the cataract's glassy screen. There reared the great, vaulted hollow of a cave, its rough ceiling reaching high into shadow. And to the rear of the cavern, an outline of something not defined by nature.

Had they not gleamed with a faint light of their own, they would have been barely visible in the misted gloom, but they stood displayed to their full height of about sixty feet—double doors of cast green-gold metal set in an archway, magnificently decorated and uncompromisingly sealed.

In here, between stone and water, the shout of the falling river deafened the intruders. The Ertishman did not even attempt to speak but laboriously led the girl across the slippery floor of the cave's mouth and out by a path on the other side of the cataract. Pastel daylight greeted them as they exited the cavern. Sinking to a water-polished stone beside the boiling basin he had already named "the porridge pot," the Ertishman panted heavily.

"Up there," he shouted, waving a hand at the cliff rising at his back, "is a small tunnel into the mines hidden behind those doors."

When he had recovered his breath they walked back along the riverbank. A short distance downstream they found a suitable camping place, beside a quiet pool where ancient trees with tangled roots hung over the banks. Here they rested, while he explained further.

"The bloke with the map described the doors to me. I think I can crack them. The old tales tell of such wizardly barriers, which open not to a key such as ye can put in your pocket, but to a rhyme or a riddle's answer. The clue is written on them, for those who can read it.

"My friend with the map, he and his comrades discovered this place by accident. They had a trained capuchin with them. They could not open the doors, so they delved with sticks and made the little tunnel in the cliff. The creature wormed its way in, bringing out lump after lump of andalum-foiled king's-biscuit—as well as some of the stuff that was not protected, which flew up into the skies and was lost. The tunnel was too tight for a man's girth, but they met with stones in its walls and had no picks or shovels to dislodge them and make the passage wider. They departed to fetch equipment from Gilvaris Tarv but met with ill chance. The map-maker's comrades were surprised by wights of unseelie odor—he himself escaped, only to be later waylaid, and his sildron was stolen. He ended up in a cell, sick with some disease borne by the rats there or possibly by Culicidae's poisonous tongues. That was where I found him. He spoke truth, it seems, but I had to see for myself. I need proof of this mine. With evidence of its wealth, I can get a secret expedition of trusty stalwarts to return here with me and load up ore by the barrowful. I could not bring a pick and shovel on the black brig, nor a capuchin—the boyos would have eaten it, like as not, and the shovel as well. But if I can crack those doors, we will not need any of that. Doors were made to open—there must be some way." He sighed and scratched his chin. "By the fires, there stands a portal! Such gates could have been fashioned only by the greatest masters of wizardry!"

That night Imrhien could ward off slumber no longer but was engulfed in the black drowning pool of it and did not surface until middle-day. On awakening she thought she dreamed at last, for a feast was spread beneath the trees. Chewing noisily and dribbling down his beard, her companion tossed a rosy orb into her lap.

"Hoe into it, Your Ladyship. Plenty more where that came from—trees and vines full of fruits, all different colors and flavors. A right banquet. Strangest plants I've ever seen, but I have been gorging on them like twenty-eight pigs with no ill effects.

"Yet," he added, suddenly recalling meals aboard the pirate brig.

The rosy orb had the sweetness of ripe strawberries. The inside of a thick-rinded one was doughy and smacked of new-baked bread. Ere long, a large pile of cores and rinds built up beside the picnic.

Afterward, Imrhien climbed a short way up the vine-hung cliff and easily found the capuchin's entrance—the passage, dark and small, bored back into the wall of stones and clay. She was narrow-hipped enough to fit through, but the closeness of the fit and the complete lightlessness and mystery of what lay beyond were too terrifying to contemplate. A long branch poked into the tunnel met with nothing.

She clambered down and found Sianadh sitting on the rocky floor of the cave behind the waterfall, his shaggy head tilted back. He was studying the doors intently.

A marvelous eagle with a seven-foot wing-span dominated the archway directly over the meeting of the portals. Proud and regal it was, with eyes that glittered. Every pinion was carved in fine detail. The rest of the arch was covered with all manner of birds and beasts represented accurately, in masterly design. The doors themselves were framed with twining leaves and bore extensive runic inscriptions. These, the man was trying to decipher.

"I be certain that these runes hold the key," he yelled against the torrent's rage. "There must be some trick or password to open these doors. I propose we remain at Waterstair for as long as it takes to discover the key."

At these words, an odd sensation gripped his companion: a shuddering coldness. She ran out of the cave into sunlight, but it was several minutes before the sickness passed. When she returned, the Ertishman was still staring at the doors, oblivious of her erstwhile disappearance.

"The writing on these doors be not Ertish or common Feorhkind," he shouted, "or any I have seen. It is some ancient high script, from which our younger languages, mayhap, have derived. Reckon I have a fair chance of figuring it out. I be not unlearned. Then we open the doors, dig out as much as we can carry, and return to the city. We sell what we have brought, deck ourselves out in fine and courtly array, and bring my nephew Liam and his most trusted comrades back here to excavate the rest."

*The city.* People would stare, there, and revile a deformed waif. But then again, all hope lay there—perhaps a cure for skin poisoning, perhaps yellow-haired folk in the street crowds—relatives, name-givers.

The girl went off to gather fresh food. The unidentified fruits, after being picked, lasted only for half a day before they withered. But they were delectable, and she craved them with a hunger she had never known, as if for the first time she tasted truly nourishing provender, food that made her limbs wake to a tingling strength that penetrated to the very roots of her hair. The closest fare to these delicacies had been the passionfruit near fuath-haunted Fincastle's Mill.

As she finished piling up the provisions for their next meal, the sound of the waterfall drew her. She went to look at it again, to marvel at its power and beauty. "Waterstair," Sianadh had called this place—a name deciphered from the barely legible word scrawled on his map. Imrhien noticed now that above the fall's lip the escarpment rose even higher. On a cliff above the cataract, long threads of water hung glinting like the tinsel on Persefonae's gowns. This was indeed a many-stepped stairway. Perhaps there was another entrance up there, behind or beside the higher waterfall. Although Imrhien's feet were still chafed and bootless, curiosity motivated her. The vine-covered, creviced cliffs would be easy to climb, worth exploring. She found a toehold and kicked into it.

From the top of the cliff, between the sun-washed tops of the trees of the river-vale below, a bird's-eye view opened. To the east, hills rolled away for miles toward a hazy horizon. In the west, the dark mass of the pine forest marched grimly into a violet distance.

The sky opened out overhead. Six thousand feet high, the clouds that Stormriders called "altocumulus castellanus" were unfolding vertically in towerlike extensions. Above this skyscape of salt-white castles, fibrous cirrus streamed across the sky in feathered filaments, as strong jet streams at thirty thousand feet swept ice crystals from the clouds.

But at Imrhien's back there was no view, for it was blocked by a rearing face of soil and stone, draped with greenery. It was the second step, rising nearly as high as the first, and the river spilled vertiginously over it on its way down from the melting heights of cold Crowsteeple. A long pool footed this upper cataract, a pool in a granite bowl with sheer sides and no path leading behind the gush. But a glorious vine spilled over the rock face, bearing clusters of perfumed purple pearls. While gathering them in handfuls, Imrhien discovered, behind the cascade of leaves, an opening.

This was no confining, lightless hole like the capuchin's tunnel, but a tall, clean passage of split rock lit by glowing ears of fungus that clung to the walls. As she followed the corridor's curve, the sound of applause grew loud in her ears. She had began to believe that she approached a hall filled with thousands of clapping hands, when it turned out to be merely water, falling from a height. After rounding the last bend, Imrhien brushed past a stone pedestal and came face-to-face with a crowd.

As still as stone, she stood gaping.

As still as stone, they stared back at her.

The cul-de-sac terminated in an airy, high-roofed cavern in the rock beneath the upper falls. Light slanted in through some high vent, in long crystals and golden splinters, and illuminated the occupants—a concourse, a multitude of forms and faces that might have been the source of the applause.

Of stone they were fashioned.

Stark stone, rich jet-black obsidian glossed with highlights—that was the mode of one-half of the gathering. The other half glistened pristine, with a snow-on-snow whiteness. All the figures stood as large as life, and as realistic, for they were marvelously chiseled. Kings and queens, armored knights, tall-hatted wizards, and all manner of foot soldiers—pikemen, bowmen, axemen, others with spears or swords—posed betwixt four crenellated towers only ten feet high. These towers, atop which stone birds perched, stood positioned at the corners of a quartz-mounted stage, a platform faultlessly inlaid with a checkered marquetry of black marble alternating with niveous onyx. Utterly still they posed under the silver hair of the falls. Yet flickering shadows subtly lent them false animation.

After long moments their visitor approached, prowling warily among the statues. She was like a coiled spring, ready to bounce up and flee should any unseelie activity erupt.

Oddly attractive, the figures possessed some indescribable alien quality in the sense that the sudden, swift movements of birds and the breathing of fish and the navigation of migratory seabirds are foreign to humankind yet also closer to the world's elemental forces. Perfect were they in every detail, and although there clung about them an invisible breath or emanation, an intangible quality that betokened great age, no sign of age defaced them; no water-blur, no chipping, stain, or growth. To touch them was to touch cold silk, so fine-grained and polished were the surfaces.

Each profile, each trapping and ornament, stood out as crisply as a carving that had been finished only an hour since. One would have expected to see the cavern's floor littered with stone-dust in flakes and slivers, yet it remained as clean as though it had been freshly swept.

So exquisitely delineated was the hair of their heads, the pointed petals of the rowel spurs, the thong-lacings on sword-belts, every ring and rivet of the chain mail, the pinnacles and crockets ornamenting the kings' scabbards, the long graceful draperies, the pointed shoes, the jeweled cauls covering the hair of the two queens and the veils fluttering down their backs like translucent sheets of water—so lifelike it all was that, save for their immobility, the figures might not have been stone at all, but frozen in death.

No giant doors frowned upon this rough-hewn cavity, but glassy quartzlike pebbles studded the walls at random. By the archway opening onto the passage from which she had just entered, there rose a pedestal in the shape of a salmon. On its head, the fish carried a waterlily, and in the open palm of the flower lay three left-handed gauntlets, unpaired, and—like the statues—unimpaired. Intricate runic patterns flowed over the overlapping metal joints on each finger. The fish-scales of the cuffs shone as if newly oiled. At odds with such extraordinary craftsmanship, they had been fashioned from cheap metals—red copper, blue andalum, and yellow talium. Imrhien picked up the copper one, turning it over with half an intention to take it back for Sianadh to see, but a sidelong glance at the centurieswise stone multitude made her think better of the idea. She replaced the cold metal thing and departed.

<<I watch. I see. What?>>

These signs, among the few Imrhien had learned, were the closest approximations to the message she was trying to communicate. Yet they were far from satisfactory.

"I swear, *chehrna,* that my next task after these doors open will be to teach ye every word I know of handspeak. What ails ye? What have ye found?"

By dint of drawings in the dirt and copious, extravagant gestures, the girl eventually described what she had seen on the cliff top.

"Kings-and-Queens?" Sianadh's eyes lit up. "Big statues on a game-board? What were they made of—gold and jewels? I must climb up and see. . . ."

His companion shook her head, intending to convey they were not golden or bejeweled and that he, with a cracked rib, should not risk a climb. The latter point he realized soon enough when, with a roar of agony, he gave up his mountaineering attempt, having achieved no greater altitude than eight feet.

Imrhien made a hand-sign of doors opening. Surprisingly, he grasped her meaning.

"Aye, of course, lass. Ye're saying there might well be another entrance up there—doors hidden in the walls, to open for whoso-ever moves the game pieces rightly. Aye, that's it! I reckon 'tis a test of worthiness for those who would open the doors to the treasure. Only the cunning deserve to succeed. Winning must be the key. Can the pieces be moved?"

They were too heavy. She shook her head, then remembered the gauntlets. Her thoughts churned. *The statues would move if prompted by a hand that wears one of those gloves. The obvious solution!*

Frustrated, unable to give expression to her inspiration, the girl stamped a foot in an uncharacteristic display of temper. Eloquently she appealed to Sianadh with her eyes.

He grasped her chin in his hand, gently.

"Ye have my word on it—I shall teach ye the 'speak. But first I be wanting to teach ye the playing of Kings-and-Queens. Fortunate ye be, as ye're looking at the best Kings-and-Queens player in all of Finvarna, which bountiful country—may I tread her green turf once more afore I die, and may that death be by drowning in a barrel of vintage Lochair Best—which country be renowned for the skill of its inhabitants at the Battle Royal. Unbeaten, I be. If ye get those pieces in checkmate, then by some clever mechanism a door may open in the side of the cliff, and ye and I shall soon be rich beyond our wildest dreams. And I cannot speak for ye, but my dreams be wilder than a creel full of fur-spitting gray-malkins."

Sianadh took a cake of ocher clay and drew some squares on a flat rock beside the river. Sticks and pebbles masqueraded as sovereigns and battle-hardy warriors.

"This be a checkmate layout," he said, setting the pieces in position to demonstrate. "The woods have captured the king of the stones."

<<How?>>

"Nay, ye do not need to know how it is arrived at. Only move the pieces from each army into this position that ye see here. Memorize it. It should suffice."

<<No.>>

"But up there on the cliff ye have no opponent. Ye cannot play Kings-and-Queens by yerself. . . ."

<<Yes.>>

"Yes what?" Exasperated, the Ertishman flushed to his ears. "Are ye telling me that ye have an opponent up there?"

<<Yes.>> It was an intuitive guess. *A powerful spell has been woven about the game pieces. Success will not be gained easily.*

Sianadh expelled a capitulary sigh and rolled his eyes.

"The object of the contest," he began, "be to knock off the other person's king before he knocks off yours. . . ."

Hours elapsed. Absorbed in strategies there in the faded jade shade of the glade, the two companions were not aware how swiftly time fled by, as silent as a silver horse on dainty cloven hooves. Night overtook them, and they must sleep.

The next day, Imrhien climbed the cliff and made her way to the gallery of the stone figures. The waterfall's applause seemed fainter, a muted hush as of the wind through distant woodlands. Why this should be so was a mystery. It was as though something had caught the attention of the water, which, having for centuries hurtled carelessly over the cliffs, had now focused its awareness on its surroundings—as though Waterstair had drawn breath and were waiting. Timidly she stepped to the fish pedestal and took up the gauntlet of talium, cold and ganoid. Its casing slid over her slender hand like a shell encompassing some pale and vulnerable sea-creature. The game pieces watched, with mineral eyes.

The girl expected that at any moment something shocking

might occur—the crowd would come alive and attack her, rend her to shreds with their blades, run her through with their spears—or the cavern wall would gape and a ghastly hand would whip out and snatch her up to be devoured, or the roof would collapse, entombing her forever in the dark, with the statues pressing in on her, leaning hard against her rib cage until the last breath was crushed out.

Drawing courage like a sword, she walked across the tiles to an infantryman in ice-white mail who, spear in hand, stood guarding the alabaster queen. There was no face for her to look at, only the bleached visor of his sallet. At his back the tall lily-queen, proud-visaged, stared ahead as at some distant cloud-palace—a formidable lady.

An impulse to beg for indulgence, if not mercy, welled up in the girl, but she bowed in lieu of that and, with her gauntleted left hand, pushed the queen's guard in the back. At once a slot opened in front of him, with a slight sound of stone scraping on stone, barely audible over the sigh and silk-rustle of the falls. He slid along it with a faint clockwork whir and halted at the next square. The slot closed smoothly and clicked.

Imrhien had not been slow to react. She had gone flying off to the side of the cavern. Braced against the wall, she fixed the game pieces with a wide-eyed stare. After a pause, another grating noise eventuated. The black queen's infantryman had matched the white's move. Almost it seemed the two repositioned soldiers glared balefully, brandishing their weapons as though they would lift them, strike, and lift again, and then the ringing clash of battle would commence. Would they bleed milk and ink?

Imrhien held herself ready to flee.

Yet frozen the warriors remained. Not another move was to be had out of them.

After a few minutes of the same, the girl stepped forward and pushed another soldier in the back. She had begun to lead the charge—the wintry army's attack against night.

That afternoon, down in the twilight Cave of Doors, she came upon the Ertishman. The lower cataract shouted white noise. If you stared at the racing water for too long, you felt as though you were falling upward. Imrhien gazed at it gloomily, stumbled, and steadied herself against the wall, grazing her elbow.

"So," shouted Sianadh over the shouting, "ye lost the game."

Morosely, the girl nodded. The black army had beaten the white. The game concluded, the combatants had moved back to their original positions and the discarded gauntlet had corroded to nothing, in a rain of blackish flakes. In horror she had flung it from her hand even as it decayed.

Sianadh sourly scrutinized the rune-doors one last time. They left the cave and sat together in the leafy shade along the riverbank. Ferns overhung the water. In the clear depths long leaves of water-plants stretched and swayed languorously along the current. The river eddied against fallen branches, bubbled around rocks, sang to itself.

"No matter, no matter," muttered Sianadh, half to himself, "I have solved much of this runic riddle, methinks. The symbols over those great doors be like Ertish in some ways, and the words I have deciphered have an echo of meanings known to me or guessed. But I do not know enough of them to make sense of it. See what ye can build of them—there is something about 'quiet raiment,' and 'rising up.' Then the words speak of the 'houses of champions' and something else about 'strength' and 'singing melodiously,' and a good deal about 'water.' Can ye fathom it? . . . Nay?" He sucked his teeth thoughtfully. "Below this riddle be written a set of twenty-nine runes that form no words at all. Alas, I need further clues. But I'll not surrender, I'll strive all the harder for this setback. Now, let us practice the Battle Royal with our set of wood and stone, and mayhap ye will win your game before I solve my puzzle. Remember now—ye strategically position the pieces and then strike. When ye can fight using tactics as cunning as my own, almost, ye shall climb Waterstair again."

She climbed Waterstair again. This time she picked up the blue gauntlet, the gauntlet of andalum. Night versus day, shadow against light, the carven armies struggled in the age-old contest, yet there was a dance to it—the one side the shadow of the other, the other the reflection of the one, as perhaps is true of adversaries of flesh.

Yet in the second conflict, the andalum gauntlet failed also. Like the talium, it aged swiftly to dust in the aftermath of defeat, as chalk-white matrix and coal-black matrix rasped softly back into formation. What would happen if the challenger lost a third game? Would the last glove merely crumble and no opportunity be left for adventurers who came in later days? Perhaps the rocky corridor might bar itself against the loser alone but remain open to others, while three new gauntlets climbed the stone pedestal with their fingers and lay there like waiting armadillos. Perhaps a sudden rockfall would, after all, crush the failed challenger, as punishment for lack of cunning and for the temerity of challenging the clever makers of the statues.

"One chance left." Sianadh sucked his teeth again. "Yan, tan, tethera. Third time lucky, as they say."

For three days they played Kings-and-Queens, hour after hour. How pleasant it was, at night, to sink into dreamless sleep where no warriors of light and dark slew one another in the ballet of silent, civilized, symbolic warfare.

Sunrise washed the treetops with dilute gold.

"May all fortune be on your side, Imrhien. And if ye do not win this time, I shall never forgive ye!"

The Ertishman's strong bellow, proving his lungs undamaged by their cracked cage, reached to the cliff top. Imrhien waved back, then threw aside the vine-curtain and slipped down the rock passage, eager yet dreading the last attempt.

*This time I shall command the black army.*

The glove slipped easily over her hand. *Red gauntlet, with you my dark warriors shall win.* She lifted her head and regarded the black host. Grimly they stared straight ahead, as always—at least, it was to be assumed that the knights whose faces were obscured by helms were also gazing blankly into the distance. *Coal-ebony-sable lady, warrior queen of night, go with fury into battle. Shadow, eclipse light.*

There would seem an inevitability about this last trial. *Third time lucky . . .*

She pushed the black queen's wizard's spearman.

The game, slow and subtle, tense and attenuated, stretched from morning to afternoon and then to evening. Imrhien pondered every move, plundered each one for its utmost variety of possibilities. She sustained herself with water from the river, fruit from the vine, thoughts of hope for Sianadh and his optimistic plans.

On the walls of the statue-cave, the luminosity of the quartzlike embedded gems and the fungous growths increased. Night had drawn its dim veil. The girl took it as a good omen. Yet she knew that even then, victory might go either way.

Night dragged on. Through darkness the game progressed. The challenger allowed herself no sleep, although the grass was soft and inviting and the heat of Summer high. Instead she sat cross-legged, her clouded eyes masking inner visions of a thousand scenarios, a thousand thundering battle-plains. The snow queen proved herself a canny adversary, Winter of course being a hardened veteran of many battles. Prisoners of war lay scattered on the border tiles around the platform, their prostration revealing the swivel hinges under their bases that had attached them to the board's hidden mechanisms and would probably do so again. Morning saw Imrhien and her swarthy battalion hard-pressed, defending against a brutal assault from the white host. Night was retreating now, both within the cavern and without. Winter closed in around the tall, dark king, threatening to freeze him to death.

Late afternoon suffused the hollow with an amber softness, like tufts of saffron-dyed wool. Imrhien's head swam with weariness.

And suddenly, the black king lost his lover. The queen of night was taken, and he was left undefended, threatened on all fronts. There was nowhere to run. Night had fallen on the battlefield, and there could be only defeat for the tall dark monarch.

Imrhien's shoulders tensed. Her hair tingled on her scalp. She waited for some final blow, some catastrophe to sweep away the unsuccessful challenger. They stood, the game pieces, their visages changeless. No smile of triumph warmed the ice-pale faces, no look of despair weighed down the polished black brows. The slender snow-lily regina and her knights held the dark lord prisoner.

Nothing happened.

The red gauntlet, the copper, began to fray upon her hand. She threw it down, relieved, tired, dispirited, fed up. *Third time unlucky*.

She fled the cavern and cast herself on the grassy apron at its mouth. Such foolish ambition, such presumptuousness! How could she, a novice, hope to defeat the wisdom of ages? Let her leave this place. Let Sianadh forget his foolish dreams. The concept of wealth easily gained was but a madman's cipher. Reality was only poverty, ugliness, and homelessness. Beneath this cliff, under the very ground on which she lay—and overhead also—existed nothing but dirt, cold stones, blind worms, and sunless hollows, fathoms deep.

She rolled over and lay sprawled on her back, summoning the strength to climb down and face the Ertishman. High in the rich mazarine blue of the evening sky, the first stars were pricking through. Some sparkled more brightly than others. Her thoughts strayed. Sianadh had said he could see these same stars in his home country. What constellations described themselves up there in the daisy fields of the sky, and how were they named? One group of stars stood out, white points so brilliant that they were like the dazzle of sunlight on water.

She counted them—yan, tan, tethera times tethera. These stars burned with a brilliant silver-white flame in contrast with the fainter garnet-red and topaz-yellow sparkles in their vicinity. Even their positions seemed significant—a line joining the bright stars might form a curve here, a point there—

It came to the star-gazer that a marked resemblance existed between the gemmy scatters on the cavern walls and the starry patterns in the sky. Those bright shiners now—what had the Ertishman once told her concerning them?

She leaped to her feet and ran back into the cave.

Nothing had altered. The fallen lay where they had crashed. The statues that remained standing loomed gray in the waning light. Reaching up, Imrhien touched the glowing gems of the wall, each in turn. The point of a beak, a ceres, an avian head, an eye—now her hand swept down the long, graceful neck to the curve of the wing. The nine stones gleamed like white fire caught in globules of water. One after the other, she brushed them with her fingertips, confirming, in awe and wonder, that they matched the constellation pulsing overhead, the sign of the Swan. She fancied each one sank a little into its socket and sprang back. These stones had been placed *just so*.

This, *this* at last was the key.

Had it been so simple, all along?

The grumble of heavy stone was a phenomenon she had expected, but its source was not. It had split in half, the tessellated game board, and was sliding apart. Jumping back to a safe distance, the girl watched the crack widen to reveal broad stairs spiraling down under the ground. An entrance—but where might it lead? To a treasure hoard or to some ancient dungeon, long inhabited by monsters or unseelie wights? The hammering of her heart filled her senses, drowning all other sounds. Sianadh—she must go back for him. She could not venture down there alone, could not go at all into that well of cold stones, blind worms, and sunless cavities. She stood still, unwilling to leave what had been so hard-won and might vanish if she looked away. . . .

In subterranean darkness, the walls of the spiral staircase shone softly yet were not studded with the same bluish phosphorescent fungi as the stone passageway. This glow was mellow gold, like the leaves of poplars in Autumn. It radiated up from below.

*Something lurks down there, for certain, to make such a shining!* It seemed not an eerie light—rather, it looked benign yet somehow untamed—like the shine of a lamp in a window at night, but not as domestic; like the glimmer of candlelight upon ripe bullion it was perilous to covet; like the soft light of a harvest sunset or long, low shafts of morning at the waning of the year.

Sianadh was unfit to climb. He could not help her. Was she to go back to him now, confess cowardice, in the face of his blustering bravado? After he had risked his life for her more than once, could she not do the same in the cause of pursuing his dream? A sudden recklessness seized her. She bowed low to the statuettes made of moonbeams and the figurines wrought of captured shadow. Before she could change her mind, Imrhien plunged down the stair beneath the stair.

Here where the sun never shone, a bone-coldness permeated—the intense frigidity of stone that had never quickened to the touch of the day-star. Yet even though the river flowed somewhere high above, no dampness reached out clammy fingers or slid weeping down the walls. The air was not dank or musty or tinged with the odors of subterranean centuries—soil, stone, roots, pale, soft-bodied things that hid from light—instead it was as sweet as the free and blowing airs of the upper world, which carried the scent of flowers and leaves and the subtle freshness of clear skies. Whoever had designed the system of ventilation shafts had achieved a wondrous feat—it was surely an efficient arrangement, built to last. The engineers of this substructure could only have been masters of their art.

Knowing little of mines, the intruder treading the stairs understood enough to suspect that this was not one at all. Exactly what it was, beyond a long, terraced spiral bathed in dim golden light, could not be guessed.

It was hard to estimate how far down the stairway took her. She was wondering whether the corkscrew drove headlong forever into the deeps when an archway opened before her and her skin prickled as though an unstorm were rolling in. After leaping down the last few treads, she stepped through the opening to behold a staggering, muted glory.

The arch gave on to a gallery halfway up the wall of an immense, high-vaulted chamber. On the floor below, thousands of baffling shapes gleamed faintly. They were piled high and crowded as far as the eye could penetrate. From them emanated the pale golden shining. Imrhien's hand flew to her pocket. The four-leafed clover remained reassuringly there—this was no glamorous illusion. The stairway now led her down the inner wall. Slowly she progressed, scarcely breathing, her hair crackling and lifting of its own accord as though she moved underwater, her gaze caressing the mass of treasure, of incalculable wealth, revealed in this cold subterranean shining. Around the trove pulsed an eerie force like the unstorm and the world's storm combined, dangerously exhilarating, invisible, but already dissipating up the stair as if fleeing through this new rupture.

If a cornucopia of gorgeousness had been spilled at her feet, all sense of time was snatched away in exchange. How long she wandered in the treasury, she forgot to remember. At every turn, some new and wondrous object appeared to hand—gold cups and plates ornamented with jewels, silver-gilt candlesticks, ornate nefs, porringers, cast-gold aquamaniles shaped like lions with their tails arched across their backs to form handles, all manner of tableware, carven chairs inlaid with ivory or gold and silver wire, richly chased and engraved caskets filled with jewels, ropes of pearls, bracelets, rings, torques, gold-mounted cameos and intaglios, fine chains and gem-crusted girdles, shirts of mail, gauntlets, helms, greaves, cuirasses floridly engraved, etched and embossed with gold or silver—an entire armory—and weapons of an unknown metal, honed spite-sharp; damascened swords with ornately pierced or chiseled guards and mounts, gemmed scabbards fretted with precious metals, battle-axes, halberds, partisans, glaives, spears, pikes, lances, and jewel-pommeled daggers—a complete arsenal. Among these were many curious things whose purpose could not be guessed. All possessed the same virtue as the statues at the overhead entrance, a supernatural beauty that could not possibly have been wrought by the hand of man. And all remained untouched by dust or decay, as if Lord Time were powerless here.

Garments were here also, folded in chests. It was not until her teeth began to chatter that Imrhien became aware of the aching cold eating at her bones like poison. She donned a sleeveless shirt of some lightweight gray fabric, a garment that seemed narrow enough to fit. In a moment of panic she thought her stair lost and sought it wildly, for it was out of view on the far wall. While she searched, her gaze came to rest upon the wall close at hand, in which was set a pair of double doors about sixty feet high.

She approached them and put out her hand. With a light touch they swung open, outward.

Beyond lay an even greater cavern—so vast that its ceiling and walls would have been out of sight even had they been lit by a conflagration of torches. What towered there surrealistically like white flame made the treasure in the first cave seem almost mundane by comparison. Mounted on shadowy crosshatchings of gantries, stanchions, transoms, and davits was a thing out of legend, a marvel. Fashioned in the shape of a swan, gleaming, ready to unfurl and fly across the water with her sails and rigging all in place, here towered a full-size three-masted barquentine.

She was all white, except where she was silver. Her beams of bleached wood were everywhere carved like feathers, each pinion white-enameled. Taffrails, binnacle—every article of metal that would have been made of brass on another craft was here fashioned of polished silver, untarnished. Sails lay heaped along the yards like snow. The figurehead was a swan, and it lent the only color to the white ship. The ceres was a startling band of garnets like drops of blood, and almonds of jade formed the eyes.

Beside this queen of ships, the girl felt herself diminished to a child's toy. Caged in supporting fretwork, the aero-keel rose in a perfect curve far above her head, to where the great hull opened out like a giant lily. The graceful lines of the long planks were sculpted into feathers, as streamlined as the flanks of a bird.

Walking beside this vision of splendor, gazing up in awe, Imrhien saw that the elegant swan figurehead faced a second set of tall doors. These also gave under the slightest pressure of her hands and swung back to admit a blinding blare of light and noise and a roaring, living giant with a spear, his arm drawn back, ready to strike her down.

Beside a river that clove its way through miles of wilderness, far from human habitation, peppercorn trees spread their boughs, dripping swaths of long leaves over a glade carpeted with springy turf.

Here stood a chair.

High-backed, this incongruity was fashioned from some dark, rubicund wood—possibly mahogany—inlaid with hammered red gold, embellished with garnets, studded with blushing rose-crystals. The feet had been carved to represent sprays of leaves, but the arms and sides and three-pointed back blossomed with a relief of poppies.

A second piece of furniture faced the first—another chair, this time of blanched pearlwood. It was the twin of the first in size and design, but ornamented with green enamel and diamonds, sculpted with lilies. Between them squatted a low table of small dimensions; it was fashioned of walnut with silver and amethysts, and its motif was the cornflower. The table was laden with a motley array of silver dishes and golden bowls—and cups, each one hollowed from a single burning crystal, and chalices twined with gold-leafed grapevines whose fruits were emeralds. Among these fake fruits, a cocktail of real fruits had been heaped. Their juices filled the cups and also filled an upturned helm that lay under some bushes next to a standing armor of lustrous yellow metal damascened with fine silver foliates.

From the open mouths of exquisite boxes and caskets and gable-lidded arks with cock's-head hinges, jewelry spilled out across the grass. Red gold in alloy with copper, yellow gold, and pale electrum had been used to produce the effect of different shades of gold, thin layers that were chased in relief and carefully inlaid to create contrasting patterns over the sides and lids of many containers. On others, a gold or silver ground had been elaborately carved out, then filled with transparent enamel to give the appearance of intaglio gems. The rest were decorated with lavishly ornate combinations of mother-of-pearl, ivory, amber, horn, bone, leather, lacquer, silver, and precious stones.

Handfuls of coins, flung in childish glee by Sianadh, lay glinting in the ferns like leaves discarded from metal trees, bright argentum, and scalding gold.

Seated on the poppy chair, the big red-haired man now tossed over his shoulder an empty goblet of chased silver and leaned toward Imrhien in the lily throne. His hands danced, portraying every word.

"We" (indicating himself and her) "are as rich as" (beginning with both extended index fingers pointing forward apart from each other, he brought them together, then raised his right hand up from the left and ended with a claw hand, palm down) "all" (making a large loop with his right hand) "the double-dealing" (pushing his index finger across his chin) "filthy" (with the knuckles of his hand under his chin, he wiggled his fingers) "fat pigs" (rocking his thumb and little finger on the opposite palm like a fat person waddling, then holding his downturned right hand under his chin and moving the fingers simultaneously up and down) "of Luindorn merchants" (forming the L-rune, followed by the miming of counting money) "put together." (His fists made a clockwise horizontal circle.) Throwing back his head, the Ertishman roared with laughter. Then he settled himself back in the chair—which was padded with torn grass for comfort—and took up a brimming cup, sampling it with a satisfied air and watching the girl over the gleaming rim as she repeated every sign, almost to perfection.

"Ye left the fat out of the pig part."

Having corrected his student's error, he went to check on the helm of fruit juice, which, optimistically, he was trying to coax to ferment into something stronger. Imrhien remained reclining in the priceless chair, reveling in the glow of success. Idly she flipped gold coins in the sunlight. They winked light and dark as they spun. She had never even touched gold before—not that she could remember.

There had been one appalling moment, when she had opened the rune-doors from within and stepped out under the lower waterfall, only to be mistaken for an unseelie wight and almost killed by the startled Ertishman. In her fright she had mistaken him for a spear-wielding ogre. But since that time, joy had reigned—peppered with the odd frisson of alarm, a feeling that had become almost familiar to the girl during her journeyings with Sianadh. Now Imrhien recalled with amusement the astonishment written on his features, as she emerged from the opening portals of the "mine." In the instant of recognition he had frozen like a rough-hewn copy of a game piece, arm upraised, mouth gaping. Then the staff had dropped from his hand, accompanied by assorted Ertish expressions dropping from his lips. It was several minutes before she could get any coherent conversation from him, and *that* had been barely intelligible.

Then he had surged between the open doors at a limping run—a gait that (he grudgingly admitted later) had been caused by his climbing the bluff in search of her, passing out owing to the effects of the exertion on his damaged ribs, and waking to find himself lying flat on his back with a swollen ankle. Fortunately, the sight of abundant wealth seemed to act as an effective remedy for agony. Sianadh, crowing, lost himself for most of the day in the ship-cavern and the inner storehouse beyond. Infected by his excitement, or perhaps by some innate quality of the treasure, his companion forgot her weariness and joined him.

There had been another terrifying instance when, emerging with a silvery candlebranch in hand, Imrhien had been wrenched off her feet, to hurtle into the air at a breathtaking rate. Too late she had realized that the silver was, in fact, sildron. In releasing the object, she had fallen instantly some ten feet, to be clumsily caught by Sianadh, who deposited her on the ground in a careless heap.

"The caves be floored with andalum, girl! Be careful what ye bring into the open. *Oghi ban Callanan,* ye nearly broke my back to match my ribs and foot—ye'll be the death of the Bear!"

She frowned, misliking his choice of words.

Now a nine-branched candlestick would be floating somewhere in the upper layers of air, to be scooped by the salvage nets of some passing trade-ship or pirate jackal.

By the end of the day they had wedged open the doors with stones, furnished and redecorated their campsite, and gathered a conglomeration of fruits. It was time to feast in celebration of success.

"Two days and two nights, Imrhien, ye were away up there. And ye wonder why I went looking for ye! What a laugh—to think the doors would open to anyone who pressed the buttons in sequence. The game-board must simply have been set there for the door-makers to amuse themselves! Seems odd to me, but as they say, other races, other customs—eh, Imrhien? Ah, but no matter. All that stuff be irrelevant now—'tis the time for reveling."

Thus began under Waterstair a happy period, a kind of golden era. Imrhien and Sianadh explored the trove, sometimes wandering awestruck in the caverns, at other times bearing chosen pieces into the sunlight. Their camping spot took on the effect of a splendid palace interior, sumptuously furnished, stamped in rich colors against a green backdrop of fern and foliage. Grass-heads tufted against inlaid mahogany table-legs. Precious stones glittered, heaped carelessly upon gray river-rocks. Birds alighted on crocketed chair-backs and on damasked helmets of war. Beetles crawled up the stems of chalices worth a peasant's lifetime of labor and sometimes halted, looking as if they were part of the exquisite decoration thereon. Flowers bloomed like dyed silks in the same mosses that couched golden torques with eyes of ruby. It was indeed a surrealistic pageant.

The armors shone with the nacreous colors of seashells—gleaming greens, opalescent blues, silvers swift and pure, lustrous moon-gray, and the soft golds of sunrise.

"Do ye see these armors, d'ye see from what materials they be fashioned?" asked Sianadh, fascinated. "Not so much as a steel rivet amongst them. Many of these metals I have not before seen, but I have heard of such—the platinum and iridium so beloved of the Icemen, here in alloy silver white; chromium, gold, and silver; copper as bright as Muirne's hair, dimmed by no patina of verdigris; yellow bronze and talium. I know not these even rarer types—here a metal as green as the ocean and there another blue as the evening sky—perhaps cobalt salts have been used—'tis a glasslike surface and seems like ceramic, yet is not brittle. No iron or steel can be found anywhere in this trove. Its makers misliked it for some reason. . . ."

He scratched his head deliberatively.

"I can only reckon on one reason." He looked up. "*Doch,* there's a wasp in the wine!" Distracted by concern for his fermenting fruits, he hurried off without elaborating.

During these days of leisure, when there seemed no need for much haste, Sianadh was wont to recline negligently among piles of gold and jewels, telling stories of his travels in the Known Lands of Aia, various scurrilous escapades—into which he had been drawn as an unwilling, innocent, and wrongly suspected participant—and of his sister, Ethlinn, who at the age of sixteen had fulfilled her ambition to become a fully fledged carlin, to their mother's sorrow. On Littlesun Day in her sixteenth year, Ethlinn had received her carlin's Staff from the Coillach Gairm, the eldritch hag of Winter. She had given up her powers of speech in return for the ability to wield the Staff. Sianadh spoke often of his youth in Finvarna. When he talked of his native land, a light would come into his eyes and a lilt entered his voice. His eyes misted, and he would gaze as if at some far-off place.

"The gaunt cliffs along the west coast of Finvarna be the westernmost edge of the Known Lands. There the gulls scream and crowd like snow on the heights. Beyond them, thundering, the terrible ocean stretches out darkly westward and northward to where the Ringstorm rages. All of Finvarna borders upon the ocean. In the west my land be wildly beautiful, desolate, a land of mountains, lakes, bogs, and rivers. Often 'tis shrouded in low curtains of cloud. Isolated, inhospitable, and rugged be the west—mysterious and wight-haunted. The people of that region work closely with seelie dwarves in metalwork: gold, silver, bronze, and copper. The land is as harsh as the folk are kindly, generous, and hospitable. We Erts welcome everyone into our homes—members of the family, friends and acquaintances, strangers, all alike. In Finvarna we do much visiting, for we be fond of news—and we dress for the occasion, and there might be a song or two when there be visitors. Above all else, we value eloquence and music. And playing Kings-and-Queens," he added, and after a reflective pause, "and hurling. That's a sport to live for. It is said the game was taught to my countrymen by the Strangers, in times long ago, before that race disappeared from the world. D'ye know of the game? . . . No? Here's the sign for it. See, it is hitting a ball with sticks, like this." He demonstrated.

"Not that I be overpatriotic, mind. Patriotism be the cause of many a young life lost on the fields of war. I be the King-Emperor's man—an Erithan first, a Finvarnan second. Yet a *place* can call to ye, it can beckon to your very blood." He sighed.

"In other parts, forest covers Finvarna, or wide-open rolling grassland, never enclosed by fences or walls. There the mighty herds of giant elk graze, and their antlers branching as wide as trees. Here and there ye might spy the ruins of small castles and tower-houses. South of the river lie rich farming lands, and that is where my mother's folk came from. So fair, Finvarna. So far. Will I see it again? Ach! Why should I be getting meself heartsick for me home? Homesickness be a scourge—it devours the life that feeds it. Me grandmother allus used to say, 'There be two days ye ought never to fash yerself with—yesterday and tomorrow.'"

Sometimes the shang wind blew, reviving no tableaux in this place where humankind rarely passed. Once or twice, at dusk, the girl glimpsed, on the edge of vision, a wild, white horse etched like ivory on the forest, its single horn a lance of moonlight—one of the elusive creatures that Sianadh called *cuinocco*.

At their leisure the treasure-finders discovered and rediscovered the secrets cached behind the rune-doors—treasures that, among their complexities, often seemed to shift position unaided. They examined and puzzled over them and chose what to take when they departed for the city. In the course of these incursions, they came upon a third and smaller side-chamber heaped with sildron bars and objects, some wrapped in andalum. To this the capuchin's tunnel had penetrated.

But the fascination that drew them most was the swan-ship, mighty and beautiful. It was a ship fit for royalty. They left her until last, then hesitantly, with profound awe and respect, boarded her via the spidery ladders and catwalks supporting the deep scoop of her hull, to tiptoe across her gleaming decks and trace with trembling fingertips her immaculate fittings. Every separate feather was delineated on the folded-back wings. They were enameled in white and outlined in silver. Except for the jeweled eyes and ceres, everything glimmered moonshine and alabaster—glistening masts, white silken sheets, and shrouds.

"What a joy, to fly this queen of swans!" Sianadh gazed up at the yardarms. "The masts be too tall to fit her out of the doors. They would have to be dismantled before she could be rolled out, and 'twould be a task for many men."

There were other joys. Sianadh had demanded to know where Imrhien had obtained the spidersilk vest.

"For"—he elaborated in his role of tutor—"spidersilk be twelve times stronger than iron and incomparably light. 'Tis stronger than a mail-shirt and more comfortable, but the cost of one would feed a common family for ten years. It all comes out of Severnesse—that country be full of spider-farms, but 'tis not a lucrative trade—so much silk is needed for just a square inch of fabric, and spiders be so unreliable."

The trove revealed a veritable wardrobe of spidersilk. Sianadh carefully selected a suitable vest, then exclaimed, "Ah, to the fires with it. I deserve an entirely new outfit."

He disappeared in a frenzied cloud of apparel, like a dog digging up a bone, and emerged clad in gray from head to ankle: a dagged doublet and full-sleeved shirt, a pleated jacket, ill-fitting hose cross-laced at the ankle, a kerchief tied rakishly over his head, and a long cloak fastened with a gold brooch. Not least, he sported a new belt of linked silver serpents' scales buckled with an ornate clasp. Each scale was intricately engraved. Over this regalia he battened an armor of ridged lamellae in which he swaggered for half a day until the heat became unbearable and, rather irresponsibly, he abandoned his outer casing under a tree like some drab cicada reaching adulthood. Of his old clothes he retained only the habitual taltry and the stout boots.

Accordingly, the girl swapped her rags for spidersilk, too, folding a swatch of it into a soft-draped gown cinched at the waist with a girdle of beaten gold. In a fit of rashness she added gold rings, bangles, a filigree collar, and a circlet for her hair.

"Ye look fine! Gold be your color. Ye were right not to choose the silver."

Embarrassed, sensing an odd discomfiture in Sianadh, she turned from the man and caught her own image reflected in a bronze mirror. Her belly knotted. A slender incarnation: narrow-waisted, exquisite as a doll from the neck down, the shoulder-length hair spilling thick and heavy as raw bullion, the face hideous as a gargoyle—such an obscenity seemed familiar, in a way that shocked her.

The rings and baubles clinked, landing in a heap, shucked quickly from her limbs. She exchanged the gown for baggy male attire.

The upper trapdoors, the two halves of the Kings-and-Queens game-board, had closed by themselves, quietly and (somewhat sinisterly) without warning. The pieces had returned to battle-ready formation, but no replacement gauntlets had appeared. Wishing to take no chance of being unaccountably and irreversibly locked in, the adventurers ensured that the lower portals in the Cave of Doors remained firmly wedged open.

The weather turned sultry.

Long gray lines of scud rolled in rapidly, ragged and low, driven by the South Wind. They blanketed the sky, pressing it down under their weight until it seemed that the firmament was supported only by the treetops. At first, the clouds released a spattering of warm raindrops, then it began to pour in earnest. Imrhien and Sianadh took shelter in the swan-ship cavern, where the rain's patter was drowned out by the muted roar of the swelling waterfall. Sianadh took this opportunity to teach handspeak and to recite the history of the world, learned by rote, embellished by a few of his own amendments.

"Since ye don't know anything, I'd better learn ye. Beginnin' with the years before the Year 1, when the countries of Erith were not united, that was when they used to fight against one another," he instructed. "As the tribes grew more numerous, these fights became wars—Eldaraigne, Namarre, Avlantia, Finvarna, and Severnesse were the main combatants, for Rimany and Luindorn had no central ruler like the others. Indeed, Luindorn was not then inhabited by men.

"At this time the Talith yellow-hairs, your own folk, were the most civilized and stately—far more so than the other three peoples. Their armies were efficient and well-equipped defense engines, but the Talith, they had no wish to extend their lands by invasion. They wished only to remain and flourish in Avlantia. My folk, the Erts, were always farmers in Finvarna. The white Icemen of Rimany, they were deadly fighters in their own country but like the Erts and the Talith had no desire to steal the lands of others. Icemen can thrive only in cold, sunless climates. If they come north, they must hide from our sun, so ye see, other lands are not much use to 'em.

"The Feorhkind, the brown-hairs like your sailor friends and those dogs of pirates, they be a warlike race. Over the span of many decades, or centuries—I forget which—they populated Eldaraigne, Namarre, Luindorn, and Severnesse, using Namarre as a penal colony at first. Some of the colony's convicts escaped imprisonment to roam the weird regions of that northern country—which is why Namarre became a haunt of brigands. All of that happened a long time ago, before the Year 1.

"James D'Armancourt the First, he was called the Uniter, and he was a powerful and wise King of Eldaraigne. He united the countries of Erith by force and by wisdom, made of them an Empire. He seized power over the other countries by clever strategy and greater numbers, both by war and by treatying with their Kings. The first King-Emperor was he, in the period called the Uniting of the Kingdoms of Erith, or 'Unity.' There came to be peace under his reign. It was decided to use a new system to number the years, whereby the Year 1 was the Year of Unity. Before this, each country had used its own reckoning and all years were numbered differently.

"Long-lived and late to marry were the Kings of the House of D'Armancourt. The son of the Uniter, who succeeded him, was wise—but the son of his son seemed to be too impulsive and reckless to hold on to this fragile balance of power. Nevertheless, he changed for the best, as youths often do when the shrewdness of maturity has grown on them, and he ruled wisely from then on. Indeed, he became known as William the Wise.

"The Year 89, during the reign of William the Wise, was a terrible year. It is said that this time marked the passing of the Faêran, the Secret Race—or at least the vanishment of most of them—to the places beyond the Ringstorm or else to the hollow hills, or wherever immortals go when they tire of our world. There were fierce storms. It was then that the shang winds arose for the first time. The people did not know how to deal with these winds until William the Wise issued laws about the making of chain mesh hoods out of the talium trihexide and the Wearing of them. Also in this year of turmoil, sildron was first discovered and became, immediately, royal property. The Houses of the Stormriders were founded, and the Windship lines as well. Although a harsh year, it also marked the beginning of the Era of Glory, when, so they say, the few Faêran who remained worked together with the Talith to design and build the cities in every country, great cities such as the one we passed through in the forests of these mountains. The first men of the Dainnan also were gathered together, the King-Emperor's special company—peacekeepers in those golden times, warriors in later days.

"The Faêran, like wights of eldritch, could not abide the touch of cold iron. And like wights, they never left an image on the shang whether bareheaded or no. The Feorhkind in their arrogance had taken to leaving their taltries off in an effort to imitate the Fair Folk. They tried to deny their passions so that they could pass through the unstorm without leaving imprints. It is said that ye can be in a shang storm without a taltry, but only if ye curb your passions, which is why Stormriders and others value control over anger and laughter and such. In backwaters and outliers like the Relay Stations, where they are so much in awe of the Fair Folk that they will not name them, or even speak of them aloud in company, many folk still think themselves noble if they show no passion.

"In the middle decades of the millennium came a time of terrible plague and war, beginning around the Year 561. It was called the Dark Era. This came about when the last Faêran who still lingered, perhaps growing weary of Erith, disappeared out of the world. The Faêran have not been seen since the beginning of the Dark Era. The remaining Talith dwindled rapidly, and their culture passed away, simply fading into the grass that grew among the ruins of their cities.

"It was then that the D'Armancourt Dynasty faltered. The King-Emperor was toppled from the throne of Eldaraigne and indeed of the Empire, and he fled into hiding with his family and retainers. Lawlessness spread throughout the lands. Weakened by pestilence, the countries were vulnerable to attack from Namarran raiders and outlaws, and evil wizards who had grown strong and formed rank alliances with things unseelie. It was then that the Stormriders and the Dainnan became warriors and remained so for three centuries.

"During the Dark Era, the Feorhkind took over the Ancient Cities. What with sickness and strife and unshielded heads, the Ancient Cities came to be haunted with afterimages and were eventually abandoned in favor of the older, less elaborate cities. Caermelor remained, having been built of dominite and the Wearing having been enforced there.

"More than two hundred years ago, the rightful heir to the High Throne arose, emerging from self-imposed obscurity. The D'Armancourt line, although hidden, had remained true throughout the long years. By then Edward the Eleventh, who was later called the Conqueror, had grown to a strength like unto his forefathers. Calling to his side the wisest men of Erith, a council of seven known as an Attriod, he amassed a great and powerful army. After a successful campaign he regained his throne and pushed the outlaws back to Namarre. Eight hundred and forty-nine was the Year of Restoration, two hundred and forty years ago.

"The D'Armancourt Dynasty first came to power over a thousand years ago, and today its strength is greater than ever. The wisdom and justice of its King-Emperors is undimmed through the generations—if anything, it seems to increase. Order was restored by Edward the Conqueror, but by then many of the secrets of the Era of Glory had passed out of mortal knowledge.

"This cache of treasure here, this be of Faêran make, no doubt. I reckon they left it here when they went away. And those fruits that grow hereabouts, they be not the germ of Erith—I would chance that they spring from seeds brought from the Lost Realm, sown or carelessly scattered centuries ago."

The tale-teller fell silent.

A thousand unaskable questions seethed in the listener's mind.

Sianadh deliberated long over what items he should select to take with them to Gilvaris Tarv.

"I cannot bear to leave any of it behind," he announced despairingly, sitting on a pile of gold pieces and clad from head to toe in yet another armor of resplendent design, "but we must soon leave this place. I need meat. I cannot go on eating this Faêran fruit forever, no matter how tasty it be. My palate craves flesh."

His attempts at river-fishing and juice-brewing having failed, the Ertishman mused wistfully and at length upon his grandmother's cuisine and the various liquors of Finvarna.

"But first and foremost, 'twill be a delight to front up to my sister's family with pockets full of candlebutter for them."

<<What?>> signed the girl.

"Candlebutter? 'Tis another name for gold—gold is warm and ripe and yellow, like butter—and it buys candle-fire and hearth-food. Ach, I can behold their faces now—Ethlinn, my sister, the boys, Diarmid and Liam, and their sweet sister, Muirne. They have lived in poverty since Riordan was slain. Uncle Bear will soon change that!"

Ultimately and with regret, he decided to take some gold neck-chains, a few modest daggers, and three small caskets, one filled with antique gold pieces and a scattering of silver, one loaded with jewels, and the last, made of andalum, containing sildron bars.

"Small enough to smuggle through the streets under a cloak, unmolested," he explained. "Heavy, but not unmanageably so. And—heark ye, Imrhien, we shall not have to carry them through the wilderness being chased by wights, for we shall build a raft!"

He paused expectantly, while the girl tried to force her hideous features into some semblance of an admiring expression.

"This scrawl of a map—such as it is—shows that this river goes on to marry the Rysingspill, which flows on right to where Gilvaris Tarv presides at its mouth like a great rotten carbuncle. We shall sit like lords and ladies on our raft and merely ride to town! What say ye?"

<<Unseelie wights.>> This sign, the representing of horns with hands touching temples, crooking the extended index and middle fingers, was one of Imrhien's latest acquisitions.

"Nay! They cannot cross running water—although," he amended, "some do dwell in water. Fuathan and the like and drowners. The most dangerous, Jenny Greenteeth, Peg Powler, and those sorts, dwell near human habitation since it is their chief delight to wreak mischief on us. But never fear, the Bear shall deal with any water wights. We have, er"—he cast about—"these tilhals still on our necks, and while we possess nothing of iron, we may yet whistle. I have been known to whistle the very birds out of the trees. Wights flee by the thousands when they see me pucker my lips! We shall find staffs of rowan-wood or of ash, the powerful trees. The Bear has defeated them once and can do it again!"

Whistling a jolly tune, the Ertishman shouldered a fine-honed, splendidly decorated war-ax and went to cut saplings to build the raft. The girl helped him lash them together with lengths of spider-silk fabric, the local vines being far too fragile for the task.

"We shall build it stout and strong in case we meet with rapids on the way," the Ertishman proclaimed enthusiastically. "With any luck we shall encounter no waterfalls—aye, but should we, that would be a ride to speak of!"

His strewn toys Sianadh removed back to the caves so as to leave no evidence.

When for the last time they swung the rune-doors together in the lower cave, the travelers wedged a precautionary stone sliver to keep them apart, just a crack, awaiting their return.

"Never trust an apparatus or an enchantment to work the same way twice!"

The waterfall flung miniature water-prisms, fracturing daylight into seven colors. An evanescent spectrum was entangled in its hair.

The raft, as shipshape as could be managed, had already been launched. It waited, bobbing on the river beside the campsite, tugging at its mooring-rope: four long-sleeved spidersilk shirts knotted together. On this craft lay the three full caskets, firmly tied on, which would also serve as seats, plenty of spidersilk ropes of various gauges, some boughs of yew in case the raft needed repairing along the way, clumsily woven rush baskets filled with pennyfoil leaves to repel Culicidae, and a small mound of fruit that would wither if not consumed at their next meal.

The spirits of the travelers were high. Whether owing to some property of the Faêran fruit, the cold purity of the riverwater, or some other factor, their various wounds and scrapes had healed quickly during their eighteen-day sojourn at Waterstair. Imrhien could have sworn her locks had grown a full inch or more. Sianadh had lost his limp, and his chest-pain had eased.

They stepped aboard, two gray-clad figures seeming clothed in twilight, and shoved off from the bank with long wooden poles. High on the escarpment at their backs, hidden figures made of light and dark faced each other, staring silently into the approaching years.

The current took the raft around a curve in the river. Looking back, the girl could not see the perpetual curtain beyond the bend, but her ears caught its long sigh receding, and between the trees she glimpsed a flicker of silver that might have been the mane or tail of a horse made of starlight.

At the journey's beginning, the river chivvied its way between low, gently sloping banks. Succulent grasses fringed it, and long-haired casuarinas, and azure jacarandas whose fallen flowers, like broken pieces of sky, were drifting in the current. The sun hammered white flints off the water. Songbirds strung glassy notes together like strings of beads.

"This little flood has no name, to my knowledge," Sianadh expounded. "It was marked on the map as merely 'a river.' I name it Cuinocco's Way. Did ye see it, the white horse with the long horn like a javelin? I thought I beheld it for one instant. Ach, we can speak of it now, but 'tis not wise to speak of such creatures when in their domains, even though they be seelie. It be not proper to name them where they might hear ye. Its presence was strong—it haunted my dreams, which was a nice change. Such majesty and strength, such beauty—I would give much to possess a creature like that. We have been fortunate. Few folk have ever caught sight of it, or of *them*—only one *cuinocco* or many, who can guess? Many have hunted the beast, but none have captured it. 'Tis known to frequent this kind of pleasant country, with galloping hills and secret glades, and where the *cuinocco* is, unseelie things do not go."

He began to hum a tune.

The water bore them along on its back. Cautious of the not entirely stable nature of the raft, they pushed away from banks and protruding rocks with twisted branches of bay-wood.

Gradually the banks rose higher until the raft was bowling along through the shadowed cleft of the ravine past the wight-haunted forest and riding south on the tipsy waters.

Their fruit withered at the end of the first day, but they did not put ashore to search for more. Sianadh refused to leave the safety of running water until the haunts of the Direath were far behind. When dusk inked the air, dimming vision, he threw a mooring-rope over an outlying branch of a willow that leaned far out over the river. The long evening stretched into a lute-string plucked by the penetrating drone of cicadas, who lurked unseen in the trees.

Now that they had passed beyond the borders of the country of the horned horse, Imrhien felt the eyes of other things, invisible eyes, watching. An uneasiness crept upon her—she began to think of the unseelie water wights Sianadh had described. The river glimmered gray under the light of the moon, and the trees gathered along the banks like black sentinels. All through the night, the travelers remained damp but afloat, scarcely daring to sleep for visions of thin, bloodless hands reaching out of the water, trailing weed, and cold eyes the color of limes, unblinking, lidless. Once, a scum-dripping horse's head emerged partway above the water and regarded them out of the pits of its skull for some while before slowly sinking underwater again.

It seemed that during the night, Sianadh's good spirits had been stolen away. The next morning, bleary-eyed and grumbling about the aching hollow in his belly, he fought to untangle the spidersilk rope from the willow's clutches while his companion moved back and forth to balance the violently rocking craft.

"I'll make a longbow this very day to shoot our dinner, or me name ain't Sianadh Kavanagh!" The Ertishman's voice rang, unnaturally loud on the still airs, skipping off the water like a pebble. "I care not if we have to eat the kill raw—and that we shall do, ye ken, unless ye be a master of that Dainnan trick of spinning wood on wood to make fire."

Imrhien shook her head. She too was gnawed by hunger but would refuse meat, cooked or uncooked, since she could not abide the smell or taste of dead flesh. In any case, it seemed doubtful whether Sianadh would be able to fashion weapons out of spidersilk and the few thin boughs of willow and yew on board, but he had made up his mind. He fell silent and sat whittling with a horn-hilted dagger inlaid with gold. The raft drifted downstream.

As they passed among celadon curtains of willow withies near the western bank, Sianadh muttered, "I wish I had not shouted out me true name back there. If there weren't pointy eldritch ears a-listening, I'm an Iceman."

Daylight welled out of the sky with the amber mellowness of honey-mead. Otters frolicked and splashed beneath trees along the riverbank. In placid backwaters, fish leaped up like silver spear-blades. Secretive holes among the roots at the water's edge indicated the presence of platypus or water-rats. A line of ducks rowed upstream. The Ertishman inaccurately projected stones at them from a makeshift slingshot, expressing a fervent wish for a baited fishhook or a bird-net. He whittled so savagely that he was in danger of cutting off his fingers, and he caught duck-feathers floating on the water with which to fletch his crude arrows.

They gathered handfuls of watercress that did nothing to assuage hunger. Imrhien leaned out over the raft-side and looked past the dapple and satin gloss of sunlight on the surface, gazing far down into the depths into a world of waving weeds. Abruptly she recoiled, almost upsetting the pallet.

Feminine forms as pale as corpse-wraiths were gliding, swooping, diving beneath the raft. Their hair was long and green, like fine seaweed. Membranous robes wafted gently around their slim white feet. Sianadh peered over the side.

"Asrai," he grunted, "seelie. Wights cannot be eaten. Do not bother with them."

By the afternoon, he had fashioned a yew longbow strung with spidersilk cord and three off-balance arrows. Imrhien had occasionally been witness to the butchering of domestic animals for the Stormrider tables, had seen injuries resulting from various accidents in the servants' quarters, and unwillingly viewed aeronauts being run through with pirate scimitars. Considering she had managed to conquer an initial squeamishness at the sight of blood, she felt oddly disturbed at the prospect of some wild creature dying, impaled on one of those barbless, sharpened shafts.

<<Wait. City.>>

"The way this ditch wanders about, it might be four or five days before we reach Tarv. I should fade away to a mere shadow of my former self if I waited until we arrived in the city to get food. Would ye be wanting to turn up in town beside a shadow, *chehrna?* Now, we must tie up and go ashore. I'll not risk losing arrows in the water, shooting at river-rats from this unriverworthy craft. Besides, there shall be better game off-water."

By now, Cuinocco's Way had meandered out from among the parklike hills on the one hand and the dark uplands on the other. On both sides, ferny banks rose sharply toward ridges densely wooded with silver birches. The trees were misted with cucumber-green and steeped in cool shadows amid the heat of the month of Arvarmis.

Long ago, an old willow-tree had fallen into the river. Most of its roots had failed to hold on to the crumbling banks, yet some were still embedded therein. Silt had built up along the half-submerged trunk, and a backwater had formed. A quiet pool gleamed there, into which flag-lilies lowered their blue reflections. The travelers secured the raft to a branch jutting from the trunk and disembarked. Halfway up the slopes, Sianadh found himself hampered by his spidersilk cloak. Impatiently he unpinned it and let it fall to the ground. The girl caught at his sleeve, gesturing back at the raft.

<<I watch. Unseelie wights.>>

Sianadh pondered.

"Ye may be right, lass. Wights be full of mischief. As soon as our backs are turned, they are likely to turn our craft upside down, or cut the rope and let it drift away with our wealth on board, to break up against some snag." He scratched his beard, furrowing his weather-beaten brow. "Yet I will need your help up there in the timber. By rights ye ought to go upwind and beat the bushes, to flush the game toward me. Ach! What a two-headed puzzle! Shall I risk my future as a rich man for a feed of raw flesh? I shall," he added quickly, hearing his stomach growl. "But ye, stand at the top of the ridge where ye can keep an eye on the raft. If anything comes near, run down and knock its head off. If any true and *lorraly* beast comes blundering out of the forest, wave your arms and scare it back toward me, so I can make breakfast of it. If owt unseelie-looking comes out at ye, get down to the running water. But never fear—either way, the Bear shall win out."

It was Imrhien's turn to frown. This idea seemed confused, harebrained, and risky.

<<You *scothy*. Not kill.>>

"*Scothy,* eh? Well, perhaps 'tis true. . . ." The Ertishman nodded philosophically. "Howbeit, I have come this far, and I will go on."

Taking a firmer grip on the makeshift longbow, he climbed up over the cliff's lip and was soon out of sight.

Imrhien clambered in his footsteps, the wiry bracken-fern

springy beneath her bare feet. She stood and waited, looking around warily. Below, the river flowed past and the raft tugged lazily on its tether. Above, the birches stood silent on the ridge top. When had such a hush fallen on the leaf-roofed landscape, such a breathless stillness? No birds sang, no leaves jostled. Even the chuckle of the river seemed to have faded.

And it seemed to Imrhien that some kind of pressure was building, that a mighty weight was crushing her like an ant, pinching her between land and sky. There was a wrongness, a flaw, in the surface of this natural world. Horror seized her by the throat, and she could not move. She stood alone, more isolated than ever she remembered, waiting for a killing to occur.

From somewhere in the birches' green fog, a shout burst the silence. Something that was moving too fast for a man crashed through the woodland, snapping twigs in its haste. As the invisible menace approached, the girl gathered her courage and braced herself, staff upraised, ready to defend or flee. Several yards away, the crashing burst out from the cover on the ridge top, then whatever had caused it dashed back in. The noise of its progress ceased abruptly.

It had been a young doe.

Imrhien went after it. She followed the deer's short trail to a small glade where the animal had fallen. She lay struggling to get up, her flanks heaving, eyes dark with fear and pain. Long red streaks striped her side, welling from where the arrow's fletched end stuck out from the shoulder. A swish of leaves announced death's arrival. Sianadh shouldered out of the undergrowth and stood with dagger drawn, triumph blazing like beacons from his blue eyes. In the same instant he looked across the body of the wounded creature and met his companion's level stare.

Her hands hung limply at her sides. Her eyes spoke.

After a long moment, the Ertishman reached down with a smooth, practiced movement, the movement of one who had been raised on a farm and knew how to use a blade cleanly. But the knife was no longer in his hand. He had sheathed it, and when he straightened, he held the red arrow. He stepped back.

A pressure split down the middle and fell aside in two halves like a walnut. Birds sang, the river gurgled. A fly went by.

With some trouble, the doe heaved herself up and stood shuddering on her long legs.

"Get along, then."

Sianadh turned away, cursing under his breath. The doe melted into the forest, leaving only crimson blossoms on bruised grass.

"She will live." The man glanced sourly at his companion from beneath beetling brows. "The shaft did not go deep, and they know where to find the healing herbs."

Imrhien tried to smile at him. Then she recalled the raft.

Made fleet by panic, she turned and ran through the trees to the cliff top. The high vantage point afforded a glimpse of the river—and of creatures crowding among the flag-lilies around the raft—creatures that had chewed at the spidersilk mooring-rope, freeing the raft from its tether. Already the vessel was beginning to depart from the banks of the leafy backwater. The girl flew down the slope to the water's edge. With a mighty effort she sprang, leaping through the air across the widening gap between rocky shore and wooden platform. At the last moment the raft swung out from under her feet. She made a desperate, useless grab at it. Water slammed up into her face, and down into a weird, breathless world she plunged.

There was at first only a close roaring—the thundering of blood in her temples and the surge of currents against her eardrums and the terrible pounding of her heart as it slaved to pump blood to flailing limbs. But the hue of that blood was darkening, and her lungs strained for air, but down here there was none—not for her.

As she sank, tiny bubbles went up in straight lines all around, as though threaded on wires. The galloping of her heart accelerated. She could think of nothing but fighting for breath, straining for breath, dying for breath. All instinct screamed at her to soar upward. But upward she could not soar, because there was a lid, hard and black, clamped overhead. Her fingers scrabbled at this cruel roof, seeking an edge, while the red night of agony roared in her brain and darkness closed in at the borders of sight, until she was looking down a long tunnel at a fading pinprick of light.

Then miraculously her fingers found purchase, and she was bursting upward, tearing through a slow and clammy viscosity, clawing free of the water's loving embrace and hanging on to solidity—a corner of the raft, now no longer a lid but a buoyant ally. With rasping gulps she drew in the gases of life, and as soon as she was able, hoisted herself up and onto the platform once more, where she lay on her side, breathing hard, coughing up water. Sunlight blocked out her eyes like white chalk.

The raft had floated well away from the shore. The winged toads that had worked it free with their little sharp teeth now leaped about on top of the water, their skinny, barbed tails lashing like whips. Sianadh was running along the shore, helpless, roaring like a bull, waving his fist. Still dazed, she could not understand what he was saying. By now the rickety craft had reached midstream and was being swept along in the thrall of the current. The wayward wights skipped on and off it, flopping their slimy bodies among the treasure chests. She chased them away. The banks began to rise more steeply. Soon the river rounded a bend and passed through a narrow cutting, overhung by perpendicular cliffs. Here it became impossible for the running man to find a foothold near the water's edge, and he was forced to climb higher, looking for a path. Picking up pace in the swift-flowing channel, the raft quickly outstripped him.

It rocked and spun like a leaf in a flooded gutter. Imrhien clung on grimly, gripping the lashings that held together the leaky craft. As she was whirled around another bend, a greater peril was revealed, lying directly in her path.

Straight ahead ranged a long ramp of semisubmerged rocks like low stairs—waterstairs—not high but many. Between them the water boiled, lathered with white froth.

This was unlooked for. Would the crudely made stage slide over the top of these gray, humpbacked behemoths of rocks? Would it slew around the heads of the greater boulders and slip between them? Or would it simply bounce up on the first one and crash down, tearing itself apart? Imrhien's grip tightened. The current picked up the raft and whipped it down a teeth-jarring stony incline, at the bottom of which the platform spun on its axis and shot to one side, crashing into a rock wall. Letting go with one hand, the girl slid her bay-wood staff out from among the knots that had tied it on board. She had the measure of this water-path now; had seen what it might and might not do. It was rough, but it might let her pass if she worked with it, precorrecting the raft's course, using the confluences and divergences of the flow to negotiate the worst of the obstacles. With jaw clenched in concentration she labored: a push here, a shove there, now rebalancing, now waiting for the moment—riding the bucking platform like a horse-breaker.

It tossed her into the air, but she was tenacious. And she miscalculated many times, but the timbers bore the brunt of it. On and down she rode in the seething foam, until with a final sickening lurch the raft dropped, battered but floating, into a smooth, quiet stretch of water, white with flowers drifting down from overhanging trees.

The treasure was still on board.

There, the raft floated placidly downstream, listing slightly. There were no oars. There was no way to get to shore. Hours drifted past.

The sun began to sink into the forests and mountains. Here, where fantastic dragonflies and glittering midges played, more of the little widemouthed toads with bat-wings were skipping over the water's surface, making free among tall rushes growing along the shore. They were quite lovely in a loathsome way, their froggy hides spangled gold and green, their tails long and thin, barbed at the tips. The veined vanes of their wings were so translucent that light shone through them. Their eyes were great, glowing, amber jewels, their teeth were many, tiny, and pointed. The girl peered at them from her tangle of dripping hair, which was threaded with long leaves of eel-grass. She fingered the tilhal at her throat, The winged toads did not attempt to trouble her. They were juveniles. At that age they were only mischievous.

Finally the raft bumped against a sandy spit. Its passenger tied it to a fallen tree that lay along the slender promontory. Then she rested, not wanting to sleep. Someone must keep watch over the treasure, and now there was no one else to accomplish the task. Hunger, too, never gave her peace, but in the dozing trances that slipped fitfully over her that night, she was half-aware of finely drawn faces, their eyes slightly upswept at the outer edges. The owners of these faces rose half out of the water to peer at the mortal girl from among tresses of long green hair floating on the river like harps strung with weed. Dreams, they were not.

By the time gray dawn drizzled out of the sky, a deep chill had seeped into Imrhien's bones. Still slightly damp, her spidersilk garments afforded her little comfort. She shivered, trying to chafe warmth into her upper arms. Lethargy slowed her down. She was lost and alone. There was, for the moment, no cause to go on, no reason to make decisions. Her head drooped. Now, at last, she slept.

The sun was hovering overhead when she was woken by the sound of a heavy body crunching through undergrowth. Quickly she unslipped the knot of the mooring-rope, but before she had a chance to pole the raft away from land, a voice yelled:

"*Obban tesh!* I have never been so glad of the sight of—of treasure in all me days!"

The Ertishman strode down the riverbank, grinning out of a filthy face, his hair a rat's nest. Of bow and arrows there was no sign, but he was cradling something close to his chest, wrapped in his shirt.

"So, here's where ye be, messing about in boats while I strut through the jungle on me pins, avoiding things that bite. Ye've led me a merry dance, that ye have! The treasure, is it all here? All safe?"

She nodded, smiling with relief. He ran along the spit with surprising surefootedness and thumped himself down on the raft beside her.

"Ye did well in that white water. I passed it a way back, expecting to see the raft smashed to smithereens somewhere on the rocks. Ye're not strong of arm, nor do ye have wizardly powers, but by harp and bow, *chehrna,* ye have sharp wits, and that's what saved ye." He patted the treasure chests lovingly. "Ye'll be ready for some breakfast by now, no doubt! I found eggs back there, up in the trees—big ones. I ate 'em, sucked out the insides. Brought some back for ye in my shirt—here. Ach, *obban!* One's cracked and ruined me good spidersilk smock."

<<No, thank you. We go.>>

"Ain't ye hungry? Suit yourself—I'll eat 'em, then. But bide a moment—did ye leave this on my cloak when ye ran back to the raft to *skitch* the 'leapers?"

He held up a flower, its petals as blue as a mountain tarn cupped close under the sky. Imrhien recognized it as the same flower she had given to the Gailledu when he had warned them against danger—not merely the same *kind* of flower, Imrhien was certain, but the *same one*. There had been a notch in two of the petals where some insect had bitten it. Yet the bloom looked as fresh as if it had just been plucked. In wonderment, and also in response to the Ertishman's question, she shook her head.

"Nay? I thought not. I'll guess our leafy friend the guardian of woodlands has been here. Mayhap he has been following us. Why should he gift me with this weed?"

Their eyes locked, briefly. At once, they both knew the answer.

The travelers moored the raft while they effected repairs to the damaged parts and constructed a pair of makeshift oars. When all was as well knit as they could manage, they cast off and continued their journey.

Sianadh did not again mention hunting, but the problem of feeding themselves had not vanished. The next few days were a season for hunger. To distract their thoughts from victuals, they used this time to learn handspeak and relate stories. Sianadh remained typically optimistic.

"When we get to the city, my sister, Ethlinn, may be able to heal ye with her carlin's lore. Or, if not, there be wizards and dyn-cynnils in Gilvaris Tarv who could do it—mighty men of powerful gramarye. Their services do not come cheaply, but that matters not, now. Ye be rich. Ye can spend what ye like on cures, garments, the best of everything. Your life be changed now. The good times be here at last."

His companion was not convinced. A feeling of foreboding grew, as every day the current bore them closer to the urban precincts.

The river widened slightly, passing through densely wooded country. Behind the trees, cliffs rose high against a brilliant blue sky. To the south, a few clouds swirled like flocks of silver gulls.

The raft drifted on.

The Ertishman turned from telling stories to expounding history lessons, but Imrhien suspected his ramblings were a way of dulling the edges of craving. For herself, the hunger pangs had died now, leaving a curious light-headedness and an inability to concentrate on what Sianadh was saying.

She thought she had heard some of his anecdotes before, at some time, but could not recall the occasion.

"Our good King-Emperor, James the Sixteenth, be both wise and strong. He rules well, but even royalty be not beyond the reach of the unseelie. Aye, 'twas a pity, the terrible misadventure that befell his Queen. D'ye know of it? . . . Nay?"

He rambled on in subdued tones, saying something about a dangerous wight that had, some years ago, slain the Queen-Empress, leaving the King-Emperor bereft and young Prince Edward motherless. Imrhien drowsed. Clouds of small insects droned. The sun's rays danced on the water.

Tranquillity was torn apart by a shrill scream.

It broke the spell of the gently rocking raft. A great shrieking and splashing arose farther downstream. Imrhien's eyes widened in horrified amazement. In the water, a young girl was thrashing about.

"Kavanagh!" the young girl cried. "Kavanagh!"

Sianadh spat out Ertish curses, expressing his bewilderment. He stood up. The raft pitched and yawed.

"*Obban tesh,* 'tis Muirne," he grated, hoarse with shock.

Instantly he began to fling off his cloak. His companion grabbed his arm, shaking and pinching him.

"What are ye at, Imrhien? My sister's daughter is drowning, can ye not see? Let go."

Violently Imrhien shook her head. The man strained wildly toward the struggling figure.

"Kavanagh! Kavanagh!" A beseeching voice, trembling with panic, choked off by mouthfuls of water.

"Muirne! I come!"

Imrhien's open hand smashed across the side of the Ertishman's face. He swore a violent oath and turned on her, wearing an ugly expression, his fist raised as though he were about to slam it across her head. At the last instant he hesitated and blinked, shaking his head as if to clear his brain of cobwebs.

*"Oghi!"*

Taking a deep breath, the Ertishman sat down. He was shuddering. His lips moved, soundlessly at first. "Iron blade and rowan-tree save me from the likes of ye," he muttered, and then he began to whistle. Turning his head, he averted his eyes from the sight of the screaming girl. The veins on his neck and temples stood out like snakes. Sweat rose in a dew on his forehead. The water-girl wailed and sank. The river closed over her head. She did not reappear.

The raft floated over the place where she had gone under. Sianadh did not utter a word but sat still, his countenance ashen. When they were past the spot, the voyagers forced themselves to look back.

A feminine manifestation rose, to the waist, out of the water. This time she did not flail about—indeed, she did not paddle or swim at all, and it was impossible to deduce how she managed to keep afloat. Instead she remained poised like a waterlily, with water flowing like silk about her lily-stem waist and her thin white arms reaching toward the mortals. The drowner, cheated of her prey, did not scream in rage. No recognizable expression crossed her delicate features. She reacted in no human fashion.

"Kavanagh, Kavanagh," she called, or chanted,

"If not for she,

"I'd have drunk your heart's blood,

"And feasted on thee."

Having spoken, she subsided gracefully, leaving a faint turbulence.

"I shall not be bathing hereabouts," Sianadh said shortly.

They drifted on, the riverscape unfolding around them. Frogs croaked among forests of feathery swamp-grass. Tall trees leaned overhead, their roots protruding into the water, vines dangling from their boughs.

*"Doch!"* exclaimed the Ertishman, slapping his brow. "I left the four-leaved clover in my old shirt when I doffed it and took on this

spidersilk. No wonder I could not see through the drowner's glamour. Being rich has addled me brains. Your wit has saved us again, *chehrna*—ye saw fit to bring along some of the leaf. Can ye spare a bit?"

Shaking her head, the girl tried to explain that she too had neglected to bring the spell-warding plant—that, like him, she had been beguiled by glamour, but that common sense had won out. It had been too coincidental, too unlikely, for Sianadh's city-dwelling niece to appear right in front of her uncle in the middle of the wilderness. Her store of hand-signs was barely adequate to convey this to Sianadh.

"Ye're certain ye have not got the Sight?" he demanded suspiciously.

Vehemently she nodded.

A shang wind, not fierce, came and went one evening. Brief showers of rain also passed over. Cuinocco's Way eventually joined up with another flexuous stream, which later flowed into a yet wider waterway. This ran at last into a proper river, the Rysingspill, which would take them on the last lap of their journey, to the city-port at its mouth. Steep cliffs and mountain gullies had given way to hills that humped ever lower under a porcelain sky the color of Sianadh's eyes.

The river neared its destination.

"Now that we have gained the Rysingspill, 'tis likely we shall begin to see river-traffic," the Ertishman warned. "Fur-trappers sometimes come this far upriver—savage *uraguhnes* who would risk other folk's lives—and their own—in eldritch haunts, for profitable trade. We could not outrun their fast boats if they took an interest in us, so we must keep an eye out and make ourselves scarce if we get wind of them. They would think nowt of scuttling a couple of gray drifters and making off with our goods."

They kept the chests covered under Sianadh's spidersilk cloak.

Gilvaris Tarv, he told her, was a colorful sinkhole of a seaport city where riffraff and brigands walked the streets, mingling with the citizens and the nobility. It was a city with no walls or guarded gates or curfew; a festering, interesting venue where fortunes were made and lost; an ebullient, belligerent center of brisk trade. The very rich dwelt there, while the very poor hung on at the fringes and sometimes fell off. Being on the east coast of Eldaraigne, Gilvaris Tarv was a popular port of call for ships out of Namarre, whose stated business was not always genuine. Port officials turned a shuttered eye to shady dealings and thrived for it.

"No use our floating into Tarv Port on a craft we can barely steer. Some merchant would run us down. Besides, it would look suspicious, and I want no questions asked. If word got about that we carry treasure, even so much as a shilling piece, our lives would be forfeit. Nay—we shall go ashore before we reach the outskirts of town and traipse in on foot, like peddlers."

They met no trappers' vessels. On the fifth day since the departure from Waterstair, the trees thinned. A low mist rose from the water. The river, now broad and lined with slate-green casuarinas, carried the raft into rolling lands. Here and there, thatched cottages squatted in groves of rowans and fruit-trees. Stone walls enclosed paddocks where a few animals grazed or fields rippling with ripening oats and barley.

It was getting dark. The Ertishman appeared jittery.

"We are close now. 'Tis too risky—we might be seen by farmers or fishers along the shore. And what would two strange-looking folk be doing floating down out of the Lofty Mountains? To be sure, we should be taken for wights."

Using their rough-bladed oars of whittled yew, the voyagers directed the raft to the west bank. It grated against the gravel of the shallows, and they came to land under a belt of casuarinas, whose swatches of long, drooping needles cascaded like unbound hair. After unloading the three caskets, the travelers untied the ropes holding the raft's logs together, pushed it away, and watched it drift downstream, slowly breaking up.

There was an indefinable sadness in this.

"Now," Sianadh said briskly, rubbing his hands, "we be peddlers out of Tarv, come to try our luck in the countryside. And now, at last, we sleep dry!"

It was indeed pleasant to nestle in fragrant fallen needles but difficult to get used to the motionlessness of land. Imrhien lay awake in the darkness, listening to the river's sighs. She thought about the city and its probable horrors.

Come morning, Sianadh was no longer beside her.

Imrhien drank from the river, washing her face and hands. Magpies chortled their euphonic greetings. Beyond the trees, the sun's morning light lay long on fields of grain, weaving a pattern like tapestry. The caskets remained where Sianadh had stashed them, shoved far back under some myrtle bushes for concealment. The Ertishman would not be far away. She waited. When he returned, cackling with pride, he bore half a loaf under his arm.

"Tuck into that, Your Ladyship! Ye've got to keep your strength up—I cannot carry the *tambalai* treasure into the city all on my own!"

She tore it in two pieces and began to eat, offering him the larger chunk. He pushed her hand away.

"Who d'ye think ate the other half?"

Who would have thought that a simple cob could taste like joy, sweeter than a feast? Imrhien could have eaten twice as much. Her friend's weathered eyes followed the chunks of bread to her mouth like the eyes of a despairing lover. For all his protests, he could not hide the fact that half a loaf had not staved off his hunger. When the first piece was devoured she feigned satiety and watched him fall like a starving wolf on what was left.

He tossed a handful of coins in her lap. She examined them closely—they were small disks made of copper. One side bore a numerical inscription she could not read, while the other was stamped with a face seen in profile. On every coin the side with the face was worn and blurred, lacking in detail.

"Put them jinglers in yer pocket!" Sianadh trumpeted.

<<How coins? How bread?>>

"I took a silver florin from amongst the treasure. Gold or jewels would give us away, of course—a silver piece was the least thing of value I could find. Ha! The least thing of value—and to think it is more than I had in the world at one time! The loaf, I bought from a penny-pinching farmwife."

Still hungry, but somewhat fortified, the travelers tied the caskets on their backs, beneath their cloaks, and set off like two tortoises. Soon they struck a road leading south, a rutted track whose high banks were overgrown with hedges on each side. Ripe blackberries dotted the briars, and these they picked as they walked.

They passed several cottages. Now and then a horsecart trundled by, bound in the other direction. Imrhien kept her head down, pulling her battered taltry well over her face, while Sianadh greeted the drivers with a cheery wave.

"Keep your taltry tugged well forward," he murmured from the side of his mouth. "One look at ye, *chehrna,* would set the tongues of the whole countryside wagging. We must not draw attention."

Her load seemed heavier by the minute. Lack of food had weakened her, and walking seemed like wading through mud. At midday they rested in a beech grove off the road. Sianadh used the pennies to purchase food and drink from a farmhouse. This time he was given richer fare. As soon as she had eaten, a strong desire for sleep surged over Imrhien, but she rose to her feet and they trudged on. Toward dusk they reached the outer sprawl of Gilvaris Tarv and passed through, into the city.

# 6

# GILVARIS TARV
## Pain and Perfidy

*I am the Wand and the Wand is the Tree.*
*The Tree seizes the Wind in its hair,*
*Holds Fire within its bones, pumps Water through its veins,*
*Grips soil and stone with its long toes.*
*The Tree stands between sky and ground.*
*The Tree is the Wand and the Wand is I.*

CHANT OF THE CARLINS

*Silence is a spell.*

ARYSK SAYING

A sparrow jumped along one of the warped black rafters, flicking its head from side to side as if searching. It paused, fluffed up its feathers smugly, and issued a small "cheep." Then it took wing and flew a quick circuit of the room before darting out through the half-open shutters into sunshine. Dust motes and a downy feather slid soporifically down a chute of chartreuse light, in past the flowering chamomile springing from the window-box, and onto the foot of the bed, bringing with them the sounds and odors of the street below.

It was not a large room to waken to. The walls were built of timber, daubed with some hard, whitish substance like clay. Here and there they were covered with stretched sackcloth that had been nailed to the joists showing through. The bed, which was wide, took up most of the space—on a stand against one wall stood a chamber-stick with a candle-end stuck in it, an unmatched ewer and basin, a wooden hairbrush, and a long-handled looking-glass. Under the window squatted a wooden stool. Everywhere, the scent of lavender permeated. From behind a thin partition came the rumble of familiar snoring.

A real bed—a luxury beyond belief. Imrhien could not recall ever having slept in one. Lying back against creamy, lavender-scented linen, she visualized the events of the preceding night, turned them over, and examined them from all angles.

Of the city, all she recalled were impressions—squares of yellow light from mullioned casements, revealing a bewildering mixture of movement, smells, sounds; a forest drowning in its own undergrowth, whose trees were the stanchions, pillars, and roof beams of buildings, whose overflow was the boil and surge of humanity—fair flower and fetid fungus. Upper stories overhung crooked tunnels of streets. Lines of pegged washing flapped like ensigns, and gutters reeked. Like bulls in a distant field, hawkers bellowed, extolling their wares. The evening was noisy with the jingle of harness, the rumble of wheels, the smack of whips, shouts, dogs barking, snatches of music. Smoke from glowing braziers thickened the air, mingled with fragrances of pastries and perfume. Armor glittered in lamplight. Dominating all loomed the light-pierced Tower of the Tenth House of the Stormriders.

The girl had walked among all this noise and glitter and stench, staying as close to Sianadh as his shadow, keeping her taltry pulled well forward and her cloak drawn across the lower half of her face. She scarcely glanced up, except to avoid tripping over street detritus or losing sight of her mentor in the deepening shadows. Along twisting streets and lanes he led her, until her sense of direction was confused. Then with the words "Here it be—Bergamot Street," they had turned the last corner into a narrow, dark thoroughfare. A few yards farther on, the Ertishman had knocked on a door. It opened. With the noise of a bell jangling, a heavy block of light fell out on the cobblestones.

Then Imrhien had shrunk back, turning her face away, but Sianadh took her arm in a firm grip, propelling her forward, and without knowing how, she was inside, in the house with the door shut at her back, surrounded by moving hands, exclamations of delight, shouts of welcome.

At this point, recollections became somewhat blurred. There had been three faces—the goodwife with the calm, searching gaze and, escaping from her wimple, a wisp of copper hair graying too much to match Sianadh's, on her forehead a painted blue disk. The broad-faced young man, perhaps twenty years of age, with the look that questioned and the ready smile, his hair rufescent as glowing embers. The lass, of a similar age to herself, with the coloring of her brother and the eyes that, when they alighted upon the newcomer, could not help revealing stark disgust and fear no matter how she endeavored to conceal it. Her smiles did not reach her blue eyes.

"How fare you?" they had asked Sianadh searchingly, between embraces.

"None of your business," he had shot back, roaring with laughter the while, lifting the red-haired lass and whirling her around so that she shrieked with genuine delight.

Then Imrhien's burden had been taken from her, and she was too weary to care where it was set. She found herself seated at a table in front of a bowl of pottage. Sianadh was eating and talking with his mouth full on the other side of the table, waving his spoon in one hand and a hunch of bread in the other. There was firelight and candlelight and a tankard of some warm liquid thrust into her hands that, when sipped, coursed down her throat and through her veins like green fire, refreshing and soothing. Someone led her upstairs to this room, and as she fell, clothed, into bed, the last words that came drifting up from below were Sianadh's: "Nay, it *ain't* got fleas, and 'tis a *girl*."

Downstairs in the morning, Sianadh's sister, Ethlinn, was drawing off water from a kettle over the fire and pouring it into a linen-draped wooden tub behind a curtain of heavy cloth in the corner. She wore shades of blue and gray—the colors of a carlin. Turning as the guest descended, she smiled, then placed the jug on the table and wiped her hands on her apron. The hands flew in intricate gestures. Imrhien shook her head. The handspeak was too fast, and there were signs she had not learned. Smiling as if she understood this, too, Ethlinn gestured toward the bath. Something about fleas rankled in the guest's mind, but she thought this goodwife had not been the one who had asked about them, and the bathwater, scented with apple-blossom, was inviting. Soon she was immersed in warm water behind the drapery, reflecting on the only other bath she could remember, feeling the long, burnished curls, once stubble, resting wet on her shoulders.

Surely this house was the best place in Erith, and if only she could find herself a face, an ordinary face at which nobody would look twice, she could live here forever, bathing in apple-blossom and slumbering in lavender.

A cure would cost dearly. Struck by sudden concern as to the security of the treasure caskets, she climbed out of the tub and dried herself, reaching for clothing Ethlinn had left folded on a stool. These were not her gray spidersilk garments but peasant garb, clean and patched, probably belonging to Ethlinn's daughter, Muirne of the disgusted eyes, who was similarly slight in build but not as tall as she. There was a linen kirtle, tight-fitting, with sleeves buttoned from wrist to elbow, a calico surcoat with a fuller sleeve reaching to the elbow, a plain girdle, a peplum for her hair, her old taltry with a newly stitched cover replacing the stained, worn one, a woollen cloak, her cracked old rooster tilhal. Girls' clothes. There was no choice, no option, but to face reality.

By the time she emerged from behind the curtain, she could hear Sianadh's laughing voice filling the room with Ertish banter, and his nephew Liam's quick replies. Muirne, setting pancakes and redcurrant sauce on the table with small, neat hands, did not raise her auburn head. Seven thin braids, like rats' tails or sleeve-lacings, had been randomly plaited into the carnelian tresses around her face. Tiny colored beads adorned the length of them.

The room was spacious, clean, and filled with a fascinating assortment of things. On the flagstone floor, fresh rushes had been strewn. Overhead, a horn lantern swung among bunches of dried leaves and flowers that dangled from low, smoke-blackened rafters. Wall-hooks supported a row of dented saucepans. Beside the oven and fireplace at the back, a door and a sunny window gave on to a courtyard. In the opposite corner, the foot of a bed showed from behind another curtain. Along one wall, benches and shelves were laden with a profusion of assorted objects and pungent ingredients: mortars and pestles of several sizes, spoons, sieves, a rack of knives, string, squares of cloth, stoppered bottles and jars, labeled, a small hand-mill, jugs, measures, cruets, a funnel, bowls, tongs, balances, scales, and other artifacts of the same ilk. Among this farrago crowded mounds of vegetation fresh and dried; leaves, stems, roots, berries, bark, flowers, seeds, nuts, fungous growths, grasses, seed-pods, stalks, and grains.

Central to the room stood a large table, well scrubbed, upon which a fair proportion of the bench's contents had encroached at one end, the other presumably being kept free for dining. Along each side of it, settles of unplaned oak provided ample seating. A partition screened the room's front end, which could be penetrated through a curtained aperture to reach the tiny shop and the front door, which opened straight onto Bergamot Street with a clang of a bell.

Ethlinn's hands wove signs.

"My mother asks if ye will be seated at our table to break your fast," said Liam, bowing slightly, stiffly. There was no hint of sarcasm in his bearing, nothing but respectful curiosity in his gaze. What had Sianadh told them of her? What, indeed, did he know of her?

"Now, *chehrna,* just for your sake, we shall use only common tongue and handspeak," said her companion of the road, "but not until we have downed a goodly portion of this fine fare. A quiet table be a busy table, and by me the cooking of Eth and Birdie here was ever beloved."

But the Ertishman's high jollity could scarcely contain itself, and it was not long before he was regaling the diners with the tale of his embarrassment at the hands of the little folk—the miniature siofra, or fanes, as they were sometimes called—at their glamour-fair. The story lost nothing in the telling, and soon all diners rocked with mirth. Then a bell rang and Muirne rose swiftly.

"I shall see to it, Mother." She went behind the leather curtain to the screened-off front of the room. Presently she returned carrying an apron full of plums.

"A scald," she said. "I made up the poultice."

<<You did well,>> her mother signed.

"And how long did it take ye to make the base for that poultice?" asked Sianadh. His sister shrugged.

"I'll wager it took hours, gathering, washing, drying, pounding, brewing, straining, and suchlike, and look what it got for ye, *tambalai*—a few plums. Nay, Sparrow-Bird. I be not at odds with ye, I know the fees your mother sets—ye were just abiding by her wish. But she charges far too little, allus has, and works too hard." He sighed. "Ah, but all that has changed now, and it be time for the telling."

Muirne deposited the plums in a dish.

"See, Imrhien here," said Sianadh, leaning on the table confidingly, "she be a lady of means. She was traveling to Tarv to get a cure for paradox poisoning, but her bodyguard met with some misfortune. Luckily I chanced along, and here we be. Ye do not have to go telling all and sundry about her visit, she wants no song and dance, just a cure." Imrhien nodded. Sianadh had a unique way of framing his explanations.

Ethlinn signed a complicated message to her daughter.

"At once?" the lass asked. The carlin nodded.

"My mother has asked Muirne to go on an errand," explained Liam. Muirne removed her apron and took up a basket and some coppers from a crock on the mantelpiece. Then she was gone, pulling on her taltry. The inevitable bell signaled her departure.

"Now we can really talk," said Sianadh. "Meaning no offense to the Sparrow, but what she does not know cannot harm her. Ethlinn and I spoke together last night when ye young 'uns were abed, and by the end of it we agreed that ye, Liam boyo, and ye only, should know the full truth of the matter."

"Ye do me a kindness, Uncle."

"Never. I know ye can make yourself useful, that is all. The rest of the matter that concerns ye be this—I came upon a lost treasure out there in the Lofties, a treasure of moonrafter and candlebutter and baubles so busy, ye cannot even dream of it. Imrhien kind of opened the doors to it, and we brought some back with us. Half of it belongs to her—we saved each other's hides at whiles all along the way—but believe me, a tenth part of it, a thousandth part of it, would keep us all in luxury all our born days."

"Mother of Warriors!" exclaimed Liam. "So 'tis to be rich, we are, is it?" He jumped up and danced a little jig around the room, his mother and uncle smiling on his enthusiasm. "Rich at last!" crowed the young man. "After being dirt poor for centuries. At last we shall have all the good things we deserve."

"Deserve!" Sianadh barked. "Deserve! Boyo, did your mother never tell ye what our granny's wise words were on that matter?"

Liam ceased his hopping and eyed his uncle inquiringly.

"She used to say nobody deserves aught in this world," said Sianadh. "Naught, neither good nor bad. Ye get what ye get, and that's the way of it. Those who talk of deserving or not deserving only end up with a chip on their shoulder."

"Ach, whatever," Liam said lightly, sitting himself down again. Sianadh winked conspiratorially at Imrhien.

"Hearken, boyo, point yer lugs this way. I be going back with an expedition to get more, a big haul, and I need your help. Ethlinn tells me that since last I was here my old cronies have drifted away—there be only one left of the trusty few, but he be crooked with a broken shoulder from some scrape with mercenaries in an alehouse. So I need your strong arms, boyo, and half a dozen trusty lads."

"But if 'tis sildron, then surely it belongs by rights to the King-Emperor?"

"Now, do not go getting like your brother. Liam, this be the Bear you be talking to. Sure and the King-Emperor's got more Rusty Jack's Friend than ye could think of and would not be wanting more. But after we take all we want, we will let the King-Emperor's Royal Court know that we have suddenly discovered a stack of riches and we ain't touched a penny. They may claim the rest, barring the reward they would give us, of course. There be some things too big for us to take, and besides, I would rather these riches fell into the right hands, the hands of ourselves and good King James and the Dainnan, not into the clutches of bloodthirsty reivers. Ain't that right, *chebrna?*"

"By all means, Uncle," Liam interjected eagerly. "I can drum up the boys we need for such an expedition, in no time at all!"

"Aye—good lad. But before we set out, none of them must know the treasure exists. It be vital that there be no chance of word leaking out into the city, and no matter how trusty your comrades may be, they be only mortal, and the tongues of mortals may slip. Tell them that 'tis a rich foreigner's hunting expedition and that we are to meet this sporting noble somewhere upriver."

"Ye ask me to lie to my comrades?"

"I demand that ye lie to them, or else there shall be no expedition. None but we four here at this table must know about what lies under Waterstair—not even your brother or your sister must know. Later there shall be time enough to reveal all, but not until we have taken all we need for ourselves. Now swear to secrecy, Liam."

The youth looked at his mother, who nodded.

"For ye, and for riches, I swear it," he said. "When do we start?"

"As soon as ye have gathered a company and provisions have been purchased."

"And are ye to accompany us, Lady Imrhien?"

She began to nod her head, but Sianadh cut across the gesture with a word.

"Nay! *Chehrna,* the wilderness be no place for lasses. Remain in safety—I shall bring back your share, to be sure."

The girl frowned, shaking her head.

Gently he said, "Remain here and undergo the cure ye have wished for. Ethlinn, can ye give her back her rightful face?"

Imrhien held her breath. She saw the woman's shoulders sag slightly, as though Sianadh had placed a burden on them. After a moment she signed to her son.

"My mother says that she cannot help. Her Wand is powerful, but it may not safely cure such a bad case of paradox without possibly causing scarring," Liam interpreted.

<<You must go to the Daughter of Grianan, who sees with one eye,>> Ethlinn signed.

"A Daughter of the Winter Sun, that means a carlin," explained Sianadh. "The carlin of whom my sister speaks is very great, perhaps the most powerful of all carlins, Maeve One-Eye. But where might she be, Eth? She travels, does she not, and is never in one place for longer than a season?"

Ethlinn's hands danced.

"Every Autumn, the dame abides near a small village by the name of White Down Rory," Liam translated, "near Caermelor."

In sudden anger, Imrhien thumped her fist on the table. Wearily her head sank into her hands. Had she come all this way across the girth of Eldaraigne, only to find that she must cross back again?

Presently Sianadh spoke.

"Mayhap there be some other healer we could try in Gilvaris Tarv—a dyn-cynnil or something?"

Ethlinn's hands said, <<No. The healer men are no use.>>

"Well then, there be nowt for it but to use our riches to organize a road-caravan to take our lass safely towards the Royal City, to see the carlin Maeve at White Down Rory. No need to worry—the cure will just take a little longer, that be all. But 'twill come—aye, that's it! While Liam and I be upriver, loading our packhorses with king's-biscuit and gold, Imrhien shall be journeying westward in comfort and safety. The best of conveyances shall be found, and in no time at all ye'll reach the other side of Eldaraigne and your face shall be restored to its former beauty—I will not recognize ye when ye come back to see me living in my golden palace!"

Imrhien forced a smile.

<<Yes, I will go.>>

But the prospect of traveling without Sianadh seemed bleak.

With that settled, the Ertishman briskly turned to business.

"Now, my young nephew—how many comrades can ye muster, who be strong of arm, worthy of trust, and able to keep their mouths shut?"

The doorbell jangled. Ethlinn rose to go to the shopfront, but before she could leave the table, the leather curtain was thrust aside and a man entered the room. He was tall, dressed in a guard's military uniform of studded leather; his brown hair was worn long, pulled back tightly into a club in the style of the Stormriders.

"By the Star," he exclaimed, "'tis Uncle Bear!"

Sianadh leapt to his feet, embracing the newcomer with bearlike hugs and matching growls. Still slapping one another on the back, they returned to the table. Liam poured another tankard of ale and set it before his elder brother.

"Imrhien," said Sianadh, "this here be Diarmid, my other nephew."

It hissed through the room, Diarmid's sharp intake of breath as his eyes fell on the wrecked face. Ethlinn signed to him. He looked down at his cup, then said formally, with a quick nod, "Your servant, my lady."

She made the greeting sign.

"Well, soldier," Sianadh said heartily, "what brings ye here? How does the art of the mercenary suit ye?"

"It suits me well, Uncle." The voice was grave. Diarmid's face resembled Muirne's with its narrow, pointed look; like his sister, he was comely. His jaw was clean-shaven, and the roots of his hair were dark red. "I make a living and have learned much."

"Still want to join the Dainnan, eh, Boldheart?"

"Aye. More than ever, that is my goal."

<<My son wishes to travel to the Royal Court when his training is complete.>>

"So, that be it? Learn as much as ye can of warrior skills amongst the hired muscle of Gilvaris Tarv and then leave them and head west."

"Aye."

"Ye've always been a King's man, through and through. And the finest of the warriors of Erith would be proud to count ye amongst them."

The front bell jangled annoyingly. Ethlinn left the room to attend to the shop, while the three men fell deep into serious conversation. When her patient had departed, Ethlinn held the leather curtain aside and beckoned to Imrhien to enter the shop. The girl now noticed that a stag's head was embroidered in dark blue on Ethlinn's left sleeve.

The state of the cell-like room was similar to that of the larger one, but more ordered. Ethlinn showed Imrhien some of the concoctions, ointments, pastes, cordials, and powders and tools of her trade. Her hands signaled slowly, clearly.

<<Let me show you something of my craft. This is the Wand of the carlin, a living thing.>> Ethlinn held up a stick of wood some two feet long, plain and smooth save for three nodes near the top, each facing in a different direction and each at a different level. She indicated the nodes.

<<Nourishment, Healing, Protection. The Wand must be

planted in the soil when it is not being carried. From the ground it draws its power.>>

She slipped the Wand back into the sheath hanging from her belt.

<<I have cures for many ailments of the mortal kind—cures that are used by the Daughters of Grianan, all over Erith.>> She touched her fingers to the painted blue disk on her forehead. <<They are powerful cures, but not powerful enough for the weals you bear.>> The same fingers touched Imrhien's face softly, with a mother's caress, as nobody had ever touched that monstrosity.

<<The swellings on your face are an ailment of the *lorraly* kind, but most severe. It is possible the one-eyed carlin might be able to heal such lesions. You may well ask, what of your voice and your remembering? Sianadh told me of that. I would give you rosemary for remembrance, to keep under your pillow and waken you to your past—I would give you gentle remedies if it were of any use. But these two afflictions, the loss of speech, the loss of memory, they are not of the *lorraly* kind. They are eldritch, and have been brought on you by gramarye.>>

A rat scuttled down Imrhien's spine.

<<Tell me more.>>

<<I know no more. Only that you have been touched by gramarye, and that, deeply. But go not to wizards for help. Despite what most folk believe, their pretense of wielding gramarye is all an illusion. True gramarye lies only in the hands of immortals, and of a few special mortals who have been given it. Eldritch wights use it, although their powers do not compare with the great forces once wielded by the Faêran, who walk no more in Erith. The one-eyed carlin trafficks with seelie wights, more so than I, who dwell in the city. She might bring benefits to you thereby.>>

<<Is she then my only hope?>>

<<Aye. Well, perhaps there may be one other chance, to find your memory, at least. . . .>>

The carlin's hands slowed. For a moment her eyes went blank and she stared sightlessly at the shelves laden with bottles and jars.

<<My husband . . .>> Unfamiliar hand-movements followed. <<You will not know the sign for his name. In his youth he went to

sea, on a merchant Seaship, sailing from port to port. But one night he spent too long singing in a Luindorn tavern—he had such a voice—and when arrived back at the docks it was too late—for his ship had sailed with the tide. He found himself work in Luindorn until the next ship should come by. Meanwhile, he taught some of the local lads how to play a game called hurling.>>

Imrhien recognized the sign for this and nodded. The carlin continued:

<<It happened that during a game, he was bowled over by an opposition player, and his head knocked hard upon the ground. When he awoke to consciousness he could remember naught, not even his own name.>>

The girl leaned forward, watching intently, hardly daring to breathe. She knotted her hands around her knees.

<<Sometimes in such cases, all it takes is for the sufferer to come upon something familiar, and then the memories slowly begin to filter back into the mind. But everything around my husband was strange to him, for he was in a foreign land. Yet he did eventually recollect the past, and can you guess what sparked off this cure?>>

The girl shook her head.

<<It was the smell of baking bread!>>

Imrhien's hopes crashed again. There had been many times when the fragrance of new-baked loaves had floated around the stairs and galleries near the kitchens of Isse Tower. Apart from causing her mouth to water, it had had no discernible effect.

A movement at the leather curtain made them look up. Sianadh was passing through with Liam. He winked at Imrhien.

"We have business to see to."

As they went out the clanging door, Muirne came in, her basket on her arm, and disappeared into the main room.

<<You have been through much,>> the carlin signed. <<Rest while you are here with us, while preparations are made for your travels. These will take time—as a wealthy lady, you will need hired guards, provisions, a carriage—and you must wait for a road-caravan to set out, so that you may go with it for protection. The roads are not as safe as they used to be. Of late, unusual numbers of unseelie wights are on the move.>>

<<May I not travel by Windship?>>

<<Indeed, you do not know the world! The Merchant Lines carry no passengers. Of civilians, only nobles ride the sky, in private Windships or sometimes upon eotaurs. Neither do *they* take passengers. The ground road is the only way, for you.

<<For myself, I do not yet know what to do with all this wealth you bring us. I have yet to foresee how it will change things. The three caskets are safe in our cellar, under the trapdoor near the hearthstone. If you wish, I will unlock it and you may go down and see them.>>

<<No. I trust.>>

A knock at the street-door; it opened peremptorily. Imrhien hurried back into the main room, beyond the view of the incoming patient. Glancing over at the table, she saw Diarmid sitting there with his long hair unbound, raining down his arms and back. Muirne was rubbing a brown paste into his scalp. Where the roots had been red, they were no longer so.

Diarmid was gone again soon after, back to his quarters at the barracks, and it was not until the evening meal had been set on the table that Sianadh and Liam returned. Then the talk was all concerning the growing militancy in Namarre, of which Sianadh had found out much during his comings and goings that day.

"I have been out of touch for too long. Smoking bones of the Chieftains, I had no idea things had got as bad as this! Unseelie wights mustering from all corners of Erith to join forces with barbarian upstarts in the Fastnesses of Namarre! They say the rebels want to overthrow the King-Emperor—what madness has gripped these *sgorramas?* And what wizards must they have amongst them, to call unseelie things to their command? How can it be possible?"

"Indeed, it is curious, Uncle, but I should say we have no cause for concern here in Gilvaris Tarv," said Liam. "The Kings of Erith be loyal, and they would send their armies to fight alongside the Royal Legions and the Dainnan if needed. But I cannot see that they would be needed. Surely the Dainnan alone might quell an uprising of mere brigands and wights."

<<I am not sure,>> his mother rejoined with furrowed brow.

<<I feel there is something else behind this rebellion—something stronger than is supposed.>>

"What might that be, sister?"

She shrugged, palms upturned.

"The Dainnan ought to be out looking for pirate Windships," said Muirne. "Did ye hear, Uncle Bear, a merchant of the Cresny-Beaulais Line was attacked and wrecked not far out of Tarv some weeks ago or more? 'Twas a terrible thing. A patrol ship found a man clinging to a treetop—Sandover was his name, he was quite the talk of the town for a while—and he told them the whereabouts of the other survivors. By then the buccaneer Windship had disappeared completely, and they were never able to trace it."

"Aye. Terrible. But—but mayhap not all pirates be that bad, ye ken," stuttered the big Ertishman. "Mayhap there were some just along for the ride, like."

"What a strange thing to say, Uncle Bear. Of course they all be evil men!"

"Anyway," deflected Sianadh, "Namarran uprising *bai doch*. 'Twill drain all the best talent from this city. Already rumor is rife that Caermelor will be calling for new recruits if the forces gathering in Namarre continue to swell. Eager young folk all over town be talking of leaving for Caermelor to assay for the Dainnan, or else to volunteer for the Royal Legions, if the Dainnan will not take them. The pay is meager—'tis said a man-at-arms gets a shilling a day, a mounted archer sixpence, a foot archer threepence, and a spearman tuppence. 'Tis the glory they want, and the honor, the excitement, and mayhap vengeance. The lives of many folk have been made dark by wights. . . ."

Muirne said, "Why should ye care if the braves of Tarv leave this city, Uncle Bear?"

"Er . . . why, Liam and I want to round up some help for a small expedition we are planning. Exploration. I mean, hunting."

Sianadh's niece stared hard at him. Then she nodded.

"I see."

Brazenly, Sianadh changed the subject.

"Sparrow, would ye like me to help ye with your archery practice in the courtyard tomorrow morning, just like old times?"

"Thank ye, Uncle Bear, yes. But methinks ye will find that my aim has improved since last ye tutored me. I shall outshoot ye now."

Sianadh guffawed. "Outshoot me! I'll lay bets on that!"

That night Imrhien retired early to bed. She could not sleep for thinking about her prospective journey to Caermelor and Sianadh's planned expedition. She also wondered when Muirne was going to come in. Ethlinn slept downstairs so that she might be at hand if a customer called in at night on some emergency. Liam and Sianadh slept in the space beyond the upstairs partition. Last night Imrhien had been too weary to take note, but these sleeping arrangements must mean that she had been given Muirne's bed and Muirne was expected to share. How she must hate that.

When Sianadh's niece came in, Imrhien feigned sleep. No sheets rustled, and when she opened one eye she saw Muirne rolled in a blanket, lying on the floor. Resentment and bitterness rose like bile in her throat. She sprang out of the bed, tapped its owner on the shoulder, and indicated the bed's emptiness, then took a blanket and lay on the floor in the opposite corner.

Muirne, obviously, was stung. Hospitality was a matter of Ertish pride.

"The bed be for ye. Ye be the guest. Please, take it."

<<The bed belongs to you.>>

"I do not want it."

<<Neither I.>>

"If ye sleep on the floor, my mother will be angry with me."

<<I not tell her.>>

Muirne gave the guest the same hard stare she had given her uncle.

"If ye sleep in the bed, I will sleep there, too."

<<Yes.>>

Muirne rolled to the farthest edge and lay like a stick of petrified wood all night, even when the shang storm came and banged open the shutters, lighting the chamomile flowers in the window-box like yellow and white stars.

Sianadh and Liam bustled constantly to and fro during the next few days, making preparations for their own journey and for Imrhien's. Using gold from the caskets, they bought all kinds of equipment and provisions until the carlin's house was so full that there was hardly room to move.

Ethlinn examined the spidersilk garments with great interest, drawing from the lining of Sianadh's cloak the wilted remains of the Gailledu's blue flower.

<<This be a thing of power.>>

Ethlinn preserved the faded flower in an egg of resin and returned it to her brother.

"A flower of souvenance," observed Liam.

Muirne always behaved civilly toward the guest, but it was plain that she found her looks offensive. Knowing this, and not daring to venture out in public, Imrhien felt the burden of the disfigurement too heavy to bear.

Then one afternoon Sianadh spoke to her alone.

"I met with an old acquaintance today, old Tavron Caiden. Years ago we were comrades, when he was working for a master-dyer here in Tarv. Always takes a little white dog with him wherever he goes—a perky little whippet. Tavron owns a chandlery now, down on Rope Street, and he be doing right well for himself and his family, I may say, especially considering he used to be poorer than a churl and living far off on some wight-infested sea-cliff—some say he did a good turn to a wight and was given gold for it, a change of fortune—but to get back to what I was saying, I asked him whether he knew of a cure for paradox, seeing as how I trust him, like, and he was slow in coming out with it, hesitant, rather, but he said there might be some hope with the wizard Korguth the Jackal, who be the greatest wizard in Tarv, and the one who charges the most, needless to say, but his reputation has spread far and wide, and in high places they say he be the equal of Sargoth of the Royal Court, or greater."

<<Indeed, a mighty wizard he must be.>>

"Aye, *chebrna*. The family of Korguth has long prospered in this town, ever since his father, when a lad, somehow acquired a set of strange musical pipes. The whereabouts of those pipes are no longer known—Korguth claims to possess them yet, but it is said they have returned to the true owner, whoever that may be. With those pipes, the sire of Korguth was held in fear by the whole town in bygone days, and none dared speak against him."

At the mention of "strange musical pipes," a shadow of fear seemed to darken the day, and a dreariness took hold of Imrhien like the ache of an old wound. Between fascination and abhorrence, she felt driven to find out more.

<<Where did the father obtain such an instrument?>>

Sianadh's blue eyes crossed slightly as he delved into memory. Recalling the tale, he settled into storytelling mode.

"His name in those days was Jack, which is where 'the Jackal' comes from, ye get my meaning. The story goes that the family were poor farmers, living a few miles from the city, and Jack—the father of Korguth, that is—would go out to the hills to watch the sheep. His stepmother gave him his dinner, which he carried with him in a cloth, but the fare was wont to be sparse and stale. On one day the fare was so bad that he had no lust for it at all, so he wrapped it up and put it away. As he sat there on the hillside an old, ragged man came along begging for food. Jack obligingly gave him all his dinner, and right glad the old man seemed of it. When he had eaten, the beggar gave thanks and offered to give Jack some gift in return for his generosity. Jack was not too unwise himself, and he suspected this old man might be some wight or other. Knowing full well how many wights rewarded kindheartedness, he asked most merrily and humbly if the old man might give him a small pipe whereon he could play a tune for the entertainment of others.

"The old man gave him a curiously fashioned set of pipes, saying, 'These have strange properties, for whosoever, save yourself, shall hear them when you play a jig must dance to the music perforce.'

"So Jack took the gift, and with it he played such pranks on his stepmother and the neighbors that they were all soon in a sorry state. After one episode a passing merchant was so bruised and battered from falling from his cart when he heard the music that the sheriff was sent for and Jack was summoned before the judge.

"The day arrived for the hearing, and Jack was there with his poor old stepmother, and the judge was in his place, and there was a goodly gathering of people besides, for news had traveled, and besides, there were many other cases to be heard. There was a fire burning in a hearth at one end of the chamber, for the season was Winter and the hour was early.

"'Here be a lad which has brought grievous trouble and sorrow upon the goodmen of the shire,' proclaims the sheriff. 'It is held he is in league with unseelie wights.'

"'How has he done this?' asks the judge.

"'My lord, he has got himself some pipes that will make you hop and dance until you are well-nigh spent.'

"The judge looks at Jack, who smiles up at him wide-eyed, like some injured innocent child. The judge, mayhap seeing some echo of his mischievous boyhood self before him, gives a chuckle. He allows no credit to the sheriff's story, so he wants to see the pipes, and then he wants to hear them played."

At this point, Sianadh aptly mimicked the voices of the characters.

"'Marry,' says the stepmother in a fright, 'prithee say not so until I am out of hearing!'

"'Play on, Jack,' says the old judge indulgently, 'and let me see what you can do.'"

As the Ertishman warmed to the tale, his smile grew broader and he began to shake with mirth.

"Jack sets the pipes to his lips," he enthused, "and the whole room is instantly in motion. All begin to dance and jump, faster and higher, as though they be out of their wits. Some leap over the tables, some tumble against the chairs, some fall into the fire. The judge springs over the desk and bruises both his shins, and he shouts to the lad to cease for the love of peace and charity. In the uproar he is not heard, and next thing Jack is out the door and on to the streets, and they all follow him, capering wildly as they go. The neighbors start at the sound and come out of their houses, springing over the fences, and some that had been still in their beds jump out and hurry into the streets, naked as they are, to join the throng at Jack's heels. A frenzy is upon them all, and they bound into the air and look not whither they plunge. Some that could no longer keep their feet for lameness dance on all fours!

"'Give over, Jack!' yells the judge, and this time Jack hearkens.

"'Well,' he says, 'I will, if the citizens of Gilvaris Tarv will promise me that they shall never do me trespass so long as I live.'

"Then as many as were there swore before the judge that they would keep peace towards the lad and help him to their power at all seasons against his enemies. And when they had done so, Jack bade the judge farewell and proceeded merrily home. From that time forth he prospered and kept everyone in the city in his fear. He rose to a prominent position and gathered much wealth, which, when he died in old age, was passed on to his son, Korguth."

The Ertishman scratched his beard. His brow knitted.

"What did they call those *doch* pipes? Ah, I have it—the *Pipes Leantainn*—the Follow Pipes. Anyhow, they've not been seen for years."

The instrument's name struck a chill through his listener. Unaware of her dismay, he continued.

"So there ye have it, *chehrna.* Now, for the sake of peace, say nothing to my sister about wizards—she cannot abide the caste! Now hearken well, for I have not been idle. As soon as Tavron Caiden gave me the good word, off went I to Korguth's palace—for a palace it be, mark ye—but his retainers said the great man is so busy that it was not possible to see him for months. When I slipped them an encouragement they said he could see us in another two days. They also mentioned his price, which was so high that I nearly fell over backward, but no matter, that be chickenfeed to us now.

"If this Korguth can cure ye, ye need not travel across the countryside but can remain here with Ethlinn until the return of our expedition. Then I will set ye up in a palace of your own—new face, new palace—the lads will be flocking around ye! What more could lass wish for? So what say ye, *chehrna?* Be ye willing to give it a try?" He grinned.

In the light of her friend's enthusiasm, the shadow of fear fled. Infected by his joy, Imrhien felt her mood lift. <<Yes! Yes!>> She could have kissed him, hedgehog of a prickly red beard and all.

Yet with the visage she wore, she would not insult him so.

In anticipation of this venture, Sianadh brought in a tailor to make new clothes for Imrhien. By then he had purchased new clothes and presents for the whole family.

"So, what exactly are you after, dear?" inquired the tailor, eyeing Muirne (who was the model for the eavesdropping guest) with a disparaging air and tapping his teeth with a tape measure. "Something for evenings? A ball-gown, perhaps? I assume the style would be Finvarnan?"

"Something . . . er, simple but nice," ventured Muirne.

"Two gowns for the goodwife, four for the lass, and two of those to be worn with high heels, so make them longer," interjected Sianadh, who had vowed not to interfere in women's matters. "Day wear. Plain cut but rich fabrics—aye, Finvarnan, of course, what d'ye think, *sgorrama?* Measure them, and make it quick and accurate. There be plenty of others who'd like the job."

He and Liam had appeared that morning in full traditional Finvarnan regalia: sheepskin boots laced crisscross from ankle to knee, calfhide surcoats sewn with copper scales, leather kilts, heavy gold torcs and bearskin cloaks, somewhat impractical at the time of year. Sianadh sported an open-faced bear-helmet, Liam a helm like a snarling hound.

Word having escaped that the carlin had recently made generous donations to several destitute families, a steadily increasing trickle of beggars began to accumulate at the door.

With all this activity, the neighbors in Bergamot Street were starting to talk. Sianadh put it about that their reclusive visitor was merely a cousin of considerable means, who was grateful for their hospitality.

Ethlinn signed, <<There will be jealousy here, in this poor quarter of town, when we are seen to rise. We must consider removing elsewhere, if trouble comes.>>

For such a long time, her facial deformities had invoked nothing but censure, revulsion, and ridicule. The possibility of being healed breathed life into Imrhien, stirred the dull embers of hope to a flame. Impatient to receive the cure, she could not rest, simmering with perturbation, pacing fitfully. She yearned anew for the human companionship that seemed to come so readily to those whose looks were deemed acceptable. Her eyes studied the faces around her with a desolate hunger. When the swellings were removed, would she be fair, plain, or ugly? How much of the damage was permanent, unable to be erased? In this ferment of excitement she soldiered through the remaining hours. It seemed two years, not two days, until at last it came time for her appointment with the wizard and her first venture into the city in daylight.

Sianadh had hired a carriage and driver, which contraption was ogled by the neighbors when it stopped at the door, carriages being a rarity in Bergamot Street. Pedestrians were forced to sidle past it, the street being so narrow, and many of them flung imprecations. Flinging them back, the Ertishman ushered his elegantly clad and deep-hooded charge on board and took his seat beside her. Shortly they were off, rattling jarringly along the cobbled streets.

"Lords and ladies!" chortled Sianadh. "Lords and ladies!"

*Do I dream at last? In truth, do I ride in a coach, clad in a satin gown like the petal of a violet and a mantle of brocade like a flower garden—or shall I waken and find myself in the Floor Five soap room in Isse Tower? And if all is as it seems, will the wizard have a cure?*

With her richly embroidered taltry pulled forward, Imrhien peered out of the window. A knot of apprehension twisted inside her belly. Between the hemming roofs the sky was strung like a canopy, pearled with an early Autumn haze. A flapping speck crossed it—a Relayer bound for the Tower of the Tenth House.

This city was such a motley medley of sights that it was hard to know which way to look. People passed hither and thither, dressed in ways she had never seen before. Among the peasants and craftsmen in their drab doublets and leather aprons strode merchants with their signatory broad-brimmed hats, and sun-freckled Ertishmen in leather-paned kilts, with auburn manes and mustaches. Sailors in rolled-up breeches, striped kerchiefs tied across their heads, traded rivalrous gibes with the "lemonleg" aeronauts of Merchant Lines. Most striking of all, hard-faced men with clawed gauntlets and wide sunray collars of linked metal strips stalked the streets in heavy jewelry and weapons. Bright tattoos swirled over their bodies. Some wore striped head-cloths hanging to their shoulders, others were crowned with tall helmets like winged birds.

"Namarrans," commented Sianadh. "Outlaws, like as not."

One went past leading a bear on a chain.

The city's architecture metamorphosed as the horses pulled the carriage from the poorer quarter to the rich. Blacksmiths, saddlers, coppersmiths, weavers, tanners, cobblers, and carpenters gave way to fishmongers, fruit vendors, and inns, then jewelers, spice-sellers, and cloth-merchants. Blowing silks and rainbow satins shone like bubbles in the breeze as it tossed hot sunlight from hand to hand.

In the better quarter, pedestrians were less numerous, vehicles more common. Like rows of gnarled old graybeards, eucalyptus trees lined the streets, richly encrusted with red velvet flowers. A wizard rode by in his whites and tall, pointed hat; a peripatetic minstrel strolled with his lute across his back and a capuchin crouching on his shoulder. With a jingle of spurs and weaponry, several mounted knights of some nobleman's retinue clattered over the cobbles. Erect and disdainful they sat, clad in chain mail overlaid with ornate tabards, accompanied by their squires. A group of fashionable gentlemen hastily retreated as they passed, lest their garb be besmirched by filth kicked up from the horses' hooves. They wore pied, knee-length cotehardies and mantles whose hems were dagged to fully eight inches deep. On their heads, loud-colored taltries tapered to ludicrously long liripipes, which they draped about their shoulders like quiescent vipers.

Ladies stepped from carriages, in long cotehardies fitted tightly to the waist, the sleeves furnished with rows of small buttons reaching from the elbows to the wrists, and tippets dangling from the upper sleeves. Wide bands of embroidery bordered the ladies' otherwise plain surcoats, and instead of wimples or peplums, the heads of older ladies were adorned with nebules: cylindrical cases of woven wire passing across the forehead and down each side of the face, allowing the hair to flow down from each opening, until the ends were confined in small mesh bags. The visible hair was usually black, sometimes brown. Glimpsed through the window of a carriage pulled by a matching team, a noble widow in her black silk mourning-mask, only her eyes showing. Tottering by on the arm of a gentleman, a simpering young lady sniffing a silver pomander, apple-shaped . . .

A bolt of lightning slammed Imrhien in the chest. She fumbled with the door-latch, shaking it violently when it refused to unclose.

"Ho there, driver—halt! Why, *chehrna*—tell me!" Sianadh's large hand held the latch firmly shut. She grasped great handfuls of her hair, shook it in his face.

<<Gold. Gold-hair lady.>>

The Ertishman peered out at the maiden who had passed by, her heavy curls like ropes of marigolds down her back.

"Aye, gold. But not Talith gold, *chehrna,* if 'tis what ye be thinking. If ye looked closelike at that hair, ye would spy that it grows out a different color. Many of the nobility dye their hair—it be the fashion. They dye it yellow or black, so as not to look like common Feorhkind. Never red—they consider themselves above us Erts, the *sgorramas*. Diarmid now, he has his locks dyed brown to fit in with his Free Company mates. 'Tis all false. Ye will not see a true Talith in Gilvaris Tarv, that I swear, for I have put about questions on your behalf. But ye will see many straw-heads, whether wigged or dyed."

Deflated, the girl fell back in her seat. The carriage jerked into motion. It bowled on until, reaching the wealthiest quarter of the wealthy quarter, it stopped before a pair of bronze gates in a high wall. Stone jackals crouched on the gateposts. After some exchange between Sianadh and a couple of guards, one of the gates swung open.

Slim cypresses and columns lined the driveway. Jasper dragons coiled around the columns, and obsidian jackals snarled atop them. This broad, paved road swept around to the front steps of a magnificent stack of masonry: the wizard's palace.

A steward conducted the visitors through high, echoing halls, across mirror-surfaced marble floors. More sentries, in Korguth's black-and-white livery, were stationed at frequent intervals.

"There be a good deal of heavy security," scowled Sianadh, who instinctively disliked enforcers of authority.

Bent over a blackwood escritoire, an elderly scribe or scholar took the full payment from them in advance and wrote something in a ledger. His quill pen scratched away, a tiny scratch like an insistent mouse eating out the hollow drum of the palace. The scribe shook powdered resin over the paper from a brass pounce-box with a domed and pierced cap.

Sianadh's boot tapped on the polished floor.

"Wait here, you." Without looking up, the scribe used the quill to indicate a chair, thus dripping ink over his sleeve and the escritoire. "The Ineffable One administers to his clients alone."

Sianadh started to say something.

"Alone," repeated the scribe, turning his gaze on the Ertishman. His hooded eyelids blinked, once.

Cursing and fuming, Sianadh sat down.

<<Good luck,>> he signed to Imrhien with flamboyant gestures, to the utmost perturbation of the nonhandspeaking scribe.

<<Thank you,>> Imrhien signed in return, being led away down the hall.

A servant bade her be seated on another chair, outside a door.

"Aren't you the fortunate girl, having a rich uncle to pay for your visit," she said primly, disapprovingly. "My master is the most charming man and the cleverest wizard in Aia."

Imrhien lifted her face. The servant flinched. Her eyes scurried away like two cockroaches.

"The Ineffable One is always very busy," she stated, sidling away. "You understand, you will have to wait until he can spare time for you. People are always clamoring to see him. Mind you, behave yourself now. People who are lucky enough to see him ought to be nice and polite."

Imrhien sat, nicely and politely, on the chair, and time labored on. Eventually the door opened and another maidservant beckoned her to enter.

The charming man's dim workrooms were as unlike Ethlinn's as night from day. Copper tubes, retorts, and round-bellied crystal containers loomed out of purple shadows, filled with colored liquids, some steaming. Little red-eyed fires glowed in braziers. A myriad of jars in neat rows held preserved eyeballs, tiny birds' hearts, embryos, and the internal organs of a multitude of species. A cluster of fox skulls hung from a hook over a dish of livid crystals. A complete skeleton of a horse stood in a corner, fastened together by brass rivets. Cases of polished wood with velvet linings lay open to display scalpels, lancets, needles. A row of bleeding-bowls stood on a shelf alongside a thaumatrope and a cautery, a variety of apothecary jars, glazed gallipots inscribed with runic labels, and large, spherical vessels footed with taps.

Some walls were mirrored, others were hung with tapestries depicting magical symbols, runes, stars, and moons. On a massive oaken desk a huge tome lay open. Across the pages slumped an intricately embroidered silk bookmark with gilt tassels. Shelves embraced more dark, leather-bound volumes, books in cases of fretted and pierced silver so intricately wrought that they looked like fine point lace, parchment scrolls tied with purple ribbon. A display case imprisoned stuffed lizards and snakes, which looked out through jeweled eyes.

The effect was of some ominous cave filled with dead or inanimate things that somehow retained a counterfeit life, so that they harbored a mechanical ability to rend, tear, slice, burn, and puncture.

A stone slab table, long and narrow, stood in the center of this grand chamber. It was raised some four feet off the floor. A spill of something caustic had pitted one of its edges. Beside it on a bench, a neat arrangement of honed instruments, knives and needles, gleamed softly in the diffuse twilight. And the smell . . . The odor of incense, masking the whiff of bad meat.

A third attendant told her to remove her outer garments and don a gray linen robe.

"The Ineffable One will appear soon," she said. Judging by her extravagant black-and-white livery, she was more exalted than the first and second. "He is a very busy man. You are fortunate he has been able to find time for you."

Imrhien nodded. If by now she did not understand how fortunate she was, she must be stupid. She was about to turn and flee when another door opened and the wizard entered, flicking crumbs from his lips.

If the abode of Korguth the Jackal was impressive, the wizard himself was more so—a tall, deep-chested man, not far past his thirtieth year, handsome. Alternating bands of black and silver striped the long, thick hair falling to his shoulders. So white were his magnificent robes that they seemed to be made of light, and he imbued with that light like a being from another, higher realm. When he saw the deformed face he showed no surprise but began speaking in a voice like a honey-cake stuffed with raisins and figs, reassuring in its mellifluous richness.

"Paradox ivy poisoning will not cause difficulty. I have had many successes with it. All you must do is mind what I tell you. Cooperate, and there shall be results. You will be as you were before the poisoning—an ordinary, somewhat plain face, I fear. I can tell from the rustic and somewhat coarse bone structure."

His eyes flickered past her to the mirror. It was then that his client realized that he had not flinched when he'd first set eyes on her because he had not *seen* her. Absorbed in himself, he perceived only a symbol, a source of income and lauder.

Yet she had almost been charmed.

*The arrogant windbag sees only himself, and the adoration of these gullible sycophants,* she thought. *But I cannot let that matter to me. He can give me what I want, and I must endure.*

"Above all, you will not complain or make screams and moans. Do you understand?"

He winced slightly, as though the very thought of such uncouthness pained his ears.

She nodded.

Then there was a drink, cold and blue like death, killing rational thought with a hard tide of paralysis. Paralysis, yet only partial numbness. They laid her on the cold stone slab, in her gray robe, and then it began: the pain, the blades, the hot needles, the searing acids of the pastes, turning each nerve to a severe metal filament that conducted along its path a charge of agony most exquisite.

It went on and on. Imrhien would have cried out, many times, if she had possessed a voice. Agony sang with a piercing, high voice of its own: a paean to pain. The whole length of her body quivered, arching in torment. Through a miasma of fire, the rich voice said smoothly, "It is necessary for it to become worse before it can get better." But it just worsened, until a time when there had been no suffering was unimaginable and all there had ever been were needles and burning. Just before the blackness came, the voice said, far off, "Tell the red uncle to come back tomorrow."

* * *

There was blood on the pillow, fresh blood and black ichor, but it was difficult to see. Her face was an inferno. With numbed fingers, the patient reached up to touch it, meeting only bandages. Somewhere, a fig-cake said contemptuously:

"It is your own fault. I'll warrant you cried out in the night, after the procedure was completed. I had expected better return of you. Now the treatment will not be effective."

Later she was lifted and carried along. A bellowing burst through numb silence, like a red blister rupturing.

*"What have ye done to her?"*

Uproar exploded all around, after which there came enclosure within a carriage. Hoofbeats dropped like long lines of clay cups, and the swaying of the upholstery sent scarlet veins of lightning through a thickness that choked.

When the cool, green relief washed over her and put out the fire, she lay and soaked in it until it turned to tears.

"'Tis your eyes," said the voice of Muirne. "Mother says your sight be in danger. We must keep your face covered for seven days. I will be bathing the skin and changing the dressings twice daily. You be scarred now beyond repair. Why did ye go to this wizard? My uncle rages like a wounded bull. He went back to the wizard's palace and demanded to see him, but the sentries would not let him in. He has threatened to ruin the mage's reputation and to kill him." Angrily she added, "They have told my uncle that if he says a word against this charlatan, he and his kindred will be hunted down!" She paused. "This man is powerful. I guess that even if we should keep silent, he means to revenge himself on us for this threat and to prevent us from ever speaking out against him. I think he means us ill. I have observed strangers watching this house. You have brought trouble on us."

*What she says is true,* thought Imrhien, lying desolate in her cage of darkness. *It is true, and I must leave this house as soon as possible lest I bring further harm. I have been a fool. In seeking public acceptance, I have lost many things far more precious.*

At night, Muirne's weight pushed down the other side of the bed as she slid in with barely a rustle and never a word. In the dark hours Imrhien would lie awake, listening to the slight scuffling sounds of the domestic bruney busy at its surreptitious housework below-stairs. By day the sparrow sometimes cheeped and scuttered, pecking the crumbs Muirne left for it on the washstand, and there were the sounds of comings and goings in the room below, and voices floated up the stairs—often the voices of unfamiliar folk who were gone in the evenings. Then the family would converse.

Liam's voice: "Aye, Mother, I ken that Eochaid would be the best lad for the job, but he cannot come with us. His father lies ill, and he must stay to keep his stepmother and young brothers. But I tell ye, the lads we have chosen be strong and skilled enough to provide defense in time of need. Uncle, Mother says she feels we are going into deadly peril with this treasure-seeking, and although she trusts the Sulibhain brothers, she mislikes the three eastside lads we be taking along."

"Hush, boyo, not so loud when ye talk of treasure. And ye should not be so freely a-spending of it in the city as ye are, gifting to your friends, buying drinks for all and sundry—the wrong folk might be getting the idea that ye have stumbled upon a good thing. I like the look of those riversiders right enough, but I trust your mother's judgment. Let us choose three others."

"But—there be no others. I mean, if we do not take those three, there will be trouble."

"Why would there be trouble?"

"Well, ye see, they be right fond of hunting, and I promised them good pay. I had to promise that, else they would not even have considered coming here to meet ye and Mother. They be stalwart, and good fighters. I thought they would be just right—I could find no fault with them."

"I can find fault to begin with—that they threaten trouble if they do not get what they want!"

"We have no choice now, Uncle."

"*Obban tesh!* Of course we have a choice! We tell them the departure has been delayed, then we leave earlier than planned, and in secret, taking only the three worthy Sulibhains. Danger there might be, but those Sulibhains be renowned for their prowess, and they b'ain't no milksops."

"Aye, but what will the eastsiders do when they learn we have given them the slip?"

"Ach, a crew of patches like those can do naught. They'd have trouble enough just pulling on their breeches. Still, I b'ain't leaving here until those wrappings come off *her* face for good and I see if she be all right."

When the bandages came off for the last time, the patient's sight was intact, if blurred. The puffy flesh of her face was too sore to touch. She avoided reflective surfaces. Ethlinn, bathing the wounds with a herbal wash, advised that the skin must be left open to the air, to dry out.

<<I shall do as you say. But I must leave this house as soon as possible. I have brought you ill luck. I have been punished for my vanity.>>

<<Think you that? No. Not true.>>

<<I will not go to the one-eyed carlin, but to some other place.>>

<<The one-eyed daughter knows the ways I do not know. She may be able to help you in some way. Promise that you will go to her. For the sake of all I have done for you, for the sake of my brother's heart. Promise.>>

Dully, Imrhien nodded.

All travel preparations were complete. It had been arranged that Imrhien, in her own coach-and-four with a driver, a personal maid, and two footmen—all of whom were to start no sooner than at the beginning of the journey—was to join with a road-caravan that was at that time forming up to drive west along the Caermelor Road. Serrure's Caravan promised to be an extensive column; as well as the usual small merchants who cooperated with each other in such journeys for the sake of the protection afforded by numbers, its ranks were being swelled by farmhands, apprentices, and town gallants who were fired up to join the Royal Legions or the Dainnan. For the armies of Eldaraigne were now mobilizing, in the face of the slowly growing threat from Namarre, and they were making preparations for battle. Playing soldiers was all the rage now in Gilvaris Tarv, and in the town squares youths practiced their fighting skills on one another, to the entertainment of the onlookers. "For D'Armancourt!" was the cry, and, "For Eldaraigne!"

Storms of both kinds hammered on the anvil of the city's roofs from time to time; these phenomena, combined with thrilling tidings of forces gathering in the northeast and the restlessness of the inhabitants, forged a sense of change in the air, as though a signpost had been passed that could not be revisited.

Diarmid blew in breathless, one dark glittering shang morning, to announce that he was wasting no more time—he was also going to accompany Serrure's Caravan on its journey westward.

"I shall hire on as a guard—an outrider. I have learned all that I can, here. If I do not go now, all the best places will be taken."

Sianadh clapped a hand on the shoulder of his tall nephew. "'Tis good news, Diarmid my young cockerel. By good fortune, Imrhien is to travel with Serrure's Caravan, too—ye can keep her company and watch over her."

Diarmid stiffened almost imperceptibly.

"With all my heart I wish to do so," he said. "But meaning no disrespect to the lady, I shall be riding as a paid guard and thus shall not be able to leave my duties."

"Ah, codswallop," Sianadh snorted. He was interrupted by Muirne, who had come running in when she heard the news.

"Oh, take me with ye, Diarmid! The Royal Company of Archers would have need of a good markswoman, would they not?"

Her brother shook his cinnamon head. "I'll not take my young sister into battle. Besides, Mother needs you here."

"'I, said the sparrow, with my bow and arrow,'" sang Sianadh. "And a *doch* good shot ye be, too, Birdie—ye won that gold brooch off me with your marksmanship, not that I wasn't going to give it to ye anyway—but a little lass like ye in the King's army—it just wouldna be right!"

"That is not fair!" chided his niece. "I would do better at court than those farm churls from hereabouts who are going to the Royal City. Why, they would not even know how to behave at the dinner table. I have heard about all the manners of gentlefolk. I know."

"Eating be eating, b'ain't it, Birdie?"

"Nay, Uncle Bear. In Caermelor, at the Royal Court, they be so—

oh, so much more advanced than anywhere else. 'Tis not done to wipe your fingers on your hair or the tablecloth, or belch, or speak with your mouth full of food, or scratch, or pick your teeth at table. Ye have to use little forks to pick up the food. Ye be not allowed to pour wine for your betters or for yourself, but to wait for them to deign to pour it for ye, if they be feeling generous. And the carving of the meats must be done a certain way, and as for the toasts—it would take ye a whole day just to learn the complications."

"Takes the fun out of eating," observed Sianadh. "I be glad ye be going to Caermelor, soldier, and not me!"

"And I would rather be going, too," Muirne said bitterly.

Ethlinn signed to her eldest son, <<Muirne and I will soon be leaving this house. It is no longer suitable for us to stay here—beggars harass us, and the house is spied on. We shall lodge for a time with our cousin Roisin Tuillimh, in Clove Street—you know the house—until we find a new place, perhaps in the middle quarter. We shall send word to you by the Yeoman Stormriders, and you must send us news also—let us know whether you have been accepted for the Dainnan testing and whether you will be sent to Namarre. For, while I am proud of you for choosing to serve our King-Emperor, I'd as lief none of my children would go to the battlefront.>>

Her eyes told more than her hands.

Imrhien's sight gradually cleared. The pain decreased to a throbbing ache. The looking-glass revealed scars and tattered flesh, a disfigurement far worse than before the treatment at the wizard's hands. She withdrew under her taltry, a snail into its shell.

A carriage arrived at the end of Bergamot Street—Roisin Tuillimh had come to visit Ethlinn. She was a tall, spare woman with a long face and bright eyes watching out from above jutting cheekbones. Her faded hair, once the shade of ruby wine, was coiffed in simple fashion. Her garb was well tailored without being ostentatious, its style unashamedly Ertish. She cared little for beauty of countenance and much for beauty of spirit. Her mode of speech was rhythmic and unusual.

"Now, lass," she said to Imrhien, "you scarce have seen the city's sights. Since first you came here, it's indoors you've chiefly bided. Yon Bear leaves upon the morrow, but today is the first of Uvailmis and I invite your company on a jaunt—to Uvailmis Market-Fair we go—perchance you'll see something you wish to purchase, some useful item for your forthcoming journey, or what you will."

Reluctantly Imrhien allowed herself to be persuaded to accompany the three women to market.

Roisin's carriage rattled to a halt in a wide square choked with a confetti of stalls and crowds. She and Ethlinn stepped out, followed closely by Muirne and Imrhien. They walked among the canvas booths and awnings, examining, haggling, purchasing. Imrhien stared at the wares spread out so enticingly.

"Do not let anyone get a good eyeful of ye," Muirne reminded her with a nudge.

Keeping her face in the shadow of her taltry, Imrhien toured the nearest booths. A commotion drew their attention; bystanders began to gather around as a man, touting at full volume, led a small horse into the square.

"No finer steed in Erith! A waterhorse of eldritch, tethered securely by a rope around its pretty neck! Ladies and gentlemen, this fine beast will run like the wind for you, work like a slave for you, carry and draw weights that would kill an ordinary hack. What price am I offered?"

Some among the bystanders now recognized the horse-seller as the proprietor of the Picktree Mill, a man known for his ability to drive a hard bargain. The miller received a mixed reaction to his offer—some drew away, muttering that it was ill luck to meddle with un*lorraly* beasts. Others surged forward—it was a rarity, the capture of something eldritch, and many folk were curious just to look. The little gray waterhorse was indeed a pretty steed, and in fine fettle. Its legs were long and sculptured, like those of a racehorse. The hooves were delicate, the neck proudly arched. Strangely, the tail curled up over its back like a half-wheel. Fluted water-leaves like thin, green ribbons twined in that glossy tail and in the mane. But the eyes rolled with indignant fear, and the nostrils flared like two wild roses, for it had no choice except to succumb meekly to whatever the holder of the rope laid upon it. It neighed its rage and sprang back as if burned when the miller shook a pair of iron stirrups near its face.

"What am I offered! The finest beast in Erith! Immortal! Tame as a pup!"

The crowd murmured warily. Few of them had ever set eyes on any wight at all, for it was unwise to look in on domestic bruneys, the wights that most commonly inhabited certain fortunate houses in the cities of men. "Is it really a waterhorse? What kind is it?" they asked among themselves. They had all heard of the Each Uisge and wanted no part of anything with a reputation for such savagery and mercilessness.

Someone knowledgeable spoke up. "Judging by the tail, 'tis only a nuggle—I mean, a nygel," he said. "Not one of the killing-horses. 'Tis harmless."

"There must be some trickery, miller," said one of the bystanders. "How could you catch so slippery a beast?"

"Do you doubt my veracity sir? Fie! No trickery—no, indeed! The wretch has plagued me this many a night, for it is fascinated by water mills, and if the mill was working during the hours of darkness, it grabbed the wheel and halted it. The only way I could drive it off was to ram a flaming torch or a long iron blade through the vent-shaft of the mill. Its other prank was to dawdle along the millstream and lure people to mount it, whereupon it would dash away into the millpond or the sea and give the unwary rider a sore ducking, half drowning him. This trickster deserved to be taught a lesson, and that's just what I have done."

"Did it ever eat anyone?" asked a nervous man.

"Never! My wightish friend here did not, like the You-Know-What, the Prince of Waterhorses, tear its victims to pieces—after it rid itself of its burden, it used to set up a great nicker and a laugh and next be seen galloping and plunging off into the distance."

"That does not explain how you come by it," another objected.

The miller had been waiting for an opportunity to describe his clever feat.

"I was but a-walking down by Millbeck Tarn, searching for my chestnut mare. This creature came up to me all friendlylike, so pretending I did not know what it was, I got on its back, but I held on with only one hand. When it galloped off with me for a joyride, I slipped my free hand in my pocket and took out the rope halter I'd been keeping for my mare and slipped it around its neck. Then it was mine! Leave the rope on, ladies and gentlemen, and the thing will do as you bid forever!"

Various offers began to be shouted.

"Two sovereigns!"

"Three!"

Excitement surged through the throng like wind through a cornfield. The waterhorse, far from its natural surroundings, shuddered, looking desperately for escape, bound inexorably by the *lorraly* fibers of the hempen rope encircling its neck.

As they bid, the faces of the onlookers were stamped with the smug superiority of those who beheld a symbol of their fear brought to its knees. All creatures of eldritch were baffling to them, alien and therefore frightening. They presented a constant threat against which most mortals felt impotent. Imrhien saw the cruelty in the faces and the trembling of the waterhorse, which was only a nygel after all, a practical joker by nature, but not a monster. The creature was guiltless, having merely been obeying its own fun-seeking instincts. Through its own naiveté it was now enslaved and reviled. Imrhien understood its situation perfectly.

The bidding rose to six sovereigns, then seven guineas. There it halted.

<<On my behalf, offer him an angel,>> Imrhien signed.

"Oh, no," Muirne protested diffidently.

"She signs too quickly. What wishes she to know, Muirne?" inquired Roisin. On being told, she threw Imrhien a measuring glance. "Be ye certain?"

A nod.

"A pony for the pony!" called Roisin.

There was general laughter, but the miller who held the rope said, "Is that a genuine offer?"

"It is."

Imrhien began rummaging in her purse.

"What? Be ye turning *scothy?*" hissed Muirne.

<<No. Please, show him the money.>>

Nobody outdid the offer. People stepped back, gawping in amazement—few had ever seen a coin of as high value as an angel. The Picktree miller made sure they didn't get much of a look at it. As soon as he had bitten the heavy golden disk to test its authenticity, he pocketed it, handed the rope halter to Roisin, and disappeared swiftly into the crowd, doubtless afraid he might have become a target for cut-purses or less subtle robbers.

The transaction completed, the bystanders now focused their attention on the new owners, calling out advice and questions. Imrhien stepped up to the terrified wight and slipped off the rope. Instantly the crowd scattered. The little waterhorse reared up on its hind legs, whinnied and dashed away, mane and tail streaming, bursting through the multitude, causing it to split and roar and curse like some many-headed monster.

"What have you done?" cried Muirne.

<<I paid for its freedom.>>

As the nygel galloped off, a movement overhead caught Imrhien's attention. A Windship passed high above, departing from Tarv Tower under full sail, coursing through the cloudless skies like a lean greyhound. Imrhien felt her taltry fall back as she tilted her head for a quick glance. Swiftly she pulled up the hood once more and turned back to the carriage. As she put her foot up on the step, she paused, sensing someone watching her. She glimpsed a short figure, with squinting eyes gleaming from the shadows of its own cowl. An odd face—very odd; disturbing.

Ethlinn followed the direction of her gaze.

<<Danger. Quickly—we must go.>>

Hurriedly the four of them reembarked, Muirne fuming about folk who not only throw away good money, but also insist on making a show of themselves for all the world to see. The carriage rattled off out of the marketplace. Ethlinn, whose eyes had been fastened to the rear window, signed, <<We are being followed.>>

"My driver knows the hidden ways and the devious," said Roisin, and she called instructions to the man. The passengers were jerked violently to one side as the carriage slewed around a corner on two wheels and bounced down a side-street. In the next instant they were thrown to the other side. Passersby scattered. Buildings flashed past.

"Be not affrighted—we will not overturn," Roisin shouted over the racket of the wheels, "Brinnegar knows well what he is at."

<<They follow yet. They are gaining on us. Stop at the next corner.>>

Roisin shouted to the coachman. As soon as the vehicle stopped, Ethlinn was out of the door with a movement surprisingly swift and lithe for her age. Leaning from the window, Imrhien saw her draw out her carlin's Wand, planting it firmly in a muddy crack between the cobbles, in the middle of the street. Then the carlin's hands moved in an unfamiliar gesture. It seemed to Imrhien that the living stave began to sprout with unnerving swiftness—that toothed briars, sharp nettles, and gorses budded and whipped out from its rind, tangling tentacles, weaving in and out betwixt walls and street, growing higher until within a few blinks of the eye they had formed a shadowy trellis of thorns. When the carlin snatched up the Wand, it broke away and the barrier remained in place. She hurried back to the carriage. As the team pulled away, a group of figures rounded the corner and ran full-tilt into the black ensnarlment. Some fell back—others became hooked and began writhing among the dim briars. The coachman's whip cracked, the horses leaped forward. Soon the stymied pursuers were out of sight.

Safely back at Ethlinn's house, Imrhien could not rid herself of the memory of the odd face in the marketplace. It seemed branded on the inner surface of her lids; every time she closed her eyes it sprang vividly before her. The mouth had stretched wide, the nostrils had been broadly flared. The hood rested on the head in a peculiar fashion, tucked up into points just above the ears. From beneath that hood, the slanting eyes had stared directly at her, with a look that seemed to come from somewhere dark and wild, somewhere alien. And the stranger had stood no more than four feet high. There was no doubt in her mind that this curious onlooker was eldritch and, furthermore, that it was malevolent.

<<I can protect myself from harm,>> signed Ethlinn, <<but I may not always be able to protect others. Amongst the group that

pursued us there were those with a wightish look—strange, since they do not love the day. I have underestimated the powers of this wizard Korguth—for I think it is he who sends these creatures after us in revenge.

<<Muirne, for safety you must go with Diarmid and Imrhien to Caermelor, at least until this madness has run its course. Until then, be careful. Tomorrow we make the move to Roisin's house, with all discretion. It is to be hoped that any pursuers will not know where we have gone. After that, do not venture out of doors until it is time to leave with the caravan.>>

Elated, her daughter began to pack immediately.

Before dawn the next day, at the street-door of the house in Bergamot Street, Sianadh and Liam said their farewells. Three laden landhorses waited, held by Sheamais, one of the trusted Sulibhain brothers. The other two members of the small company were to meet them at a prearranged rendezvous outside the city.

An ache of grief churned inside Imrhien's chest.

"I do not know when we may meet again," the Ertishman said to her awkwardly. "By the time I return ye will be well away on the Caermelor Road, with Serrure's Caravan." He gave her a rakish grin. "We went through it together, did we not, *chebrna?* We went through it and ye opened the doors for me and I gave ye a name. There be an old saying in Finvarna, '*Inna shai tithen elion*'—We have lived the days."

She nodded, swallowing the tightness in her throat.

"Good speed to ye, and all luck. I hope ye may find what ye seek."

<<For the last time, Sianadh, I beg you not to go,>> his sister urged. <<No good shall come of it. My heart tells me some doom awaits you on that path.>>

Sianadh kissed her lightly on the forehead. "Never worry, Eth. Doom has waited for me before. It can keep on waiting. The Bear will prevail."

He kissed Muirne on the back of her hand. Imrhien, he embraced clumsily, thumping her on the back like a drinking partner.

<<What does it mean, the name you gave to me?>>

Her eyes searched the rough landscape of his face. The very intensity of her gaze was a fine chain linking the two of them together.

"Imrhien—it be the Ertish word for butterfly."

Without another word, Sianadh turned abruptly. The chain snapped. He swung himself up into his saddle and rode off with the young Sulibhain. Liam, having taken his leave, followed.

Tears glistened on Muirne's face. "Mother, shall we see them again?"

Ethlinn stood with her hands pressed together, gazing down the street.

Stormriders on 'tween-city runs reported that an incoming road-caravan—many of whose members were to join up with Serrure's—had been delayed by harassment from large numbers of road-haunters. Not only was it late, but once the convoy arrived, time would be needed for repairs. This put back the departure date of Serrure's Caravan. It would not, now, leave for another week or perhaps two. From time to time other, smaller convoys were leaving—however, these being less reputable and less well guarded, Ethlinn deemed them unsuitable for her children and Imrhien.

Meanwhile, the move from Bergamot Street to Clove Street had to be made quickly—to this purpose, everything had been boxed in advance. The cart arrived late on the same night of Sianadh's departure, its wheels muffled with straw. Quickly and quietly they loaded their belongings. Ethlinn locked the door, and they drove away with a minimum of fuss. All seemed to be going well, but as the cart turned the corner out of Bergamot Street, Muirne abruptly jerked bolt upright.

"The brooch!"

<<What brooch?>> her mother asked.

"The gold brooch Uncle Bear gave me for my marksmanship—I have left it behind, hidden for safekeeping behind the wall-linings!"

<<Leave it,>> Ethlinn insisted, <<let it be. You have gold enough with the portion he bestowed upon you.>>

"But it is a prize for my skill at archery! It is special. And he gave it to me. I would trade all my gold for it."

<<I forbid you to return to the house. The danger is too great.>>

Muirne shuttered her face like a window.

Welcoming lamps shone softly from Roisin Tuillimh's large, comfortable abode. Efficiently, swiftly, the cart was unloaded and driven away.

"Weariness sits heavy on you all," said gray-haired Roisin. "Come rest awhile, partake of milk and honey to refresh, before your heads meet pillows. Some commotion I heard just now, perhaps your seelie helper the bruney. From your luggage it unloaded itself, methinks. If it stays, 'twill find 'tis never idle within these walls, I trow—my servants' hands were erst full enough with but one mistress to wait upon—oh, and of course the lynxes, my pampered pets. The maids shall be told to leave your wight unmolested and not to spy, lest it should take offense and depart. And, dear Eth, a grounding-place for your Wand has been prepared beside the rose that grows in the front court."

That night, when all were abed, Imrhien heard the soft sounds of Muirne moving about in the next room. She lighted a candle and stole in like some pale haunter of the marshes. Muirne, fully gowned in her emerald velvet, was about to descend the stair. She started guiltily, one hand on the banister, a dark-lantern in the other. Shadows enfolded her face like a mask.

"Go back to bed," she whispered.

Imrhien fixed her candle in the socket of an empty holder. <<You go to fetch the brooch. Do not. Go in daylight.>>

"I cannot go in daylight. People would see. I might be followed."

Muirne started to go down the stairs. Imrhien grabbed her elbow.

<<Wait. I go with you.>>

Muirne hesitated, then nodded, relief flashing across her features. She waited while Imrhien dressed herself hurriedly in her magenta brocade, throwing across her shoulders a cloak the color of the evening ocean. Together the two damsels went silently out of the front door, crossed the tiny courtyard, and passed through the gate into the obscurity of the street.

* * *

At night, the city seemed to be another world. Angled roofs pitched and seesawed, black cutouts against the smoky veil obscuring the moon. Soft-footed the girls went, with covered lanterns, hugging the pools of inky shadow that flowed under walls. Straw blew down the street in dry wisps. A tame lynx ran along a wall and dropped down on the other side. In the distance someone screamed. A dog yapped, several streets away. Rowan tilhals hung over every door as a traditional precaution, even though wights seldom roamed in cities. Bruneys and such seelie domestic solitaries habitually remained indoors—their natural abodes were human shelters.

As the two girls drew near their destination, a knot of drunken revelers passed across the end of a street and caroused off down some lane, flinging back aberrant echoes of their incoherence. There were no nightwatchmen in this part of Tarv, to swing glaring lanterns into the faces of late loiterers and ask questions.

Bergamot Street seemed empty. There was no sign of movement. Soundlessly Muirne turned the key in the door of the deserted house. The irritating bell failed to ring, having been removed. All was quiet. Uneasily Imrhien wondered whether it was too quiet—she could remember no night stillness as profound as this, not in this street. Usually one could detect someone coughing in an upstairs window, the susurration of voices from a back room, the thin wail of an infant. The back of her neck tingled, as at the approach of the unstorm. She listened for a footfall, for any sound to crack the hard silence, but a numbness pressed on her ears like wads of wool.

The interior of the house was unfamiliar in its emptiness. It seemed sad and somehow eerie, like an abandoned ship found drifting on the tide. With the lanterns partially uncovered, the intruders ascended the creaking stairs. The bare room above still held the lingering scent of lavender and something more, undefinable. Muirne groped behind the sackcloth on the walls.

"Here it be."

She fastened the brooch to her gown, beneath her mantle.

They took up their lanterns again, making their way down to the front door. Shadows fled before their feet. The back window of the lower room stared: a blank eye.

The oppressive feeling grew stronger when they entered the street. It felt like a warning. Imrhien wished Muirne would hurry—she was fumbling with the lock, having trouble with the key.

Then the key clattered to the cobbles with a sudden noise like the riving of a muted bell. Cold on the stones, it lay alone, and no hand reached to retrieve it. The abductors had sprung from behind, clapping one hand across the mouths of their victims, twisting an arm behind their backs and dragging them to a cart waiting around the corner. In vain the girls struggled. A whip cracked twice, and the cart clattered away.

On the street, the key floated in a pool of shadow.

The house sprouted like a toadstool down by the river, in a dilapidated section of the city. Oily water glinted between ramshackle edifices bereft of paint and tiles. The area stank of mold and rising damp.

Little did the captives glimpse of their new surroundings before they were thrust roughly through the door, divested of their jewelry, dragged to a small, cheerless room, and locked in, alone. For a long time, Muirne sobbed quietly. Her companion prowled the room. It was furnished only with a straw pallet, a couple of rough woollen blankets, and two buckets, one empty and the other full of water. In the gloom, none of these objects was easy to discern. Weak illumination was provided by pale moonlight through a barred window, high in one wall. From beyond the window came the lapping and gurgling of the river. An eldritch tingle raked Imrhien's spine—the faint sounds of scuttling overlaid the water's music. The room was also furnished with rats. The cellars of Isse Tower had harbored such rodents—she hated them with a vehemence far out of proportion to their few transgressions against her.

The rats stayed out of sight. Eventually Imrhien curled up at one end of the pallet and fell asleep.

She woke, stiff and cold, with Muirne lying red-eyed beside her. Daylight the color of gruel was leaking in between the window-bars.

"Ye," Muirne said scornfully, lifting her tearstained face, "how could ye sleep? Have ye no mind as to what has happened, to what shall happen?"

Imrhien shook her head. This she had pondered, as slumber overcame her. It seemed obvious that the wizard's minions were carrying out their threat to harm Sianadh's kin if he damaged Korguth's reputation. But if so, why had they imprisoned herself and Muirne and not simply thrown them into the river? And if the abductors were indeed the wizard's henchmen, why had they not made their move as soon as Sianadh had threatened their master? Why had they waited until Ethlinn's house was empty? It made no sense.

Muirne said, "They were after *ye,* the *uragubne* wizard's roustabouts, and they took *me* by mistake. I heard one of them say, 'Which one is it?' to which another replied, 'I know not. Take them both.' Now we shall both suffer the same fate, which, most likely, is to be taken to Namarre and sold as slaves. Ah, my poor mother!" She began again to weep.

A key rattled in the lock, and the door banged open. A burly man with a pockmarked face stood beyond it. Another, clad in servant's drab, lugged in a second straw pallet and threw it on the floor, followed by a couple of blankets and a dirty loaf of bread.

A third man strode in, his face almost invisible beneath a bushy brown beard. He wore merchant's yellow.

"Stand up and give us a look at you."

Then he swore a violent oath as the prisoners obeyed.

"So, Weasel—this is what you fetch for me out of the gutters—a henna'd queen and a bleached hag."

He studied Imrhien from head to toe.

"A form a man could worship and a face from out of his worst nightmares."

Imrhien shivered. The man had Mortier's stench.

"This could be better than I had hoped. Two for the price of one! 'Twill make for a fine show and a fine bidding after. Make sure you keep the little dancers well fed, Weasel—they shall need to be light on their feet."

As though this were a clever joke, the man outside the room laughed.

"Aye, Scalzo," grunted Weasel, the drab servant.

The bearded man stamped out of the room, followed by Weasel, who slammed the door.

<<We live. Have hope.>>

Ignoring the impassioned signals, Muirne turned her face away.

Like all caged animals and incarcerated mortals, they took to pacing up and down. Their footsteps marked the passage of seconds, minutes, days. Seven short strides were the measure of their prison; that, they learned well. Once a day Weasel came bringing food that varied little—bread, pickled fish, and sometimes apples. He would stare at them with blank eyes, offering no conversation—completely devoid of compassion and fellow-feeling. Each morning Imrhien scratched the tally of the passing days on the wall with a piece of broken brick. As the row of marks lengthened, Muirne's silences became shorter and her antipathy crumbled.

To pass the time they played games—Cloth-Scissors-Rock, guessing games, charades. They planned escapes. Muirne extended Imrhien's knowledge of handspeak, and in return Imrhien related, as well as she could, her adventures with Sianadh among the mountains. Muirne wanted to know why she had been traveling there, but Imrhien avoided the subject, having promised Sianadh not to reveal the truth of the treasure at Waterstair. Nevertheless, out of the seed of the Ertish girl's interest, sympathy grew.

Except for the passing of a mild shang wind that raised hazy specters of mist, there was scant distinction of one day from the next.

"Why do they keep us here for so long?" mused Muirne. She answered herself: "Likely they wait for a Seaship to arrive in Tarv Port—a slaver to take us to Namarre. We have missed our place in Serrure's Caravan. It will have departed by now. Yet why should I be concerned about caravans? We shall be lucky enough to stay alive."

On the fourteenth day, bickering voices arose beyond their door like angry wasps.

"We can wait no longer. Each day that passes brings more danger of discovery."

"Soon it will come! It might well be today. Why waste what we have?"

"We have delayed far too long already."

"What are you afraid of? The blue-faced crones? Poor Weasel, frightened of the grannies!"

"I say, get them out of here."

"No. A good strong ghost-maker will come this night. I feel it."

The voices faded as the men moved away, still arguing.

"Oh," said Muirne in a small voice, "how *breorig*. No doubt this be an unshielded house, and we are to be used as *gilfs* before we are sold."

<<What means that?>> Imrhien's hands demanded.

"*Gilfs*—performers in shang. Folk who choose, or who are forced, to bare their heads in the unstorm and become part of some act or event that, during later unstorms, be shown to a paying audience. These shows, these unshielded houses, be illegal. The black-hearted *skeerda* criminals who run them charge a high fee for viewing and be always on the lookout for some new act to draw back old customers—new *gilfs,* more exciting stunts."

<<How must we perform?>>

"I know not, but I dread to imagine. I have heard these things spoken of in quiet corners when older folk believed I could not overhear. The *gilf*-shows in these illegal houses—men are made to fight one another to the death or to wrestle wild animals. Sometimes they must jump through fiery hoops or walk upon hot coals, barefoot. Always they must perform acts of great daring. Through their fear, their images burn brighter on the shang."

<<Happiness burns.>>

"Oh, aye—great joy burns brightly, too, but it is easier for such *uragubnes* as these to inspire fear than joy. And not the kind of gray, sweating fear that turns folk to stone, but the full-blooded terror that pushes them to deeds they could not normally do—that makes for better entertainment. It seems we are to be used for this, when the next shang wind comes, Ceileinh save us. There be worse things than death."

No unstorm came that night, to turn the city into a jewel box—or the next. But Weasel came in, drunk, and spoke to them.

"This used to be a busy house with a profitable *gilf*-room upstairs," he confided with uncharacteristic garrulity, "until one night during a ghost-maker, when the audience was packed around the walls, watching the shows, there came a loud voice saying, 'Where is my golden eye?' and a great hairy Hand or maybe a Foot came down the chimbley and groped out into the room. The onlookers fled in terror. Since then, every time there is a ghost-maker the Voice says, 'Where is my golden eye?' and the Hand comes down the chimbley, grasping and seeking. It drove away all the customers. Scalzo has tried many ways to get rid of this Thing in the Chimbley, but with no success. So he keeps a watch-worm locked in the *gilf*-room in case the Thing comes down the chimbley one night, and then slides down the stair to these lower rooms where we sleep. Still, we do not rest easy in our beds, and we cannot open the *gilf*-room to trade. Now we find ourselves with two prisoners with no better fate in store than the slave-ships. What chance—you both have eyes! Are they golden?"

"*Manscatha!*" hissed Muirne.

"You will both be sent to the *gilf*-room as soon as the next ghost-maker comes. When the Thing in the Chimbley asks for eyes, it can take its pick of the two of you—the gooseberry eyes of the bleached hag or the robin's eggs of the henna'd queen." He shrugged. "Who kens—mayhap the Thing will not know the difference, or care. Then maybe it will be content and leave us in peace. If one of you remains unmarred, she shall be taken away to be sold."

Corpse-pale, Muirne clenched her fists until her nails bit her flesh. She could not speak. Weasel, suddenly as wooden as always, made his exit, remembering to lock the door.

Imrhien had scratched the twenty-second mark on the wall when she felt the first premonition of it—the same prickling thrill that accompanied the buildup of any massive thunderstorm. Through that day the precognition grew, slowly. As evening deepened, Muirne nervously clutched at her companion's arm.

"The unstorm! Imrhien, it comes this way!"

With that awakening, a sudden wail broke out from beyond the walls, a wild and tragic cry of grief.

Muirne shuddered. She lapsed into silence, and they both hearkened. Once, twice, three times—at the third cry, the long, grievous lament trailed off brokenly on the evening breeze. The Weeper of Tarv had dwelled by the river long before the first buildings of the city had sprung up on the banks. Rivers were the age-old haunts of weepers. If they were to be perceived at all by mortal eyes—which might happen perhaps once in a hundred years—they would be seen kneeling at the water's edge, apparently washing the blood-stained garments of those about to die. Their grim warnings were distributed among townsfolk and countryfolk alike, and they were always accurate.

Who would die this night?

Stars grilled themselves to white cinders on the cold grating of the window. With a metallic clang, the door opened. Men stood in the frame, outlined by flaring torches. An order was barked. A short man stepped forward. Sores clustered at the corners of his mouth.

"Time for the show," he remarked. He pulled the taltries from the heads of the captives, then pushed them out through the door and up some stairs. Their escort parted ranks and closed in behind them.

At the top of four flights, a man unbolted a door and kicked it wide. Two others thrust blazing torches into the darkness of the room beyond, a chamber opening out long and broad.

"Back! Get back there," they barked at something beyond the door. They jabbed forward their brands. Flickering light flooded the corners of the room as more torches entered. The captives were pushed through the portal.

A scream rose up in Muirne. It snapped from her mouth like a whipcord. She and Imrhien tilted back their heads, staring in wonder.

The flat, wedge-shaped head of a giant snake towered over them, rising out of a spiral of coils. The snake was a rainbow taken out of the sky and twisted into the shape of a corkscrew and covered all over with flattened water drops that refracted the rainbow's living light, glinting iridescent like the inner lining of an abalone shell. As thick in the girth as a man's body, the watch-worm made a hiss like steam, flicking out its forked tongue from between the wide jaws. Its eyes were fathomless, multifaceted crystals. Evanescent colors rippled down its convolutions: zircon, ruby, emerald, diamond, sapphire. The men swung torches at the creature, driving it up one end of the room, where it began to gather its coils in a coruscating slither of sequins and pearl buttons.

This chamber, this *gilf*-room, occupied the entire upper story. At one end gaped a blackened and toothless maw of a fireplace, hooded by a stone chimney. At the other squatted a massive chest, with open lid. Bits of smashed walls jutted, showing where the chamber had once been divided into smaller rooms. It was painted all over—walls, ceiling, floor—with brightly colored, amateurish murals crudely representing battles and acts of wizardry. The window shutters hung askew, the wall-murals flowing over them uninterrupted.

One of Scalzo's men was shouting: "Pack away the watch-worm—the ghost-maker's coming!"

A jinking, chinking sound was approaching, as of a million tiny bells. Imrhien's hair bristled like a sunburst, crackled like ice. Fear and elation filled her. Muirne held her arm in the grip of a steel trap. A black post stood near the center of the floor, and to this the two *gilfs* were now efficiently roped.

"Now don't you try to get free," the short man declared, "or it will be the worse for you. I won't have chits like you overlapping with my other tableaux and getting things all confused. There's been an old, half-baked one there where that pillar is—it's always looked a bit faded, so tonight we'll overlay it with something better, eh, Golden-Eyes?" Cracking a whip he had been holding at his side, he stepped back. The victims shivered.

The watch-worm was darting its huge head toward the torch-bearers. Scalzo's men stabbed forward with torches, passing the flares across the sliding metallic hide of the massive boa. It jerked and thrashed as if it were in pain and opened its fanged mouth to emit a hiss as loud as an arsenal of white-hot weapons being plunged into cold water. The dorsal spines, which had lain quiescent along its backbone, lifted like a crest, like a row of shot-silk fans, their flaring membranes radiating colors from angry carmine to violent violet. The men must leap and dodge now, flying like birds in a whirling cage, to avoid the flogging tail. The worm lunged for the door, and the short man's whip bit into its neck, just below the fins.

"Get it into the chest quick, or I'll millstone the lot of you! Hurry—then get out of here!"

With flaming brands, the men tried to chase the creature toward the cramped chest that was its prison. At that moment the shang storm struck with full force and the theater of horrors sprang to life. Imrhien was too intent on watching the snake to concern herself with the terrible scenes that had awakened throughout the length and breadth of the unshielded room.

Muirne had begun to tremble violently, her face a wooden carving of terror. Somewhere, a muffled drum, or possibly a heart, began to pound. Swept up by the ecstasy of the shang, Imrhien had no room for fear.

Then the mad roaring, down through the vent over the fireplace, into the room:

*"Where is my golden eye?"*

Terrible was the Voice, bitter and ancient, harsh with menace. Muirne's screams mingled among the yells of the men.

Beyond the screams, beyond the gold-limned cameos of the unstorm shimmering in random repetition, and the flowing scintillas of the watch-worm's gyrations—behind the backs of their tormentors, the disjointed shutters of a window fell open and two figures entered, jumping down from the ledge. At first, Imrhien thought them part of yet another ghostly scene, but when she looked again she realized that they had attacked two of Scalzo's torchbearers, taking them by surprise. Bearers and torches already lay sputtering out on the floor in a puddle of blood as dark as spilled wine. Circling amid the chaos of images, the intruders managed to catch two more men unawares. As these men fell, run through by short-swords, their accomplices realized what was afoot and turned in fury to fall upon the unexpected assailants. Swords flashed from scabbards, men went flying across the room. Now freed from the ring of fire, the watch-worm careened about the walls in lightning loops of illumination. Three of the torchbearers flung down their brands and leapt for the door, wrenching it open and disappearing down the stairs. The avenging watch-worm followed them at greater speed. Another man, in terror, jumped out of the open window.

Then a shadow fell on the hearth, a dark reflection of something moving farther up inside the chimney. It seemed to be the shadow of a loathsome claw or a hideous and gigantic spider. Scrapings of soot rained out of the core of the funnel.

A man bellowed, "Muirne!"

The Voice rumbled louder, more venomously, *"Where is my golden eye?"*

Flourishing bloody swords, Liam and another young Ertishman dashed out of the melee of shang wraiths. They slashed the ropes binding the captives.

Four men lay wounded or dead on the floor, beneath the translucent afterimage of the watch-worm, a wheeling vortex. Some of Scalzo's men were running about as though they had lost their wits, too terrified to leave the room in case the watch-worm should be waiting outside, yet afraid to remain and face certain peril. Shang images repeated themselves everywhere—even high in the roof-cavities, where sildron belts had been used on past *gilfs*. At the other end of the room, the blackened smoke-shaft began to vibrate. Bits of dislodged mortar dropped out from between the stones, building up along the mantelpiece. A thing rammed straight down into the fireplace and stood there. It looked like a giant chicken's foot blasted by fire or struck by a thunderbolt.

*"WHERE IS MY GOLDEN EYE?"*

"Shut up about yer golden eye!" a wounded man shrieked hysterically.

A wind swept through the room, followed by an eerie vacuum. The short man with the whip began to slide. He shot at speed, still standing upright toward the hearthstone. As he entered the fireplace he let out a yell and dropped the whip. In the next instant he was gone, as if something had closed on his head and pulled him upward. As quick as thought, he had simply vanished up the chimney, like a cork jetted from a bottle, his arms and legs dangling as loosely as the limbs of a wooden doll. One moment he had been rooted to the spot, a look of horror spreading across his features, and the next he was nowhere to be seen. No sound, no scream, marked his disappearance—only a small rain of soot from the flue.

"Hasten!" someone shouted.

The queer wind began to blow again. The vacuum sucked at the eardrums of everyone in the room. Another man began to slide.

The erstwhile *gilfs,* accompanied by Liam's comrade, jumped out of the window, with Liam bringing up the rear. As they slid down the sloping roof, the shanged night-roofs of Gilvaris Tarv spread out before them, the soft brilliance of their frosting reflecting a clover-field of stars above. Ahead of Imrhien, the young man helped Muirne to jump down to a lower roof. From behind Imrhien's shoulder, Liam lent a hand to steady her.

The riverside dwellings had been built higgledy-piggledy, with no attention paid to planning. Jammed up alongside each other, their roofs reached a multiplicity of heights, like some staircase constructed by a madman, randomly punctured by the burning towers of smokestacks. While the unstorm rolled away over the housetops, the foursome slithered down each canting slope and leaped across to the next, until at last they landed in a narrow laneway where two horses were tethered.

"Make haste," said Liam, untying the reins, "before they can raise reinforcements."

Even as he spoke, it was too late. Shouts, the clamor of hooves, and the crunch of booted feet erupted at the bottom of the lane, and saffron torchlight splashed the night.

Muirne was up and onto one of the horses with one practiced swing. The young Ertishman jumped onto the other steed, then leaned down and reached toward Imrhien. Liam tossed the girl up in front of his comrade. She grabbed a handful of mane and hung on grimly.

"Liam!" cried Muirne. Agitated, her horse pranced and sidled.

"Go!" her brother shouted. "'Tis myself to blame. I shall hold them off until ye get away."

"No!"

But Liam slapped each horse hard on the rump. Startled into flight, they took off up the lane at a gallop, leaping over the now gray and plumper shape of the avenged watch-worm wending its way down to the river.

Far behind, cries arose. The pursuers closed in on the man who stood alone against them.

* * *

Along winding lanes and through tunnels beneath overarching tenements the horses dashed, until they reached the outskirts of the river district. There, in a square whose center was marked by a well with a small, steeply pitched roof, their deliverer called a halt. The steeds stood breathing hard, their flanks steaming in the starlight. Sparrows, disturbed by the clatter, twittered from the eaves of a house.

"I must go back for Liam." The Ertishman leapt down to the cobblestones. "Ye both, go on back to Roisin's. Muirne, ye ken the way from Farthingwell Square."

"I will come with ye, Eochaid," Muirne sobbed in a low voice.

"Nay. What if they should take ye again? If he lives, I will bring him back. If he does not, would ye risk that the lad should have given his life in vain?"

In a cool, calm manner, Eochaid confirmed directions for finding their way to the house of Roisin, and then he was gone, running lightly down a lane between two buildings.

Many windows overlooked the square. The shutters of one of them now opened.

"Who goes there?" a belligerent voice demanded. "Is that you, Pardrot?" Other voices began to join the first.

"Come," said Muirne in a tight murmur. She cantered out of the square, pulling Imrhien's horse by the reins.

They hammered on Roisin Tuillimh's back gate. Roisin and her coachman, Brinnegar, admitted them, bundling them indoors. After that, everything seemed to happen at once.

On hearing that Liam was in danger, Ethlinn lost no time. With the Wand at her side, she ran out to the stables. She was mounted and off down the street at a gallop while the rescuees were still being bandaged and embraced and endeavoring to answer Roisin's barrage of questions.

"But what was Liam doing back in Tarv?" Muirne kept asking. "Why was he not on the expedition with Uncle Bear?"

Roisin explained that she and Ethlinn had not seen Liam since his departure with Sianadh's company. When the two girls had disappeared, the alarm had been raised across the city by a network of neighbors, friends, and carlins. Swiftly and efficiently, Diarmid had assembled a band of mercenaries to join the hunt, but all attempts had been unsuccessful. Serrure's Caravan had left without him—he had given away all thoughts of leaving the city until his sister could be found.

Word had arrived from the neighbors in Bergamot Street. Odd-looking characters had been seen snooping around the empty house and asking questions as to the whereabouts of its previous occupants. Their questions were in vain—those who knew the carlin and her family loved them too well to betray them. Lately, Roisin's house also had been watched.

"Each and every time we leave this house, we catch a sight of some ill-favored thing spying from some angle or roof's top," Roisin said. "I've no doubt they are the minions of Korguth, and it is Sianadh they are after. But we have not let them deter us—in sooth, we have been trying to catch one of these watchers, in case they might give information leading us to you."

"I saw no spies when we arrived just now," said Muirne, fretful and distracted.

"Had Ethlinn not just come in the moment before you arrived, you would not have slipped past them. She has been out after them, with the Wand. In trying to elude her entrapments, they relaxed their attention. Meanwhile, upon our very doorstep you appear, all praise to the Lord of Eagles! Brinnegar has gone just now at my despatch, swiftly, with word to Diarmid of your safe whereabouts, bidding him make haste and comb the river district in strong company, to aid Liam and Eochaid. How came Liam here to the city, we know not. Back from the expedition and alone—'tis a mystery, and one that smacks of foul play."

"I cannot bide here," Muirne burst out, wringing her hands, "I must go back to my brother. Alone, he was, against them all."

"Bide you must," replied Roisin. "You are overwrought. Swallow this draft—it will make you sleep. Swallow it, I say."

Fretfully, Muirne obeyed and was led upstairs, protesting, by one of the maids.

"Stay you, Imrhien, and keep vigil with me. I need company on this fell night," said Roisin. She stared out of the window. Dark roofs reared in blunt wedges against a distillation of stars.

Minutes slowly dripped by, eroding night as water wears away the marble of an antique fountain. Imrhien sat with her head in her hands.

They guessed the truth at once when they spied the slow procession coming up the street. Roisin uttered a sudden cry of pain. She stood motionless. There was Ethlinn, leading the way, bent over like an old, defeated woman, her hair hanging about her face. The Wand had grown as tall and thick as a staff, and she was leaning on it. Next came Eochaid, bearing Liam's broken body across his arms. At his back, Brinnegar and a score or so of other men, battle-grimed and grim-faced.

Eochaid, pale and drawn, laid his friend ever so gently on Roisin's table, covered him with his cloak, and spoke to his comrades.

"Go now, my friends," he said, "bravely have we fought this night. We meet again on the morrow."

"Brinnegar, I pray you keep watch," said Roisin to her coachman.

The men departed in silence. The four people who remained stood with bowed heads around the table where Liam lay, and Eochaid, in a flat monotone, said:

"Liam is gone. He follows Sianadh and the Sulibhain boys to the grave."

Nobody moved.

Eochaid's voice cracked. "Liam, my friend, be assured, those who slew you paid a high price for the deed. Five for one, we made them pay." He turned to Ethlinn. "The morning of this very day, Liam came to me. His horse was in a lather—he himself looked half-gone, all covered with scratches and wounds. He came to me for help. It seems the great treasure-getting expedition was ill-fated and had come to a wretched end. He told me the story of its downfall. The company was but a day out of Tarv, he said, when a couple of travelers out of the city overtook them and, hailing Liam, drew him aside. Riversiders, they were. They showed him a brooch—a brooch of gold, shaped like a dragon, which belonged to Muirne.

"'Ye caught our leader's eye, Liam Bruadair,' they said to him, 'with your free spending and high living. Where does a poor lad like ye get such amounts? Our leader, he found out ye were planning a sortie, and he reckoned ye were going back for more. He wanted a share, too, and our three eastside boyos were going to get it for him, but ye betrayed our lads and stole away without giving them notice. Have ye seen your sister of late? We have. Do as we say and she will meet no harm. If we do not return to Tarv with the goods by the end of this month, she is doomed.'

"So, it appears the abductors were not the wizard's men after all," Roisin commented dully, "but some riverbank gang of thieves and slavers. Yet those watchers have an eldritch look. . . . " Her spoken thoughts petered out, overtaken by grief. Eochaid continued the story, his face showing the strain of effort.

"Liam protested that he did not know the way to the treasure's hiding place, that he himself was being shown the route. They bade him secretly blaze marks on the tree trunks at intervals along the way, so that the rest of their riverside band, who followed stealthily, would be able to find the way.

"'When your company reaches the destination,' they said, 'ye must steal the weapons of your comrades so that we may imprison them without unnecessary bloodshed. If we find them armed, we will kill them.' They assured him that no one would be injured—that they would merely fetter his friends, load up a share of the treasure, and ride away.

"'Do not try to return now to the city to find your sister,' they warned, 'for a greater part of our band rides behind, and will prevent ye. And if ye betray our purpose to your comrades, we will overpower ye all, for we have ye far outnumbered. 'Tis your choice—we be giving ye a chance to save the lives of your sister and your friends. Will ye take it?'

"And so, with the brooch as proof that Muirne was in their power, Liam had no option but to agree to their ploy. When these strangers galloped out of sight of Sianadh and the Sulibhains, Liam, in agony of mind, at first excused their visit by telling his four comrades that they had been after him for some money he owed, which he had lost at dice. But later that same day he bowed to his conscience and revealed the truth.

"Liam wanted to leave the expedition straightaway, to go back and search for Muirne—I can tell ye, he suffered something dreadful, wondering what had befallen her. Knowing that any turning back would be prevented, the company decided to keep going and to pretend to fall in with what the blackguards had demanded. Sianadh led them upstream for eleven days. Some unseelie things troubled the company from time to time—they were but minor wights, and the lads were able to deal with them using iron and salt and charms. Liam blazed marks on the trees along the way, but did it falsely, trying to mislead the followers. In fact, the company believed they had succeeded in this, for eventually the signs of pursuit disappeared. Then Sianadh turned their steps to the place he called Waterstair, but Liam prepared to return alone to rescue Muirne.

"On the night they camped before the doors of Waterstair, the brigands crept up and set upon them. They fought hard, but they had little chance against so many. Of course, the *manscathas* were treacherous. Two of them pressed blades to Sianadh's throat. 'Tell us who else knows the way to this place,' they said, 'and we will spare your life.' But he would not tell, and they threw him down with the dagger in him. One or two of the Sulibhain brothers got away into the forest, but Liam never saw them after. He slew one of the attackers with a skian, but four came after him. Wounded, he had to flee. Eleven days it had taken to ride upriver, for the way is pathless—ten it took him to ride back, even through the wilderness, and injured. In his haste he gained a day, for he scarcely rested.

"If ever I saw a man in torment, it was Liam after that *clahmor* ride. He blamed himself for the loss of those good men, and the single thought that burned in him like a flame was to rescue Muirne."

Eochaid fell to his knees and wept. "Ah, but if I had been at his side, this would never have happened! Before he left, Liam gave me a bag of gold to keep my family. He was always generous. But my stepmother is lame, a cripple, and 'tis not only gold my family needs, but my strong arms. I could not leave them. I could not go with him."

Ethlinn gestured.

"She says the guilt of it is not with you," Roisin said quietly. "Pray tell, how were you and Liam able to find Muirne?"

Swallowing his tears, the young man replied, "Liam knew . . . certain men. He never caused trouble, you understand, but he drank and diced with some who did—some whom Diarmid would never mix with. As soon as Liam told me what had happened, we went straight to them. Rumor spreads quickly among the dregs. The gossipmongers had it that two midcity damsels were being kept by Scalzo's men in an unshielded house near the river, a house with a *gilf*-room on the top floor. An unstorm was hitting the city when we reached the house, so we went straight to the top room, with the idea of covering our entrance in the confusion of ghost-shows. And we found them there. Ye know the rest."

Ethlinn raised her head. Her face was milk-gray, deeply graven. She signed to Roisin, who translated to Eochaid.

"Ethlinn wishes to know if Liam informed anyone else about the existence of the treasure cache in the cliff, this 'Waterstair.'"

"I can assure ye, my dame, he told me only, and the Sulibhain brothers who went with them to Waterstair. They are slain now and will never speak—and I have passed the knowledge on to no one."

"Did he describe how to reach the place?"

"Nay."

"So, the secret of the treasure's house resides with Imrhien and with this band of racketeers and their leader, this Scalzo. I doubt they'll broadcast the information any further, if they can help it."

Again, Ethlinn's hands flew into motion.

<<Soon Diarmid will come here. He was with us when we found Liam lying in the street. He and his party went hunting after revenge on those who did this. Diarmid and Muirne must not be told about Waterstair. They must not learn the true reason, the lawless reason, for Sianadh's expedition. Give them only part of the truth. Let them believe that a small group of racketeers stole the lasses for slaves, and that Liam heard of this and turned back, and in the course of battling for their freedom, he fell.>>

<<But why not tell Muirne?>> Bewilderment and disbelief wrapped Imrhien in a temporary cocoon against sorrow.

<<Muirne cannot keep secrets. She would surely tell Diarmid. I know my son—he is unable to restrain himself—he and his mercenary comrades would be hot for revenge upon the larger band of

eastside brigands, those who attacked Sianadh at Waterstair. Diarmid would try to wipe them out. But if Scalzo has houses in the river quarter and links to the Namarran slave-trade, his band is evidently powerful and well organized. Diarmid's crew is not equal to the task—it would take the Dainnan to break them. Besides, it would burden my children's hearts to know the part Liam played in their uncle's undoing.>>

Lightly she brushed her son's cold brow with her fingertips.

<<Diarmid must never seek this treasure. It may be that it is accursed—all who have sought it have met with evil chance. As for these things that have been spying on us—I know not whether they are Scalzo's or the wizard's, but I suspect they are connected with something else only to be guessed at, for they are unseelie and perilous. No mortal man commands the wights of eldritch—not for long.>>

Beyond the window, darkness was beginning to seep from the city. Above walls and roofs emerging in glimmering gray, the stars were fading. Far off, a rooster crowed. Another answered. The carlin turned her gaze upon Imrhien.

<<Diarmid and Muirne wish to be part of the gathering of royal forces in the west. As earlier planned, they must leave this city with you, when you travel to visit the one-eyed Daughter of the Winter Sun. I want my remaining children to be safe, far away from here. I have lost a brother and a son. . . .>>

The carlin's hands fell to her lap like dying leaves. Her dark pools of eyes gazed out beyond the walls, beyond the city, to a green hill where peppercorn trees let down the veils of their soft and dusty tresses.

It was there they brought Liam at the dawning of the day.

# 7

# THE ROAD

## Thicket and Thorn

*The sea's a road—a waterway that's rolling*
*To ev'ry far-flung country of the world.*
*Scant landmarks grid its restless, billow'd surface—*
*Chaste, lonely isles and jutting rocks, shell-pearl'd,*
*Sly reefs and green-tress'd banks at ebb of tide*
*Where sirens sing and armor'd fishes hide.*

*The sky's a road—an airy course unfathom'd,*
*And overlooking ev'ry other track.*
*Below, great lakes and mountains stand as signposts*
*For birds, and those who ride on sildron's back.*
*The cloud-wreath'd paths, the highway of the swan,*
*Are routes that boots can never tread upon.*

*All land-bound paths, from thoroughfares to byways,*
*All winding strips of rutted soil unsow'd,*
*All avenues and Seaship routes and skyways*
*Are intertwined. The universal Road—*
*One line to draw you under hill and o'er,*
*One fare to bear you homeward to your door.*

SUNG BY A TRAVELING MINSTREL

The Caermelor Road had threaded its way through farmlands, past garths and granges, crofts and byres, alongside hedged meadows where cattle pondered or shepherds with crosiers in hand followed their flocks, past pitch-roofed haystacks, ponds teeming with ducks, tilled patches of worts in leafy rows, and burgeoning fields of einkorn, emmer, and spelt where hoop-backed reapers toiled, by vineyards glutted with overflow of clammy juice and moss-trunked orchards already ravished, the last windfalls rotting on the ground, their sweet decay choired by sucking insects. It had passed from these tamed lands to rolling country, where trees stood in lines or clustered in holts and spinneys. Stained copper, auburn, xanthe, crimson, and bronze, their leaves fled down lightly in glimmering showers, to form deep-piled carpets.

Serrure's Caravan having departed long since, Chambord's now wound its way along this road: a score of covered wagons, some tarpaulin-shrouded carts piled with merchandise, a few coaches, horsemen, and patrolling outriders. Archers perched on the tailboards of wagons and on the box seats of coaches. Everything bristled with protective accoutrements—bells, red ribbons, rowan, horseshoes, ash, iron.

Across bridges the column went jingling, following the Road over little brooks bubbling like apple-cider, skirting the shoulders of hills. The pale grasses by the wayside nodded with ripe seedheads the color of rose-wine; the meadows were hazed with their pink. Filbert thickets burst with rich bounties of nuts. Overhead, the soft hue of the sky paled into mist at the margins. Dandelion-puff clouds raced past, their fleet shadows rolling like ocean waves across the land. The sun glowed as warm and golden as a ripe pumpkin. From the south, a crisp wind brought the high and lonely cries of dark birds riding the thermals effortlessly, their wings stretched to full span.

Imrhien sat beneath a wagon's canopy, wearing a widow's veil of mourning for concealment. As the wagon jolted along, rocking her with sudden lurches from side to side, she toyed with the new stone tilhal Ethlinn had given her, strung on a thong of leather about her neck. Her thoughts turned to reflections on all that had passed. Of her original quest, begun when she had left the Tower, what had she achieved? Now that her facial features had been rendered irredeemable, how could she hope that any who had known her before her amnesiac days would recognize her again? Of all the goals for which she had set out in search—a less uncomely face, her birth-name, memories—she had gained none. Yet the world was no longer such a mystery, now that its delights and terrors had been tasted. She had found true friendship. And lost it. That did not bear thinking of, and she quickly turned her thoughts elsewhere, lest the ache of despair overwhelm her.

On that morning, that terrible morn after the night of disaster, Ethlinn had taken her aside. Her hands had trembled, faltering often.

<<Imrhien, there is danger in Tarv for you now. You must leave without delay. It is only a matter of time before the leader of the eastsider racketeers, this Scalzo, finds out that Sianadh came to Tarv accompanied by one answering to your description, and deduces that you are likely to know where the treasure lies. It is well that they were not aware you possessed this knowledge while they held you prisoner, for it is certain you would have been slain. You have, now, a quest to undertake. It is for you, Imrhien, as the one who has set eyes on Waterstair and knows the way—it is for you to go to the Royal Court at Caermelor carrying news of Waterstair to the King-Emperor. The law of the Empire must be set in motion. Then these black-hearted men who, even now, with bloodstained hands, are despoiling the cache may be undone.>>

<<Do you bid me go before the King-Emperor himself? Had you not charged me with this commission, mother, I would have vowed to do so on my own. My thoughts concur with yours. Justice must be done.>>

<<Journey first to the one-eyed Daughter of Grianan. Her wisdom is deeper and stronger than my own. She may be able to restore your face or she may not, but perhaps she can shed light on

your history, and I feel that this is of great importance. You must be as well prepared as may be for your encounter with the Royal Court.>>

Gone were the plans for the coach-and-four and the servants. Their departure must be made as unapparent as possible. Thus, on the following day, the three of them—Imrhien, Muirne, and Diarmid—had taken the next road-caravan out of Gilvaris Tarv, Diarmid riding patrol with the guards while Muirne traveled in the wagon with Imrhien and a few women and children. The Ertish lass sat silent, brooding, now and then fingering the wooden, sparrow-shaped buckle carved by Eochaid, which he had given her as a parting gift.

It was more than eight hundred miles in a straight line across the breadth of Eldaraigne from Gilvaris Tarv to Caermelor, but farther by the winding Caermelor Road. Usually caravans took four weeks to complete the journey. Northward, another road led west out of Gilvaris Tarv toward Rigspindle, there to join the King's High Way running along the coast to the Royal City. The Rigspindle Road was said to be safer than its southern counterpart but was avoided by many merchants—that coastal road, with its convolutions, added too many miles.

Among the caravaners, talk was rife concerning the steady stream of unseelie creatures that, according to rumor, were passing through the countryside, heading north and east, toward the Nenian Landbridge joining Eldaraigne with Namarre—creatures that, when crossing the Caermelor Road, worked wickedness upon any travelers they encountered. Only hours before their departure, news had reached Gilvaris Tarv of a caravan making its way out of Caermelor that had been totally destroyed upon the Road. Its guards and passengers were slain or vanished, its vehicles cracked apart like ripe filberts, its merchandise and belongings strewn unheeded across the highway—wights had no use for them. Then there was doubt about the wisdom of Chambord's decision to use this Road, and some would-be travelers had turned back, but Chambord ordered the guard to be doubled and had pressed on. He had deadlines to meet.

Every night there were sounds, sometimes lights, glimpsed

ahead of the caravan or behind. Occasionally figures dwarfish or grotesque, manlike or formed like beasts, alone or in troupes, fled furtively out of the trees and across the Road. So far, none had troubled the cavalcade—the charms they carried were protection against wights of the weaker sort, although it was whispered that they had negligible effect on the mighty.

A wightish encounter, Sianadh had said once, bore little similarity to attacks by human aggressors, which were usually direct confrontations involving brute force. Wights, he had told Imrhien, had to obey their own natural laws. Just as men could not become invisible or shift their shape in the manner native to wights, so wights—save, perhaps, for the most powerful—could not move against mortals unless certain conditions were fulfilled, certain actions taken or words spoken. If fear was shown, or if a mortal should be foolish enough to let his senses be tricked, or should he break certain silences or reveal his true name or answer questions ignorantly, or if he should transgress against wights by trespass or other means, then the creatures of eldritch could strike. Then the unfortunate man might be torn apart, drained of blood, crushed, hung, or slain by any manner or means, or he might simply die of fright. Yet even then, there was a chance he might still be saved by fleetness of foot, quick-wittedness, valor, intervention from others, or pure luck.

The caravan was a week out of Gilvaris Tarv when scouts came galloping back to report that the Road ahead, passing through a narrow gap between hills, was obstructed by fallen rocks. Men on horseback or on foot were able to get through, but there was no chance for wagons and coaches. At the head of the convoy, Chambord's captain, mounted on a black gelding, raised his hand. Drivers reined in, and the caravan ground to a halt. The merchant spoke to his captain. Orders were relayed down the line.

"We are to detour off the main Road. We are to take the side road that runs through Etherian and loops back to the highway."

A ripple of excitement ran through the caravan. Not wishing to rouse Muirne from her reverie by asking questions, Imrhien clasped her hands and sat still. Beside her, two women held converse.

"Etherian! Well, I never thought to see that land. I wonder if 'tis as strange as the tales report. I should like to see those queer little folk what live there."

"I hope its entertainment makes up for the extra miles on this journey," grumbled the other.

Soon after, the lead wagons turned aside to the south. Trees thinned, then dwindled and disappeared. The sky opened out, a hemisphere of rich lapis lazuli lightly frosted with cirrocumulus in vast, sweeping bands so thin that the sun shone through like a giant dahlia.

The day wore on. The dying sun colored the uplands with glowing rose and hazed them with somber gold. Late in the afternoon, the cavalcade rounded a knoll to behold a sudden, majestic sight.

Spread out before and below them lay a massive canyon, some three miles across, slashed deeply into the surface of the land. So far away was its opposite end that it disappeared into a veil of motes and dust. The sunken floor was lost in shadow. Half a mile away on the rocky wall to the left hung a silver ribbon twined with streamers of mist. The roar of this towering cataract was lost in the vastness of the gulf its waters had created.

Yet, in sculpting this chasm, the river's power had not been enough to erode certain formations—cores of adamant, resistant to water and wind. These cores now stood by the tens of thousands, tall and spindly columns scattered throughout the canyon. Their flat tops, two hundred feet or more from their roots, were level with the gorge's lip and the surrounding countryside. It appeared like a giant forest of thin and limbless trees, all cut off at the same height.

A precipitous path hacked into the sides of this monumental cavity. As the caravan snaked its way down this road, it could be seen that dwellings existed atop the columns, angular houses of pebbles and clay, and these were linked to one another by spidery suspended bridges and attenuated ropes.

Channeled by the rocky walls, the wind here was strong, an almost palpable force. The canyon's shape scooped up its currents, forcing them to rise against the cliff walls and throwing them skyward with a plaintive whistling. On these ascending airs, dark forms hovered and swooped. They were not birds, that was plain to see by their shape—some looked like pointy triangles underwired by struts in which manlike shapes were cradled, others appeared to be large bats.

"There they are—the Clanneun," said one of the women, pointing them out to her child, "the bat-winged folk. Do not be afraid, they will not harm us."

That night the caravaners made camp by the river that flowed through Etherian, lighting their fires and setting guards to watch. Darkness fell swiftly in the depths, and the singing of the silver waters, fed by a thousand filaments down the cliffs, rang louder.

From the conversation of the other passengers, Imrhien gleaned that the Clanneun, being diminutive of stature and possessing membranes attached between arms and body, could stretch out their arms to glide for short distances, like bats and flying foxes. When they needed to carry their children or other burdens, they used the kitelike contraptions or the bridges or ropes with pulleys, to traverse from column to column. It seemed they lived mainly on cliff-side vegetation and on flying insects, of which there were many in the darkling air. These they captured in fine nets strung between columns or plucked out of the air as they glided from platform to platform. They collected their water from the rain and the dew or from the tops of the cataracts. Never did they stoop to the canyon's floor, where unseelie perils sometimes lurked. Not much else was known about them. Their culture and language were their own—they did not mix with other peoples but lived apart in their strange land, neither molested nor molesting, safe in their aerial abodes.

"Do not throw stones, or loose arrows," came the orders. "Leave the Clanneun to themselves, that we may pass through their domain swiftly and in peace."

Diarmid stopped at the fire beside Imrhien's wagon to inquire politely after the welfare of his sister and her companion, then disappeared as quickly as he had arrived. He ate, slept, and worked with the other guards. His words were sparse and his appearances sparser.

The next morning they broke camp early and thus were able to cross Etherian and climb out at the other end of the canyon before the end of the day. The difficult cliff path with its hairpin bends brought the convoy up into thick and gloomy forest.

"Word is that we shall not reach the main Road again before dark," said one of the women in Imrhien's wagon. "We must soon stop in the nether fringes of Tiriendor for the night. I mislike these lonely backwoods, far from the main Road. I'd as lief be back in Etherian—queer it was, but it did have a more comfortable feeling."

Indeed, a sense of disquiet and fear emanated from the woods. Horses and hounds were restless. Children whimpered peevishly. Folk turned their heads to the north, then glanced quickly back over their shoulders. Imrhien guessed she was not alone in sensing some kind of pulling toward that direction—a leaning, as of grasses bowing beneath a northbound jet stream. The air strummed like a taut wire at breaking point.

"The glades of Tiriendor have a wightish feel," someone muttered. Someone else tried to begin a song, but the words and tune fell flat and trailed into nothing.

The caravan rumbled to a halt in the middle of the road, with the half-leafless boughs of elms trembling overhead. Wheels were chocked, horses were unharnessed, fires were lit. After rechecking their protective gear, the caravaners snugged in for the night.

Around midnight, strange knocking sounds suddenly erupted from among the trees a short way off the road. From another approach, a great, shaggy black dog, nearly the size of a calf, appeared at the verge of firelight. It stood staring at a group of guards with its large eyes like flaming coals.

Not a man spoke. They stood like propped cadavers. Their own hounds growled, hackles raised, but would not attack. One man slipped away to bring the caravan's wizard. When he came, the black dog turned and padded back into the forest.

The wizard trotted up and down on a gray palfrey, chanting incantations. A barrel-chested cockerel flapped on his gloved hand. The guards whistled tunelessly, eerily, well into the night.

The period just before dawn, which the Erts called *uhta,* brought an intense shang wind. Orders were that the caravan must stay put until it had passed over. The unstorm engendered the usual colored lights, but no tableaux.

"Nobody ever passed this way to make ghosts," said a traveler. "I am surprised there is a road at all."

"'Tis an old byroad," said her companion, "very old, made in the times when they knew how to make 'em last forever."

As soon as the last light and chime had died away, the caravaners bestirred themselves. Although gray-shadowed leaves partly concealed the sun, the knowledge of its rising cheered most people. Toward noon they struck the main Road again, now past the blocked section. From here it began to slope steadily down—more and more often it crossed bridges. The Forest of Tiriendor, however, refused to be left behind and crowded as closely to the edges of the Caermelor Road as it had to the Etherian back road.

That afternoon, livid clouds swarmed in from the northeast and covered the face of the sun. The trees locked their branches together over the roadway. Shadows congested. The premonition of danger that had begun the night before now intensified. Muirne sat beside Imrhien on the wagon's tailboard, her eyes darting from right to left. She had strapped her quiver to her back, and now she drew an arrow from it, nocking it to the bowstring.

"I saw something just now, by the wayside. It ran away. I want to be ready."

Grief and loss seemed to have hardened the Ertish girl. Some of her diffidence had evaporated, and so had the antipathy she had shown to Imrhien. Grateful for the friendship that had existed between them during their time of imprisonment and knowing that after all, the wizard's patient had not been to blame for it, Muirne had come to regard her Talith companion with friendship. For her part, Imrhien respected and admired Muirne's skills in weaponry and horsemanship.

Imrhien touched her arm and pointed. <<See!>>

"What? . . . Aye, I saw. It was another like the first. They move quicklike." She narrowed her eyes. "Nasty little *skeerdas,* I'll warrant."

Diarmid cantered past.

"Be aware, Muirne," he called. She waved acknowledgment.

"'Tis curious for wights to be sticking out their noses so much in daylight hours," she mused, watching her brother ride on down the line. "Their glorytime be the night. Either there be something after chasing them, or they simply be about in great numbers. Or both. No matter—the guards say we shall be clear of these woods by nightfall."

As she spoke, a commotion erupted from up ahead, a splintering crash and the neighing of frightened horses, shouting, the dire clash of iron. Some guards sped past, others held to their stations in case this was a planned diversion, the tactics of ambush.

"The second wagon has gone down in a rut," called a voice. "The axle is broken. None of the others can get past."

The disabled cart was past mending. Its contents had to be distributed among the other wains before they could go forward, and the detritus cleared from the Road. This caused a delay, which meant that the caravan was still plodding among the trees when darkness gathered. Greenish phosphorescence winked on all sides, misleading the eye. Horses blundered off the roadside and into tree trunks invisible in the murk.

Orders were shouted.

"Halt and make camp on the Road."

Once again the drivers stationed the line of wagons, coaches, and carts along the middle of the Road. The horses were taken out of the shafts and tethered alongside. Campfires burned rosy between the wains, chasing away the shadows for a few feet around. Beyond these globes of light the silent darkness pressed heavily, a wall. Guards moved along the camp's perimeters. After the evening meal, some caravaners lay wakeful within their wagons, others sat by the fires, speaking in hushed tones. Save for the random jingling of harness and the crunch of boots, all was quiet; no hunting owls or melancholy night-birds cried.

Seated in their customary place on the wagon's tailboard, Imrhien and Muirne stared into the profound shadows interlaced between the trees.

"Mother of Warriors, save us," Muirne whispered. "Last night was bad enough. I'll not sleep this night. This has the feel of an ambush."

They stoked up the fires and, with the cold certainty of doom, kept vigil.

The encounters began at midnight.

It was very dark. In the total silence, not a whisper or a sigh could be heard. Eventually, somewhere in the deeps of the Forest of Tiriendor, a wind went through, rustling the leaves like the sough of the ocean. And then the firelight lit up a pearly Something coming down the Road. It was not fog. Alive, woolly, like a cloud or a wet blanket, with a terrible cold and a stale smell, it slid up and all over the wagons, the carts, the coaches, the horses, the hounds, the caravaners, in every nook and cranny, and was gone, rolling and bowling and stretching out and in, down the Road.

Nerveless, aghast, the caravaners leaned together in a lethargy bequeathed by shock.

Shortly thereafter, sounds of bubbling laughter and cheerful conversation flew out from the trees like a flock of brilliant birds. Alerted, shaken to their senses, the guards drew out their blades, the ringing rasp of their steel cutting briefly across the darkness. The other travelers stiffened, bracing themselves, grasping their charms, and muttering incantations. Lights shone out from between the trees, accompanied by strains of music and snatches of song. The rhythm of the tune was so rapid, the cadences so lilting and compellingly harmonious, that those who heard it felt their toes twitch in their shoes, tapped their fingers in spite of their dread, and quickened to the beat. There came into view, where the lights shone forth, a large circle of dancers—charming young damsels, it seemed, skipping with grace and delighted abandon, laughing, singing, breathless in their exuberance. Their filmy robes flew about them like banners of mist, green, gold, and silver; their hair was caught with sparkling flowers; and each face was comelier than the next.

"An old trick of the baobhansith," murmured Muirne. "All folk know of it, and none would be foolish enough to fall."

But they were oh, so guileless, those damsels—so lighthearted and innocent, the music utterly enticing, the movements of the dance thoroughly alluring. A thrill, akin to the exhilaration of shang yet not it, roused in the pale-haired watcher. Against all reason, it seemed that what she desired urgently in that instant was for Diarmid to come galloping up, so that she could jump up behind him, her arms about his waist; then they two would ride to join the circle, escaping the fear and dreariness of the stolid wagons.

Uproar broke out farther down the line.

A report rippled down the column. One of the younger guards had slipped into the forest before he could be stopped—for a better look, he had said over his shoulder as he departed—not to enter the circle, oh no, he was no fool—but just to see the pretty creatures at closer range. Knowing too well what fate awaited the bedazzled youth, two of his comrades had plunged in after him. The captain had issued orders that on pain of flogging, no more should leave the Road, but it was too late for the three. All the caravaners could see them clearly, dancing in the lighted circle, their feet scarcely touching the ground, whirling their delectable partners in time to the piped reel. They were grinning like death's-heads.

"See how they laugh," said someone in horrified fascination. "The baobhansith have done nothing to them."

"Yet," added another.

Stung to a restlessness of yearning by the music, Muirne's companion sprang down and walked, barely noticed, up the line. The attention of the caravaners was directed outward.

Something moved in from the side of the Road to where two guards were standing. Instinctively Imrhien shrank back into shadow. She saw a shining of wet leaves after rain, a moonbeam—it was not one of the caravan women approaching. Such loveliness was never of mortal ilk.

Metal pealed. The blades of the guards flashed to the ready. Stepping back a pace, and with a small gasp like the cooing of a dove, the object of their attention held out a reproachful hand, soft and white as the poisonous spathe of the arum lily.

"Do not affright me, Han! Will you not conduct me across the Road, that I may join the Dance?"

"Hypericum, salt, and bread . . . ," began one of the men.

Her pale, narrow hands flew to her ears.

"Oh, sir," she sobbed, "do you take me for some wight? I had thought you a gentleman, alas. Well, then I shall try my own way if no help is to be found."

She turned away a little too quickly, but the guard who had been silent sheathed his sword and moved to her side.

"If you are no wight, what do you here?"

"Have you not seen me, Han? I am a traveler."

"I have not seen you before. But as a traveler you may not leave the Road."

"Oh, but my sisters are in the woods—how shall I reach them?" she sighed, looking at him from the corners of eyes that glinted as green as jealousy.

"Weep not. I shall help you find them. Wait for me, Greb."

The other stood uncertainly, dazed, his blade lowered and forgotten.

"But . . ."

The couple vanished among the trees. A moment later the second man followed. Unable to shout a warning that might bring back their ability to reason, Imrhien ran after them for a short distance. The tree-boles rapidly crowded in between her and the Road until, on reaching a spot where only one thin blade of firelight sliced through them, she halted. Her hair stood up. A great horror squeezed her throat, and she began to retrace her steps, but it was hard going, as if something heavy dragged at her legs, as if she were wading through the deep and treacherous mud of the fens.

At her back, a terrible scream ripped through the night.

Imrhien regained the grassy verge. Muirne was there, pulling her onto the Road.

"*Daruhshie!* What be ye a-thinking of?"

A man staggered out of the trees, corpse-white, silent, shivering convulsively.

"'S death!" cried the guards. "It is Greb! What has happened, and where is Han that was with him?"

Greb collapsed into the arms of his comrades and was borne away. At that moment, the lights that had been glowing away under the trees suddenly went out and the music stopped dead, cut off in the middle of a bar. The same heavy blanket of silence descended, muffling even the caravan's bells, which hardly dared to chink.

"Come back to the wagon with me. There be more evil things abroad here than could be dreamed of in a thousand years." Muirne had firm hold of her friend's arm.

A far-off rumbling began, as of something approaching swiftly out of the east.

"A wickedness! A wickedness be coming this way!" The Ertish girl moved faster.

"Aroint us!" the folk among the caravans cried desperately. "Avaunt, avaunt!"

With a rattle of wheels, a crack of a whip, and a clatter of hooves, a macabre vehicle passed through the trees on a course parallel with the Road. It was a coach-and-four, lit by a lurid, flickering light of its own. Dimly through verdigrised windows could be discerned a trio of occupants. The driver wore a three-cornered hat.

As the rumor of the coach's passage faded, Muirne whispered:

"*Oghi ban Callanan*—there be no road for wheels out among those trees. No road at all."

Before she had finished speaking, the sound of bitter weeping began afar off. The sobs, like those of a grieving woman, were filled with despair and depthless anguish.

Dismay infected the caravaners like plague.

"It is the first cry of a weeper," they gasped. "We are surely doomed!"

The mournful cries broke out afresh, closer this time, not as loud but far more sorrowful, as if the weeper were heartbroken and could never be consoled. And again, for the last time; the lamenting seemed closer, almost in the wagon with them, and soft.

"Tethera. The third cry," said Muirne, tonelessly, unnecessarily.

Some of the horses began to jump and snort as if pricked by invisible spurs. Somehow they had worked loose from their pickets. Around and between the wagons they raced, kicking up their heels and bucking, scattering the caravaners and their fires. Soon all the horses had been contaminated by this frenzy. Imrhien thought she could spy, through the haze of dust and sparks, small dark things sitting astride their backs, grinning with malicious glee. Pointed caps adorned the riders' oversize heads, jammed between sharp, upstanding ears. Their legs were skinny and their feet grotesquely large. They appeared like caricatures of little men, parodies sketched by a humorous artist.

The caravaners' hounds set up a yelping and a barking. They leapt crazily in and out of the kicking hooves, snapping at the riders. The archers yelled that they could see nothing to shoot at. Men ran, shouting and swinging lanterns, trying to catch the frantic animals; others rang bells, crying advice and warnings. The whole caravan had betrayed itself in the throes of pandemonium.

Screaming and frothing, the wizard's palfrey hurdled the remains of a campfire and hurtled away down the Road as if whipped mercilessly, with all the other horses in fervid pursuit. Some of the men ran after them and, like the horses, were swallowed up in darkness. None returned.

Orders were passed down the line.

"Keep your lanterns lit. Stay in the wagons. Turn your clothes."

Diarmid swung himself up into his sister's wagon. The lanterns shone on his pale face. His eyes were caverns of shadow.

"What report, Diarmid?"

"No need to fear, Muirne," her brother said loudly, for the benefit of the other occupants, who craned forward to hear. "The wains are built of rowan and iron. They are solid protection as long as we stay within them. Come cock-crow, we shall go forth to find the horses. They will not have strayed far."

"In truth, Diarmid, how fare we?" said Muirne in a low voice. "Tell me softly."

Her brother hesitated, then spoke in a murmur.

"Badly, in faith, badly. Many men are lost—how many I cannot reckon. The horses—mayhap we shall never find them. My hope is that the worst is yet over."

But it was not.

To keep the silent night at bay, the caravaners continually jangled bells and droned incantations. They whistled until their lips were as dry as the wizard's rooster's throat was hoarse. For a time, this appeared to have effect—eldritch sights and sounds died away, retreated.

As though gathering their strength.

The waiting was unnerving—the total lack of any sign of activity, of any clue as to what might happen next, or when.

Fear grew steadily on all those who sheltered among the wains, a dread so heavy that they could scarcely lift their leaden hands to shake the bells or force their numbed mouths to shape the rhyming words. A groping horror came down the Road, reaching out to seize them. In every breast a great need arose, to dash away from it, away up the Road out of its clutches.

"Hold fast! Stay in your wagons!" bellowed the guards.

Several of the caravaners wrenched themselves from the grasp of their fellows and fled, gibbering, unable to endure any longer, driven from their wits by terror. Those left behind leaned from the wagons, calling in vain entreaty, straining their eyes against unrelieved darkness.

From far away reverberated the dismal "holloa" of a Hunter.

Other things issued from the dark then, and it was the signal for the onset of Chambord's Caravan's doom.

They barreled in with a wild and eldritch uproar, the pack of the Hunter. Baying and howling, the hounds rushed in, with the power of a windstorm and the fury of thunder, snorting fire. Too numerous were they to be stopped by the hail of arrows, for when one fell another two took its place. Blood lust boiled in their eyes. Bone-white glistened their coats and fangs. Their tongues and ears burned with an inner radiance, crimson as fresh gore. As for the caravaners, gone was all thought of protection, all thought of resistance—this was the final reckoning, the last grasp at survival. The hour of destruction was upon them.

Lanterns were flung away, shattering like broken flowers on the Road. The night was filled with the deafening howl of the pack, which drowned the noises of flight—the crashes, the running feet, the appalling cries, the bloody rendings.

When pallid dawn glimmered reluctantly, its light washed down over a strange scene. Twenty-eight abandoned vehicles stood in a row. About them, nothing moved. Nothing at all.

* * *

When the tumult of the hounds had first reached the ears of Imrhien and her two friends, Diarmid, grim-faced, had reacted swiftly, saying, "That sound—'tis either the Wild Hunt or the Dando Dogs. Either way, the end is nigh. These we cannot withstand. Now 'tis time to fly or perish. Leave behind all chattels. Come."

<<The other passengers—we must help them!>>

"A man will be hard put to save his own skin." Diarmid had then raised his voice so that all might hear. "As you value your lives, fly now, for death approaches! Make your own ways—each man for himself."

Panic ensued. Imrhien had been pushed from behind and had fallen onto the Road. Picking herself up, she narrowly avoided being trampled by those who, in their heedless terror, jumped down from the wagon. By the light of the remaining lantern swinging on the wagon's side, people ran hither and thither, uncertain which direction to take, lest they run straight into the maws of the unseelie dogs. Some were knocked to the ground in the confusion. Some called out, "Avaunt!" Others yelled, "Bo Shrove!" Through this milling group they struggled, Diarmid with his sister on his right arm and Imrhien on his left. Two guards collided with them, breaking Diarmid's grip and separating the trio. In the dimness Imrhien could not find them again. Faintly through the din, she thought she heard their voices calling her name and each other's. Imagining she saw them diving headlong into the trees, she picked up her skirts and ran for her life.

There in the Forest of Tiriendor, a kind of blindness sealed her eyes, and she lost all sense of time. Eerie howls issued from all around. The flesh crawled and shivered at the back of her neck. She stumbled on, not knowing which way she was going, certain that at any moment grisly jaws would seize her. But as she lurched forward, crashing into hard objects, impeded by her garments catching and ripping on things unseen, the cries of the pack became dimmer and drew away. Eventually they faded altogether. The pursuee stopped, unable to go any farther. Exhausted, she sank to the ground and passed involuntarily into a twitching half-sleep, like animated death.

Never had morning been more welcome. Dawn, to banish the evils of night.

The light of day revealed Imrhien's surroundings to be no murky wood of gnarled and snarling trees. It was an ordinary forest, though very beautiful. She looked around in growing awe. To waken here was to waken in the heart of a great jewel shot with vermilion, amber, topaz, chartreuse, russet: the blazing hues of maples touched by Autumn's artistic gramarye. Strung between the finer twigs hung thousands of spiderwebs that, having caught the dewdrops, shimmered like starry nets, refracting the light, now winking silver, now violet.

The return of awareness brought memories of loss like a blow, with redoubled force. Now, once more, was she alone. The grieving for Sianadh that was ever present, at this time extended to embrace the entire caravan, draining her initiative and leaving a hollow emptiness. There was only one hope to cling to—that Muirne and Diarmid, or some of the others, had survived.

The dew, so eye-catching on the webs, was cold and clammy on the skin. Shivering, Imrhien moved stiffly from the red-gold drift of leaves into which she had fallen, brushing herself off with bruised and aching hands. Her aimless, panicked footsteps of the previous night had plowed a path through the forest carpet. She retraced it until it lost itself among ferns. Still she stumbled on in the same direction, hoping it would take her back to the Road. Of course, there was a strong possibility that she had been running in circles the night before and therefore might strike off in the wrong direction—parallel to the Road or even toward the heart of the Forest—but there was no way of knowing. She had to do something, to search, however despairingly—to move her limbs so that warmth would return to them. Had she been able, she would have called out a greeting to whoever might be near. For surely someone from the caravan must be within earshot. . . .

In a little glade, tall flowers glowed—crimson lilies whose cups had filled with dew. She tipped them and drank nectar-tinct water.

High above, birds twittered, cheeped, chirruped, and whistled from every branch. Oh, to put on a sildron harness, to be able to go glissanding as nobles did for sport—as, it was said, the Dainnan sometimes did. At a height of fifty to seventy-five feet, clearing the smaller vegetation and about halfway up the taller trees, glissanders would take hold of a branch and propel themselves forward to the next. Momentum carried them a long way, down in the shelter of the trees where there was little air turbulence, but if glissanders found themselves suspended helpless, stationary, with no branches nearby, they would use the ropes they carried, throwing an end to the nearest bough, then pulling themselves in, hand over hand. Sildron repelled the ground but would not, of itself, propel—no wizard had yet been able to invent a suitable bladed rotor for personal propulsion in glissanding, and the idea of it had been discarded long ago. Imrhien considered the sildron she owned, which was now sitting uselessly in a box in the valuables-coach of Chambord's Caravan. Special tools and expertise were needed to shape the metal, none of which had been available to Ethlinn's family—otherwise she would have had a flying-belt made in Gilvaris Tarv, with an andalum cover to slide over it.

A crackling of boughs over to the right arrested her musings. Something pushed through the foliage—a giant, covered in dusky fur. The bear passed by, ignoring her, and lumbered away.

Strangely heartened by this sight of a beast that was not eldritch, the girl pushed on.

At her back, the sun rode higher. From time to time there came distant sounds that might have been the barking of some creature. Not knowing whether the Road was to the right or to the left, the wanderer decided to continue heading west, merely because the original destination lay in that direction; to keep going until the Road swung around and crossed her path or until she perished from hunger or from assuaging the hunger of some other creature.

A second disturbance in the lower boughs made her heart knock. An icicle of fear lanced between her ribs. Another *lorraly* beast or some apparition of unseelie, come to finish a task?

A branch moved and a head appeared, turning to scan the surroundings. A man's head, brown-haired. She might have wept for joy, for it was Diarmid. He had not caught sight of her, apparently, and began to move away quite swiftly. Distracted, she tried to call out, but only a sigh issued from her throat. A half-formed warning floated in her thoughts but was drowned by the need to catch his attention before he disappeared.

She snatched at a dry branch and swung on it with all her might. With a resounding crack it broke off. In the instant she tumbled with the branch, Diarmid's skian flew past her ear and stuck, quivering, in the bark of the trunk. The warning, belated, formed itself clearly across her vision: *If you take him unawares, he will think you a creature of unseelie.*

An outline blocked out the leaf-framed sky, the silhouette of a man with sword upraised in both hands. As she flung up the broken bough to defend herself, he cried out in amazement.

*"Obban tesh!"* Ertish—a lapse.

His sword lowered, he helped her to her feet, gazing upon her with eager relief.

"Is Muirne with you?" His face fell when she shook her head.

"Which way did she go? Did you see her? Which way is the Road?"

His visage regained its remote and grim expression as he received her negative answers.

"I have called her name many times. . . ."

Finally he said, "There be nothing for it but to go on westward until we find her, or discover the Road, or both. Black was the day I first heard the name of Chambord."

He pulled the skian out of the tree trunk, and together they went forward.

The leather harness of an outrider fared better in harsh environments than the Autumnal traveling raiment of a wealthy city lady. Stout though the broadcloth fabric of Imrhien's outfit was, it had been pierced and rent in many places. Her jacket, kirtle, overgown, and petticoats hung in rags. Her mantle was gone, but miraculously the taltry had survived. Some of the gold coins that had been sewn into the linings had fallen out, but the small traveler's pouch that hung concealed under her ripped bodice was still safe.

It contained a key, a ruby, a sapphire, a bracelet of pearls, and an emerald. She and Muirne and Diarmid had all donned these pouches as a precaution against robbery. The remainder of their wealth lay within locked caskets inside the reinforced valuables-coach of the abandoned caravan.

"I have studied woodcraft," said Diarmid, "in readiness for the tests for admittance to the Dainnan Brotherhood. With my knowledge, we shall survive." These statements were most reassuring, and it was comforting to think of them later that day when it began to rain and the two lost wanderers sheltered under a dripping tree, their stomachs gnawed out with hunger. Diarmid stared silently out at the steady, pattering stream. Certainly he was a more taciturn companion than his boisterous uncle.

*Ah, Sianadh,* thought Imrhien, *if rain were the sky's tears, it should be weeping for him.* The steely face of the man beside her barely masked his own grief—his brother, his uncle, and now his sister had been torn from him.

When the showers tapered away, Diarmid started to dig a pit-trap in the middle of a track made by some animal, but the sticks he used to penetrate the soil kept breaking off, and he was forced to stop.

"I have not the right tools," he said.

He rubbed two more sticks together to start a fire so that they could dry their garments.

"The wood is too wet."

Imrhien helped him search for wild fruits.

"These crab-apples are not edible. They are too bitter."

That night they slept in a pile of leaves, taking turns to keep watch, huddled together for warmth. Diarmid remained stoic against the fact that his strong sense of harmony and symmetry was injured every time he was forced to glance in her direction. Despite his kenning-name "the Cockerel" among the mercenaries, which he insisted was because he was a favorite with the ladies—but which some said was more to do with the resemblance of a cockscomb to the roots of his hair—a coldness existed between them that went deeper than the chill of the flesh. To Diarmid, all folk were either friends or enemies, men or women; she properly fitted none of these categories in his eyes, and he did not know truly how to behave toward her. She would not have wished it otherwise, except that some comradeship might have been pleasant.

In the morning, Diarmid said, "Today is the fifth of Gaothmis. If we go on at this rate, we shall not reach Caermelor until early in Nethilmis."

Flagging, his companion admired his optimism.

That day he made a noose-trap with his belt and strips of broadcloth slashed from Imrhien's overgown. They waited in silent concealment for hours, but no untame thing was so obliging as to ensnare itself, save only five wine-red leaves. The sight of them almost plucked some deep string of remembrance in the inner core of Imrhien, but at the last, it failed. She retrieved the belt and makeshift rope, and they went on.

"Hunting and trapping wastes time. We shall gather as we go."

The ache in Imrhien's stomach felt familiar. *Should I ever regain civilization, I shall learn how to survive comfortably when forced to be far from it.* Reality was so different from the tales heard in the Tower kitchens. Fictional wanderers always discovered food with ease along the way, fruit and berries dropped into their hands; no matter what the season, they habitually slept on the ground without suffering from damp and dying of cold. All utter myths.

Finding deep brakes of hazel seemed a stroke of good fortune. Eagerly they began to raid them for ripe nuts that lay scattered on the ground. The thicket gave a frantic heave and exploded. Its wild heart burst out, wearing a malevolent face, and the face shrieked:

Gin tha' steal or gin tha' beg,  
Tha'll get no cobs from Churnmilk Peg.

A green-skinned, ragged, haggard crone *grew* out appallingly at the marauders. She careered forth like some preposterous weed, brandishing a knopped hazel-club in a knobbled hand. Her sly, upswept eyes were the shape of narrow leaves and as hard and brown as hazelnuts. She had a furfuraceous chin, a parasitical gall of a nose.

* * *

Peg shall beat tha' if tha' stay—
Nut thieves, nut thieves, go away!

Her rictus of a grin exposed lichened teeth, but Diarmid stood his ground. The guardian wight ground her teeth and lifted her hands. Splintery slivers of fingernails extruded like thorns from her sticklike fingers. Confronted with this evidence of vegetable malignity, Diarmid revised his thoughts and stepped back.

"You wicked old thing—have your way, then."

Hastening from the hazel brakes, the wayfarers continued on their way. Sounds of rhythmic churning came grinding from out of the wight-protected thicket, receding as distance increased.

"Not a powerful wight, but too much like an old woman in looks. I never strike women."

<<Much like an old woman, but not much of a poet.>>

Stone as usual, Diarmid did not smile.

They went hungry on that second day, and the morning of the third showed every sign that their plight would be no different. Furthermore, the night had been cold—so cold that the wayfarers, in their damp garments, had hardly slept. With chattering teeth they had walked to and fro during most of the dark hours, too sleepy even to keep a proper watch for peril.

But as they plodded through that morning under a misty roof of leaves, Imrhien knew that they could not continue much longer in this manner. It had been different when she'd traveled with Sianadh—then it had been high Summer. Now the seasons had turned, bringing the danger of perishing from exposure. Cold and hungry, she desired only to lie down and sleep. Stubbornness and pride drove her on.

Although lack of nourishment made them light-headed and scattered their wits, it did not dull their senses. If anything, it sharpened them, so that when the fragrance drifted to their nostrils it seemed the most piquant and mouthwatering scent they had ever inhaled. Their wits assembled themselves promptly. Simultaneously, the walkers moved in the direction from which allurement drifted.

"It might be a trap. Keep watch in case we are surrounded. Have you the self-bored stone tilhal my mother gave to you?"

She nodded. Self-bored stones were eagerly sought. Pierced by a central hole worn by the natural action of a flowing stream, such a charm was an invaluable asset if confronted with shape-shifters or the glamour—to look through the hole was to strip away illusion. Imrhien drew out the tilhal, in readiness.

Their senses drew them to a little sunny clearing. At its edge, they peered warily out from behind flaming leaf-curtains.

Springy turf ran down to a small, reed-fringed pool. A short distance from its mirrored surface, a pile of sticks burned on a flat stone, the flames ethereal in the sunlight, sending up a slender column of blue smoke.

Between water and fire, a man reclined on his elbow, carelessly flicking a stalk of grass. That is to say, one who looked like a man, but since humanlike form was the true shape of many eldritch wights, Imrhien could not be certain. She was not close enough to see whether there was some defect, the inevitable sign of eldritch. She held the self-bored stone to her eye. Through it he appeared unaltered.

"Dainnan!" breathed Diarmid. "He wears Dainnan gear. Not a wight, then?"

<<Maybe not.>>

"Good morrow." The stranger's voice carried clearly across the clearing: "In fellowship, come forth."

Startled, the spies glanced at one another. Diarmid nodded, squared his shoulders, and assumed the watchful demeanor of a guard. "Stay behind me." He let his right hand fall to his side, setting it lightly on his sword-hilt.

They emerged into the open and approached. The stranger did not move from his position. He smiled up at them, a dark smile that struck within Imrhien like the note of a great bell. A dazzle ran straight through her like a silver needle.

"Sit you down by the fire," he invited, "unless you prefer your teeth chattering in your heads."

In that brief glimpse, it came to Imrhien that to describe this stranger as "handsome" would be doing him an injustice. It would be as inadequate as applying the word *pretty* to a sable sky jeweled with stars, and those stars lowering their reflections like glimmering nets into a wintry sea.

Lean and angular was his face, the features chiseled, high-boned. Beneath straight eyebrows his dark eyes seemed to burn with a cold fire, piercing. His jaw was strong and clean-shaven, although brushed with rough shadow. The hair, glossy black as a raven's wing, was swept carelessly back from his brow, the front locks pulled loosely back and knotted together behind his head and falling, bound, nearly to the waist. Unfastened—she imagined—it would be a cloud of soft darkness, a cascade of shadow.

As young and yet as long-enduring as Spring he seemed to Imrhien, and all in that flash she had noted he was tall and broad of shoulder, with the hard-thewed look of a warrior. There had been no defect.

Quite the reverse.

The warmth of the fire reached out welcomingly to penetrate the chill flesh of the wanderers. They moved closer to the blaze but remained standing. Imrhien did not know if she breathed.

"Thank you," Diarmid replied guardedly, "we are but passing by. Have you seen other travelers these three days, perhaps a red-haired lady?"

"Do you enjoy giving your host a crick in the neck?"

They seated themselves.

Reaching her hands out to the flames, the girl stared fixedly at them, avoiding the stranger's eyes. The pounding of her pulse was a choir of a thousand voices, as low as the rumble of stone shifting beneath the foundations of the mountains, as high as the birth-places of the stars. Her thoughts were so vivid, she felt that they could be read easily by a blind beggar. She blushed, like the fire.

When she had first come near, she had imagined this lone traveler might be one of the ganconers, the Love-Talkers, male counterparts of the beautiful, ruthless baobhansith. Soon the tone of his comments put her mind at rest.

"Have I recently seen other persons as half-perished as you two? I cannot say that I have." He spoke in a musical baritone, his words clearly articulated.

Imrhien's mind was numb. As from a distance, she thought, *His voice is as beautiful as the rest. Surely he speaks with extraordinary power.*

"I pray you, speak more plainly," said Diarmid, bristling like a hound at bay.

"You wish me to give a direct answer, to prove I am no wight who has destroyed those whom you seek?"

"Yes."

"Then, no."

After a perplexed pause during which both Imrhien and Diarmid wondered what kind of validation his answer implied, the Ertishman parried, "What proof have *you* that *we* are human?"

"The obvious signs."

"Such as?"

"The new beard out of match with the rest—a human mistake."

Diarmid's hand flew to his red-sprouting chin. "And she?" he demanded, nettled.

"She."

Another pause. Imrhien burned in the knowledge that the dark, thoughtful gaze was bent upon her. She dared not look up.

"Lady," the voice said gently, "will you speak?"

"I speak for her. She is mute," interjected the Ertishman.

"Well, lady, is that so?"

She nodded, eyes downcast.

The stranger took a stick and raked a pile of coals heaped by the fire, uncovering four ash-coated lumps in the shape of small, flat loaves. Their savory fragrance burst out like an assault. The girl wanted to reach her hand through the translucent flames and snatch them out.

"What bakes there?" Diarmid's voice had an edge to it.

"Enough to share."

With deft precision, the Dainnan hooked the loaves out of the embers onto a waiting dish formed from a scoop of bark. Beside the bark dish lay a leaf plate holding several varieties of fruits and berries. The Dainnan took up an orange-red pomegranate and sliced off the top.

"You may not speak, but perhaps you will eat."

<<Thank you.>> Automatically she made the sign and accepted the fruit with trembling hands. He passed another to the Ertishman.

Diarmid had devoured his portion when Imrhien had scarcely begun. The presence of the stranger killed her hunger. The scooped-out pith and seeds of the pomegranate tasted sweet, but she could only nibble at them.

"Do not stint yourselves."

The famished Ertishman needed no second invitation. He reached for a loaf and broke it open, heedless of burnt fingers. Steam jumped from the pale gold dough inside, like shredded cloud.

When all the food was gone and washed down with clear water from the spring, he sighed and wiped his mouth on his sleeve.

"A noble repast. I am indebted, sir."

"Perhaps you are in my debt, but it is only your names you owe me, guests, in good courtesy."

"Captain Bruadair of Chambord's Mercenary Guards, at your service." Given with a seated bow.

By this, the giving of his family name, Imrhien knew Diarmid had put behind him any doubt about the stranger's humanity.

"This damsel, the companion of my lost sister, is called by the kenning of 'Imrhien.' And you, sir?"

"My Dainnan name is Thorn."

"You are Dainnan, yet you travel alone?"

The stranger smiled. "How much do you know of the Brotherhood? Alone, in pairs, in groups—the Dainnan travel as needs must. In my case it is expedient—one alone is often overlooked, giving him a better chance to gather information unobserved. I travel on the King-Emperor's business."

"We were journeying to Caermelor when our caravan was waylaid by unseelie wights on the Road. All folk were driven from it or destroyed."

"Wights?" the Dainnan said sharply. "What was your reckoning of their number?"

Diarmid told him.

"So many and so strong." He looked grave. "My undertaking—about which you are doubtless vexed—while royal business, is no secret. It is to measure the strength and numbers of unseelie wights pouring up from the south in this strange new tide. As it happens,

I am near the end of my mission and on my way back to Caermelor. Join me and teach me this intriguing speech of hands you have between you. I will show you how to find food."

Imrhien now noted that no rucksack was in evidence—only a bow and quiver lay nearby on the grass. The stranger journeyed lightly burdened.

"Sir, that is a skill I already possess," Diarmid said, simmering with pent-up resentment.

The Dainnan shrugged. "As it please you."

<<You do not speak for me!>>

Diarmid added hastily, "But in courtesy we will go partway, at least, in your company."

"If only in courtesy, let me assure you there is no obligation. I travel faster alone."

Thorn rose to his feet, lithe as a great cat, and kicked the fire out. Tall and straight he stood. Imrhien studied him from the corner of her eye, cataloging every detail.

He wore a shirt of fine wool with wide sleeves gathered at the shoulders and rolled up to the elbows; over this, a tunic of soft leather reaching almost to his knees and slit on both sides along the length of his thighs, to allow freedom of movement. Beneath the tunic, leather leggings. At each shoulder, the Royal Insignia was embroidered—a crown over the numeral 16 with the runes *J* and *R* on either side. Around his right forearm was wrapped a supple calfskin bracer laced with leather thongs. From a baldric swung a silver-clasped horn, white as milk, and a smaller, sun-yellow horn mounted in brass. At his belt, a water-bottle, a couple of pouches, and a coil of rope. From a weapon-belt depended a sheathed dagger and a smaller knife, as well as a short-handled ax.

He picked up a second baldric, heavily embossed, slinging it across his chest from his right shoulder. A longbow and quiver protruded from behind that shoulder now, and arrows crested with bands of green and gold, fletched with dyed goose-feathers.

"May we accompany you, in any case?" Diarmid asked, his face set, stonily trying to betray no emotion, no weakness.

"Would this arrangement please you?" This was addressed to Imrhien. Again she nodded in response to Thorn's question, again without meeting his eye. Something was knotted in her, hurting. If only she did not have to besmirch those eyes by presenting them with such a face to look at. If only she could shape-shift and become the wind, unseen to tug those strands of black hair.

Thorn picked up the cloak on which he had lain and whistled softly. A goshawk flew down to his shoulder.

"Come, then."

He strode from the clearing, and they had no heart but to follow.

Imrhien called to mind all that she had learned of the Dainnan. An elite brotherhood of warriors were they, a company of men who were more than royal bodyguards, for their role was as peacekeepers in these times, and they had been soldiers in times of war. When they were not at court they roamed throughout the lands. In Summer they lived in the open, in Winter they sometimes billeted with the people. Their leader was the famous Tamlain Conmor, Duke of Roxburgh, who was sometimes called the greatest warrior of Erith. Most youths aspired to the ranks of the Dainnan, but those who wished to join had to pass strenuous tests. The first prerequisite was expertise in Erithan historical sagas and poetry, yet this was easy compared with the famous tests of fighting skill and valor, of swiftness, agility, and fearlessness, that the Dainnan demanded. Only the cream of the candidates succeeded.

He traveled light, this Dainnan. Obviously, woodcraft stood him in good stead to survive in the wilderness. He went swiftly but with astonishing silence, causing neither twig to snap nor leaf to rustle. Although revived by the mouthfuls of food she had swallowed, Imrhien had difficulty in keeping up—her tattered skirts hampered free movement. Before her, Diarmid crashed along like a berserk bull, occasionally turning impatiently to offer her his arm—had they both always been so clumsy?

Thorn paid no heed to their noise but drew them aside now and then to reveal the secrets of the season—the shriveled, twining tendrils that must be tracked with patience as they wound through rocks to the point at which they entered the ground, indicating the presence of tubers, which he dug up with a sharpened stick; the white-barked wild fig-tree, its slender branches extending from the crevices of a rocky outcrop, bearing clusters of long, dusty green leaves and reddish orange fruit; in moist gullies, the tree-ferns with their "fiddleheads," or unopened fronds, never to be eaten without first being roasted to remove their acids.

Once, he pointed to a liquidambar tree, alone in a clearing: 150 feet of brilliant ruby, gold, and deep purple.

"What can we eat of that?" Diarmid asked.

"Nothing."

"A man cannot draw sustenance from beauty."

"I can."

Foods, medicines, dyes—all could be obtained from the wilderness, Thorn informed them in his beautiful voice, and Autumn was the richest season, in other ways as well. The gorgeous hues of the Forest of Tiriendor hung festooned on all sides like jeweled curtains. Spreading tupelos boasted bright red leaves and vivid blue fruits. The flat, fanlike sprays of the white cedars' aromatic foliage were turning from dark green to orange gold. High above, crimson glory-vines climbed rampant, sunlight shining through their stained-glass leaves.

The sun was sinking when they came to yet another rill—there had been no shortage of watercourses along the way; indeed, it seemed they had been leaping over them constantly. Along the banks of this one, among a profusion of fishbone ferns and sword-leafed irises, grew grass bushes, heavy with seed-heads.

"Panicum grass." Thorn, on bended knee, stripped the tiny seeds off the stalks. Following his example, Imrhien soon had a skirtful of seed. He held out the leather pouch for her to pour it into, then brought the fingertips of his open hand, palm facing inward, down and forward from his mouth.

He smiled, as he often did, and Imrhien imagined how that breath-stopping, white, wolf-smile no doubt made slaves of every lady of the court. So—he had already learned "Thank you" from her earlier inadvertent gesture.

"See," said Diarmid, indicating with outflung hand, "that tree is leafless, yet it bears bunches of yellow berries, like beads. Beauty that can be eaten."

"Taste them and die. Melia's berries are poison. Sometimes the most beautiful things are the most ungentle," replied the Dainnan. "And conversely."

The goshawk flew off from time to time, but always it returned.

"No jesses, no bell, no hood," Diarmid remarked, "yet surely at night the bird must be tethered?"

"Not by me."

"It is trained well. An imprint?"

"No."

When chill evening drew in, they made camp by a rocky pool formed by the streamlet. It was overhung by red-gold maples whose discarded leaves floated, suspended on its glasslike surface. They piled up dry sticks collected along the way, and Diarmid used the Dainnan's tinderbox. Flames budded along the dark twigs like luminous flowers. Beside the fire, Thorn excavated a hole a foot deep and a little more in diameter.

The Dainnan showed them how to rub the grass-seeds between their hands and let the breeze winnow the outer glumes away. He used a stone to grind the seeds into a thick paste with water in the hollow of a rock. This he poured onto the hot ashes in six small flat loaves, covering them with glowing sticks. By now the fire had burned low, forming coals. He lined the cooking pit with these, placed the washed tubers inside, and covered them with coals and warm soil. When the upper surfaces of the loaves had been toasted, he turned them over, heaped hot ashes over the top, and left them to cook through. While they waited for the baking to be completed, Diarmid and the girl roasted fiddleheads and feasted on figs. Thorn unstrung his longbow and stood rubbing it down with wax.

The goshawk watched them from the branch of a she-oak. He had caught a quail and was mantling its limp form, covering it up with the twin fans of his outspread wings. After a time he folded himself together again, stood on one leg, gripped his prey in the talons of the other, and began to thoroughly pluck the little corpse. Efficiently he tore the skin away and drove his hooked upper beak into the flesh, closed the two halves of his beak like a pair of scissors, and tugged off a bite-size chunk of bloody meat, gulping it down whole.

"Your hawk—you do not fly it?"

"Errantry does not hunt at my command, only to feed himself."

"And he comes back to you? Does not return to the wild? It is extraordinary."

Thorn made no reply. Somewhere in the dusk, crickets whirred their last memories of a lost Summer.

"Had we a vessel of clay or metal," mused Diarmid, "we might have collected the sap of maples to boil on the fire. And with your arrows, we might have brought down a squirrel or two."

"Why chase after one's supper when there is plenty to hand that does not flee? We do not starve."

"And save the steel barbs for wights, eh?"

"I prefer my hide in one piece."

"Your longbow—I have not seen its like before."

"It was made under my direction, by the Royal Bowyer to the Dainnan."

"May I see it?"

Thorn passed the bow across, and the Ertishman studied it closely.

"An unusual design," he said. "The limbs are not round, but rectangular in section."

"Yet wide enough to compensate against torque as the bow is drawn."

"Not straight-limbed—a recurve bow, with a sculptured handgrip and arrow-rest."

"Made to fit my right hand."

"This material fitted along the bow's back—what is it?"

"Laminations of horn and whalebone behind the yew. They improve performance and prevent it from breaking. It draws a hundred and forty pounds to twenty-eight inches and will send a broadhead over seventeen hundred and sixty yards."

"A land mile—good sooth! Impressive indeed. In Tarv they tell of a champion of old who could achieve nine hundred, but I thought it a mere wives' tale. I should envy to see this done."

"Maximum flight is only a measure." Thorn held up an arrow more than a cloth-yard long and squinted along the shaft to check for warping. "The effective range of this bow as a weapon is no more than two or three furlongs."

"But it must be over six feet in length—is that not overlong for a hunting bow?"

"Its height matches my own—two inches above six feet."

"Surely it must prove difficult to carry through the tangling trees."

"Its measure is a personal preference."

"I thought the Dainnan used crossbows."

"For weaponry in dense-wooded country, aye. But the longbow is lighter and more rapid in fire. In open country, archers may stand shoulder to shoulder, needing much less room than crossbowmen."

"And I note your darts are balanced with goose quills. Is it true what they say, that the arrows of the Royal Family and the Royal Attriod are fletched with the feathers of peacocks?"

"It is true."

Diarmid digested this information in silence, caressing the polished moon-crescent of the mighty bow with gentle hands. Then he said:

"How long is it, sir, since you were at Caermelor? What can you tell me of the preparations of the Royal Legions to do battle with the northern hordes, should they push down into Eldaraigne?"

Thorn seated himself between his companions with his back against a tree-bole, and stretched out his long legs toward the fire.

"I can tell you that the King-Emperor does indeed intend to send battalions northward as preparation against invasion. The Dainnan are everywhere at this time—even scouting in Namarre to pick up what information they can regarding this Namarran brigand Chieftain who is said to have arisen, who seems to have the power to unite the disparate factions of outlaws and outcasts—indeed, it is thought that he must be a wizard of great power, to draw even the fell creatures of eldritch to his aid—that, or he promises them great reward, such as the sacking of all humanity, save only his own supporters. If so, he is sadly deluded, for unseelie wights would as soon turn on him as on the rest of humankind."

"Never before in history has man been allied with the unseelie," Diarmid said gravely.

"Never."

"And are there as many as it is rumored, sir, answering to that northern call?"

"I know not the numbers of which rumor speaks. But yes, there are many. The Forest of Tiriendor was ever a favored haunt of things eldritch. One of them watches us now."

Diarmid stiffened, motionless as a stone's shadow.

"'Tis only a urisk," said Thorn, smiling, "a seelie thing. It dwells by this pool, as it has dwelled for many lives of men."

They followed his gaze across the water. The remains of the day reflected up from the mere into dusky shadows, forming an outline of a slight, goat-legged manlike creature with stubby horns protruding from his curly hair. He sat with his arms about his hairy knees, staring at his observers with a mournful look.

"They crave human company," Thorn explained dismissively, "but their appearance drives men away."

<<The Dainnan says the wight has lived here long. Does the Dainnan then know these lands well?>>

Diarmid relayed Imrhien's question. She was rewarded with Thorn's attention, which caused her heart to flop over like a gasping fish.

"I do," he said.

<<Does he know how to reach the Road?>>

"The Caermelor Road lies some two miles to the north of here," the Dainnan replied to Diarmid's translation. "Lady, do you think it would speed our journey to go that way, along a clear path? For certain, your skirts receive too much attention from bushes and briars. But the main Road holds added peril for mortals—it is a focus for unseelie spite. Besides, my work is not yet quite finished, and it takes me from the beaten track onto other roads, those that may not be so obvious at first—animal trails, watercourses, the paths of the sun and stars."

"I'll warrant the eye of a Dainnan sees many roads," said Diarmid.

After about twenty minutes, the tubers were lifted out and put on a platter of leaves to be peeled and eaten, after which the loaves were ready also. Firm and nutty, their substance was satisfying.

"If we stay south of the Road, we must pass through Mirrinor,"

Diarmid said between mouthfuls. "I fear it may be more perilous than the Road itself."

"Mirrinor, Land of Still Waters—perilous, yes, but I have passed through it before, unscathed, and intend to do so again. My business takes me there. Also, it is a land of great beauty."

After she had eaten, an irresistible drowsiness overcame Imrhien. The fire's warmth seemed to soften her very bones. With one last glance at the mossy place where the urisk remained sitting in his loneliness, she lay down on Thorn's cloak and instantly fell asleep. The last words she heard were Diarmid's—"I shall keep first watch."

Discordant sounds began the morning—shrill whistles, plaintive screams, and ear-piercing cackles. Errantry was greeting the sun. After calling, he began to preen on his perch, arranging his contour-feathers neatly with his bill. His tawny plumage was strikingly barred and mottled, his eyes gold-orange disks ringed with black, centered with darkness like twin eclipses of the sun.

A silver-clasped horn lay on its side in the grass. From its mouth spilled fat blueberries. Beside it, a rich tumble of golden-orange persimmons, their glossy leaves still attached. Two leftover loaves lay on a curl of bark, dark with wood-ash. The sun was sailing, sending diagonal shafts down through the trees. The urisk was gone, and so was Thorn, as she had known he would be. No one had woken Imrhien to bid her take a turn at keeping watch. She considered it very gentlemanly and guilt-provoking of them and went downstream to bathe. When she returned, Diarmid was sitting up, yawning.

"Fair device!" he exclaimed, his eyes alighting upon the container of blueberries. "This horn is wrought more cunningly than any I have seen." He picked it up, turning it in his hands. Berries scattered like beads of lapis lazuli. "Its aspect is antique," he murmured to himself, "yet it is as unblemished as if newly made. Such curious and exquisite craftsmanship! Methinks this is some family heirloom, perhaps fashioned during the Era of Glory."

After he and Imrhien had broken their fast, Thorn returned. He looked unweary. Stepping out of the woods dressed in the subtle green brown of Dainnan garb, he seemed part of the Autumn morning, and as comely.

"Good morrow, sleepyheads. Half the day is gone—we shall have to run like the very deer to catch up with the sun."

He broke some seed-pods from boughs overhead and passed them to Diarmid, along with his knife.

"The seeds of the tallow tree have a waxy coating that lathers in water like soap. My blade is sharp enough for a close shave. The tree does not grow everywhere—pods should be carried."

Foam-faced, Diarmid leaned over the pool, trying to see his wavering reflection. He nicked his chin and cursed.

<<I can help you.>>

Imrhien took the knife from the Ertishman's hand and scraped his jaw clean. They buried the blackened remnants of the fire in the cooking pit and set off.

Motes of sunlight pelted down like sparks. Flames of trees tapered upward. The three travelers were dwarfed by these towering, heatless infernos, like tiny salamanders crawling through a blaze of glory. Always, Imrhien's thoughts dwelled on Thorn, their intensity tempered only by an ever-present thin blue trickle of grief for loss, which ebbed and flowed at random, as grief will.

For the next few days, Thorn was rarely to be seen. At one moment he would be walking beside them, matching their strides with his long legs and explaining the forthcoming section of the route or pointing out some new source of food. At the next he would be gone, melting silently into the woodland, not to return for hours. It seemed to Imrhien that when he was there, the sun smiled and the breeze laughed, and when he was gone shadows hung drearily on the trees and, in desolation, no birds sang. At times the goshawk Errantry rode at his shoulder—at other times the bird could be seen through the filigree of leaves overhead, a dark speck high up and far away. Errantry was a brilliant aerobatic flier; like all raptors, a proficient hunter.

Like jewel boxes were the tall trees of Tiriendor, like towering cones of variegated glass. Now and then a gust would release all the loose leaves simultaneously from their many tiers. Snapping free at the same instant from upper and lower ranks, they would shower down at a constant rate, a curtain of falling scraps of color. In the midst of flying leaves, Imrhien tilted back her head and gazed in awe.

Thorn said, "There is a word for that—*fallaise*."

*Would that my mouth could utter it.*

"A useful term," he said, caught ethereally in a shaft of amber light. "It might describe a fall of gauze, jewel-stitched, or a flock of bright birds descending, or a mantle of wind wafting stars, bits of a rainbow caught in a torrent, a burst of fiery sparks against the night, a thrown scattering of gems . . ."

*And glints of sunlight netted in blowing hair.*

This close, there was about him a fragrance of hyacinths, blue as the quintessence of evening, wild as the sky before a storm. Again Imrhien turned away lest he recognize the consuming intensity of her emotion.

With fierce determination, Diarmid noted everything the Dainnan taught them, taking pride in locating the fruits of the forest and delight in collecting them, to eat along the way or to be tied up in Imrhien's voluminous overskirt to be shared later. In this, at last, a tenuous link formed between Imrhien and her reluctant companion.

"Mark you the quandion tree," the Dainnan instructed as he strode along, "its red fruits and their kernels may be eaten. An infusion of the roots is used against travel weariness, decoction of the outer wood is drunk for sickness of the chest, bark shavings are soaked and the liquid applied to itches, paste of the seeds is rubbed on wounds."

Thorn often pointed out certain useful plants growing among others or certain birds of beauty in the trees. More often than not, Imrhien and Diarmid would stand puzzling at masses of seemingly undifferentiated or uninhabited foliage until the Dainnan plucked a leaf or the bird hopped along a branch. After that, they would perceive what he had indicated, and it became easier to do so as their eyes became attuned to the shapes and colors of the forest.

"Many things are hard to see unless you know how to observe.

You will learn. The Forest at first seems empty to many folk, but after a time your eyes will be drawn to plants that can give you sustenance—they will seem to leap out at you."

And that was true enough.

A fierce thunderstorm struck, but the bruising of the air had forewarned of it. Thorn was away on one of his reconnaissances. Diarmid and Imrhien sheltered together under an overhanging rock in a hillside, the Ertishman uneasy with this ungentlemanly proximity, his sense of propriety offended.

When the rain abated, Thorn appeared, dry save for some droplets caught in his hair like crystals in a web of darkness. He offered his hand to Imrhien, to help her out of the shelter. Unexpectedly, lightning seared along her arm. Thunder roared in her temples. The storm that had raged outside seemed as nothing to the one within.

At nights, by the fire, she and Diarmid demonstrated the handspeak to their mentor. An eager student, he only had to be shown each sign once and he would remember it. Then the Dainnan and the Ertishman would often fall to discussing the relative merits of archery equipment, the complexities of design, and the finer technical points.

Wights, half-glimpsed and surreptitious, snuffled through bushes or darted across their path by day and glared from beyond the circle of firelight by night—mostly trooping wights, seelie and unseelie: gray trows, tiny siofra, hyter sprites. There were deer or goats with an uncanny look of knowingness in their eyes, and some solitaries—puckles and madcaps. Once or twice the sound of spinning wheels came from somewhere beneath the roots of trees, and strange singing.

"In your wanderings, do they not trouble you, the wights?"

"I know all their tricks. All of Roxburgh's knights must know their nature and, in particular, be able to have the Last Word. It is part of the Dainnan Trial, to be well learned in eldritch lore."

"The Trial—is all they say about it true? Is it so difficult?"

"No man is accepted into the Dainnan who does not know the lore of medicinal plants and survival in the wilderness. He must know in advance the location and identity of food plants, and the seasons and conditions of their ripening. Eldritch lore, Erithan history, the Twelve Books of Rhyme, tests of skill and strength and endurance, knowing the stars' names and how to tell the time by them as well as by the sun and moon—all these are part of the Trial. I surmise 'twould be not unpleasant to you, to become one of the Brotherhood."

"Indeed, sir. Prithee tell me more—I would hear about the Nine Vows to which the Brotherhood is bound."

"Even so, my friend. As you surely know, a Dainnan warrior must never lie, and must remain faithful to his pledged word even in the face of death. He must honor and protect women. He must take no property by oppression, or fall back before nine fighting men. A Dainnan must not look for personal revenge, even if all his kindred were to be killed. But if he himself were to harm others in the course of his duty, that harm is not to be avenged on his people.

"Before any man is taken into the Dainnan, he must leap into a hole in the ground, up to his middle, with a shield and a hazel rod in his hands. Nine men stand at the distance of sixteen paces from him and hurl their spears at him all at the same time. If he is wounded by one of them, he is not thought suitable to join with the Dainnan. If he passes that trial, his hair is fastened up and he must run through the woods of Eldaraigne with the Dainnan knights following after him to try if they can wound him. Only the length of a bough is permitted between himself and themselves when they start out. If they catch up with him and inflict injury upon him, he is not allowed to join them, or if his spears have trembled in his hand, or if the twig of a tree has undone the plaiting of his hair, or if he has been sundered from something of his own flesh—a torn piece of skin or a hair caught on a twig—or if he has cracked a dry stick under his foot while running.

"After that again, he will not be accepted among the Dainnan until he has leapt over a staff the height of himself, and ducked under a barrier the height of his knee, and taken a thorn out of his foot with his fingernail, all the while running his fastest. But if he has done all these things, then he is fit to be given a name from the wild places of the land, and to join Roxburgh's knights.

"It is good wages the Dainnan get, and a great many things along with that. The Brotherhood is served by a great retinue of bards, physicians, minstrels, messengers, armorers, falconers, austringers, bowyers, cooks, door-keepers, cup-bearers, and huntsmen, besides the best serving-women in Eldaraigne, who work year-round making raiment of *dusken* at Sleeve Edhrin. But as excellent as the pay is, the hardships and the perils to be borne are greater. For it is the duty of the Brotherhood to prevent strangers and robbers from beyond the seas from entering Eldaraigne, and it is exacting work enough in doing that. An active life it is, full of delights and dangers."

When he had heard this, Diarmid fell quiet and thoughtful.

Images of the tall Dainnan would not let Imrhien sleep easily, after the first night. The knowledge that he lay on the other side of the fire was a torment that kept her wakeful despite an aching need for rest after a hard day's walking. At first she had been shy with him, afraid to meet his eyes lest she should read the familiar disgust there. But when at last she braved a glance, she witnessed no disgust, only perhaps a hint of guarded curiosity and eyes that were, more often than not, crinkled with good humor. After that she had continued to avoid his gaze lest he should read what lay in her own thoughts. How he would laugh, should he learn she was under his spell. How even Diarmid the grim-faced would laugh.

Yet, a creation such as *he,* how could he but know he was admired by all who beheld him? Surely he must be accustomed to it.

When he was not with them, she would curse herself for acting like some simpering palace courtier, some silly, smitten wench. What did she know of him? Only that he was, to the eye, like water to the desert. This was not love—it was infatuation. She would not be shy, she would not go to the opposite extreme, either, and be cold to him, a game played by many a lusty lad or lass among the Tower servants—she would play no games at all. Never had she done so, and there was no reason to begin now.

When he returned, all rational thought lay in ruins, all plans in confusion, smashed by one slow turn of his raven-black head. Then she cursed the day she had first set eyes on him, the day the worm of hopeless yearning had begun its gnawing and all promise of peace had fled forever.

The land sloped ever downward. Brooks and streams became more numerous, and after four days they came to Mirrinor.

# 8

# MIRRINOR

## Wights of Water

*We're calling. Come hither, we want you to follow*
*Down where we dance in the water-green hollow.*
*We'll sweep you to carelessness, wrap you in dreams and*
*Your land-chains we'll sever. You'll stay here forever.*

*Fair dancers, sweet voices, you gleam and you glisten.*
*Don't call me, don't beckon, I'll turn and not listen.*
*You'd trap me and drown me and wrap me with bindweed,*
*Sink deep in green hollows. Don't call me, I'll not heed.*

*Your dancing's entrancing, my feet must start gliding*
*Out to the green water where lilies are riding*
*In your arms entwine me, come take me I'm crying,*
*My breath leaves my body, I'm sinking, I'm dying.*

"THE DROWNERS," A FOLK SONG

Mirrinor—it was the Place of Islands, the Land of Still Waters, where every lake was strewn with islands and every island strewn with lakes. Indeed, it was hard to tell whether the region was mostly above water or below it. Tall snowmint trees grew profusely in Mirrinor, evergreens reflecting down deep into the sky-filled lakes, slender white pillars rising straight up, two hundred feet high, their streamers of peeling bark draping down to the ground. Festooned were the snowmints with long vertical blue-green leaves, volatile with peppermint. And leaning out from the rims of meres, golden willows wept golden tears to drift among waterlilies and rushes. Frogs loved Mirrinor, and blink-fast dragonflies in resplendent livery, and small midges and gnats and shy green water-snakes and Culicidae and strange, strange things that lived underwater and sneaked around its margins.

The travelers came to the shore of a sheet of water and looked out across its mirrored surface to the far islets.

"We cannot cross all this water," Diarmid said. "We shall have to go back to the Road. It passes through the northern fringes of this land, crossing over stout bridges."

Thorn did not reply. He had paused for an instant beside a plant growing out of the water in a dense, tidy clump. Its sturdy, erect stems each carried a heart-shaped, shiny green leaf, and the flowers, vivid blue, were packed densely on a spike growing from the base of each leaf.

*"Spargairme,"* he murmured, reaching out and lightly brushing a spike. "Pickerel weed, in the common tongue. A fair bloom of the water gardens."

There did not appear to be anywhere to go, besides along the lake's willow-lined shores, but soon Thorn was leading the way seemingly on top of the still waters, along a narrow, natural cause-way hitherto concealed: a grassy path raised just above the level of the lake. The Dainnan, surefooted, soon outstripped his followers. Imrhien had picked up her ruined skirts and was endeavoring to walk as swiftly as possible without losing her balance and falling among the swaths of silver silk spreading wide on either side. How deep were they? As deep as the sky was high? Looking down, she could see only the blue heavens, where clouds drifted. It seemed she walked between two skies. And what lurked in those depthless depths? What wights waited there with long, cold, bony fingers? At her back, Diarmid impatiently muttered something under his breath. Ahead, the Dainnan had already disappeared among the leaves of an island. Her hands being occupied, Imrhien could not speak to the Ertishman.

In the next instant there came a mighty splash, and she whirled, wide-eyed, to see that Diarmid had disappeared. Ripples spread out, sparkling, across the lake. Imrhien dropped to her knees, straining to see past the shining surface, plunging her arm in up to the shoulder, fingers outstretched, searching.

Suddenly he burst upward in an explosion of spray, gasping, shaking weeds from his hair and eyes, spitting muddy water. Then, to her astonishment, he actually stood up and waded back to the causeway. Rising to her feet, Imrhien turned and saw that Thorn had returned and come up with them.

"Some of these meres are quite shallow," he remarked, "fortunately."

*"Doch!"* cursed Diarmid. "The money-pouch slipped from my neck and is lost in the mire."

"Do not distress yourself," said Thorn.

Not wishing to increase Diarmid's discomfiture, Imrhien did not stare at his dripping hair and clothes. Instead she hastened along the causeway in Thorn's wake, hiding her amusement—Diarmid had made a comic picture, after all—and they reached the small island.

There grew paper reeds, whose tall, graceful dark green stems were topped by mop heads of pendulous threadlike foliage. Concealed among them, a boat. Carvel-built, clean-lined, and painted green, she was an exquisite little craft. Her high prow bore a modest carving of a winged toad, and a name was written on her side, but Imrhien could not decipher the runes.

"She is called *Llambigyn Y Dwr*," said Thorn, as if he could read Imrhien's thoughts, *"Waterleaper."* His marvelous smile pierced like a spear straight through her heart, only more painfully. She wondered how long she could endure.

They launched the boat and climbed aboard. Diarmid seized the oars and began to row mightily, as though the water were his foe and he were beating it. His sodden clothes stuck to his back. Seated in the bows, Imrhien snatched a glance over the mercenary's heaving shoulders, toward Thorn, standing spear-straight and relaxed at the tiller, scanning the waterscape with hawk's eyes.

As softly as breath, the goshawk Errantry glided in to alight on the carven prow, gripping the carved wooden waterleaper with his strong, scaly feet and spreading his wings to their full span for a moment before folding them. The momentum of his flight gently rocked the boat. He rode with them, his eyes shuttered by the milky translucence of his nictitating membranes. A long, vaned primary molted from his wing tip and drifted down to lie lightly on the water.

Now and then, Thorn spoke quietly to the rower. "Pull a little to port. . . . Now straight. . . . A snag there—to starboard." He scarcely needed to touch the tiller. In this manner, the little boat moved across the waters of Mirrinor with her silver wake trailing after in an ever-widening V.

A matching V of wild geese went honking by overhead, and then the boat entered a network of leafy channels among wooded islets. Here, in backwaters, the small bright green disks of duckweed floated decoratively on the water with a short root hanging from each disk. Pillarlike snowmints soared straight up on either side. Beneath the long, pale curtains of their bark the dark fronds of brake-ferns pushed up, crowding to the edge. Willow leaves floated like the torn and jaundiced pages of antique books. Dragonflies, blue and gold, skimmed over the bright yellow flowers of brass buttons spreading on the surface. Leapfrogging juvenile waterleapers kept pace with their namesake, then scampered away as though they tired of the game.

From time to time the trees parted, and through gaps between islands, wider expanses of water could be seen. Like great mirrors lying on their backs, or windows looking onto some deep, upside-down world, they imaged black swans drifting on their reflections in perfect symmetry, high above drowned cloud formations. Lying back against the lofty curve of the prow, Imrhien trailed a fingertip in the water and felt the wonder of this beauty like an ache in her bones, for all beauty was Thorn's, and all she saw seemed part of him.

The Dainnan took a turn at rowing. Diarmid stood stiffly at the tiller, determined to steer faultlessly if it became necessary. Thorn was so close now to Imrhien, an arm's length. To distract her thoughts, she turned her gaze away and looked out over the side of *Waterleaper,* as she had often gazed from the raft with Sianadh. The oars moved rhythmically, making scarcely a sound. Here, the water was very deep. She had been looking down at them for the space of several heartbeats before she saw them, as if viewed through clouded green glass, looming out of obscurity—the towers and belfries and gables of a drowned city far below. The boat glided over the dim rooftops, a bird in the city's refracted skies, and it seemed to Imrhien that from out of the depths she heard the profound tolling of a bell.

On they voyaged, and there came never a breath of wind to ruffle the surface of the lakes. All was still and calm. Later, Imrhien volunteered to take a turn at rowing, to prove she was no useless encumbrance of a passenger—and, for a space, to have Thorn at her back, lest he should come to read too much in her eyes and his kindness turn to contempt. Diarmid refused her offer, affronted, as if it were in bad taste that a girl should presume to a job he considered a man's, as if this reflected on his own ability to propel the boat. Thorn overruled him.

"Take the oars if you would, lady."

She was clumsy at first, but the skeptical glances of the Ertishman at the tiller hardened her resolve. Soon she had mastered the art of it and sent the little boat sculling along, if slowly, at least in a straight line. Long-legged insects walked over the water, held up by surface tension, and concealed frogs began a *bink-tonk* chorus, calling to mind the moss-frogs spuriously or genuinely bettering the wine in the Tower's cellars. Gelatinous whiteness gleamed from reedy inlets; great, silent rafts floated there, woven from bulrushes. Packed tightly into these rafts lay scores of semilucent eggs, each as large as a melon.

The sun began to subside in the west. Birds piped from every bush. Errantry spread his wings and sped aloft with a hushed whirr.

A sagittate flock of swans winged its way out of the south and alighted on open water. With arched necks, admiring their reflections, they paddled to an island nearby and climbed out, waddling up onto the sedges to shake themselves. It was difficult to see them under the curtains of leaves, but they appeared to cast off their feathers like cloaks. Soon a flock of dark-haired girls clustered where the swans had stood. They moved off together into the trees, the echoes of their voices wafting like music out over the water.

"Mortals also must find a roosting-place for the night," said the

Dainnan. "If you have blistered your hands to your satisfaction, lady, you may allow me to take the oars now. Captain, stay on course. We make for that craggy tor, the Isle of Findrelas."

Imrhien shipped the oars and exchanged places with Thorn. The boat rocked—he steadied her, catching her by the waist with an arm of steel and whipcord. From the points of contact between them, the jolt of energy seared her again. Her face burned, but then, whichever side of her was turned toward Thorn was always suffused with heat and the far side was always cold—it was as though he were a fire to her.

The saw-toothed crag of Findrelas was a larger island than its neighbors. *Waterleaper* made landfall on its northern shores.

After they had disembarked, Thorn tied the boat's painter to the bole of a snowmint.

"Made fast, she's more likely to be here in the morning," said Thorn, hoisting his baldric over his shoulder. "There are thieves about, over lake and under."

"Should we not haul the boat right out of the water, to make the task less easy for thieves?" asked Diarmid. "We might conceal it beneath these bushes."

"A boat like this must not be left high and dry. If she were to leave her element, her timbers would shrink. The next time her hull entered the water, it would leak."

"In sooth, sir, my knowledge lies not in nautical matters. But this may prove useful," said Diarmid, retrieving a wooden, brass-studded bailing-bucket from stowage under one of the seats. "We must make camp farther inland, away from the water's marge. Many egg-rafts lie anchored there. Culicidae Vectors will appear in great numbers at dusk."

"What you say is true," Thorn acknowledged, "but no place on Findrelas, in Mirrinor, is far from water."

They trod now on a mosaic of fallen leaves like painted tiles in tints of richest ocher, terracotta, copper, and bronze. Again Thorn led the way, stepping lightly, stopping at whiles to break off certain seed-bearing stems or leaves or strips of bark, which he tucked in a belt-pouch.

"Quandion, star boronia, the resin of snowmints—medicinal plants. And guardians against mosquitoes."

His students took careful note of the characteristics of the plants, for later identification. A campsite was found on a low rise, surrounded by russet thickets of golden abelias.

"Here shall we make our fire," said the Dainnan, "but there is much to be done first."

The fernlike foliage of the surrounding swamp cypresses had deepened to rich bronze-red at this season. Among their twisted roots, bright leaves lay like sparks smitten from Autumn's anvil. Farther from the campsite, the trees opened out on a wide pool edged with bulrushes and the ensiform leaves of water-flags. The pool was choked with blue, pink, and white waterlilies and a water-fern whose shiny leaves, spread flat on the water like four-petaled pansies, were stamped with a scalloped center of umber, bordered with bright green and limned by a thin line of scarlet.

"In the water, supper awaits," said Thorn, throwing off his tunic and shirt. "Corms of waterlilies, rhizomes of bulrushes, spores of nardue."

"That is women's work," Diarmid objected. "Lend me the bow, sir, and I will hunt for meat."

"If by 'women's work' you mean it is not dangerous," replied Thorn, "then you are mistaken. Be aware of what might well lurk beneath this pretty surface."

"I do not fear water wights. And I have been beneath Mirrinor's waters before, without trouble."

"What, then, would you hunt? Eldritch beasts cannot be eaten."

"There is *lorraly* game in Mirrinor."

"The only game worth the chase are deer—and they are not to be found here."

"I have seen otters. I am told they make good stew."

"You would hunt otters? Then let me not hinder you." Thorn thrust his unstrung longbow and quiverful of arrows into the Ertishman's hands. "Go."

Although he smiled, the Dainnan's tone, always hitherto laughing and lighthearted, had turned cold like a sudden storm, and as perilous—yet it held not anger, but contempt.

Diarmid hesitated. "I would not leave you weaponless, at the mercy of the unseelie."

"Fear not for me, my friend—I do not need weapons to survive."

"And the girl . . ."

"I have two arms."

Diarmid met the other's cool stare, then dropped his gaze.

"Tomorrow. I shall hunt tomorrow." He relinquished the longbow and arrows.

"As it please you."

Thorn pulled off his boots and was soon up to his middle in the icy water. So smooth, so perfect, was the musculature of his arms and shoulders that he seemed not to be of flesh, but carved of wood the color of honey. With the midnight shower of his hair cascading down his back to meet the water, and the quatrefoil leaves of nardue brushing his sides as he waded among the bulrushes, he appeared like some eldritch incarnation that had arisen to entrap maidens with his beauty and drown them in long, tangling weeds. For one chilling moment, the watching girl felt terror. Diarmid plunged in after the Dainnan. Her fear past, Imrhien did not linger but left them to dive for these delicacies and went off carrying Thorn's hatchet to gather firewood and bring it to the chosen site.

Her shoulders ached from the unaccustomed effort of rowing, and the oars had blistered her hands, but the wooden bailing-pail from *Waterleaper* made it easier to carry small kindling. Placing it on the ground beside her pile of wood, she caught a movement at the corner of her eye and looked up to see an unexpected sight so far away from farmlands—a white cow ambling out from a stand of golden abelias. A lovely little cow she was, with round ears, very friendly looking, but Imrhien was taking no chances. She continued chopping wood with the iron hatchet, showing no unease, feigning unconcern. The cow lowed softly, halted, and regarded her reproachfully with large and liquid eyes, its udder distinctly distended. Since it stood between her and the pool where her two companions were diving, Imrhien was considering whether to remain where she was or throw the pail at the cow and make a dash for safety, when Thorn returned with Diarmid.

"Do not keep her waiting too long," smiled the Dainnan. Dripping wet, he threw down his shirt, which was tied in a bundle and full of lumpy objects. "She is in need of milking."

<<Seelie?>>

"She is of the *Gwartheg Illyn*. Her milk will be sweet."

As soon as Imrhien put down the iron hatchet and emptied the pail of kindling, the white cow approached, as though offering herself to be milked. Imrhien had milked goats at the Tower—this was not much different. The creamy liquid jetted forth easily, and before long the pail was brimming. Meanwhile Diarmid, using his new-learned Dainnan trick of fire-making, had caused a few flames to begin to flicker among the kindling. The Dainnan carried a tinder-box, but Diarmid had entreated him to demonstrate the stick-twirling art of making fire without flint or steel and now practiced it at every opportunity. Imrhien had mastered it also.

Tentatively the girl stroked the neck of the little cow. Then a voice called, clear and loud through the twilight. A tall figure in green stood on a crag above the lake. She chanted out:

Come thou, Einion's Yellow One,<br>
Stray-horns, the Parti-colored Lake Cow,<br>
And the hornless Dodin,<br>
Arise, come home.

At the first sound of the seeming-lady's call, the white cow had pricked up her round ears and trotted off. As the song went on, other cattle emerged from various places and moved up the hill-side toward the singer, gathering to the summons. They surrounded the green lady, who formed them into ranks and led them down into the dark waters of the lake surrounding Findrelas. Only a cluster of yellow waterlilies marked the spot where they disappeared.

Diarmid, as if waking from a dream, turned his attention back to the fire, coaxing it to take hold, blowing life into it.

"The herds of Finvarna are said to have the blood of elf-bulls," he said between breaths.

Thorn had disappeared again, but soon he came back, singing in full and mellow voice:

'Tis the thrill of the chase with the wind in your hair
And the riding to hounds with a company fair
'Tis the thunder of hooves over meadow and hill,
'Tis the song of the arrow that flies to the kill,
The hunting of the stag, O! The hunting of the stag!

'Tis a soft Summer's eve with the moon in the trees
And the glimmer of stars and a rose-scented breeze
'Tis the laughter and music that ring through the night
And the feet that move swiftly in patterned delight
Dancing on the grass, O! Dancing on the grass!

"A trivial ditty to which no salt-worthy bard would admit," he concluded, "but what it lacks in poetry it amends with gaiety." He bore armfuls of vegetation, including a small, perfumed flower which he dropped in Imrhien's lap. Hunger, which had been troubling her since she recalled they had eaten nothing since dawn, abruptly disappeared in the standard manner for lovesick fools, leaving only the soreness of shoulders and the sting of blistered hands.

"Waterlily corms and bulrush rhizomes must be roasted under the coals," explained the Dainnan, seating himself by the fire. "The seeds of waterlilies are sweet—as are these, the seeds of wild ginger—eat them raw. Nardue is not so palatable. And if not prepared rightly, it starves instead of nourishing." He scooped foaming milk from the pail, using the silver-clasped horn. "This instrument is stoppered now, but there is more to its purpose than a drinking vessel." They shared the warm drink around their circle of three. Sedge corms had been harvested, too, and there were peeled waterlily stems and the very new, white shoots of the bulrush, to be eaten raw.

"Can the roots of water-iris be eaten?" Diarmid asked, noticing that Thorn had brought a handful.

"No—they have other purposes." Thorn tucked the bulbs away in a pocket of his tunic.

The goshawk returned after a long absence and went swooping after crickets. His master ignored him, intent on crushing leaves of star boronia.

"The wood of white-leaf crackles in this corner of our fire. Its ashes, mixed to a paste with water, are a treatment for blisters. Crushed leaves of star boronia, steeped, wash away soreness of the sinews. So, you both may sleep comfortably this night. The smoke of quandion leaves drives away mosquitoes and similar winged pests. Throw them on the fire when you hear the Vectors' whine. The nights are cooler in this season, which is not to their liking—yet, sensing mortal breath, the Vectors will come."

It was dark by now. The goshawk perched on a high branch, dining on something limp and ratlike. The fire crackled. Imrhien raked the cooked food out of the coals. A loud, harsh cry like the roar of an angry bull funneled out of the dark distance. Three times it came. Diarmid peered into the shadows, his hand on the longbow.

"'Tis the call of the boubrie only," said Thorn.

Diarmid's wariness dissipated. "Boubrie birds—I have seen them. They eat only sheep or cattle. It is far from its usual haunts, this one, unless it can stomach eldritch cattle."

"Mayhap it simply passes by."

The cry sounded again farther away, plaintive, anguished, and lonely in the night.

Supper finished, Diarmid and Imrhien soothed their hurts with the infusions and pastes prepared by the Dainnan, who, wilderness-hardened, needed no cures.

"Errantry shall be the nightwatchman and shall awaken us at the slightest hint of peril."

As if in reply, the hawk uttered, "Swee-swit, swee-swit." He flicked his tail, scratched the side of his head with a talon, then sat hunched on his bough, one leg tucked up inside the apron of his panel.

They stoked the fire and lay down to sleep.

It was a clear night. All over Mirrinor, frogs were chorusing. Acutely conscious of Thorn reclining nearby in idle vigor, the archetype of male beauty, Imrhien lay looking up at the stars. "The Uile" was the name she had once heard Sianadh give to that vastness: the All that cradled Aia, the boundless ocean of suns, moons, and strange worlds. Far above, the Swan constellation unfurled its wings protectively over Erith. A myriad stars above, a myriad frogs below.

The stars drew down so low that she could have reached up and touched the nearest; and the deeps of the star-filled sky were so dizzying that she might have fallen into them.

The whine of a Vector penetrated her reverie, and she sat bolt upright. Errantry gave a warning whistle and began to chatter in shrill anger. The fire was still bright—she tossed leaves on it, and pungent blue smoke billowed up. The Vector was close, and others were closing in behind the first, stretched waifs on wings of starlight. The bizarre, almost human look of them was eerie. Improbably thin were the attenuated, delicate dancer's legs—the ankles no larger in diameter than the thickness of a man's thumb, the limbs twice as long as a woman's. They were human in form, yet not in proportion. And not in movement, either, for they could not turn their heads at all; their large-eyed faces were directed straight ahead, their fragile flower's stamens of arms terminated in innocent, tiny hands. Their childlike and gossamer appearance belied their nature. They could alight on a sleeping man without waking him and insinuate their poisoned needles deep into his flesh, sucking his blood, injecting itches, fever, the parasitic worms of filaria, and slow death. Devoid of human emotions, they resembled engines of clockwork going about their business, patient, ruthless, relentless, maddening.

Where they met the smoke the Vectors moved away, but they always returned, drawn by their senses. In a circle they hung in the still airs, their piercing, high-pitched drones unceasing. More of them gathered. Diarmid threw extra leaves on the fire.

"'S death—they'll have us at any moment!"

"The leaves must last us until morning," said Thorn.

<<Unless the wind comes to blow away these vampires.>>

"Does the wind ever blow, in Mirrinor?" asked the Ertishman. He had drawn his skian and was slashing futilely at the Vectors, who gently drifted out of reach on every air current engendered by his vigorous movements.

"Rarely."

But even as Thorn spoke, the air stirred. A light breeze arose and strengthened. The Vectors were thrown together, then torn apart. They hovered as best they could on their weak aerofoils, but the breeze caught them up and carried them away, and the night became still again.

"They will return."

Diarmid and Imrhien huddled down to sleep, uneasily. The girl dozed sporadically. Whenever she opened her eyes, they were filled by the white light of stars that stippled the sky like a glimmering net thrown from one horizon to the other. Against the stars, the tall, dark figure of Thorn stood quiet and vigilant.

Sometimes she would study him covertly from under her lashes, marveling. His was not the comely regularity of the classic statue carven to the measurements of ruler and quadrant and the laws of arithmetic. His was the lawless beauty of the cloud-crowned mountain, the violent ocean, the blowing stars—a wild beauty, in that it was impossible to pin down, to describe, or to measure.

Vectors came and went in the night, always heralded by Errantry's cries. With scented smokes, Thorn warded off their blood-seeking tongues. By dawn, the quandion leaves were all gone. As were the Culicidae.

At *uhta,* in the insipid light of before-day, Imrhien raised her head. White vapors from the lakes curled through tawny abelias and tall snowmints, settling in fine droplets on their leaves. All the trees seemed to be floating free of the ground, suspended on a sea of pale cloud. Away eastward, the sun would soon be rising crimson out of the mists to paint the Autumn trees with gilded rose. Errantry began his raucous morning oratory. His master was already awake and moving about—she wondered whether he ever slept. Diarmid was beginning to stir.

A noise nearby startled them. Something huge came crashing through the golden abelias, and a head reared over the top of the bushes. Like a gigantic black waterbird it appeared—the neck was almost three feet long, the bill half as long again and hooked like an eagle's. Webbed were the feet and armed with tremendous claws. This creature gave a deafening bellow. Two small white forms shot out of the trees and across the clearing. Thorn had the longbow in his hand and an arrow nocked before the girl could blink. The great bow sang, and the first arrow was scarcely on its way before a second whined after it, and two hares tumbled on the ground, rolling over and over, a shaft through the heart of each of them. The boubrie crashed off toward the water's edge, bellowing.

"Here is your breakfast," said Thorn, retrieving the hares and slinging them on the ground beside the smoldering fire. He placed his booted foot on the still twitching carcasses and pulled out the arrows. "They were doomed. Had I not taken them, the wight would have done so."

Diarmid, with difficulty, mastered his amazement.

"I thought you did not hunt hares, Sir Longbow."

"Never did, never shall."

"Then, these are eldritch things?"

"Think you I cannot tell the difference? No. *That* was not hunting."

Thorn took the bloody arrows and went off toward the waterlily pool.

The Ertishman turned to Imrhien. "Know you how to dress these?"

She shook her head, not untruthfully. Let he who would eat them, prepare them—she would be no scullion, not anymore.

The boat was found where they had stowed it. Spiders had spun sticky, glistening webs all over its sides. As the travelers put out from shore, Thorn commented on the fact that the small island on which the swanmaidens had landed the night before was no longer to be seen. Only an empty shining sheet of water stretched there now.

"'Tis one of the floating isles," he said, "of which Mirrinor has many. Findrelas, however, has its roots firmly planted beneath the lake."

Diarmid took first turn at rowing, his hands bandaged with strips torn from Imrhien's petticoat.

Bridges linked some of the isles of Mirrinor, although they were few in number and varied in design. One or two were ancient constructions of greenish stone, moldering and crumbled. Three or four were rickety wooden pontoon-bridges, and others were simple affairs suspended across the water, attached at either end to tall trees.

"Few men ever dwelled in this region," said Thorn. "None have dwelt here for more than a few years. Only some edifices of stone remain, which once they built. Other creatures made the wooden bridges. Those builders cannot cross running water, but the waters of Mirrinor stand still."

Here in this place forsaken by mortalkind, wights and other wildlife were numerous. A pony's head broke the water's surface and regarded the occupants of the boat. Weeds were tangled like green ribbons in its mane. The waterhorse swam to a northern shore and heaved itself out, disappearing from view into a clump of trees. In the time it takes to draw one breath, its alternate shape of a rough, shaggy man came out on the other side of the thicket and trotted away into the distance. Close at hand, naked little folk no more than twelve inches high, thin and pale as the sickle moon, dived off lily pads and gamboled in the water. Startled by the boat, they fled with melodramatic cries of dismay. Mallards quacked in the reeds.

A sparse shower of rain passed over, leaving an archway of pastel colors in the skies. Thorn disconnected the bowstring and thrust it under the front opening of his shirt to keep it dry. At evening, mists arose languidly from the meres. Through them, the haunting strains of solemn music came drifting to the ears of the voyagers. A shadow loomed. The white haze thinned and drew back for a moment, revealing the mouth of a channel between two islands. On either side of this waterway tall, funereal trees stood in rows. From this gap a light barge emerged, propelled neither by oar nor by sail. Its smooth passage stenciled two glimmering furrows along the water's surface. Folds of rich cloth-of-silver were draped over the barge's sides, the hems trailing in the lake. Cradled within lay a knight, clad in armor the color of moonlight. His hands were crossed upon his breast, his helm was open. Dark were the lashes of his shuttered eyes against the pallor of his face. In the bows of this vessel a shrouded figure stood, motionless. As the barge glided on, the veils of mist closed in, hiding the vessel and muffling the haunting melody, which faded slowly into the ageless quietude of the water-world.

Diarmid broke the hush.

"By my oath, what was that which passed yonder?"

"It was *An Bata Saighdear Ban,*" said Thorn. "The Boat of the Pale Warrior."

In response to the Ertishman's puzzled frown, he added, "Forever, that vessel glides upon the waters of Mirrinor."

"Once, was that fair knight a living man?"

"No, never."

"And he who rides at the prow?"

"Neither."

Water gurgled softly beneath the timbers of *Waterleaper*'s hull.

"How long should it take to cross this place?" asked Diarmid.

"Ten days, maybe eleven."

Their course took them along channels through water-meadows luxuriant with bog-bean and sharp-flowered rush and the golden kingcups called marsh-marigolds. Their vessel swam through flooded jungles of coppiced trees: alder, willow, casuarina, and poplar, where birds, otters, and beavers flourished. A pair of lynxes came to the water's edge to drink, majestic and aloof.

At nights, viridescent lights, ringed by pale circles in the mist, bobbed beyond the flicker of the campfire. The vapors would swirl apart to reveal black waters and close in again. Then they would melt and the sky could be seen overhead, thickly encrusted with twinkling white stars like seed-pearls sewn on a velvet cloak. Sometimes Diarmid spoke softly of Muirne, trying to regain her with memories, certain—he said—that she had survived and would be found again, safe and well, certain that they would be reunited. Culicidae Vectors always came, lured by breath and warmth. They whined for blood all night at the edges of the smoke. Once, one of them hovered very close to Diarmid, and he woke to Errantry's shrill scream, lashing out instantly. The frail, venomous Vector dropped from the air, and he crushed it with a stone. It flattened out to nothing, a mere spindly outline with a crimson splash at its center. The other Culicidae droned on monotonously as though nothing had occurred, as though they cared naught for their own kind, which indeed they did not.

One bright morning, busy filling the water-bottle at a limpid spring, Imrhien caught Thorn's smile as he rinsed his knife farther downstream, and she flicked a tendril of water at him by way of reply. He returned the splash. Caught up in a sudden spontaneous joy whose founts she had not guessed, she dropped the bottle and scooped water at him with both hands. Fine droplets flew back and forth like diamonds, catching the light, in a game such as children play. They both returned to camp shaking their dripping hair. She, between shock and shame and delight, could not name her inner turmoil.

On two nights, shang winds came and blew the Vectors away, without much disturbing the surfaces of the lakes. Mirrinor then glittered gorgeously, like a million green-and-silver candelabra, like fires of burning emeralds and ice crystals.

The shoulders of the mercenary and the girl ached from daily rowing and were nightly soothed with herbal balms. At times Thorn revealed to them much lore of the wilderness. At other times he would fall silent for hours, looking out across the water-plains and myriad eyots of Mirrinor as though he saw beyond, to a place no other eyes could see. It seemed there was some secret sorrow deep within him, hidden behind the mirthful gray eyes, although no word betrayed it.

Once, after they had tied up the boat and were making their way along the shores of some islet, danger came on them from an unexpected quarter. All had seemed peaceful, until the trees began to roar and toss before a blasting wind. A huge shadow obliterated the sun's pearl, and with a scream as of seven hundred madmen, something came down at Imrhien on leather wings twenty feet in span, sharp-taloned on their leading edge. Leaves were torn from their stems with the force of its wing-beats. The long, pointed beak gaped red-gulleted, showing double rows of teeth. Small, pushed-in eyes blazed from beneath bony ridges. Feet like bunches of scythes extended to rend its prey. Then the scream rose suddenly to a new height, like a metal auger puncturing the skull, and the tyrax lurched across the sky, crashing down into the undergrowth. The feathered shaft of an arrow protruded from each eye, and the twang of a bowstring stayed on the air like a memory.

Thorn stood, straight as a spear, and watched the great reptilian flier fall. The end of the longbow in his hand rested lightly on the ground. The beast thrashed for a few moments, then stilled.

Diarmid moved warily to look at it and returned, shaking his head incredulously.

"I thought our days were numbered. Two shots, and both dead accurate."

"'Tis the best way to slay them—shafts through the eyes."

"Aye, Sir Longbow, but I have never seen such marksmanship."

"A Dainnan must be skilled in archery."

"Such skill is beyond measure. It seems that in all things you can never fail."

Thorn threw him an odd look, almost angry. "Fail? Oh yes, I have been known to fail. I have failed at crucial moments. And for that, I have paid dearly."

He slung the bow over his shoulder. Diarmid found courage to speak again.

"Shall I retrieve the arrows?"

"Leave them."

They moved off together, Imrhien glancing over her shoulder at one long wing tip of the tyrax, devoid of feathers.

"Is the bow, then, the chief weapon of the Dainnan?" Diarmid asked, intrigued.

"No."

"The sword, then, is it the sword?"

"It is not the sword."

Diarmid fell silent, at a loss.

"The finest weapon of a Dainnan is his own being," said Thorn. "His mind and body, wit and brawn. When deprived of all other weapons, he is yet able to survive and carry out his duty to the King-Emperor. Had I not been armed, I would have found another way to confound the assailant."

They moved beneath tall golden poplars standing straight as candle-flames and as radiant.

"When threatened," the Dainnan said, "a Dainnan must look to see if there is anything lying around that he may use as a weapon, such as a stone or a stick. If an attacker carries arms, he may be relieved of his weapons in many ways."

"An unarmed man against a knife-wielder? 'Tis hard to credit. . . ."

Impatiently Thorn halted and sloughed his equipment. "Draw your skian."

Readily Diarmid obliged. The two stood facing one another, poised, watchful. Around them, sun-colored leaves rained down like torn silk. A radiance burned from within them.

"Now, try to use it."

The mercenary's knife arm moved a fraction of an inch. That was all the time permitted it. Thorn's left hand grabbed it by the wrist, striking its owner on the chin with his right elbow. Diarmid's head fell back.

This happened within the space of three heartbeats: Instantly the Dainnan pushed the knife hand back and away from him, forcing his adversary to bend forward, whereupon he reached over Diarmid's shoulder and, controlling the mercenary's elbow with his chest, applied a reverse bent arm-lock, all the time pushing the knife up and away from him. A strong nudge with the knee in the pit of the stomach caused Diarmid to double over farther. Thorn pushed down on his shoulder, using the arm-lock to throw him forward and off balance, simultaneously stepping across to block Diarmid's left foot. The mercenary fell forward onto his face and left hand. Mounting pressure on his right wrist forced his fingers open—he dropped the skian. Thorn picked it up, released him, and stepped back. Diarmid stood up, breathing hard.

Five slow heartbeats passed. The Dainnan offered Diarmid the weapon.

Sheathing it, the Ertishman grimaced.

"I should like to learn that trick."

Thorn nodded. He said to Imrhien, "Women may learn also. Even those possessing no great strength may be trained to defeat an assailant using Dainnan techniques. The method turns an adversary's own strength against him."

As they traveled on together, the Ertishman's resentment gradually dissipated. He listened with close attention to the Dainnan's words. At odd moments, Thorn taught him some of the precepts of the Dainnan Brotherhood and showed him basic methods of weaponless fighting: holds and blocks, kicks, throws, and locks.

In reply to Diarmid's petitions for use of the bow, Thorn said, "No man can shoot with another's bow, any more than he can fight with another's sword. Besides, mine is made for a left-handed archer. Howbeit, if you are so zealous, I will teach you a little, and you shall practice and mayhap there will be some gain in it for you."

The Ertishman took every opportunity to accustom himself to the bow.

So near to each other were these three voyagers of different peoples—so near in presence, yet vast gulfs separated them. He was rare, this warrior of the wilderness—extraordinary. That, Imrhien knew well. Oh yes, he was of the finest.

A thought took shape.

<<Think you,>> Imrhien signed, <<that Thorn has wizards' powers of gramarye?>>

She and Diarmid, upon the sixth evening in Mirrinor, were alone together. They were helping each other to set up at an island encampment, the one to whom she alluded having disappeared on one of his forays.

Diarmid looked startled.

"Powers? I see no reason to think so. He is skilled, yea, more than any man I have met in the flesh—but not more skilled than a man may be. Yet"—he scratched his chin thoughtfully—"it might be so. Mayhap he has studied somewhat of the Nine Arts. Wizards, or part-wizards, may become Dainnan as well as any."

<<The elder race, the . . .>> She had no sign for "Faêran." <<Fair Folk, the immortals. Is it possible he is of their blood?>>

"The Fair Folk? Ha! Such immortals passed into legend long ago. Besides, like wights, they could not stand the touch of cold iron. Sir Thorn wields a steel blade, steel-barbed arrows—his belt buckle, too, I'll warrant, is of the same metal. Nay, I've no doubt he is a mortal man, but such a man—one of no ordinary ilk. A man for men to follow. Perhaps a wizard, I know not. But 'tis not couth to speak of him this way, behind his back, as it were—I will not discuss this further."

Later that same evening, the mercenary took Thorn's longbow, slung the baldric and quiver over his shoulder, and went hunting. While he was away, Imrhien remained beside the fire with the Dainnan, who had asked her to teach him more handspeak. He coaxed her to smile with his satirical portrayal of the upper classes—including his peers—by feigning to guess the signs for "duchess," "wizard," "Relayer," "Storm Chieftain," "Dainnan." If she could have laughed aloud, she would have done so. He inspired her to devise lampoons of her own—she could not remember when she had felt so free of spirit as now, delighting in his company, except for the angst of knowing it would not last.

Diarmid was long away and still had not appeared by the time Errantry flew down to his master's shoulder and interrupted the game. Early darkness had closed in. Imrhien was struck with sudden concern.

<<Our friend has not yet returned.>>

<<I search,>> the Dainnan signed. He rose to his feet. <<Remain.>>

<<I will go with you.>>

He threw her a quizzical glance, then gave a quick nod and snatched up a flaming brand from the fire to use as a torch.

By its light, Diarmid walked unlooked for from the outer darkness.

"Good morrow, *cirean mi coileach,*" said Thorn. "We are glad you could join us."

"Ah—good morning." The Ertishman stared blankly. His face was as pale as the night mist that now coiled up from the waters. "I was lost, for a time. I found my way back again," he added unnecessarily, handing the longbow and quiver to Thorn.

<<Are you hale?>>

"Aye."

He would say no more, and soon they lay down to sleep.

Magpies glorified the sunrise with their crystalline warblings. Imrhien opened her eyes in the misty morning to see Thorn standing guard by the sleeping mercenary. Diarmid lay in a twisted position, with arms outflung, as though he had met with violent death. His face was still drained of color; only the rise and fall of his chest betrayed vitality.

"In the dark hours he walked," said Thorn. "I brought him back, with some force. He would not come of his own accord. Wait by him. If he should wake and escape, sound the yellow horn, which is here at hand, unstoppered. I go now to stock the boat with provisions."

He made the hand-sign for "I return soon" and departed silently.

Diarmid slept as if he had breathed of the fumes of poppies that had lulled him into blissful unwariness. When he did awaken, it was so abruptly and noiselessly that he was gone before Imrhien noticed. Too late, a rustle of leaves alerted her. Holding the brass-mounted horn to her lips, she blew as hard as she could. A single, brazen note sounded, warm and warning, as penetrating as strong wine. As the note seeped away into the mist, she cast the instrument to the ground and ran in pursuit of Diarmid.

Following the direction in which he had headed, she soon found herself running along a shoreline bordered with ancient alders. Streamers of vapor curled slowly over the lake and twined through the black tree-stems. She saw the Ertishman standing a little way off, knee-deep in the shallow margins of the lake where slim rushes trembled. He was not alone. He was speaking earnestly to one who stood in the water before him, and that one was the essence of all Mirrinor's fairness fashioned into feminine form. Slender as reeds, pale as mist, lovely and delicate as waterlilies, was she. Emerald hair dripped down the length of her body. Her clinging gown of lettuce green was convoluted and scalloped as if it were made of watercress and eel-grass and duckweed, which perhaps it was. Slyly, shyly, she reached out to the young man, took hold of his hand and began to step backward, drawing him into the lake. The frail tissues of her emerald gown spread out and floated on the water. Without taking his eyes from her, Diarmid followed meekly. Imrhien's feet flew across the strand and splashed through the lake toward him. She closed her arms about his waist and hauled hard. It made no difference—he was too strong for her, or the watermaiden was too potent, or both. In an effort to bring him to his senses, she tugged his hair, slapped his cheek—but it seemed he was in a trance, oblivious of all she inflicted upon him.

Not so the drowner.

She bent her jade gaze on Imrhien, and her pale hand shot out, imprisoning the girl's wrist in a grip like the jaws of a steel trap. With

Diarmid, Imrhien was drawn irresistibly down. She struggled and splashed, beating at the wight with her free hand, but the water rose to their waists, to their shoulders. Long grasses sprouting from the deep mud tangled their feet, pulling them farther into the depths. Before the water closed over her head, the last sights Imrhien saw were the slanted, unblinking eyes of the drowner and her verdant tresses spreading gracefully on the surface, a cloud of fine silk threads.

Underwater, Imrhien tried vainly to kick away the gulping grasses, to wrest free of the inhuman grasp. All the while her last life's breath, and Diarmid's, bubbled up in front of their eyes like an ascent of tiny pearls. Thin strands tightened themselves about her neck. A terrible pounding began in her head, and a pain spilled like molten metal in her chest. Her own hand waved before her eyes, pale and thin like the drowner's, nerveless now as vigor failed.

Then a blade glittered suddenly, cold and bright. With a mighty heave and a gut-wrenching surge of propulsion, Imrhien was thrust up into the air and the sunlight, gasping and choking. All was confusion for a time, until her head cleared and she found herself outstretched on the shore. Beside her lay Diarmid, his body racked by spasms of coughing and retching. Kneeling on one knee close by, the Dainnan wiped his dagger clean. Water streamed from his clothes and dripped from his occult hair.

"When you have both rid yourselves of your lungs," he said, "perhaps we may resume our voyage."

Diarmid's wits returned in full immediately after this ordeal. He and Imrhien were left with no other legacy of the encounter but aching purple bruises around their wrists—the imprint of the Fideal's fingers—and thin weals about their throats. For it had been the Fideal herself, none other, who had tried to lure the man toward his doom. Of all ancient eldritch things that dwelled in water, and were the bane of men, she was one of the most feared.

"I was too easily gulled," Diarmid berated himself.

"She is powerful, the Fideal," said Thorn.

"Yet I should have known. When I first sighted her she was sitting on the surface of the lake, combing her hair. I thought her one of the Gwragedd Annwn, then doubted and came away. But I could not forget. . . ."

"Forget now."

The Ertishman looked at the Dainnan with a mixture of respect, dread, and wonder. "To slay such a wight is beyond the power of mortal men, Longbow."

"The Fideal lives."

"You did not slay her?" Diarmid was taken aback.

"Only did I sever the waterweeds that held you both submerged. With the dagger I slashed them. The Fideal is of the weeds, the weeds are of the Fideal. But she lives on, to bide in Mirrinor or perhaps to travel along the secret subterranean waterways that flow beneath Eldaraigne until she finds some other pool or tarn to haunt. During untold lives of Kings she has bided in her sequestered retreats of ooze. Mayhap she will leave them soon and, like the rest, be drawn by the Call from the North. Who knows?"

For five days more, the *Waterleaper* clove the meres of Mirrinor. Many strange sights and sounds came to the voyagers, but they avoided further peril until they reached the farthest shore. Leaving the trusty vessel beached among crab-apples and firethorns, they stepped ashore on marshy ground.

Brilliant yellow flowers peeped from acid-green turf. Ahead of them, to the west, lay a tumble of low hills that curved around in the south but dwindled in the north. The sky was softly veiled from the brink of the horizon right back across Mirrinor. A soft breeze sprang up and ran naked among the grasses.

"Mirrinor's edge," said Thorn. "From here the land begins to rise. A day's walk shall take us well into Doundelding. Once through that region, we shall be almost at the gates of Caermelor."

The sound of the city's name rang like a death knell in Imrhien's skull. Thorn would be claimed by the city, and rightfully so. He was a King-Emperor's man, one of Roxburgh's warriors. For Imrhien, then, Caermelor would mean the termination of color, passion, and light, and no matter what else it offered, their journey's end must bring days as desolate as wastelands, doomed to be scoured eternally by hungering winds.

# 9

# DOUNDELDING
## Secrets Under Stone

*Precious stones, buried bones, roots and rivers, caverns cold.*
*Clay and sand beneath the land, silver, tin, and shining gold.*
*Dig and sweat—don't forget—danger lies in sunless halls.*
*Miner brave dig your grave, far below the mountain's walls.*

"Wight Warning"

A long and winding path of stepping-stones led the travelers across the boggy ground to the foot of a hill, where it petered out among groves of stunted walnuts, ten or twelve feet tall. Through the leaves a dark fleck could be seen high above, circling. The goshawk Errantry was never far away. The ground underfoot became rough and stony.

After a time they reached the top of the hill. Round pouches of green velvet hung from the boughs of the walnuts; some had split into segments at the lower part, releasing the stonelike fruit within. Peering out through the gnarled trunks, the travelers could see across the folds and valleys of a gray and rocky region, rather barren. It was scattered with piled boulders like crouching monsters and misshapen mounds and indistinct forms like pointing fingers, which might have been towers. Yet it was not an unlovely land.

Its slopes rolled away toward a jumble of low hills, mauve-hazed, among which one mountain stood out higher than the rest. Steep was its peak, gaunt and sharply pointed like the tooth of a predator.

"There rises Thunder Mountain," said Thorn, "and its utmost pinnacle, Burnt Crag. A perilous place, especially when storms gather about the heads of the hills."

On the hilltop they stooped to gather walnuts from the ground, which they cracked with stones, stowing some in the pouches for later. Diarmid raided some of the sticky outer casings for any contents that had not yet been spilled.

"Whence came this?" He stared in surprise at the dark brown juices staining his fingers.

"The green purses of the walnut render a dye that is well-nigh indelible," Thorn explained.

Halfway down the slope a spring ran out of the hillside. They drank from it, Thorn refilled the water-bottle, and the Ertishman pointlessly washed his hands.

"I have heard tell that mining men dwell in the far west of this land," he said, shaking dry his stained fingers, "and only in the far west, for in all other regions, Doundelding is empty of human life. But it is said that the whole length of this land is riddled with hollow galleries and caves from one end to the other."

"Then it is said truly."

"It is also told that these underground tunnels and chambers are the province of many strange creatures. Should we not strike north for the Road?"

"We walk aboveground, not below it, at least, for now. At this time, the Road is most perilous of all. With the passing of unseelie forces toward the north or northeast, many more than usual are crossing it. Since it is a traffic-way for Man, their ancient enemy, the Road has become a focus for their malevolence. My knowledge is that few caravans are getting through unscathed. Here, we are south of the Road. Already many things that would wreak mischief and harm will have departed from this place."

"What summons them, sir?"

"I cannot say."

"Might we not entrap one and make it tell us—one of the petty wights?"

"That I have done—aye, and the not so petty also. Yet they themselves do not know what calls, only that they are beckoned northeast, out of their caves and pools and ruined keeps, and they must go, in troops or alone, causing harm to any Men they encounter along the way. If the migration continues, in a few months the southern lands will be empty of all but the most witless or stubborn or puny of unseelie wights."

"Then Men shall walk free of fear at last!"

"Until the malevolent tide now mustering in Namarre finally bursts its banks and spews forth, united, led by a commander."

"But surely no wights have ever submitted themselves to a leader?" questioned Diarmid. "To my knowledge, they have never, as a race, formed an alliance. The trooping wights obey the orders of their own Chieftains, the Hounds hearken to their Huntsmen—but eldritch allegiance extends no further than that."

"Yet once it did," replied Thorn, "but that erstwhile Lord of Unseelie is now no more than a shade and can never rise again. It seems that another has arisen who has mastered the wicked ones, whether they will or no. Whether wight or wizard I cannot say, but he must be a mighty one indeed."

By evening the travelers had reached a grassy dell. A silver fox ran across, paused and looked at them for an instant, then raced on into the darkness. Birches pressed in, patterning a black lacework against pale sky. Here they made camp. Lacquered beetles medallioned the ropy roots and trunks, reflecting in amber the glow of the campfire. Some way off, a crow croaked harshly.

Moonrise came early. Beside Burnt Crag the night orb came up like a copper cauldron and seemed to hang suspended over the hills, at the lip of the horizon. It was then that the music started up—thin music like the piping of reeds but backed by a rollicking beat made by rattling snares and the deep thumping thud of a bass drum—music to dance to under the face of the moon.

And, in a clearing not far from the campsite, were those who danced to it—a circle of small gray figures moving awkwardly, without grace.

Thorn laughed softly.

"Come—let us see the henkies and the trows," he said, "they might bring us joy this night."

Diarmid demurred, but Imrhien stepped out bravely beside the tall Dainnan, and they went together to join the dance.

The quaint, dwarfish folk were silhouetted against the towering shield of the rising moon, black intaglio on burnished copper. Some capered in a bounding, grotesque manner, others danced exquisitely, with an intricate though uneven step. From tales told in the Tower, Imrhien knew a little about trows and henkies. They were relatively harmless seelie wights, and their dances did not lure mortals to their deaths in the way of the bloodsucking baobhansith and others. Whether they would take offense at being spied upon was another matter.

The Dainnan did not try to conceal their approach but moved openly across the turf. Tall against the moon's flare, graceful and lithe as a wild creature, he seemed at that moment to belong more to the eldritch night than to mortalkind.

The dancers, engrossed in their fun, did not seem to notice the arrival of visitors—the pipers continued to pipe and the drummers to drum. Not as stocky as dwarves, these wights ranged in height from three to three and a half feet. Their heads were large, as were their hands and feet. Their long noses drooped at the tips, their hair hung lank, stringy, and pallid. Rather stooped was their posture, and they limped to varying degrees. Imrhien was reminded of club-footed Pod at the Tower—Pod the Henker, he had named himself. All the wights were clad in gray, rustic garb, the trow-wives with fringed shawls tied around their heads. In contrast with their simple clothing, silver glinted like starlight at their wrists and necks.

The Dainnan turned to Imrhien and swept a bow worthy of a royal courtier.

"Lady, shall you dance with me?"

She wanted to run and hide, but she stood, unable to move, ashamed. It came to her with full force how ugly she was, how unworthy. Besides, she could not dance, did not know how. But could she deny him? In an effort to purchase time, her hands formed a sign.

<<Now?>>

"It is more difficult if you wait for the music to stop. We shall not dance as they dance—the gavotte is more suited to this rhythm; do you know it? In the gavotte, couples must move together without making contact. Follow my lead."

His voice, his glance, were compelling. With hammering heart she followed him into the circle of movement. Were it some spell of the trows or some memory rekindled, suddenly dancing seemed easy. Her feet skipped almost of their own accord. She lifted her ragged skirts above her ankles and found herself stepping to the music as lightly as if her toes were not touching the ground. The knot of anxiety that had bound her now sprang apart and was thrust aside by an upwelling of joy. This sequence through which Thorn led her was a courtly dance of dignified gestures, although not slow and ponderous. It was a dance of curtsying and exchanging places with one's partner and pirouetting in a stately manner. Soon the little gray folk were imitating the two tall figures in their midst, producing their own limping version of the gavotte. Imrhien would have been inclined to smile at their antics, had her heart not been filled with terror and joy in the knowledge that she danced with Thorn.

The melody and rhythm altered, and the tempo increased. Another dance had begun as soon as the first had ended, without even a pause for the traditional courtesies. Imrhien stood aside with Thorn to see what sort of choreography the trows were practicing this time. Someone struck up energetically on a fiddle, as though he meant to saw it in half. The music moved on apace. One small trow-wife stood apart from the others, gazing at the revelry. She could be heard singing a pathetic little song to herself:

*Hey! co Cuttie an' ho! co Cuttie,*
*An' wha'ill dance wi' me? co Cuttie.*
*She luked aboot an' saw naebody,*
*Sae I'll henk awa' mesel', co Cuttie.*

The trow-wife began to dance alone, if "dance" were the correct term for it. Her limp was so pronounced that she seemed only to be staggering about, teetering on the edge of balance. *I know how she must feel,* Imrhien thought sympathetically, *scorned and outcast.*

Forcing her heart to slow its pelting, she signed:

<<It is a shame that the little trow-wife must dance alone.>>

Thorn laughed. "Who could dance with such a clod-foot?"

<<Yet it is not her fault!>> The girl was indignant now, astounded at his inclemency.

"What must be, is. Her plight is her own."

<<Have you no pity?>>

"Why submit to fetters when one might be free and joyous instead?"

<<I shall dance with her!>>

Thorn bowed with a flourish, but when he looked up she saw bemusement in his eyes. As she hastened forward, Imrhien wondered whether it was life at the court or life in the wilderness that hardened men so.

She went to the trow-wife and held out a hand. The wight turned her funny little face up to Imrhien's, then reached up a big, bony paw to rest lightly on her arm. They began to sway in time to the music and then to step, the trow-wife clumsy and the girl agile, then Imrhien pulled her into the whirling circle. New life entered into the other dancers. They bounded higher and higher, giving little yips and yelps of excitement.

This was a wild, stamping dance of rural origin—there was nothing courtly about it. The girl could not copy the henkies' grotesque squatting goose-step or the trows' intricate hobbling, but it mattered not—each capered in his own manner. Partners were tossed from one to another, progressively around the ring. Faces blended into a blur, and the excited cries reached a new pitch. How long the dance went on, Imrhien could not say, but at the end she felt refreshed instead of tired, and warm with a tingling of the blood.

Thorn's white wolf-smile flashed out of the darkness. Little folk milled around their tall visitors, bowing deeply, speaking in a strange tongue. They did not appear at all irked by the presence of strangers in their midst—quite the contrary, it was evident they were delighted.

<<One more dance,>> Imrhien signed, glowing.

"One more. With one partner."

At his words, Imrhien was moved with a joy beyond understanding.

In their enthusiasm, the musicians had recruited a second fiddler to play harmonies. They danced, then, the Dainnan and the girl—so close, so very close, but never, ever touching. Neither did a lock of his hair flick her shoulder or the hem of her dress brush against his boot; that was how precisely they danced. Later, looking back on this night, Imrhien could not clearly recall the slow beauty of the inhuman harmonies or her wonder at the clear eyes that smiled down on her, only the way the wind lifted his long dark hair like spreading wings.

As they were leaving the revelry, a lone trow-boy wandered up to them, weeping sadly. He spoke in the common speech, but with a thick brogue, as though his tongue had difficulty getting around the words.

"Hae ye ony sulver, ma'am? Hae ye ony, sir, Your Lordship?"

"Go—get along to the dance," said Thorn, not ungently.

"An it please ye, they will na' tak' me back, sir! They will na' let me in. I be banished frae Trowland and condemned to wander forever among the lonesome places."

"Why were you banished?"

"Och, an' I stealed summat, sir, but I meant no harm, and it were sae bonny, all o' sulver. But it were the King's spoon, sir, the King o' the Trows. I gived it back, I did, but they'll nae let me in again, save for once a year on Littlesun Eve when I be allooed to veesit Trowland for a *peerie* start—but a' I gets is eggshells tae crack atween me teeth followed by a lunder upon me lugs and a wallop ower me back. So I wanders *wanless,* poor object!"

"But so it must be, for that's your law."

The trow-boy went away, weeping afresh.

<<Poor little fellow. The trows have indeed a stern code of honor—>>

"When it comes to themselves!" Thorn interjected. "Trows are no paragons of honesty—they will steal from other races. Yet their ethics dictate that they must never thieve anything from one of their own kind. It is a precept more far-reaching than any statute of mortal men. Laws can be made and unmade. They can be disputed by those who are bound by them. Like all wights, trows may break their code, but they are unable to disbelieve or challenge it. Their code is in their making, as natural and immutable as the laws that govern the tides and the phases of the moon, the rise and fall of the sun, and the budding of blossoms in Spring and the blossoming of frost in Winter. And trows are partial to silver," he added. "If Diarmid has not been watchful, he may find that the hunting-horn is betrayed."

They returned to the grassy dell to find that the silver-clasped horn had escaped being stolen. Diarmid related how Errantry had hurtled screaming from the trees to attack the sly gray hand that had reached down to snatch it. Frightened off, the thief had fled.

The goshawk kept vigil all through the hours of darkness, sparing the travelers the duty of taking turns at the watch, but Imrhien harbored more than a suspicion that Thorn scarcely slept and that if he did, it was only lightly. If ever she woke at night, she would see him sitting with his back to a tree, gazing up at stars thick as frost overhead, or perhaps standing outlined against their incandescent glory and looking out across the distant hills while a soft breeze lifted streamers of his hair and spread them out in a great, dark fan. Or he would not be there at all, but she would know somehow that he was not far away and that his watchful eyes would spy any danger, and that she and Diarmid were safe with him, for now. Beyond that, there was also a knowledge that under certain conditions they might not be safe with him, and that if aroused, his ire would be terrible, his retribution swift and sure. Like fire, he was a powerful ally but would be a dangerous enemy.

Often she wondered about Thorn. She had glimpsed the mote of callousness in him, born of a kind of amorality. Deeply he cared for beauty and for honor. He was kind, and he loved laughter—but he could find no sympathy for cripples or outcasts. Save for one. Then perhaps he did not consider her to be a cripple or an outcast. If not for pity, then why had he danced with her? She was not foolish enough to believe that one so proud and comely, so enamored of beauty as he, could enjoy looking upon her face—or that one accustomed to the witty repartee of courtiers and cityfolk parrying with their fine-honed words like rapiers could enjoy the company of a mute. What, then? Only that maybe it was a game to him, to play with hearts like hers and drag them on a string.

* * *

The sun rose incarnadine. Its early rays tinted a creeping Autumn mist that softened the landscape, hiding in secret rifts, smoking from secluded valleys like rows of cottage chimneys.

For breakfast there was nothing except a handful of walnuts and clear water from a rocky rill. They set out soon after waking. The sky was a sheet of bleached satin. In its luminous heights a hawk circled. Suddenly the bird folded his wings and fell out of the sky with a speed that made the air whistle through his pinions. The thump of collision was borne to the travelers from three hundred yards away. A sparse drift of feathers hung where once a pigeon had flown. The wind teased them out like the tail of a kite, scattering them across the sky. Errantry lifted on the crescents of his wings, carrying off his kill.

"Hawks dine well, but we have left the lands of plenty behind us," sighed Diarmid as they reached the crest of a long, windswept shoulder. "These lands are barren. Here I shall seek wood-pigeons, grouse, and rabbits."

"Look down there," said Thorn, indicating with a sweep of his hand. "Bunya pines and lillypilly trees grow in the valley. Upon Alderstone Edge, apple-berry vines climb over the ruins."

A ridge on the other side of the valley ran for miles, from north to south. At intervals along its top stood crumbling pele towers. Nowhere near tall enough to be Relay Stations or Interchange Turrets, they were square and stubby structures of ancient stone, in various stages of disrepair.

"I'll warrant those are the old Watchtowers of the borders," said the mercenary, "built long ago, when Doundelding was divided east from west. The borders are long since blurred and forgotten, but the Watchtowers remain. The foundations of those towers are said to delve down a long way and to be rooted in eldritch places."

"Our way lies over that ridge," said Thorn.

The going was difficult, for the ground was uneven and the grasses grew thick and tussocky. They reached the first stand of bunya pines about midmorning. The Dainnan threw down his gear, took off his boots, and began to drag strong vines off neighboring bushes. Above their heads, the bustling bunyas reared some three hundred feet into the sky, seeming to topple against a backdrop of scudding cloudlets. Their topmost boughs, like skinny outstretched arms ending in leafy hands, stirred the wind.

The Dainnan placed the dagger between his teeth and slung a vine around the nearest trunk. After knotting the rest of the creeper around his waist, he ascended without apparent effort. He would lean back against the vine, take two steps up the side of the tree, then lean in to take the pressure off the vine and simultaneously shift it farther up. By repeating these actions, he reached the heights where the huge cones grew and threw them down as he cut them. When they hit the ground, thumb-size nuts exploded out across the grass.

Once he had belayed the vine to a stout bough, Thorn passed it under one thigh and over the opposite shoulder so that it could be paid smoothly and gradually as he rappeled down.

"Bunyas are always prolific," he said, springing down to land on the grass, "but every three years they are more so. Fortunately, this happens to be one of those years."

They feasted until they could feast no more, then packed the pouches full of nuts and went on their way. Soon they encountered a sunken path winding between grassy banks. It led them to a line of stepping-stones across a stream and then up a slope scattered with lillypillies. Great, luscious bunches of fat pink berries dripped among their dark glossy leaves—these came easily to hand when the harvesters reached for them.

The little path wound uphill, toward the summit of Alderstone Edge. It was after noon by the time they reached the highest point. On the other side, the land dropped sharply away to a sparsely wooded valley pitted with craters. Huge boulders lay on their sides and in piles, some cracked open as if they had been flung carelessly by some giant hand.

"Emmyn Vale," said Thorn. "Once its slopes were fair, covered with pine and sloe and heather. Now they are bleak, the seasonal haunt of felhens and other wights."

The barren slopes of Thunder Mountain loomed closer now. To left and right, the line of ruined Watchtowers marched at wide intervals along the spine of land. The wind was strong up here and cold, galloping out of the southwest. Heavy clouds obscured the sun, darkening the landscape. They seemed to bode ill. Far off, a bird of prey, possibly Errantry, folded its wings and plummeted like a stone. A cawing of crows or rooks came creaking on the breeze.

"This is too steep," declared Diarmid, looking down. "We must find another place to descend."

The smoking clouds thickened. It was as though a shang storm were on its way, but without the sensation of fizzing in the blood. Yet no glimmering airs of gramarye came rushing to scatter powdered lights over the landscape—instead there came a lull in the susurration of the wind.

Thorn stopped and stood quite still, as if listening.

"What is it?" Diarmid presently asked.

"Dunters."

"Dunters?"

"A noise of them issues from the old towers."

Roofless, jagged, the nearest pele tower stood open to the sky, its window-holes watching.

"Walk staunchly past the tower walls," said Thorn. "Do not stop or show fear."

Imrhien began to hear a constant noise, which swelled as they approached the ruin—a noise like the beating of flax or the grinding of barley in a hollow stone quern. Closer to the tower, it grew so loud that it was almost unbearable. It vibrated in Imrhien's ears and fibrillated in the cavities of her skull, it trembled in the very ground and the bones of her feet. As they drew level with the ruins, the grinding stopped abruptly.

A thick dough of silence fell, heavy and deafening.

<<Keep walking.>> This she signaled to Diarmid, who had hesitated, his hand on his skian. They moved on.

The pele tower stood still and quiet. There was no sign of movement from its blank windows and overgrown walls, except for the nodding tendrils of apple-berry vines. Whatever lurked inside made no sound, but Imrhien sensed a watching and a waiting so intense that it suffused the surrounding airs with a tension as brittle as dry leaves. As soon as the travelers had moved a few paces past the building, the noise broke out anew, as loud and constant as before. The pressure abated. The girl breathed a shaky sigh of relief.

With distance, the dunters' grinding gradually died away.

"What do they look like, the dunters?" asked the Ertishman.

The Dainnan raised one eyebrow. "No mortal has ever seen them."

The ground beneath their feet began to drop away rapidly toward the valley floor.

"Can you climb down here, lady?" Thorn asked Imrhien. She shook her head doubtfully. The slope was precipitous. Hampered by ragged skirts, she was uncertain whether she could negotiate it.

"Then we shall go farther on this downward path. We shall bear north along the land's spine and make for that squat tower yonder. If I read its shape aright, that is the Twenty-ninth Keep. Once past it, the fall to the lowlands on the west side is gentle—you shall have no trouble there. But if we must pass through the Twenty-ninth Keep, beware. For years a redcap was wont to skulk therein, and he maybe lurks there still. If so, then doubtless his cap is by now quite faded. In this unoccupied region it must be a good while since he colored it with redcaps' favorite dye, and he will welcome the sight of mortals."

They turned then to the north and followed the ridge top until they came to the next pele tower. The wind had risen again, and wisps of dark cloud began to move in from the southwest. Under a marbled sky, the Twenty-ninth Keep loomed, a square, buttressed fortress of verdigrised stone. At its top some crenellations still remained—perhaps even some part of its roof. Certainly the south wall, facing the travelers, had well withstood the ravages of time and tempest. Starved arrow-slits squeezed themselves between massive stones, some of which, higher up, jutted out to form slight ledges on which entrepreneurial plants had taken root. The stonework was fretted all over with vines.

The Twenty-ninth Keep straddled the narrowest part of the ridge. On either side of it the ground fell away in a sheer drop—the only way past was through.

They stopped at the doorless archway, curtained by vines that had lost most of their foliage. Only shriveled, dry leaves remained clinging and small oval fruits—apple-berries. The wind rattled the vine-stems and soughed eerily high in the chinks of broken stone. There was no other sound.

The Ertishman squinted up at a weather-blurred inscription over the entrance.

"By My Name Shall Ye Know Me," he read slowly. "Could this be some riddle?"

"No riddle," Thorn said. "Those who built the towers were wont to scrape epigrams above the doors. Such sayings are scribbled upon every border keep."

Diarmid eyed the broken threshold—a garden of weeds, strewn with rubble.

"I shall go first," he said, a little too loudly and quickly.

Drawing his skian, he stooped under the curtain of basketwork and entered. Imrhien came after, with Thorn following at her back. She saw him glance briefly over his shoulder.

The interior was gloomy and bitterly cold. Shafts of gray light emanated from places where mortar and stone had fallen away to reveal the outside world, a vista of racing sky. The vines had run rampant overhead, growing and dying over many seasons, falling in under their own weight so that they formed a dense network of desiccated, blackened sticks and yellowing tendrils. Untidy birds' nests, abandoned, decorated the walls.

The pitted floor displayed decorations of another sort—it was scattered profusely with human skulls and dismembered skeletons. These lay, pallid and stained, on top of the dark red-brown splashes that covered the floor and streaked the walls. Stepping carefully among the bones so as not to rattle them, the intruders came warily to another archway that gave on to an inner room decorated similarly to the first.

On the far side of this yawned a further opening, dark enough to be black even against the twilight of the inner chamber. A stench oozed from it, and a sense of a presence, a consciousness brooding, *knowing*.

Diarmid stepped through.

Imrhien had scarcely set foot beside him when a hoarse yell cracked the silence like an egg, and a yolk-yellow brilliance flooded their eye sockets. When their vision adjusted they made out a short, thickset old goblin with long, prominent teeth. His skinny fingers, armed with talons like eagles, were wrapped around a spitting firebrand in one hand and a pikestaff in the other. Grisly hair streamed down his shoulders. He glared at the intruders with large eyes of a fiery red color. His feet were clapped into metal boots, his domed head jammed into a dull red cap. They saw, at his back, a sooty fireplace, a chopping block, and an ax. On a stone table, a bantam rooster crouched dismally in a wicker cage.

"An Ertishman!" cried the wight. "And me cap in need o' new color! All the redder for't, carrot-beard."

Veins bulged on Diarmid's neck and temples. He thrust his chin forward, aggressively. With a few well- or ill-chosen words, the goblin had aroused the mercenary's ire. This seemed to bring out a formidable and hitherto unrecognized talent in the taciturn young man.

"Why cam' ye by my door?" The redcap brandished his pikestaff menacingly.

"It lay in my road," Diarmid replied evenly, weighing the skian in his hand and the words in his head. The wight spat contemptuously at the knife.

"Yer cold iron afears me not. I sha' fling stones upon ye."

"I'd rather you flung loaves," countered the man.

"I wish't ye were hangin' up on yonder battlement!"

"And a good ladder under me," Diarmid parried instantly.

"And the ladder for to break!"

"And for you to fall down."

The advantage was with Diarmid—he had pronounced the Last Word. The wight gnashed his teeth, fuming and stamping, at a loss for utterance. Inspiration dawned on his filthy brow like a marsh-light rising from the fens.

"I wish ye were in the sea!"

"And a good boat under me." The Ertishman remained undaunted.

"And the boat for to break!"

"And for you to be drowned."

"But I wish ye were in the lake!"

"And I swimming," said Diarmid, his zeal blazing now.

"And the water frozen."

"And the smith a-hammering at it."

"And the smith to be dead!"

"And another smith instead!"

This was a master-stroke—the Ertishman's line had rhymed with the wight's, beating it hands down. The redcap's face transmuted from scarlet to puce. His chest swelled as if it were about to burst. It was obvious that despite the apparent imminence of defeat, he was still scratching for words. Like overripe plums, his eyes popped and rolled in his head, finally alighting on his ax. Brutality was ever a ready defense for the slow-witted.

"I will hack you with my ax!"

"You'll only chop stone," said Diarmid with a sudden sidestep to show how swiftly he could react.

"I will fight ye anon."

"Aye, and not long till I defeat you."

The goblin stood stuttering, openmouthed, dribbling and dumbfounded. Vanquished.

The Ertishman could not resist this opportunity to add one final triumphant insult.

"Giff, gaff, your mouth's full of chaff."

It was too much. His malignant adversary gave a bellow of rage ending in a hysterical shriek, and the torch went out. In that last gleam, Imrhien had seen Thorn striding forward. She thought he spoke a word, but she could not be sure. As soon as the light vanished, Imrhien made for the wicker cage. She could see nothing, but her seeking hand fell upon it. She tucked it under her arm and ran for the far wall, where an exit surely must exist. Heart-stoppingly, she came up against cold, slippery stones and felt along them blindly, colliding with someone.

"'S death," swore Diarmid, "is that you, wench?"

His hand closed around her arm, propelling her sideways.

Whether it was having the Last Word that saved them, they did not stop to discuss. Moments later they pushed past a heavy drapery of foliage to emerge on the north side of the Twenty-ninth Keep. The sun was beginning to descend. Forty yards farther on, the three travelers followed its example—for here, as Thorn had indicated, the gradient was amiable. As they slithered down the slope, the bantam rooster jounced and jolted in its cage under Imrhien's arm. When they reached the valley floor, the travelers did not pause but put as much distance as possible between themselves and Alderstone Edge before nightfall.

The wind had buffeted them all the way down the ridge side, and it did not cease its gusting. They found shelter on the lee side of a stack of boulders and soon had a fire going whose vigor matched that of the turbulent airs. There they reclined in relief and great merriment.

Diarmid recounted his battle of words and the way he had triumphed He waxed eloquent in front of the responsive half of his audience of four. The cockerel, a black one with copper and green tail-feathers, sat glumly in the cage. Imrhien was loath to release it until they were farther from the Edge. Errantry sat with hunched shoulders, eyeing the rooster with utmost contempt. With a slight spasm, he regurgitated a pellet of unrecognizable parts of rodents.

"You should have seen his face, Longbow!" Diarmid enthused. "And you might have heard the clashing of those teeth from miles away! I can only surmise that his previous victims panicked at the sight of him and could not collect their thoughts, for 'tis not hard to outspeak one with the wit of a flea. Besides, I am practiced at that sparring—when I was a lad, I used to trade words with my—with my uncle." He sobered at his own words, remembering.

<<Once I heard Sianadh word-fighting against some wicked men. He won.>> Imrhien, too, remembered.

"He always won. Ertishmen are famous for their skill with words; Finvarna is the birthplace of most of the greatest bards. But the Bear could outspar even his own countrymen."

"This man you speak of is lost to you?" asked Thorn, regarding their faces gravely.

Diarmid nodded, his heart too full now for words.

After a few moments, Thorn said, "As we entered the keep I looked back and saw in the sky nine Stormriders, far south, heading west. It is unusual for so many to ride together. There are momentous stirrings in the world—the sooner we reach the city, the better."

*Not the better, the worse—for I shall lose you then,* thought Imrhien, and she recalled also the vengeful wizard's henchmen and the eastsiders who might hunt her for her knowledge of Waterstair.

Might these pursuers have found their way to Caermelor by land, sea, or air? Or might they have sent messages to spies already in the Royal City?

For supper there were bunya nuts, lillypilly berries, brown-capped mushrooms that had pushed up between the roots of trees, and apple-berries that the travelers had plundered in passing, up on Alderstone Edge. On greenwood spits, the mercenary roasted two pigeons he had brought down with the longbow—for the loss of three arrows, to his chagrin.

"We ought to dine on the cockerel," he mused, eating a pigeon's heart. "What did you save it for if not for that?"

Imrhien pushed a few grass-heads and luckless worms through the cage's slats.

<<For its own good.>>

She would not let him have the bird.

Beyond the shelter of the rocks a tide of leaves swept past in a sudden gust. Above the towering summit of the Edge thunderclouds were building—turbulent currents boiling within their dark hearts. Tenebrous and menacing their roots, brilliant white their heads, where the strong winds blew away the ice crystals to flatten the tops and make anvils of them. To the west, Thunder Mountain's lofty peak seemed to have accumulated its own mass of grim iron-gray vapors.

A long drawn howling came down the wind, treacherously switching directions—not a howling of hounds, but a deep ululation that might have been generated in the throat of some unimaginably immense, wild creature. Like the boubrie's bellow it was clearly not human. It carried its own complaining unharmonies, to raise the flesh on one's scalp like fingernails scraping on slate.

"The Hooper?" Diarmid asked overcasually as the howling faded.

"A brother of it. In this part of the country it is the Howlaa that helpfully warns of storms. Also belatedly, in this case."

In the gloom to the west, a jagged thread of white light like molten wire appeared for an instant, linking the roiling clouds with the tip of Burnt Crag. Thunder rolled and crashed in the distance. A blast of wind hooked around the boulders and snatched at the fire, sending fountains of sparks into the night. Plump raindrops fell, one or two, and expired in a hiss of steam.

"We must seek shelter," said the Dainnan, kicking dust onto the fire. With a practiced movement he detached the bowstring and slipped the coil beneath his shirt.

Sky-hammers boomed on nearer cloud-anvils, and the ground trembled. A bloom of sheet lightning illuminated the land with stark blue white. In that instant, it revealed an unexpected and ghastly sight. Not a hundred paces away from their encampment, a mighty boulder hung in the black sky, as though frozen in the very moment of its flight. Lightning's illusion was shattered when, with a deafening blast, the chunk of mountain crashed down almost upon the travelers. Dirt and pebbles sprayed everywhere. The ground quaked.

"This way!" Thorn shouted. Imrhien's ears rang with such clamor that she could scarcely make out his words, but in another flash-frozen moment she saw him with all his gear, and the goshawk on his shoulder, moving away. She grabbed the rooster's cage and went after. The Ertishman was not far behind.

A swath of crackling blue light showed that the first gigantic missile had burst apart, and a second was being hurled up into the air from a distance. Dangerously close, a third crag crashed, along with a hail of smaller ones the size of human heads. Rain began to fall in sparse, heavy drops. The travelers made haste, dodging among outcrops and weedy hillocks and piled slabs until they struck a track, deeply cloven into the ground, that led downhill. On either side, the banks rose up, high over their heads. The walls of rock blocked out the storm's flares, but not the tremendous blasts of thunder and thrown rocks, and not the deluge. Still the track burrowed down, narrowing, until the walls arched over, forming a tunnel that dived under the hill.

It was pitch black.

"Wait! I can see nothing," said Diarmid, to Imrhien's intense relief—in the dark, she was truly mute.

"Halt here," Thorn's voice, reassuring, from shadow in shadow. "Soon, you will see."

Vision slowly cleared. They stood in a rough-hewn tunnel inclining down toward the innards of Erith. That they could see at all was a mystery, until Imrhien noticed the luminous ears of fungus growing on the walls, the same kind she had seen growing at Waterstair.

"We must go on farther," said the Dainnan, "in case the inaccuracy of the Foawr collapses the entrance."

They walked several yards farther down the adit and then stopped to rest. Through the rock walls, the bass vibrations of the battle outside could be felt. The ground thrummed.

"The Foawr." Diarmid slumped wearily against a wall. "Who can outspeak those giants? For they have heads of granite and tongues of basalt, the wit of a flea upon a flea and, I surmise, the knowledge of no more than three words—and those most likely in some thick and cloddish language. Not that a man could get close enough to speak to them."

"Not that they are much aware that Men exist," added Thorn. "This vale is one of their battlegrounds. Storms rouse them to fight, but they do so for no reason other than that they have always done so."

"Then, Longbow, when the storm passes, will they make peace?"

"Maybe." Another crash brought pebbles showering from the ceiling. "Maybe not. They are blind to reason and may rouse at whim."

The cold of underground, where sunlight never reached radiant fingers to warm stone and rock and bring dawn to endless night, seeped out of the clammy walls and into Imrhien's blood. The rooster looked half-dead in its prison. Somehow, the spontaneous act of rescuing it had engendered in her a burdening responsibility for its life; she ardently desired that it might live. It kicked feebly when she took it from the cage and held it wrapped against her body. The icy, oddly reptilian feet scratched her, but after a few moments its struggles subsided and it lay quiescent. Thorn's cloak seemed to have qualities of gramarye, for she fancied its fabric radiated warmth. Its owner drew the garment around her shoulders, flicking a fold over the bird.

"Chanticleer has the best bed of all, this night," Thorn said with a swift smile that twanged Imrhien's senses like bowstrings.

The bird stank of stale fowl-manure. Her arms, enfolding it, were grimy and scratched, wrapped in ragged sleeves. Her dress was nothing but dirty tatters, and her face and hair must present a spectacle similar to Diarmid's—smudged, bedraggled, unkempt. The last time she had washed had been days ago in Mirrinor, splashing cold water over herself, for it was not safe to plunge into those eldritch pools to bathe. How Thorn remained unbesmirched—by some Dainnan trick or perhaps some wizard's art—was a conundrum.

"Take a drop of this." The Dainnan unstoppered a red crystal phial and offered it to Imrhien. "It will keep the cold from you."

She tasted the contents and passed the phial to Diarmid. The Ertishman swigged and nodded.

"That's a draft to warm the cockles of the heart, no doubt of it. What is it? For it is neither ale nor mead nor sack nor malmsey nor any cider or spirit that I have tasted."

"It is *nathrach deirge,* called also Dragon's Blood—an elixir of herbs."

"What tongue is it that sometimes you speak, sir? I have never heard it."

"It is an ancient one."

"I have heard the Dainnan must be learned in many tongues."

Time stretched out in the darkness. Wrapped in Thorn's cloak, with the elixir coursing warmly through her veins, Imrhien began to drowse. Just as she was about to drift away she thought she heard a knocking or tapping some way off. Too tired to care, she was soon asleep.

Her slumber was profound—a deep black pit that sucked the light out of its surroundings, so that no dreams could float above the chasm; a fathomless mine-shaft sunk into the hard layers separating the sunny, living, wind-tossed world from the carious world of grave stillness, eternal silence, and unrelenting cold.

Imrhien's eyes flew open.

The long call that had jolted her to wakefulness dwindled away, then broke out again. Harmonics bounced off the limestone walls and ran up and down the adit, crossing and recrossing each other in a cacophony of ear-splitting reverberations.

The rooster was crowing.

Imrhien clapped her hands over her ears.

"Cursed fowls!" groaned Diarmid. "Is a man not permitted some rest?"

The girl tried to hush the cockerel. It fluttered from her grasp and leaped onto her head, where its feet became entangled in her hair. It crowed a third time, then quietened, making little noises in its throat. In pain, the girl batted at the bird, which jumped awkwardly to the floor. Blood ran down her forehead and into her eye, from where its spur had pierced her scalp. A couple of feathers descended lazily in the light of the fungi.

"What ails the fowl? 'Tis the middle of the night!" Diarmid complained.

A tang of wood-smoke and a savory scent drifted down the tunnel. Imrhien looked around for Thorn, but he was nowhere to be seen. She struggled to her feet and made a grab for the rooster, which eluded her. Leaving it to its own devices, she walked with the Ertishman back along the tunnel's rising floor, through the entrance, and up out of the culvert into the open air. The cockerel followed several paces behind.

The sun had not yet lifted above the horizon. A gray predawn pallor washed over Emmyn Vale. Once again, *uhta* was on the world—that breathless hour between the marches of night and the threshold of day when nocturnal incarnations paused in their business, turning their eyes to the east, pricking up their ears; when birds began to stir sleepily in their nests, chirping tentatively as they made ready to greet the sun; when unseelie shapes and nightmares went skulking back to crannies and subtle places, there to hide from the solar glare and wait for nightfall.

There was no sign of the Foawr other than the aftermath of their battle—splintered trees, twisted bushes, gaping raw wounds in hillsides, gleaming facets of new-broken rock. Black mouths gaped from hillsides and under boulders, the entrances to the myriad caves that riddled the ground on which they stood. Daylight revealed that the adit ran into the side of a small grassy hill. The sight of a door leading underground disturbed Imrhien, stirring a queer mingling of horror and excitement.

A fire sprang like a red lily in a stony clearing among the heather. Thorn stepped silently from the dusky trees, holding a brace of bunya cones. Errantry was perched on his shoulder. The Dainnan knelt by the fire and began to skin a dead rabbit that lay there already.

"The Foawr have done us a favor," he said cheerfully. "A bunya pine lies shattered, its cones rolling—easy pickings."

The bantam rooster scratched vigorously in the dirt, throwing dust over Diarmid's boot.

"First the bird wakens me, then it befouls me," the Ertishman said grimly, unaware of his pun. "It desires a short life."

"Such birds can be useful," said Thorn. "Even in dark places they can tell when dawn arrives in the world outside. Many wights fear the sun, including the Foawr. At a cockerel's proclamation of the sun's imminence, even powerful wights may flee in dread."

As she sat warming herself by the flames, Imrhien cast her mind back to her old tilhal, the wooden rooster. It had been falling apart. She had lost it to the eastsiders when she and Muirne had been taken—Ethlinn had given her the self-bored stone tilhal to replace it. The wooden rooster had been of no value, but they had taken it anyway, probably using it to fuel their fire. How much of Waterstair's treasure had they plundered by now? Where did Sianadh's body lie—had they possessed the decency to bury him, or had they left his remains to be devoured by wild things? That great treasure lawfully belonged to the Crown. What would the King-Emperor do when he learned of its existence?

Imrhien was tempted to tell Thorn of her mission. As a warrior of the King-Emperor he would be able to help—perhaps he might secure an audience with His Majesty. She was only a tattered wanderer with a maimed face. What chance would she have of speaking personally with the King-Emperor himself? At best, her information would be relayed up to him through the hierarchy of courtiers. Yet that mattered not in the long run, she supposed—for as long as the King-Emperor received word of Waterstair and of the evil deeds of the eastsiders, her mission would be complete. She need do no more, for then the Dainnan Brotherhood would be sent forth to dispatch justice.

<<*Trust no one. Tell no one of your mission,*>> Ethlinn had insisted, <<*until you reach the court. Then, speak only to the King-Emperor or to his two most trusted men.*>>

Imrhien had made the "promise" signal, and thus she was bound, if not to her word, then to her sign.

Behind the ridge the eastern horizon was now brushed with orchid-pink, but the sun's first ray was not yet visible when from behind a hillock came a grunting and a snorting as of a wild pig. Something came over the hill and stood still for a moment, as if sniffing the air. It was a giant, barrel-chested man-thing, with a black pig's head and two great tusks like a wild boar's. This formidable apparition started to walk down the dark slope, lifting its feet high with its thick ham hocks of legs. The feet were large and blunt, all the toes, however many there were, arranged in a straight row. Although it was ponderous, it moved swiftly, grunting and snuffling all the while.

Thorn remained unmoved by this apparition.

"He has not seen us," he said. The goshawk stood on one leg and nibbled a strand of his hair.

Presently the pig-man moved off among the hummocks and was lost to view.

"Now you have beheld Jimmy Squarefoot," said Thorn. "When he is a giant pig he is ridden over land and sea by the Foawr. In his present form he is a stone-thrower, like them, but he does no great damage. He is out late—before the first sunray touches the land he must find shelter—"

He broke off and leapt to his feet. Errantry flew up with a whirr and a clap of wings. Imrhien and Diarmid lifted their heads, alert for danger.

"Longbow, what approaches?"

Thorn silenced him with a gesture. A noise grazed the edges of hearing. After a moment the Dainnan lifted the brass-mounted horn to his mouth and sounded a long note. Then he said:

"From the north I hear the winding of a Dainnan horn. One of the Brotherhood calls for aid. I must answer."

He turned toward his companions, speaking with urgency.

"That call comes from a long distance. I must travel swiftly, and so cannot bring you with me. I may be gone for several days. It is not safe for you to remain here—you must press on by yourselves. Without my company, you must travel under the ground for this part of your journey. This region of Doundelding's surface is an eldritch crossroad. Numbers of unseelie wights may pass through here on their way north, but belowground you will encounter mostly the seelie. Follow the adit down and then straight ahead—it winds through many mines, up and down—whenever it branches, take the left-hand path, save for the third and seventh branches. If you follow these directions, you will emerge in the west of Doundelding. If not, you will lose yourselves in the labyrinth and perish. Now, I must make haste. Drink only flowing water, never water that stands. Provision yourselves well and light *no fires* in the mines. Take these."

He thrust the red phial, the cloak, and some other gear into their arms. Placing a hand lightly on Diarmid's shoulder, he looked down at him—for the Dainnan was the taller by an inch or two—and said gravely:

"Captain, I would enjoin you to protect this damsel, but where native wit is of more use than a strong arm, she may prove the protectress. Yet, guard her with your strength, I do charge you. Both, come safely through."

Diarmid opened his mouth to protest, but again Thorn silenced him.

"There is no time. Already it may be too late."

<<Shall we meet you again?>> The girl's hands fell to her sides, palms turned outward, empty. He stepped so close, then, that the pine-fragrance of him infused her senses. His glance pierced like a shard shawled in velvet, for there was a gentleness to its edge. Softly he spoke:

"May our parting not be for long, Gold-Hair."

Errantry rose on his pinions with a sound like rushing wind. The Dainnan tilted back his head, his eyes following the bird's flight. His profile was drawn finely against the blushing sky of sunrise.

Then he was away.

As the sun lifted itself up over the blasted vale, Imrhien and Diarmid breakfasted in morose silence. Morning brought with it the first stirrings of a shang wind. The rooster pecked and strutted around authoritatively, obviously in charge now that the goshawk had departed. It had taken a liking to Diarmid, who kept pushing it away with his elbow and elaborately refraining from cursing it, to prove himself gentlemanly. Imrhien hardly noticed. She thought she must have swallowed a stone during the night, and it had lodged in her chest, just above the heart. She had become aware of it only after Thorn had gone. Her throat constricted, and she could not eat.

Few birds called from the surrounding countryside. A cold wind was blowing—the place seemed cheerless. As the travelers picked around the fallen boughs of the bunya pine, collecting as many nuts as they could cram into the pouches, the tinkling of a million miniature bells came over the hills. It was as though a meadowful of snowdrop flowers with tiny clappers were bowing under a breeze. The strange clouds of the shang blotted out the sun. Soft airs plucked at their clothes. Imrhien wanted to run on the hilltops, to spring into the air and see if the wind would buoy her up, would lift her into the sky and away from the ache of loss. Diarmid would disapprove—not that she cared.

Instead she tied on her taltry.

Rocks glittered with points of silver light. On a hillside a bloody skirmish was taking place between two bands of see-through warriors in old-fashioned mail and plumed helmets. They were up to their knees in turf, the ground level having altered since their day. Closer still, a young couple in peasant garb ran up a slope, he dragging her by the hand—she was exhausted. Fear was written on both their faces as they stared back over their shoulders at whatever had pursued them, long ago. Who they were and what they were running from was now lost and forgotten.

By the time the unstorm had passed, the travelers had packed and were ready to leave. They looked about for the entrance to the adit, and that was when consternation first set in. For there were numerous underground entrances puncturing the hills, and most of them were adits with cuttings running down into their mouths.

"We are left to ourselves for half an hour and already we are lost," Diarmid expostulated as they searched. "Perhaps any one of these would do . . . I surmise that all are interconnected."

Imrhien shook her head. Thorn's directions had been specific—the wrong entrance could lead them in the wrong direction, into peril.

Eventually they sat down, at a loss.

"We shall have to find it before nightfall," the Ertishman said grimly. "That Jimmy Squarefoot will be abroad, and who knows what else may roam after sunset."

The girl gave a start and looked around wildly.

"No need to be troubled yet!" he said.

<<No, no. Where is the rooster?>>

"I know not. I care not."

Imrhien went looking for the rescued bird and saw it sitting on a hilltop. When she came near, it scuttled away down the other side of the hill. Following its trail, she came to the very entrance of the sought-after adit—she recognized it by a jutting limestone protuberance resembling a giant's nose. The rooster was already inside, darting after flies. The girl climbed back to the hilltop and waved her arms to hail her companion. In a moment he was beside her, and she led him to the tunnel where the bird was pecking.

"Then it has a use after all, the witless fowl," he grunted, but his smile revealed his gladness.

Imrhien gazed for one last time toward the north. Then, saying farewell to the open skies, they walked down into the dark.

Gradually their eyes adapted to the dim luminescence of the fungi. The rooster shortsightedly blundered about and crashed into a wall. Grudgingly Diarmid rescued it, setting it on his shoulder with deep misgivings. It pecked his ear affectionately. Imrhien tapped on Diarmid's arm.

<<We must beware of pits and count the intersections.>>

Diarmid squinted. "I can barely see your hands. Say you that we must watch our step in case we fall down some winze or ventilation shaft to a lower level? Aye, I'll not disagree. And we must look for branching passages. What was it now—take the left, except for the third and seventh?" She nodded.

An hour later they had not yet passed one side-opening, and still the tunnel descended. From afar off, the sounds of tapping and knocking started up again. There being no night or day in this worm's abode, the travelers at last halted when they had agreed it must be around noon. Snail-trails of water ran down the walls—it was difficult to find a dry place to sit. Brown mud smeared their faces and hands, caked their hair and garments. Rummaging in the food-pouches, they found little more than bunya nuts, with a few withered lillypilly berries, overripe apple-berries, and crumbled mushrooms. The nuts were rich and sustaining, but Imrhien knew they would tire of them before long. She crushed a few for the rooster to peck, which it did, peevishly.

"Those knocking sounds," said Diarmid, his voice loud in the still darkness, "they would drive a man mad."

Behind his back the rooster gave a sudden screech. Both travelers jumped. The bird shot off down the passageway.

<<The crumbs of nuts—they are gone.>>

"Aye, and there was quite a pile of them. The fowl could not have eaten them all in such a short moment. Mayhap we have company." The Ertishman's voice dropped to a whisper.

They peered out into the gloom but could see no moving thing.

<<It seems we are alone. . . .>>

Diarmid gave a shout and grabbed the food-pouches off the floor.

"I left a handful of bunya nuts right there. They are gone! Leave no food on the living rock. Let us get out of this place."

A screech issued out of the darkness ahead and the rooster came running back. Imrhien scooped it up. Its eyes, usually wide and indignant looking, were more so.

They walked on for a minute or two, then placed a couple of nuts on the limestone floor. Nothing happened until they looked away. Then there was a faint scraping of stone on stone and the food was gone. A dim drone of bagpipes came to their ears from somewhere to the left and below.

<<Under this floor, things are dwelling. Doubtless, every stone is a trapdoor.>>

"Let us hope that they are not after food other than the vegetable kind."

It seemed wiser to eat and drink as they walked.

The drone of the pipes drew nearer. Such underground piping was not unfamiliar to the girl, for she had heard such dim upwellings somewhere in the forests north of Gilvaris Tarv. The music crescendoed, rising from beneath the feet of the listeners to send cold thrills juddering through them. The piper moved along some sublevel crosscut to the right and passed farther away into distant labyrinthine reaches. After the music had faded, even the knocking ceased. Silence pressed more heavily than before.

The passage forked.

"That's one!"

They took the left-hand path.

The rocky floor ramped down more steeply now. On the slippery, uneven surface it would have been easy to lose one's footing. Down here, far from human aid, a broken limb could eventually prove fatal. This passage twisted and turned until those who followed it had lost all sense of direction. After what seemed hours it led them to another intersection. There, they rested, for surely it must be evening, somewhere far above their heads, and the first frosty stars opening in the sky.

The tappings had resumed as they walked. They rang louder now—instead of one or two knockers there seemed a multitude, all banging at different rhythms and tempos, some in the walls, others underfoot or overhead. They might have been nearby, or far off in some other section of the mine, their tappings amplified by some echo-chamber effect along a conduit. The travelers sat down on the cloak, abruptly realizing how weary they were.

"If anything can keep us from the thieves beneath the floor, 'tis this Dainnan cloak," Diarmid muttered, "with whatever wizardly qualities it is endowed. Mayhap it is woven of wight-spun yarn." To be completely certain, they let no crumb fall. The rooster refused to set foot on the ground under any circumstances and ended up perched on Imrhien's knee while she fed it from her hand and cupped water for it.

"The tin mines of Doundelding are ancient workings," Diarmid mused with a yawn. "Digging has been going on here for centuries. The old mines, now hardly ever worked, intersect with the new on many levels, and the whole lot is laced with natural caverns. Back in the Tarv barracks, Sergeant Waterhouse used to tell tales of this place."

There was no doubt that the Ertishman had become more informative and agreeable since the advent of the Dainnan's company. However, Imrhien's eyelids were so heavy that she could scarcely follow what he was saying.

"You sleep," she heard him say, "I shall take first watch."

* * *

It was hard to waken when Diarmid shook her to take her turn at the watch. The cockerel, having slumbered peacefully, skipped from her hip to the man's, sank its neck into its feathery chest, and closed its eyes smugly. Imrhien struggled to stay alert in the eternal gloom, listening to the sporadic *tap-tap,* now near at hand, now far off. Sometimes she paced up and down, longing for an end to this timeless night.

Deep in the ground, with miles of limestone hanging over their heads, they had only one timepiece to mark the rise and fall of the sun. The cockerel opened its affronted eyes, extended its neck, shook itself, glared all around, and puffed out its chest by way of ritual. Opening its wings and pointing its beak to the ceiling, it let fly with its fanfare. Such a crowing would have carried a long distance, had it been blasted forth over fields and farmlands. Here in this enclosed place it rolled around, making the rocks ring with its echoes.

When the triumphant cry finally faded, all sound ceased. The rooster fluffed up its feathers and shook itself.

Bleary-eyed and now wool-eared, the travelers breakfasted and went on their way.

The path always ran downhill, always lit by fungus, always slicked with damp. Occasionally it would narrow, or widen, or turn this way or that, or the ceiling would soar away out of sight, or the walls would be streaked with layers of color, or the way would suddenly widen into a cavern, its roof supported by pillars of living rock, or the sound of rushing water would come chuckling and gurgling from behind the walls.

At the third branch, they took the right-hand passage and the floor leveled off, no longer descending. The passage ran straight for many miles, without a turnoff. They dined while on the march, unwilling to rest on these treacherous floors and eager to reach the end of this journey as soon as possible.

In this long, straight hall the travelers felt vulnerable. If danger approached from ahead or behind, there would be no choice of escape route. Besides, the stark walls offered no caverns or niches in which they might take shelter. Often they glanced back over their shoulders, fancying they could hear following footsteps.

"Anything that dwells down here knows exactly where we are," grunted Diarmid, "our modest friend made sure of that." Yet he allowed the bird to ride on his shoulder.

They were beginning to despair of ever finding another branch when they came upon two in rapid succession.

"Four and five! After the seventh, how many until the end, I wonder?"

Discouragingly, the way sloped downward again. The sixth fork appeared, and they entered the tunnel on the left. Everything seemed to be proceeding according to plan until they reached a section of the passage where, high in the right-hand wall, a small opening gaped, large enough for a man to crawl through. Dimly discernible by the glow of the cave-fungi, it was partly concealed by jutting rock. No steps led up to this hole, only several rough-hewn footholds. Perplexed, Diarmid stood scratching at the itchy new growth of his beard. Imrhien tugged at his sleeve and pointed.

<<That is the seventh branch,>> she insisted.

"I am not so sure. It is not like the others. I think it is some exploratory drift, leading to some old stope, or simply a dead end."

Vehemently she shook her head. <<Thorn would have told us.>>

"No—he would expect us to choose the obvious path. This passage leads straight on."

<<That passage is the left-hand branch. I choose the other.>>

Diarmid's jaw tightened. "I do not."

They had reached an impasse. Presently Imrhien began to scale the wall. She had not climbed more than three feet when Diarmid's hands seized her around the waist and dragged her down.

"Foolish wench! You will not go that way." She tried to pull free, but he would not release her. White anger flared in her skull, and she slapped her open palm hard against his cheek. He released his grip abruptly, and she fell back against the wall.

"Go, then." His clenched hands trembled. They were dark with walnut-dye and mud. "But you will go without the water-bottle or any food."

Although she guessed he was bluffing, she knew also that he had the upper hand. If she called his bluff, he might easily force her to accompany him, dragging her along by the hair if he so desired. Struggling to cool the boiling of her rage, she pushed past Diarmid and strode down the path he had chosen, hoping against her own conviction that it might be the correct way after all.

The passage inclined downhill. In antipathetic silence they marched for an hour or so. As ire dissipated, Imrhien became aware that she had heard no knockings for quite some time. The only sounds were the echoes of their own footfalls and the occasional melancholy *drip-drip* of water from the ceiling.

A barrier loomed before them: a rusted gate of thickset iron bars, like a portcullis. It blocked the whole passage.

<<What now, Captain?>> Mockery flashed in Imrhien's eyes.

The Ertishman did not reply. With his hands and eyes he searched the crevices of the surrounding walls and floor. He found a lever and hauled hard. Somewhere an ancient mechanism stirred. With a squeaking and creaking of moribund pulleys and springs, the portcullis began to lift. It clanged into place above their heads, leaving the way clear. At this, the rooster balked and set up a tremendous racket, hissing and stretching out its wings. Diarmid regarded it with a baleful stare, as though it were a traitor, and strode forward. Taking a deep breath, Imrhien followed.

Farther along this path, the luminous fungi dwindled and disappeared, to be replaced by small blue lights emanating from a species of glow-worm clinging all over the rock like encrustations of gems. The air thickened and became stuffy. The travelers had for so long trodden upon a firm surface that they had become careless about where they put their feet. This proved a mistake.

Diarmid's booted foot stepped out into empty air. After that, it seemed time slowed down. A shaft was gaping in the floor in front of them, and the young man was falling into it. He tried to throw his weight backward, teetering on the brink. Imrhien thrust out her hand, *so slowly,* she thought in terror, too slowly as he wavered there between life and death. She felt as though her hand passed through flowing water instead of air, or as if time's current moved backward, retarding her actions. He was gone, almost, hovering there in the gelatinous liquid of suspended moments, and all she could reach was an outflung fold of his jacket and his flying hair. Grabbing a handful of both, she braced herself and then jerked back. The force was enough to swing the fragile balance, and the Ertishman fell backward to the floor.

The continuum resumed its normal flow. Diarmid lay, sobbing for breath. After a moment they both crawled to the shaft's edge. Nothing could be seen down there. It might have been as shallow as a wine vat or as deep as a well.

A ledge ran between the abyss and the wall.

<<We must turn back.>>

"No. The ledge is the path."

He would heed her signs no longer, would not even look at her. Keeping his back firmly against the wall, he began to negotiate his way past the shaft, sliding his feet sideways along the narrow shelf. The cockerel took to Imrhien's shoulder. Yet again, she had no choice but to follow the Ertishman.

Once past the shaft, they went on slowly and cautiously. The air grew stuffier, the glow-worms more plentiful. They had traveled some seven hundred yards when they rounded a bend to find themselves confronting a breathtaking scene. Here loomed a mighty cavern hung with fantastic stalactites. The slow erosion of water on limestone had produced shapes of curtains, giant birds' wings, and organ pipes. Some of the pendant formations had joined with stalagmites to form fluted pillars. Like the interior of some surrealistic palace built by a mad King, the whole scene was pricked out with the jewels of billions of silent glow-worms dreaming sapphire dreams. Imrhien touched her companion's shoulder.

<<Where lies our path now?>>

He pointed to the ground.

"See, there is a channel, worn in the floor. From this door it leads across the cave."

Indeed, a curious groove had been gouged into the cavern's floor. Measuring perhaps three feet across, it was defined by parallel sides and an inner surface that was perfectly concave, smooth, and polished. Imrhien looked around. They had unwittingly been walking along this arcane incision—it continued back the way they had come. There was something unsettling about it.

However, Diarmid's mind was made up, and he struck out again.

They crossed the coldly glittering limestone cavern, dripping with its sculpted drapery and frozen swans' wings. The groove led straight into an opening on the opposite side, and soon they found themselves back in a passageway. The stuffy air gave out a prickling feeling and a curious metallic stench.

<<Death lies ahead.>> Imrhien was smitten with a sudden premonition. <<Turn back.>>

The Ertishman ignored her.

Another cavern opened out before them. Its roof was low, hanging just above their heads. In the center sprawled a great black lake, a sheet of polished obsidian mirroring in its depths the azure stars clinging above. The chamber was like the hollowed interior of a dark crystal shot with flecks of lapis lazuli. Faintly illuminated, the floor-groove ran to the left, curving around the shore. As they pursued it, Imrhien thought she saw a dark shape hump itself out of the oily waters and slowly subside.

Utter horror seized her. What were they doing here? Diarmid was leading them to certain doom—why had she not fought him with greater stubbornness, perhaps somehow stunned him with a rock and fled?

But he was pressing on. She looked back, into the shadows, and it seemed more terrifying to fly that way alone. In a foment of dread, she followed close on his heels.

Past the lake-cave, the bitter-tasting stink intensified. They were both gasping for breath. A low vibration came humming through the rock, a deep, whining drone of pent-up energy punctuated by crackling sizzles and the smell of something charred. The hair stood up on the back of Imrhien's neck. Iron-clawed spiders tiptoed down her spine. Ahead, from around a corner, issued sudden flashes as brilliant as shards of pure sunlight struck off a glacier. A zigzag bolt of energy hit the wall, gouging a crater of melted slag. Diarmid turned to his companion. His eyes were sunken wells in a face drained of color. His lips parted, and a strangled whisper issued from them:

"This is *not* the way."

They began to retrace their steps, running. Yet they had delayed too long.

Beyond that last bend, something large and mailed began to

move, something that had gouged the long groove into the rock floor over countless years of passing to and fro.

Far beneath Doundelding, an ancient secret had lain curled at the root of a rich vertical lode that stretched all the way up through Thunder Mountain to the summit's surface. High on that summit jutted Burnt Crag, a toothed pinnacle that sucked in the veined flares of lightning from any storm for miles around. The crag was a focal point redirecting the energy down through the conduit of ore, down to a prehistoric sentience that attracted levin-bolts from the atmosphere. Deep beneath the ground it stirred, for it had been disturbed. It moved to seek the source of the disturbance. The body unraveled sinuously. The leading terminus swayed a little, blunt and glowing. It gathered speed.

In its path, two small figures fled. Having reached the worm-lit cave of the lake, they dashed along the water's edge with a recklessness born of panic. Out of the wet shadows of the subterranean cistern reared an amorphous vitality. It lunged at them in passing. The two figures ran on, one sobbing with terror, the other gasping soundlessly. Their backs were intermittently lit with a blue-white glare. By the time this following light drove past the lake, searing its reflections into the water, the surface was flat, blandly innocent, save for a lattice of ripples.

Through the mortified splendor of the stalactite cave ran Imrhien and Diarmid, along the smooth curve of the serpent's track. A metallic, slithering rasp roared through the underground halls, the sound of a thousand habergeons of chain mail being dragged rapidly across riveted sheet iron. It was punctuated by crackles and fizzing hisses like hot fat spitting in water. Smoothly their pursuer gained on them.

Almost, they had not remembered the shaft. It seemed to spring open deliberately at their feet, as if to catch them unawares. Now must they slow down and move with agonizing precision. Diarmid thrust the girl in front of him.

"You first."

He breathed in hoarse gasps.

Holding herself flat against the wall, she sidled across. The flow of minutes and seconds seemed once more to decelerate. Diarmid came after, moving as though in syrup, straining against some invisible pressure that turned his sinews to lead. A whine of energy spiraled down the tunnel. Bluish brilliance brightened on the walls. Mailed coils grated across polished minerals.

Diarmid was halfway across when a bolt sizzled the air, breaking off a chunk of limestone from above the pit. It hurtled past his ears. There was no echoing crack from below to indicate it had reached the base of the shaft. The Ertishman, with a great leap, now cleared the chasm. After landing awkwardly on the other side, he rolled to his feet, then winced and stumbled. As they sped toward the iron portcullis, they finally heard a dim echo of the broken-off rock hitting the pit's floor.

Any hopes that the pursuer would be hindered by the shaft were soon dashed. The roar and hiss of its passage slowed for a heartbeat, then surged forth afresh, closing in. How they managed that final sprint to the iron gate was later a source of amazement to Imrhien. Their lungs were inflamed bellows, exploding. With every step, Diarmid cried out in agony. As they rounded a bend the gate came into view, hanging high above their heads. It snapped into blue-white relief. Light flashed. The air thrummed and fried. They threw themselves past the gate, and Imrhien reached for the lever. Diarmid flung her aside and grabbed the handle in both hands, bearing down on the mechanism with all his might.

Driven by an engine of rusted cogs forced into action, the portcullis began to descend, squeaking and clamoring with the reluctance of old age. It was halfway to biting the floor when, like an outrageous firework, a force came roaring around the bend and slammed into it. A current surged. Sparks exploded in a blistering snarl, and Diarmid was flung backward up the passage, where he lay motionless.

Rent and twisted, metal screamed. The passageway was described by a jerky sequence of utter darkness and scalding brilliance, each flicker and instant of blindness lasting no more than a heartbeat. An ominous hum of power reverberated through the walls and floor.

By degrees, these phenomena began to fade. Incredibly, the gate had descended and held, according to its age-old purpose. The avenger had been thwarted. With the sound of ten wrecked chariots being hauled over rocks by spans of oxen, it departed.

The girl's eyes were dazzled by retinal afterimages. She could barely discern the man where he lay. He did not move. But she touched him and discovered a pulse, light and rapid. Now, in the twilight, she could see the dark blood welling from his forehead, the blackened hands, already swelling. She untied the pouches from his belt and ransacked them, careless of the food spilling across the floor. The bandages for the rowers' hands had been washed and rolled up. After tearing off a length, she wadded it and applied pressure to the head wound, moistened his lips with a couple of drops of water, bandaged his hands.

*Survive,* she begged in her mind. *Sianadh, Liam, and Muirne are gone. Do not go, too—you are the last of Ethlinn's kin. The last of* my *people.*

Lovingly, the dark chill of underground embraced them. Diarmid would not waken—she was alone. The scattered food had already disappeared; not a nut remained. Where was the rooster? Had it been left behind? As if in reply, a slightly singed bundle of feathers jumped from its perch on a high shelf to her knee. She held it close. Its small company would be welcome during the long hours of vigil.

And long they were, those hours, sitting beside Diarmid, hoping for a word or a sign. His face was flushed. She applied wet cloths to it. He was burning. His breath came in shallow gasps.

Imrhien had forgotten how loud was the dawn call of the faithful cockerel. In the end, it was that which woke Diarmid. He sat up, muttering, dazed. The last reverberations of the bird's clamor sent bits of gravel scurrying down the walls.

A rumbling began. Somewhere, some delicate balance, dependent on bits of gravel, had shifted. The walls and floor began to shake. Imrhien seized Diarmid's arm and tried to pull him to his feet. Pebbles were falling. The ground muttered as she led him up the tunnel, he limping badly. Where had it been, the little opening high in the wall? Had she gone past without noticing it?

But there it was, the seventh branch. Or possibly not.

<<Climb,>> her hands commanded.

Torment showed in every line of the man's body, every twitching muscle of his face. He did not speak, but clambered up the rough ledges to the aperture, which was not tall enough to allow him to stand. With a pitiful cry, he forced himself in, headfirst. As the girl and the cockerel scrambled in to join him, the ceiling of the passage below collapsed with a roar. Dust puffed in at them. Coughing, they crawled away on hands and knees.

*This will be aptly named, should it turn out to be a dead end.*

The passage went on, however, with a purposeful air, rising on a shallow gradient. Soon the walls fell back, the ceiling flew up, and they were able to stand. By the soft light of glow-fungi, Imrhien saw that Diarmid's bandages were soaking red. The Ertishman had crawled over stony ground on burned and blackened hands.

His fortitude was impressive. He propped himself against a wall, allowed her to hold the near empty water-bottle to his mouth, and shook his head when she asked if he wanted to rest. He was resolute. They shared the last drops of water and marched on.

It was a relief to hear the knockings again; the girl felt certain now that they had regained the right path. Diarmid's ankle had been injured, and he could put very little weight on it. They were forced to halt several times, but they had covered a surprising amount of ground by the time they reached the freshet. Clear water sprang out of the walls, ran noisily down a narrow gutter beside the floor, and disappeared through a chink in the rock. Gratefully the travelers and their bird drank of it. They bathed and refilled the water-bottle.

"Unlace my shirt for me," said Diarmid, "please. 'Tis so hot here." The air was chill, but he was aflame. Carefully, so as not to touch his wounded hands, she helped him remove his mercenary's jacket. She rinsed his hair with cool water. The roots were growing out red.

"You are kind." His eyes were bright, feverish. They seemed unfocused.

She put on his jacket—it was easier to carry it that way, and the rooster seemed to like perching on the epaulets. There had been refreshment but no relief for Diarmid at this stop. Stubbornly he pulled himself to his feet, and they continued on their way.

To Imrhien it felt like late afternoon, a time when aboveground the sun's rays would be lying in long bars of bullion across the meadows and woods and the rooks would be flying home to roost. Down here there was no reason to feel this, no indication of the sun's invisible journey in the outside world.

The knockings amplified in volume and number, and as the travelers climbed the rising floor, they came to where the walls of the passageway were no longer featureless and unbroken. Small caves and diggings honeycombed them. Hope burgeoned in Imrhien, for she detected the sounds of miners hard at work in drifts nearby, separated perhaps only by a thin partition of rock. Yet she could not call out to them, and Diarmid was past speech.

The rumor of their industry was everywhere: hammerings, blastings, the squeak of wheels, the rattle of a windlass, shoutings of orders, a burble of voices, and laughter. The travelers picked up their pace. Even through the mists of pain the Ertishman seemed encouraged by the evidence of human aid close at hand. But within another hundred yards or so, their expectations crashed into ruin.

They came upon a side-cavern lit by dozens of tiny lanterns held by diminutive manlike beings who milled to and fro. Each of these wights was about eighteen inches in height, dressed after the manner of tin-miners, and grotesquely ugly. Their faces were cheery, however, as they bustled back and forth with picks and shovels and crowbars across their shoulders, or pushing barrows, or carrying buckets on poles. One of them rounded a corner quite close by and stopped in his tracks. His jaw dropped as he confronted the two mortals.

"Methinks," wheezed Diarmid to Imrhien, "they are seelie." He fixed his gaze on the tiny miner. "Can you"—the Ertishman paused for breath—"show us the way out?"

"Ooh, *Mathy,* what's that behind ye?" exclaimed the little fellow, pointing over their shoulders, his quaint eyebrows popping up with surprise. In their weakened condition, the travelers fell for the trick. They took their eyes off him. When a split moment later they turned back, not one of the miners was to be seen—only their tiny tools lying where they had been dropped and a lingering echo of tittering and squeaking.

Disheartened, the travelers moved on. They could hear the wights emerge behind them, even before they were out of sight, and return to their scurryings. It would have been useless to round on them, trying to catch them unawares. The wights were apprised of their presence now and would be gone in a puff of dust before the mortals could try to seize them, or draw breath, or even blink.

These small folk seemed very occupied with the business at hand, but the girl had seen no ore in the buckets and barrows, and despite all the wielding of picks and shovels, not one of the little miners had been actually digging. Despite all their great show of labor, she could find no palpable trace of their work. They were, in fact, performing nothing.

Imrhien's head ached and she could not remember when she had last slept. Leaving behind the scenes of pointless industry, the travelers drew into a side-cavern and lay down. Diarmid fell asleep instantly. Imrhien tried to keep watch but eventually succumbed to slumber. The singed rooster dozed, with one eye half-open.

Another sunless dawn arrived without altering the stasis of time in the realm below the roots and foundations and graves and riverbeds of the surface. After the dying harmonics of the *cock-a-doodle-doo*—more starved and feeble now—there was no answering rumble, no shifting of unbalanced rock into undercut interstices. The supports held strong in this section of the mines.

All their food had been stolen or buried under the rock-fall with the pouches and Thorn's cloak, but Imrhien still had the phial of Dragon's Blood tucked into her belt, and there seemed to be some kind of sustenance in this elixir. She shared it with Diarmid. Its warmth warded off the eternal chill of underground.

Drearily, the bird pecked about. Eventually it found a few stray glow-worms, which it swallowed. Imrhien shook Diarmid awake and spilled water into his mouth. His condition had grown worse; his lips were cracked and caked, his eyes glassy. He spoke no word at all. She propped herself under his arm to give support. Thus they went haltingly forward.

The passage still sloped straight up, arriving among more and larger side-chambers. The small tinners could be glimpsed flitting elusively here and there. Farther on they became scarce, until they vanished altogether.

The hubbub of mining continued, dimly, behind and ahead. After about an hour the passage went past an aperture lined with crystals. Lights glimmered from within. Overcome by exhaustion, Diarmid sat down to rest against the wall outside this niche. Curious as to the source of the light, Imrhien looked into it and spied three wightish miners—yet they were different from those they had first encountered; not so ugly, they had the faces of hearty old diggers. These were real mine-workers. The one in the middle was sitting on a stone, his jacket off and his shirtsleeves rolled up. Between his knees he held a small anvil, no more than three inches square, yet as complete as any ever seen in a smith's shop. His left hand clutched a boryer about the size of a darning-needle, which he was sharpening for one of the tinners, while the other was waiting his turn to have the pick he held in his hand new steeled.

Diarmid groaned. Imrhien turned to check on him. When she looked again, the trio had, not unexpectedly, vanished.

But it was certain that they had now come into the working levels of the Doundelding tin mines. Sometimes they caught sight of a small railway running parallel with their course on a ramp at about knee height. Wooden trams rolled along it, propelled, it seemed at first glance, merely by flickering azure lights that had hold of the rope traces and drew the vehicles up the incline with ease, despite the fact that they were loaded with shining ore. These lights were tricksy; if one did not look directly at them, it could be imagined that they centered around small figures wearing bright blue caps—but it was hard to be certain.

The hearty wightish tinners, all with their sleeves rolled up, were chipping and hacking away at the lode with their picks. Their yellow lanterns shone on piles of freshly excavated tin ore. It was as useless to approach them as it had been to approach their unproductive mimickers farther back. As soon as Imrhien took her eyes from them for an instant, or even if she blinked, they were gone. Their elusiveness was severely frustrating; often she was on the verge of tears, begging them with her stained and blistered hands to come back, to help, to show them the way out. Only one fact gave her courage—surely, with those miniature trams rattling up and down so frequently, she and Diarmid must now be close to the surface.

At one point, the floor of the passage ended in a narrow stair leading upward, and they had to climb. Several flights later they could drag themselves no farther. Rolling into a side-cave to rest, they sipped a drop of Dragon's Blood and were overtaken by slumber so swiftly that they had no knowledge of the transition.

The rooster crowed hoarsely, as if it had an ear of wheat stuck in its throat. It seemed to have little heart for crowing, merely going through the performance out of a sense of obligation. Imrhien lay on her back, the unyielding floor of cold adamant pushing up against her shoulder blades. Shivering slightly, she stared up at the fungus-lit roof. The warming effects of her drink from the red phial were wearing off. Had it been five days since they had left the world of light and air? Had it been four, or six, or twenty?

Dutifully she struggled to her feet. Without the elixir's fire in her blood she must keep moving to ward off the cold. It was becoming harder and harder to waken the Ertishman. After much shaking and splashing, he revived. He did not ask for food, merely water—then he heaved himself upright and set forth. There was a strong will driving him, but it would not be enough to keep him going for much longer.

The stair wound on and up, hour after hour, then became a steep ramp, then a short stair followed by a shallow incline. By now their path had diverged from the straight rail-track of the trams, and the miners' knockings had contracted to the right. Suddenly a breath of sweet air met the travelers, filled with a fragrance of leaves and grasses. On its perch, the rooster lifted its drooping head. Imrhien turned excitedly to Diarmid, but engrossed in the struggle to stay on his feet, he had noticed nothing.

Eagerly Imrhien dragged the dazed Ertishman forward. She expected at any moment to encounter a portal giving on to the world's surface, but once again hope dissolved into disappointment.

Unpredictably this slope ceased its climb, leveling out to the horizontal. The sides of the passageway were no longer formed of solid rock, rough-hewn. Here, the great, twisted roots of trees intruded, forming archways over the tunnel and twining in and out of the walls. Worms glistened like tubes of pink glass, antlered beetles lumbered along crannies. The cockerel attacked these small beasts voraciously. A rat skittered into a rock-mouth. At the sight of it Imrhien felt sick.

From up ahead issued a whirring and a whizzing. It was mingled with a chorus of song in treble-pitched and bass voices: euphonious singing, high and sweet like starlight, deep and cool like a mountain lake. The sounds seemed to be emanating from behind a wooden door set in the wall of the tunnel. When they reached this door, Imrhien pushed it open a crack and peeped in cautiously.

She saw a wide cavern, well lit, in which numbers of queer old wives sat spinning, each on a white marble stone. Every shape of deformity was upon them, and they all had long, long lips with which they held the yarn. One old wife was walking up and down, directing them all. Approaching one spinner sitting a little apart from the rest, who was uglier than all of them, she said, in hardly intelligible tones:

"Bundle up the yarn, Scantlie Mab, for 'tis time to tae tak' it wheer it belongs."

The watcher closed the door softly so as not to disturb the wights. There had been no sign of an exit from that chamber.

<<Can you go on?>> she signed to Diarmid.

The young man's glazed glance alighted on the hand-signs without seeing them.

They went on.

Ahead, light glimmered—not the luminosity of lanterns or underground life forms, but the mother of all radiance—the light of day.

It strengthened, blotting out the fungi, whitewashing the walls, stabbing at their eyes. The cockerel ran forward with a strange cry. To Imrhien, it seemed that they were stumbling forth into a blaze of glory, an inpouring of pure whiteness beyond which there was only more whiteness, brighter and more brilliant.

They had reached the surface.

# 10
# ROSEDALE
## Briar and Bird

*How far is the Vale of the Rose?*
*Not too far, as fly the Black Crows.*
*She is there, who waits at sunrise—*
*Ever her gaze turns to the skies.*
*How far is the Vale of the Briar?*
*The Black Rook is a swift flier.*
*He is there who waits at twilight*
*Until the day has fled into night.*

THE SISTER'S SONG

The tunnel emerged under a flat rock protruding from a hillside, where bracken-ferns and sweet-briars overgrew the entrance. Above and behind loomed the hilltop. To the right, a green slope rose to obscure the view. To the left and straight ahead stretched a belt of scattered birches. Directly over the trees, a dandelion sun fell toward late afternoon in a floss of clouds like thistledown. A ragged line of birds winged its way across the landscape. Atop the birches, rooks were perched like untidy black fruit. They uttered their rasping calls and suddenly took to the skies.

A breeze, heady and sweet as any wine, tweaked fronds and made them nod agreement. The cockerel pecked and strutted about the travelers' feet. The Ertishman's weight sagged a little more on Imrhien's back. She had thrown his arm about her shoulders in order to support him. She braced herself. Slowly they made their way down the hill, with the fowl in tow.

There was no path or track, but their eventual goal lay toward the west, so they followed the sun's path down into the trees, their boots swishing through piles of bronze and gold leaves. The gaps between the slender, papery stems afforded a view of a land sculpted into unnatural formations beneath its grassy mantle: flat-topped mounds dropping steeply away on all sides, giant pyramids, broad stairs cut into the sides of hills, sunken pits with straight sides, filled to the brim with rainwater. Once, as they halted for a brief respite, Imrhien looked back. Thunder Mountain reared against the sky, its sharp peak mantled in cloud.

Faintly, so faintly that Imrhien had to hold her breath to catch it, a familiar grinding noise came rumbling down the wind. On a rise to the south of the birch-grove stood an old wooden gravity-mill, overgrown with rambling briar-roses in faded profusion. So smothered in prickly stemmed vines was the old mill that it was scarcely recognizable as an edifice. Long, symmetrical mounds stretched out beside it. The ground appeared to have been whipped out from under the northern half of the building, for on that side the walls sagged and a rusted railway track that had risen on a transomed ramp to its top floor had half collapsed. Most of the supports were broken, and the remaining section hung in midair. Below, other rails, still attached to their sleepers, leaned in suspense over sunken hollows. Over all these walls and roofs and through the windows trailed the wild roses, rich with orange-red hips and patterned with the last lingering leaves of Autumn. This place was the source of the steady thrum of dunters.

More fortuitously, a cottage peeped from a clump of trees nestled on the slopes and banks below the abandoned mill. A rutted lane ran toward it, between hawthorn hedges twined with dog-roses. Thin blue smoke twisted from the chimney—a welcome and enticing sight. Toward this, the travelers bent their erratic steps, summoning the last of their strength.

As they approached, a soft, clear tinkling came to them in gusts. The thatched roofs of the cottage and outbuildings looked out from among spreading rowans bubbling with coralline berries, from whose boughs small bells of bronze depended. They rang prettily as the breeze swayed them. A stone wall meandered in and out of the borders of this coppice. A wide wooden gate opened out of the wall into the lane. It swung open easily, giving on to a stone-flagged path edged with rosebushes. This path led to a second gate in a low hedge, over which rambling roses had been trained in an arch. Beyond a trellis stood the house, covered with wisteria and columbine and climbing tea-roses whose green leaves were barely touched with the burnish of the season, plump rose-fruits pendant on their stems like ovoid lamps. Sunlight through the rowans damasked the brick chimney on the western wall, although rain-clouds were by now boiling up from the east. Iron horseshoes hung on nails over the front door and every window.

Diarmid staggered, steadied himself with one hand against a porch-post, and regained his balance. In his eyes, Imrhien read the determination to achieve one thing—to stay on his feet until they found a haven.

*Prithee,* she silently begged the occupants of the cottage, *do not turn us away. Do not despise the ugliness of my face. Give us shelter.*

She knocked three times on the door.

From within there came a sound as though someone pushed back a stool or chair. A voice called, "Is that thee, Da'?"

Diarmid moaned, almost inaudibly.

A bolt slid back with a click. And another. The door opened and a young woman's face appeared. With a short scream, she slammed the door. Presently she reopened it, wide-eyed.

"Who are thee? What's thane business?"

The man swayed. "Please—"

With an exclamation, the girl flung the door wide.

"Tha be 'urt! Why didn't tha say so!"

And with that, she put her small shoulder beneath Diarmid's free arm and helped Imrhien to half carry him indoors. The cockerel barged past, jumped on a spinning wheel, and flew up to the rafters.

They laid the sick man on a bed in the corner. The girl locked the door and bustled about the room, hanging a kettle of water over the fire, bringing clean bandages, setting food on the table. Kneeling beside the Ertishman, Imrhien watched her. She appeared to be about Muirne's age—perhaps twenty Winters old. Beneath her red head-scarf, her hair flowed walnut-brown and glossy. A dozen string-thin braids were twined decoratively among the tresses. Her cheeks and lips blushed with the tint of roses. She wore a well-laundered kirtle the color of oatmeal, covered with a spotless white pinafore apron tied in a bow at the back. Setting a bowl and a pile of clean linen before Imrhien, she said:

"Wash thane man's 'urts now and I'll give tha some salve afore tha binds 'em up."

Imrhien made the sign for "Thank you" and began her task.

"Tha doesn't talk. Wha's the matter wi' tha, my dove? Got a spell on tha?"

Diarmid cried out inadvertently as the old blood-stiffened bandages were peeled from his hands. Doggedly Imrhien continued her ministrations.

"Talk now, sir," the brown-haired girl said gently, "and tha will nae feel it so much."

Diarmid, stung to confused wakefulness, began to babble. Somewhere in the clutter of words, he managed to force out his own name and Imrhien's before he fell back, groaning.

The girl handed the salve to Imrhien, and she finished her work.

"Let 'im sleep. 'E's too hot, anyway. Somethin's got at 'im."

Imrhien nodded.

"Come to table, my dove. Tha look 'alf-starved, don't thee? Anyway, they call me Silken Janet and tha's come to Briar Cottage, in Rosedale. Welcome to thee."

To lie, bathed, with clean-rinsed hair, between utterly clean—if coarse—sheets, with a belly filled with warm bread and milk—this must surely be close to contentment.

Yet tired as she was, Imrhien could not sleep. Thoughts of the dark-haired Dainnan would not leave her in peace. She watched the fire-glow and candlelight flicker on the spinning wheel, underlighting the rafters where the rooster slept in a small, self-assured bundle. In another corner, Diarmid tossed and moaned. Silken Janet had swept the hearth with a goose-wing and set out a saucer of milk by the doorstep "for 'edge'og what comes by at nights," but she had not gone to bed; indeed, only two beds were to be seen in this one-room cottage.

"I'll make meself a bed o' bracken and hay," their hostess had explained—but she had not done so, and she seemed restless. She paced up and down, stopping sometimes at the shuttered windows as if listening and then kneeling by Diarmid's side to dab his forehead with cool water in which mint leaves had been sprinkled.

Raindrops had begun to patter on the thatch. Farm animals mooed or bellowed or clucked at intervals from somewhere out in the night—this did not perturb Silken Janet. She smoothed her hands down the front of her apron, picked up the goose-wing, and swept the hearth for the umpteenth time.

The wind took hold of the shutters and rattled them. Janet's head jerked up.

"Is that thee, Da'?"

There was no reply.

Imrhien raised herself on one elbow.

"So, tha's awake. Good. I'm goin' out." Janet untied her apron. "Tha can mind the house and yon man, and keep the fire a-goin'."

*This damsel would entrust her home and hearth to strangers,* thought Imrhien. *Is she perceptive, or merely naive?*

Janet removed some neatly pressed clothes from a chest.

"Tha canna put yon dirty rags o' thane on tha back. Take these o' mine. If anybody raps at door while I'm gane, don't let 'em in. After sunset, in these parts, tha might hear strange noises. There's some rum creatures roamin' these parts—nor rowan nor iron nor tinker-bells can fritten 'em off. Tha might chance to hear a sound like a child cryin', or some such, but if tha opens the door to help it, a girt black bull or a shadowy goblin dog might rush across the threshold, or worse things. And if tha hears a flappin' as of wings against the window, do not open the shutters or look out. Wicked creatures can have mickle fair voices. But they canna get in if tha don't lift the latch to 'em."

After giving these warnings, she lit a lantern and drew a hooded cloak around her shoulders. "But if anybody raps thrice, that will be me or me da', so let 'em in. 'E's been gane too long, me da'—'e went out after 'em bullocks what got loose out o' stalls today. Busted t' fence and went a-rovin', they did, and 'e went after 'em. Ain't come back. Musta got hisself strayed. I'll find 'im."

She picked up the lantern and took hold of a staff that had been leaning behind the door.

"It'll be cold out. Keep fire stoked and mind what I said—do not open door unless tha hears a three times knockin'. Like wha' *tha* did. No wight can cross over threshold uninvited."

<<You must not go out in the dark and the rain. It is too dangerous.>>

"I canna hear tha hands, my dove, and by t' look in thane eyes, I think if I could, I wouldna heed 'em. Fare tha well and lock t' door now."

Janet drew back the bolts and with a swish of her cloak was gone, closing the door carefully behind her. Her footsteps hurried away down the path.

Imrhien thrust the iron bolts home on the inside of the door, dressed herself in Janet's calico gown, and knelt at Diarmid's bedside to bathe his feverish brow.

When his fretful movements ceased and he had eased into a deeper sleep, she opened the small traveler's pouch she had carried on a thong about her neck all the way from Gilvaris Tarv. Throughout her arduous journey it had remained intact. The key to the caskets of treasure, the three jewels, and the bracelet of dove-white pearls gleamed in the flame-light. She took out the rope of pearls, placed it in Janet's clothes-chest, and shut the lid. Then she threw a stick on the fire and seated herself on the stool by the fireplace, stirring the embers with the poker, listening to the song of the rain.

Flames filled her vision. The fleeting shapes within them were castles on crags, twisted forests, shimmering dragons, crowds of ethereal beings. She tried to recall Thorn's face, but his image floated beyond her grasp.

The night advanced, and Janet had not yet returned. Lulled by the warmth and quietude, Imrhien began to feel sleepy at last. Once or twice she trickled water into the sick man's mouth when he half woke. He would gaze at her, saying, "Muirne?" and drift back into delirium. Only the plink of raindrops and the soft jinking of the rowan-bells disturbed the night's peace now.

Imrhien leaned the poker against the chimney corner. She fought the desire to close her eyes. Silken Janet had trusted her to "mind the house," so she must not betray that trust; must not lie down on the soft bed and succumb to the urgent need for sleep that now oppressed her.

The rain drummed. Diarmid lay helpless and insensible, his mouth ajar. Sweat-beads stood out on his forehead, and his fingers twitched feebly.

There was a knock at the door.

Imrhien jumped.

Three times the blow fell on the painted wood.

The girl did not run to the door straightaway. She could not call out to whoever stood on the doorstep, could not ask them to speak their name. It must be Janet's father giving the prearranged signal. Or Janet herself—but then Janet would call out, surely. Strange—there had been no sound of footsteps coming down the path.

A sudden thought made her hesitate. By chance, she herself had knocked thrice when she and Diarmid had first arrived.

What if—by chance—some malevolent visitor did the same?

Instinctively she drew her taltry over her head, pulling it forward so that her appalling visage was blotted out under a cowl of shadow.

Again the three blows landed on the door—louder this time—demandingly, insistently. Imrhien came to a decision. This was the signal about which Janet had tutored her so earnestly. She must not fail her hostess. Taking a candle with her, she walked toward the threshold. The iron bolts hammered into their brackets as she drew them back. She opened the door.

A dark-haired man strode in, shaking a glittering spray of water drops from his cloak.

Thorn.

Imrhien dropped the candle. It guttered out.

But no, he was not Thorn—her eyes, made inventive by longing, had deceived her. Here was a man less in stature, a stranger, drenched and dripping. Young and comely he was, with curling hair, and he spoke to her in some foreign tongue. He seemed to be asking to be allowed to warm himself at the fire. This struck a chord in the girl.

*Only hours ago it was I who sought shelter, I who could not make myself understood. Janet has shown me such hospitality—*

*should I not do the same for this man, even though this is not my own house?*

Bread and milk still stood on the table, but he would eat nothing she offered him. He merely lay down by the fire and fell asleep. She resumed her seat on the stool. The candle and the lamp had both gone out, but Imrhien blew up the fire—quietly, gently, so as not to disturb the sleepers. Its light flared, ruddy and cheerful. She glanced at the stranger.

His appearance was striking, unusual. His hair must be dyed, and freshly so, for the roots were as black as the rest—but the structure of his face did not seem to fit the Feorhkind mold, nor did he seem to come of any other race she had yet seen. By the fire's brighter illumination she now noticed a sight that paralyzed her. Half-hidden among his dark curls were fine, pointed ears.

So. He—*it* was a waterhorse.

So.

And it had come by night—doubtless it was one of the nocturnal kind, which could not bear the light of day.

A long, cold shudder rippled through her.

At any moment, this thing might take its horse's shape and drag her out into some nearby lake or pool to devour her beneath the waters. If only dawn would come, she would be saved. She sat as still as ice on the stool by the fire, and that was not an easy thing to do. Diarmid lay silent—for how much longer, she could not guess. Any movement or groan from him might waken the malignant thing. The night grew darker. She remembered that she had left the door unbolted, but it was too late now.

The rain drew away and left her alone. Outside the windows, the eaves dripped monotonously. The rowan-bells gave no sound. Every moment was stretched taut, to its limit. Imrhien had no way of reckoning how many hours remained until dawn. She dared not move a fingertip. If only he would stay asleep until then . . .

Too soon, a log cracked and flared, and the stranger roused. He sat up and drew from his sleeve a long string of emeralds, which he dangled enticingly before Imrhien. His slim fingers beckoned her. His twilight eyes were fraught with liquid reflections of desire and death: panes staring out from some remote and drowned place. She pushed his hand aside, and he caught her gown. She jerked away, knocking over the poker, which clattered loudly to the hearthstone. At this sound, the little black cock sitting on the rafter woke and crowed. The unseelie thing dashed out the unbolted door. Horse's hooves trampled the path outside, rushed through the gate, and galloped away down the lane to the west.

In the wake of the unseelie being, a sudden, violent wind gusted. The door swung wide on its hinges and banged against the wall. She ran to close it but stopped with her hand on the latch. A glimmer of light was bobbing down the lane from the east. Two figures with a lantern held high were approaching swiftly. In at the garden gate they entered: a woman and, at her side, a tall man striding toward Imrhien in haste.

Lamplight flowed over the broad shoulders of the tall figure and struck ruby glints in the mazy skeins of his midnight hair. Behind Imrhien's ribs, a storm raged. At the sight of him, a scintillation flared through her flesh, branching out to sear along every nerve, snatching breath.

"Did it harm you, the Glastyn?" asked Thorn, lifting the lantern so that its amber glow flooded Imrhien's face. "We saw it race from here as we came to the gate. Did it harm you?"

She shook her head, could not make any other sign, could only look at him, drinking in the sight as a parched wanderer slakes his thirst at a desert well. She noted every detail over and again: the diamond plane between the jawline and the high cheekbones, the firm set of the mouth, the eyes whose cold fire seemed to penetrate all, the natural grace of his stance, the hand, long and strong, which held the dark-lantern. Indeed it was he.

"Turn around," he said.

She spun on her heel.

"Yes, you are hale, I see. And the Glastyn runs from you as though horsewhipped. Remarkable. The captain—is he in the house?"

<<Yes, but—>>

"Wait indoors." Without further explanation he was away, rounding the corner of the cottage.

Silken Janet laughed and accompanied Imrhien into the house. She shook out her wet cloak by the fire.

"Close door, me dove, 'e will be back in a trice. 'E's just gone tae 'elp me da' put the bullocks tae bed. Found me da', I did. At any rate, thane 'andsome Dainnan found 'im and then brought us both 'ome, bullocks and all. Dainnan were seekin' tha. Asked if we 'ad seen tha. Said both o' thee would be comin' out o' mines. Is tha unscathed?"

Imrhien nodded.

"Is tha certain?" Janet peered anxiously at her guest. "Tha might be shock-shaken now. Sit here at table. 'Tis white tha be, white as me pinny. That wicked 'orse-wight might 'ave 'ad tha in another ring o' the bell. What must tha go openin' doors for?"

Wearily Imrhien tapped three times on the table. Then she leaned her elbows on her knees, resting her head in her hands.

"There I go, axin' too many questions," said Janet. "Never mind, I'll leave tha be. 'Ow fares me dove?" She bent over Diarmid's sleeping face. "Nae good, nae good. Janet's come now. Janet'll take care o' thee."

She threw some sticks on the fire and swung the kettle over it. As she busied herself with preparations for a midnight supper, she kept up a flow of chatter.

"Glastyn were right 'ere, eh? Wicked thing. Is tha carlin, then, tae get rid o' sich a wight? . . . Nay? I thought tha carlin. Carlins 'ave tae give summat in return for their powers. I thought tha gived tha voice or tha face. But tha got nothin' in return, eh? 'Tis a wicked world. 'Ow dreadful—that unseelie thing in me own 'ome. Gives me the shudders. Da' and me shall 'ave tae choose a better signal than three knocks—folly o' me, that's anybody's!"

Boot-heels crunched down the path. Preceded by a gust of cold wind and a swirl of dying rose-leaves, the two men entered, Thorn ducking his head to clear the low lintel. Janet's father bolted the door in a practiced manner. Snow-haired, his grim face tanned and creased by windblown sunshine, he yet retained a measure of the good looks he must have possessed in his youth, except that he was a little stooped, as though he had struggled for years to carry a great burden on his shoulders. He was clothed in a faded red cap, stout boots, breeches tucked into gaiters, a tartan waistcoat, and a matching worsted jacket. His hair was shorn just below his ears. He held an iron-shod staff, and on his finger gleamed a thick gold signet ring. A lean, restless hound trotted at his side.

This man held out a hand to Imrhien, palm up. She gave him her own, and he bowed over it, speaking with a mixture of the cultured accents of a gentleman and a country burr.

"I bid thee welcome, my lady Imrhien. Sir Thorn has told me of thee. Roland Trenowyn, at tha service."

Thorn had gone at once to Diarmid's bedside.

"How can this be? He has the mark of the Beithir on him!"

He placed his hand on the Ertishman's brow. "He burns. But the fever has turned already, and he has the strength to fight. I judge he will be well by morning. If this is the brand of the lightning serpent, then you took a wrong turning in the mines. I'll warrant it was not *your* heart, lady, that led you to the serpent's lair."

"Beithir!" exclaimed Janet, kneeling by the Ertishman's side. "So that's what struck 'im. Ain't seen anythin' like it before. Poor dove."

"Come, Janet," said her father, "if Sir Thorn says he will recover, let us not keep our guests waiting for their supper. Pray, do us the honor of joining us at table, sir and my lady. Our fare is humble, but all that we have is at your disposal. Whatever you ask for shall be provided, have we the means. . . . "

All voices faded. The floor tilted, and the room went black at the edges. Imrhien made a grab for the corner of the table for support, but it swung away. Overwhelmingly, the past few days had come crowding back—the attack of the Beithir, she half carrying Diarmid through the mines, the long nights on hard beds of stone, the narrow escape from the Glastyn, and now meeting again with Thorn.

It was as if a great wave of terror, despair, and joy had been gathering itself together as she sat at the Trenowyns' table, rising ever higher over her head. All at once this accumulation reached breaking point.

A darkness came roaring in from the perimeters of her skull. The wave came thundering down.

The rooster crowed. Deep in the cobwebs of sleep, Imrhien heard Silken Janet speaking.

"Now, me dove, tha can come out wi' me tae the 'en'ouse. That's the place for thee, instead o' wakin' folk with thane racket. Come on, tha goosegog, I got a 'andful o' corn for thee!"

After some squawking and fluttering, quiet resumed. Long, long waves of black slumber came rolling over.

It seemed that not a minute had gone by when Imrhien was woken by a rattle at the window and opened her eyes to see Janet flinging wide the shutters. Long diagonals of sunlight streamed in, and sweet birdsong, and the earthy smell of moist loam and wet leaves. On the eaves above the windows, doves repeated, "Coo-coroo-coo." Somewhere outside, hens were cackling and something mooed. Imrhien felt refreshed in mind and body. A whiff of baking bread scented the air.

"Good mornin' to thee"—Janet smiled—"and a fair mornin' it is. Thane captain said so, too, not long since."

Diarmid pushed aside a curtain in the corner and stepped out, without any sign of favoring his leg. He was freshly scrubbed and shaved, dressed in some of Trenowyn's clothes—woollen breeches, leathern gaiters, a linen shirt, and a twill jacket, looking quite the country squire, except for the hair that fell past his shoulders, red and brown.

Imrhien jumped up and ran to him.

<<How hale you look!>> Indeed, he did look well. Although the gash on his forehead was still scabrous and puffy, a rosy hue stained his cheeks—not the flush of fever, but the bloom of health.

<<Show me your hands.>>

<<They are healing,>> signed Diarmid. <<It is the fairest of mornings, and I am forever in your debt.>> He bent his knee, kissed the back of her hand, and stood again, palms outstretched. The ruined tissue had been sloughed. Over his palms new skin had already formed, pink and fragile. Only, on each of them, was emblazoned a white mark like forked lightning. <<The unguents of our hostess are marvelous!>>

He stilled his hands and asked in a low voice, "I have heard that you were in danger last night. How is it that you escaped from the Glastyn?"

<<The rooster crowed untimely. Thinking dawn was nigh, the thing fled.>>

"'S death!" Diarmid said in astonishment. "Then the raucous bird has repaid its debt in full! Where is it now?"

<<In the henhouse.>>

Laughter and footsteps came up the garden path. Silken Janet leaned out of the window.

"So, there tha be! Did tha 'ave a comfortable night in 'ayloft?" She unbolted the door. Her father entered. Thorn stood outside on the path with Errantry on his upraised wrist, the fierce talons clutching the leathern armband. The goshawk spread his wings wide to keep balance; the great draft of their movement sent his master's unbound hair tossing like long grasses underwater.

Janet eyed the bird with some alarm. "Do tha bird fly at rooks, Sir Thorn?"

There was an edge to her voice.

"Not if I forbid it." The Dainnan looked directly at Janet and smiled. Then he turned his attention to the goshawk. "So-ho, Bold-and-Fearless!" He threw his arm upward to help the bird take off, watching him rise with a whirr and a clatter of wings and fly over the trees. Then he stepped indoors.

The five of them sat down to a hearty breakfast. There being only four seats, Thorn elected to sit on the window ledge. He leaned his back against the frame, one booted foot on the sill, the other swinging. At his back soared a washed blue sky—often he would turn his head to look out at the wind-driven clouds scudding over the treetops, as if to be between walls made him restless.

Janet had set before them ripe blackberries, gooseberry tart, rhubarb and pink quinces in honeyed syrup, bread and butter, scrambled eggs, cream and honey, green cheese flecked with sage, frothing milk, mellow, yellow mead, and dandelion wine. The guests complimented her on her table and did full justice to it. There was so much to eat and so much to tell that the sun had climbed toward its zenith before they were finished.

The travelers had immediately asked for news. Trenowyn reported that the King-Emperor's Legions were in full strength at Caermelor, while recruits for the army and for the Dainnan were being summoned now to rally at Isenhammer. It was rumored that conflict was forthcoming, for the gathering forces in Namarre had grown strong in numbers, and while they had not yet mobilized, it seemed certain that they would soon strike south. At these tidings, shadows of concern darkened the faces of both Thorn and Diarmid.

The Dainnan had searched for Imrhien and Diarmid—they had remained longer in the mines than he had reckoned, and since the underground ways led to many openings, he had suspected they had taken a wrong turning. While seeking them, he had first encountered Roland Trenowyn, whose beasts had strayed far. He had helped the farmer drive them home, and on their way they had met Janet.

Diarmid questioned Thorn about his unexpected errand in answer to the call of the Dainnan horn.

"It was Flint of the Third Thriesniun who sounded that call," replied the Dainnan. "He and a scouting party found themselves in dire peril, caused indirectly by certain wights who dwell beneath the ground. What do you know of the Fridean?"

"I know plenty," put in Trenowyn. "Doundelding is as riddled as a worm's nest with underground tunnels and caves. The Fridean delve them, as they are wont to delve beneath many remote regions of Erith. He who stands above Fridean diggings might betimes catch their music rising from beneath his feet. He who unwisely lingers above Fridean diggings when a boulder falls nearby might well find himself undermined. For the Fridean do not delve with accuracy in the manner of eldritch miners. My friends the knockers shore up the walls of their tunnels and secure the ceilings with crossbeams. The Fridean merely dig in straight lines without reference to consequences. When they encounter a hard substance they cannot penetrate, they turn a corner and continue in a straight line in another direction. In this manner they build labyrinths, sometimes close to the surface. Should their tunnels collapse, as often happens, they are never troubled."

"And should tha go intae the hills and sit upon a bare rock tae tak' a bite, and should tha let fall a morsel or two," declared Janet, "then t' crumbs will be gone afore tha can say Jack Robinson."

"Then we have met the Fridean in the mines!" said Diarmid. "And was it those wights who threatened the lives of Sir Flint and his men?"

"No," said Thorn, "for they do not harm mortals. But at the dawning of the day, one came nigh whose joy it is to destroy creatures that live, and that was the Cearb, who is called the Killing One. Where the Cearb walks, the ground quakes. The Dainnan were unaware they traveled above a hollow maze the Fridean delved long ago. Great cracks opened beneath their feet, and as they fell, struggling, the Cearb came at them, for it is one of the Lords of Unseelie and has no fear of the sun's rays. Yet it may be outrun by the fleet of foot—lured away by a decoy so that others may escape."

"Wert tha able to save 'em?" asked Janet, agog.

"Indeed. The call was sounded early, and I was able to reach them at the crucial instant," Thorn said. Enigmatically he added, "This time."

He would say no more on the subject.

Thorn and Trenowyn having spoken, it was Diarmid's turn. Having dined with a prodigious appetite, he related the tale of the sacking of Chambord's Caravan, of their meeting with the Dainnan and subsequent wanderings through Mirrinor and Doundelding, and all that he could recall about the mines, prompted by Imrhien's handspeak. Silken Janet sat silent throughout, wide-eyed, too rapt to think of bringing a morsel to her lips. Few travelers ever passed through Rosedale—the words they were prepared to spare were fewer.

"Well!" she exclaimed when the tale was told. "Ain't never 'eard nothin' like it in all me born days! So, tha saw trows beyond Emmyn Vale, did tha? Ain't never been that far afield, but there's lots of trows 'ereabouts, ain't there, Da'?"

"Here? In Rosedale?" asked Diarmid.

"Aye, sir. Once, Da's cousin's family came to stay 'ere unexpectedlike, and there's six o' 'em, with four growed-up lads, and I was in such a tither findin' places for them to bed down and food for table that I clean forgot tae do some o' me tasks. The trows 'ave it that every hearth shall be swept clean on a sevennight, that no one shall be found near it, and above all that plenty o' clean water shall be found in 'ouse. All these things were neglected—I was bedded down near fireplace, 'avin' given me bed away, and when the trows came they were mighty enraged and made such a noise that I awoke. The guests were so drunk, they kept on sleepin', and Da' was snorin' away after 'ard day's work.

"Anyway, I wake up and what should I see but two trow-wives seating themselves not far from where I lay, and one with a lovely little baby. The one without t' baby sought for clean water but found none and revenged 'erself by takin' the first liquor she came across, which chanced tae be a keg o' swatts I 'ad a-steepin' in t' corner.

"Now, Sir Captain, tha would know what swatts is, bein' from Finvarna and all, but 'tis not a common drink in Eldaraigne." Janet turned to Imrhien. "Da' and me, we 'ave a dish called sowens, which we make by steepin' oat-husks in water. When 'tis fermented a little, we boil it to make it ready to eat. But the water that covers sowens is called swatts. The trows poured some o' swatts in a basin and washed their baby in it, and then baby's clothes, and then poured the mess back into keg, sayin', 'Tak ye dat for no haein' clean water ae da hoose.' They then sat down close by fire, hanging baby's clothes on their big feet, spreadin' their feet out before fire to dry t' garments in that way!"

Even Trenowyn's somber visage lightened at the picture Janet painted. Diarmid smiled and Thorn laughed; at his laughter, Janet's cheeks flushed. She resumed her tale with renewed enthusiasm.

"Now I was watchin' all this, and I knew that if I kept me eyes fixed on them, they could not go away. So I kept starin' and listenin' to their conversation in 'opes o' 'earin' somethin' worth rememberin'. But the trow-wives began tae fidget, bein' desirous o' departing before sunrise, and at last one o' them stuck tongs in fire and made 'em red hot! As soon as tongs became glowing, she seized 'em and, approachin' me, pointed a blade at each eye, grinnin' in the most 'ideous manner, while she brought t' tongs closer to me face. O' course I blinked and screamed, and the trows, takin' advantage of the moment when me eyes were closed, fled. Next mornin' when we all went to take sowens from the keg for breakfast, there was nothin' left but dirty water!"

"The trows are quick to take offense when housework is not done," commented Trenowyn, "but that is the only time such a thing has happened, and 'twas not the fault of Janet."

"Tha's got to be careful with trows," continued Janet, "for they'll sometimes carry off animals, or even men, women, or children, and leave in their stead some semblance, a seeming-thing. That 'appened 'ere once. One fine day, me da' got up to see 'ow the sun rose, for by that 'e can tell if 'twill be a fine day for the cartin', and goin' out to the side-gate, 'e saw two gray-clad boys goin' along the lane below the 'ouse. 'E thought they were with some travelers come by the mines, but when they came benigh 'ouse they left lane and went up to where our brindle cow Daisy was lying on grass. They walked up to Daisy's face, then turned away again, running, and cow ran, too, following as far as her tether would stretch. I came to the gate then, and I swear I saw all three run up the 'ill and right over top. But when we went to look, Daisy was still there. She died that same day, so 'tis clear the trows took the real one and 'twas but a Seeming that was left to die."

"Aye," said her father, "but there was worse than that from the hill-tings, before." He and his daughter exchanged glances. She nodded, shuddering. "One Winter night," said Trenowyn, "I was away from home on a short journey. When I was returning across the hills in the darkness and had got down close to the outer gate, I met a gang of trows carrying a bundle between them. I had a kind of strange feeling as I looked at that bundle, but I allowed them to pass and hurried on toward the cottage.

"As soon as I entered the door, I saw that Janet was gone, and that the trows had left an effigy of her in her accustomed chair. Quick as thought, I seized the trow-stock, which looked like Janet in every way, I assure you—and flung it into the fire."

"'S death!" exclaimed Diarmid. "How could you be certain 'twas not your daughter?"

"Well," said Trenowyn, "if a man cannot know how his own child greets him, then what kind of father be he?" He turned away his head for a moment, and they could not read his expression.

Presently Thorn said, "What happened next?"

"The effigy at once took fire," said Trenowyn. "It rose into the air, flaming, amid a cloud of smoke, and vanished up the chimney. As it disappeared, Janet walked in at the cottage door, safe and sound. Soon after, we bought some potent charms from a wizard in Isenhammer, and the trows have never been back in this house since, of which I am glad."

"Conceivably you earned their respect," Thorn suggested.

"I . . . don't know about that, Sir Thorn," Trenowyn stammered, embarrassed. "Mayhap I have earned the respect of the knockers, but I never thought of that with the trows."

"And what manner of wights are knockers?" Diarmid asked.

"They are small seelie miners," replied Trenowyn, "those you spoke of, Captain, which you saw dwelling beneath Doundelding and under the hills on the marches of Rosedale. And they be bread and butter to us, good sirs. Not like those thickheaded coblynau, who do nothing. The wee knockers—some call them bockles—know where the rich lodes be. They dig it out and pack it into the trams. The bluecaps are the tram-putters. They bring the ore to the surface every night, up to a place behind Tinner's Knoll—you canna see it from here. They tip their loads into my wain, which commonly I leave at the mine's entrance. When it is full enough I hitch up the bullocks and drive to Isenhammer to sell the ore. Isenhammer, where the big furnaces be, is five days' drive from here—two days out from the King's Cross. I shall be making a trip three days from now, if tha wants a ride in. Once a fortnight I go down the mine and leave payment for the knockers and the bluecaps in a solitary corner, keeping a bit back myself for cartage. That's how we live, by that and the farm-beasts and Janet's bit o' garden wi' the roses. I never cheat the knockers, and they always do right by me. Doesn't pay to try to cheat wights. They be industrious and require, quite rightly, to be paid for their work. If I should leave a farthing below their due, they would get mighty indignant and would not pocket a stiver. If 'twere a farthing above their due, they would leave the surplus revenue where they found it, and I can tell thee they would be just as angry about that!"

"Perhaps the lodes are still rich," said Diarmid, "but small wights cannot dig out great quantities. Why do men not delve the mines of Rosedale and Doundelding for themselves? By the look of this valley, methinks the diggings are long abandoned."

"You are not mistaken, sir. Men used to mine here, long ago, but no more. Mining men will not go near where bockles are delving, no matter how much payment is offered. There used to be an old gravity-mill in Rosedale, too, for concentrating the ore. The underground creeping got to it, not long before the knockers and bluecaps moved in—so they say—and the mill subsided, but that was before we came here."

"I bring in a few extra coins," interjected Janet. "In Summer when the roses bloom I 'arvest 'em and brew attar of roses to perfume the fine ladies of Isen'ammer. I make rose vinegar, rose 'oney, rose oil, and rose-petal beads. This cot smells so sweet all Summer, don't it, Da'!"

Diarmid was charmed. "How may beads be manufactured from flower petals?" he asked. "Surely 'tis not possible!"

Janet laughed. "Ain't tha never seen it done? Tha mun put the petals in a pan with a few drops of water, and add a rusty nail to give t' beads a better color. Tha must heat 'em once a day for three days, and they turn to pulp. When 'tis cool, tha mun roll pulp with thy fingers, press out drops, and shape 'em into beads around a darnin' needle so that there be an 'ole through the center. Then tha mun leave 'em to dry, turnin' 'em twice a day. Rose-petal beads smell sweetest when worn—the warmth of skin brings out t' perfume." She showed them the necklace of rich red beads she wore about her own white neck.

"A pleasant Summer task," said Diarmid, "working amidst flowers."

"Janet is always busy throughout the year," her father stated.

"At other seasons I spin nettles that grow around 'ere," Janet said, "or flax for folk in Isenhammer. Da' brings it home in wagon, big sacks o' lint, and I spin it into skeins, then 'e takes it back to town when 'e goes."

"Do you dye the yarn?" Diarmid slid in another question.

"Aye," Janet said, "when there be call for 't. Got some nice woad growin' in me garden, for the blues, and some madder for reds. Canna grow worts or herbs in me patch, but woad and madder do well."

"Do you have any, er, brown dye?" the Ertishman asked casually.

"Ain't got call for brown. Might be able tae get it from oak—"

Thorn drew something from his pocket and tossed it across to Diarmid. "The root of iris," he said.

"That makes black, don't it?" said Janet. "Ain't never used it, but I've 'eard. 'Ow is it mordanted?"

"With an iron mordant, to which salt and elder has been added," Thorn said.

From beyond the window came the grating calls of a flock of rooks, like groans of agony. Thorn turned his gaze toward the windy sky; Janet and her father also. A flock of birds rushed up from the boughs of a tree and flew away, long stitches of black thread unraveling. In the sudden silence, a shadow crossed Trenowyn's face.

"Got beasts to tend," he said gruffly. After excusing himself, he called the hound to him and went out. Silken Janet went to stand at the window.

"'Ow many rooks were in that tree?" she asked softly.

"Seven." Thorn glanced at her sharply.

The merry breakfast had come to an end on a strangely jarring note.

Imrhien and Diarmid helped Janet to clear away, a task that was evidently unfamiliar to the Ertishman. He seemed preoccupied.

<<You should go and see how our friend the cockerel fares,>> he signed. He was using handspeak more often now, out of politeness to Imrhien, since he owed her his life.

"What's all that flappin' about? What are tha sayin'?"

"The cockerel—see?" Diarmid wagged his hands.

"Oh, aye, 'e's round in the 'en'ouse. They be all bantams in there. Do 'im good. Our other one died two months ago; pretty old 'e was. So thane black rooster ain't got no rival. I let 'em out in mornin', tae 'ave a peck round garden."

Imrhien indicated that she would perform this task today.

<<You may keep the rooster,>> she added.

Diarmid conveyed the message to Janet, who clapped her hands, overjoyed.

The rooster did indeed appear unrivaled. Imrhien opened the door of the henhouse and watched him strut out into the garden, bossing the fussy hens, snatching caterpillars from under their beaks, ignoring her, his rescuer, with the air of a preoccupied patriarch. When she passed by the cottage and glanced through the open window, Imrhien saw Janet washing Diarmid's hair in a bowl of black water. She continued on and went to sit on the well-head's coping, in the sunshine. Stone frogs goggled from the well's mossy wall, and the slates of its pitched roof were furred gray green with lichen.

It was a fine Autumn morning. Behind the cottage, steep, grassy shoulders of land climbed to the softest of skies. To the west, beyond a sunken fence, a meadow rolled down to a little glad brook that ran chuckling through it, coming out of the hills over cold gray stones. There, a cow and two bullocks grazed. Northward, a gentle combe overgrown with sweet-briars sloped to a timbered height on the other side. The miniature silhouette of a ship sailed up there, distant, lost in the clouds, for an outer Windship route crossed Woody Hill.

To the east lay the mine hills. Tall chimneys of brick or stone like pointing fingers stood in groups, the wood of their miners' houses having burned down or been taken for firewood long since. The sound of dunting carried in the still air from the old gravity-mill. Dull red berries spattered the stark hawthorns along the lane and bordering the fields; poplars reached skyward, their stripped boughs trimmed with the yellow lace of lichen to match the flowers of the gorse. Lorikeets flashed like emeralds as they flew up, startled, from long cream-colored grasses, and the afternoon light in the meadow glowed on the coat of the curly brown cow.

The open air invigorated Imrhien after the stuffiness of the mines. She drank it in great cold drafts. Her old traveling taltry was pushed back, and the breeze from the north lifted her hair about her face in strands of shining gold. It had grown rapidly and was now as long as Diarmid's, reaching halfway down her back in soft crimps and ringlets like rippled sea-sand strewn with copper corkscrews.

She would wimple her hair for the journey and for coming in to the city. *Ah, the city,* she thought. Caermelor was so close now—White Down Rory even nearer. This face with its dreadful knots and bulges—the skin and flesh had been distorted for so long. How long? How could it ever heal? Her goal had been to find a history, a voice, a presentable face. Deep in her heart, now, something mattered more, but that was a vanity of vanities, an ache, a wound that could never heal.

The source of that pain came walking lightly toward the well with the goshawk on his shoulder. He was singing the second part of a familiar ditty in a clear voice, flawlessly modulated:

'Tis the voices in unison lilting and clear,
And the weaving of harmonies sweet to the ear
Sung to a melody stirring and keen
And the music of harps in the woodlands so green!
Singing 'neath the trees, O! Singing 'neath the trees!

'Tis the smoking hot platter of meats heaped on high
And the dishes of pastries that gladden the eye
The fruit of the forest, the wine in the cup
Good cheer and good appetite—long may we sup!
Feasting one and all, O! Feasting one and all!

With his customary grace, he swung down beside her, his presence igniting a keen and strange delight. His shirtsleeve brushed her wrist. She did not know if she fell into the well and it was a well without nadir or whether she remained seated on the stone coping.

"We are close now to our destination," Thorn said, patently oblivious of his effect on her. "Trenowyn leaves in three days' time with a cartload of ore for Isenhammer. If we wish to ride with him, we can wait. I prefer to leave tomorrow on foot—too much time has been lost already."

<<I also.>>

"What is it that takes you to the Royal City?"

She hesitated, torn between keeping her pledge of secrecy to Ethlinn and confiding all to this dark enchanter whose laughing eyes now rested on her. There could be no harm in telling everything to Thorn, yet a promise made must not be broken. Regretfully she sighed.

<<I seek a village close by the Royal City. Its name is White Down—>> Would the Dainnan understand? The sign Ethlinn had taught for "Rory" was the sign for the roar of a bull, there being no other equivalent in handspeak.

"White Down Rory? Why then, our ways must part at the King's Cross. There, the Bronze Road crosses the Caermelor Road, coming up from the south from White Down Rory, and wending north to where the blast furnaces stain the skies with their smoke. Have you ever been to Isenhammer?"

She shook her head.

"At night, the visitor who approaches that town sees the sudden glow of liquid orange as pots from the furnaces are tipped over, emptying the molten slag down the hill like lava from miniature volcanoes. There is a certain splendor to it."

He took from around his neck a golden locket on a chain. The size of his thumbnail, it was curiously wrought in filigree. The detail of the intertwining leaf-patterns and the quality of the workmanship were beyond anything Imrhien remembered seeing.

<<What is kept inside?>>

He smiled, but this time there was little joy on his countenance. "Only this."

He unsnibbed the tiny clasp and opened the locket. A fine, dry dust lay there. Thorn gazed long upon it with sightless eyes, as if stirred by some memory. The substance looked like ordinary sand or powdered clay, but, as her own eyes rested upon it, Imrhien was seized by a terrible longing or hunger, the like of which she had never known. She reached out to touch it, but too late, for with a quick breath, Thorn had blown it away. The breeze took up the light burden and scattered it over the garden, over the rooster sitting on a trellis, over the hens. As they flew, the fine particles sparkled in every color, glorified the air with a rainbow, and faded with a sigh as of a myriad voices. With a mighty spring, the goshawk flew up from Thorn's shoulder and disappeared in the sky.

"Janet shall have no trouble growing the finest herbs this year, and every year after that," the Dainnan said softly.

He closed the locket and hid it again beneath his shirt.

The rooster fell off the trellis, very ungainly, in front of the hens.

For no reason that she could fathom, Imrhien was left with a deep sense of loneliness and bitter loss. Thorn regarded her gravely. His hands shaped the language of signs:

<<Come, walk with me to the orchard while the day is yet sunny.>>

All sorrow lifted. Willingly, light-footed, she went beside him, past the cramped stone dairy that had been built half under the ground for coolness, past the byre, out through a side-gate in the yew hedge, past the humming bee-skeps to the little orchard. The grasses of Autumn were toast-colored, the last of their clinging seed-heads as fine as sprinkled powder.

In the orchard, a few withered pippins still clung to the branches or lay windfallen in the grass. The quince and apple trees stood almost leafless now, the pear boughs had long since stretched naked against the sky, but beside them, as a windbreak, stood a line of ancient candlebark gumtrees, as green as ever.

Thorn's voice rose in song once more, as strong and warm as spiced wine and as intoxicating:

Autumn is mellow, a lady of leisure
Dew in the morning, that's Autumn's treasure.
Red on the maple, gold on the willow,
Dress'd in bright colors, Autumn is mellow.

Bonny, bonny Spring is a lassie fair,
Flowers at her feet and blossoms in her hair,
Lambs in the pasture, birds on the wing,
Rain on the leaf-buds—bonny, bonny Spring.

Merry, merry Summer is a maiden gay,
Sun on the cornfield and heat in the hay.
Tawny-tressed Summer is brown as a berry
Through the long evenings, Summer is merry.

Winter is wise, with hair like the snow.
Under her mantle the wild creatures go.
Frost on the hillsides, clouds in the skies,
Rest and find peace, for Winter is wise.

"Are you then the personification of Spring, Gold-Hair?" he inquired.

Lowering her deformed face, she let the pouring glory of her hair curtain its hideousness and parried his question with another.

<<If Spring is gold-tressed and Summer brown, then Autumn ought to be red-haired, red as the vine. The song says Winter's hair is white, but which season is akin to you?>>

This was a chaffing question, since it was obvious he garnered the roots of the wild iris wherever he found them and carried these vegetables with him, in order to rinse his hair with black dye when the color grew out. He had chosen the midnight shade, one of the two colors most popular among the pedigreed citizens of Gilvaris Tarv, who copied the trends flourishing at the King-Emperor's Court. Doubtless, even the Dainnan were not immune to the vagaries of fashion.

In reply to her banter, Thorn only laughed. They stood together beneath an antique apple that leaned out with twisted boughs like yearning arms. A breeze rustled its leaves and made dapples of sunlight dance on the lichened bark.

"The changes of the year are worthy of song," he said, gazing up at the tree. "They lie fair on the lands. Each possesses its own rare beauty. To those who understand them, the wild lands and the seasons are generous, providing shelter and sustenance of spirit and body. There is no need to hunger or thirst in the lands of Erith."

<<Not all wanderers are such proficient gatherers and hunters as the Dainnan. Many starve.>>

"As you have starved? Allow me to advise you, Gold-Hair. When all else fails, there is always Fairbread—Wayfarer's Loaf, Farbrod, or Hob's Cob, as it is also known. It is a victual with many names—some call it the Bread of the Faêran. Have you heard of it? . . . No? Most folk fancy it no more than the subject of old wives' tales. It is real, but hard to see unless you know how to look. You understand that if folk step upon a stray sod, they cannot find their path? With Fairbread, it is as if the eyes of all men are under such a misleading spell all the time, unless they cast it off. It is the fruit of a mistletoe that loves only certain trees—apple, alder, hazel, holly and willow, elder, oak, banksia and elm, birch and blackthorn. Never does it grow on other trees, and not always on those I have cataloged for you. But if moss or lichen loves the tree's bole and clings to it like a tight-laced bodice, then there is a good chance of Fairbread. These fruits can only be seen in certain lights—in the first and last rays of the sun, and never when the wind blows from the east. You must stand beneath a tree, such as this apple, and look to the left. In the half-light your eyes may trick you—but if you glimpse, at the edges of sight, leafy sprouts and amongst them small, soft spheres like softly glowing lamps, then you may reach up and pluck them. This is the Fairbread and provides much sustenance. But touch it not if it is seen by night. Washed with starlight or moonlight, it may intoxicate the blood, and perilously."

<<This is useful knowledge for travelers!>>

The greatest of the orchard's windbreak trees had, in its youth, grown three main stems; over time they had thickened to massive girth. One had fallen long ago and lay on the ground, yet it thrived still. It had turned its new sprouts up toward the sky, sending out boughs that overarched to form the roof of a living bower. The branches of the other two trunks spread wide and wept downward. Their ends lay along the grass like many-fingered hands, tufted with verdant hair, the younger shoots yellow green against the dusky jade of their elders. Leaning on its elbows, the whole tree formed a natural chamber, thatched and walled with long leaves, and from the outside it resembled a leafy knoll.

An old rope swing dangled from one of the branches that reached like a rafter across this green hall. Imrhien seated herself on its wooden plank, but Thorn climbed into the branches above. He lay sprawled across the boughs, hanging on by some Dainnan art or gramarye, and pushed on the ropes.

"Unless you wish to fall, you cannot speak while you hold fast. Thus, I must sing to you."

But the lyrics of the song he sang were shaped by a language she did not understand. It sounded like no Ertish dialect or any other tongue she had ever heard spoken, save only when Thorn had named the Dragon's Blood or identified certain trees and flowers. The timbre and cadence of the words possessed a potent loveliness. Alien they were, but harmonious, thrilling. Although Imrhien could not know their meaning, they fell on her ears like sweet rain from some cloud-borne realm of crystal palaces a thousand feet tall, intersected with shafts of clear radiance and purple shadow. They whispered beckoningly to her, deeply stirring. They gave her half-glimpsed visions of wonder and lured her among stars larger and brighter than any that lit the skies of Erith, to a country beyond the shores of the known lands that was filled with peril and delight unguessed. Her imprisoned memory dragged at its chains, straining to be free. Slowly Thorn swung the ropes that lifted her, and then faster, higher, and his song changed like a swift river leaping and dancing down from high mountains, like a free bird, swooping and soaring, riding the back of the wind.

Imrhien swept back and forth through the sunlit air. First it would pour into her face like a gush of transparent mountain water, dragging her hair and garments backward; then for a heartbeat she would be weightless before falling backward with a rush, her hair billowing about her face in streamers, her skirts a flurry of fabric folds flapping at her feet. The exultation made her breathless. Through the long falls of leaves she flew, as though borne by sildron or upon a shang wind. She kicked her feet and would have laughed aloud, had she been able, but Thorn laughed for her, perceiving her joyousness as she tipped back her terrible face and let her hair swing out, careless as a child, until the tilting of the world made her dizzy and she clutched hard at the ropes, not knowing or caring whether sky and ground were above or below, because she would fly forever, as long as those hands held the ropes and she was holding them, too.

When Imrhien returned to the cottage, Silken Janet was clucking disapprovingly around Diarmid, holding up a little burnished bronze mirror for him.

"I've dyed thane eyebrows but will not do thane lashes—the dye can blind 'e. Black, 'e says, so black 'e gets, but it don't suit tha, beggin' thane pardon, sir. Thane own shade's so comely, so rare. I've always thought, 'ow nice 'twould be tae 'ave Ertish blood and that lovely 'air like polished copper. I'd swap it for mine any day."

"Do I appear Ertish now, madam?" said Diarmid, taking the mirror and peering into it so closely that his eyes crossed.

"Not at all, without that lovely red—the bone-shapes o' your folk and mine bein' much the same."

The answer seemed to please Diarmid. Janet added:

"O' course, tha has got them lovely blue eyes like forget-me-nots." Abruptly, Diarmid slammed down the mirror. Outside the window, startled rooks cawed contemptuous accusations among the trees.

Trenowyn came in carrying two longbows, his highly strung hound trotting at his heels.

"Thought I might get us a partridge for our supper."

The Ertishman picked up a bow, examining it. "I should like to shoot those blasted rooks that are racketing by your gate."

There was a crash. Janet had dropped a bowl. It lay in rocking shards. Trenowyn's face was deeply graven stone, gray and haggard.

"Never shoot a rook," he rasped, as if his throat had withered and dried, "never."

Diarmid shrugged, clearly bewildered. "I jest." He replaced the longbow on the table.

Slowly Trenowyn's glare faded. He took up from where he had left off, as though nothing untoward had happened. "I also want to check on the wagon—to see how much ore they have put in it by now. Don't want it too heavy for the bullocks. Is it to your liking, sir, going after game fowls?"

It was to Diarmid's liking. The men went off hunting together.

Toward evening, Imrhien was walking in the garden when she heard voices. Between the rowans she could see Silken Janet standing before the tall Dainnan, twisting her apron in her hands as though troubled. The tiny bells intended to ward off wights tinkled like the shang unstorm. Amber light glowed on the western halves of the trees, casting blue shadows. Limned in sapphire and amber, these two made a pretty pair. Imrhien's heart lurched. She hesitated in the shadow of the trees, unwilling to disturb their conversation yet fearful of what it might portend. They did not look her way. On the breeze, their words were carried to her.

"I thank thee, sir, I thank thee with all my heart," Janet was saying earnestly.

"You must be brave and steadfast," said Thorn, looking down at her with a curious mixture of mockery and softness, "but I trow you are that."

"I shall try, sir, I shall. I cannot tell tha what this means to me!"

She curtsied awkwardly but sweetly.

The Dainnan reached into Janet's hair and pulled a silver piece from behind her ear. "An odd place to store money," he said.

"'Tis not mine, sir!"

"No?"

He tossed the coin in the air, and it vanished.

"Oh, sir! How did you do that?"

"Lose it? No matter—'tis easily found." He plucked a coin out of the air. And another coin, and another. He cupped both hands around the silver pieces.

"Blow on my fingers."

She did so; he opened them, and a white dove flew up into the rowans.

"How swiftly money flies from our grasp!" said Thorn.

The girl clapped her hands. "That's clever! Such pretty gramarye! Art tha wizard?"

"Call me wizard if you like."

With a smile he left her, striding off among the rowans. Janet came hurrying back to the cottage and caught sight of Imrhien.

"Oh, me lady, come indoors now, me dove. 'Tis getting cold, and fire's lit. I'll 'ave some supper on table soon—rose-hip tart, if tha does like it."

Janet would not hear of her guest lifting a finger to help. She sang as she busied herself in the larder, and when the table was laid and they were waiting for the men to arrive, she drew up a stool near to Imrhien and sat down, clapping her hands. Her eyes shone.

"Me lady, me dove, I 'ave tae tell somebody, I do, I'm fair burstin' with me tidin's. But I'll start from the beginnin'."

Then Silken Janet told a strange tale.

Many years ago, her father and mother had lived on a large estate outside Isenhammer. By the time they had been married twelve years, they had twelve sons. Despite the accumulation of expensive wizard's charms, no daughter had been born to them. A daughter was what they craved, however, and when at last Janet was born, their happiness knew no limits.

In those days, Isenhammer's most famous wizard sold a special water that, if used to bathe a child, promised lifelong protection against unseelie wights. It was most costly, but Janet's mother and father were determined to have it for her.

"Take this gold, all our savings, and go to the wizard's house," they said to the twelve boys. "Get the precious water of gramarye to bathe your sister." The boys went off together and bought the water, but on the way back they dropped the vessel containing it, and it broke. Fearing to return to their parents' house without the water, they loitered in the road, unable to decide what to do. Meanwhile their parents had been wondering where the boys were. Their father's annoyance increased, aggravated by the accusing cries of some rooks outside the window.

Evening closed in.

Trenowyn stood at the gate, looking up the road. He bade the servants to throw stones at the black birds and they flew off, but the sun was going down and still his sons had not returned.

"Where are those boys?" he raged. "How dare they delay like this! I wish they would all turn into rooks and fly away, curse them."

As soon as the words were out of his mouth he regretted them, but it was too late. Something wicked had been passing by in the road or perhaps lying in wait. There was a nickering in the hedgerows that might have been laughter, and twelve big black birds came flying toward him. The servant made to throw stones, but Trenowyn stopped him. The rooks alighted on the fence, gave a cry of sorrow, and winged away into the south. Janet's father knew then that they were his boys, transformed by his own fault.

Over the next few years Trenowyn hired every wizard of any repute, begging them to put forth their powers and locate his sons. All their attempts failed, and Trenowyn's fortune was soon whittled down to nought. His wife could never forgive him for his hasty ill-wrought curse, and in some oblique manner she let her blame spill over onto Janet, for whose benefit the boys had been bringing the water. She lost all joy in life, and after a time she went away, leaving both husband and young daughter. At last Trenowyn had to sell the large empty house. They came to live as common carters and spinners in Rosedale.

"When I set eyes on thane 'andsome Dainnan, I bethought to meself, Now, me dove, there's one who is wise. I might ask 'im if he knows 'ow tae get me brothers back. And so I did."

Thorn had told Janet to take her father's golden signet ring and to journey to the southern shores of Eldaraigne. There she must board a Seaship to take her across the straits to remote Rimany—for he knew of a mountain in that land, well out of the way of Rimanian Windship and Stormrider routes, and on that mountain, it was said, stood a castle wherein dwelled twelve black birds, served by a dwarf. Only within the castle walls could these birds become human, for an hour a day—then they must fly out the windows. Only if they walked out through the door could they stay in human shape, and only a maiden could unlock the door. So smooth and clear, so polished and gleaming, was this mountain that it seemed to be made of glass. This had earned it the name of Glass Mountain, but in truth it was a great frozen cliff of water, a glacier in the snowbound wastes of the southern land.

"'Ow should I get up a glass mountain?" I asked, and 'e told me I should go tae t' old Arysk carlin as dwells near the foot of it, and tell 'er Sir Thorn sent me, and she would give me a pair o' shoon, all made o' iron, with spikes, and with them I could climb up! Ain't that a wonder!

"When I reach the castle, I mun go carefully. Sir Thorn says the twelve birds will be quite wild now, after eighteen years. They will not recognize their sister and, thinking me a stranger, they be likely tae set upon me and tear me tae pieces.

"I mun go quietlike tae t' castle door, which will be locked. Then I mun blow three times intae t' key'ole and stick in t' little finger o' me left hand. Door will open, Sir Thorn says. 'Tis a finger-lock on that castle door, see, me dove. Once inside, I mun use me wits tae 'elp me brothers. By the ring they will know me, but if they see me before they see the ring, I will be killed." She waxed pensive. "Ah, but I wish tha could speak wi' me, lady me dove, an' tell me thane thoughts, for I never 'ad much company 'ere, an' I would so love a good chat. I be all keyed up now and ready to go. That cold land, Rimany, where the Arysk folk do dwell—Sir Thorn told me about it, an' I fain would fly there at once, if I 'ad wings.

"Sir Thorn said I mun go alone to t' Glass Mountain," she said to Imrhien, "and 'e knows the lore of the wights, knows all their rules. So I shall not tell me da'. I never 'ave deceived 'im afore, but if I told 'im, 'e would want to go by 'imself, or at least go with me. Meanin' no disrespect, if any were to go with me, I'd as lief it were Sir Thorn. Ain't never seen 'is like before." She sighed. "And never will again, I 'spect. Now there be a man tae make thane 'ead swim and thane 'eart bubble like a brook."

Trenowyn and Diarmid arrived with a brace of gorcocks. Later, Thorn came in and they sat down to dine together. It was a merry meal, even more so than breakfast; Janet's eyes were bright and rested often on Thorn. Her laughter joined frequently with his, until even dour Diarmid and her grim father had to smile, blaming it all on the strong mead. They sang many songs and told many tales. Imrhien could only listen and watch, but she made the best of it and tried not to feel shut out, alone in the dark.

The next morning, all were up early. In the treetops, magpies were warbling their strangely poignant bell-calls. Clouds rested on the heads of the hills. Janet, having milked the curly brown cow, sat astride its back and rode out to the meadow, singing at the top of her voice. Imrhien said good-bye to the cockerel, in handspeak. It looked at her with a glassy eye, surrounded by hens.

Janet and her father pressed all kinds of food and drink and spare clothing on their guests. "And if you would wait two days more," said Trenowyn, "you might ride with me when I drive to town. But there is not yet enough ore in the wagon to make the journey worthwhile, and if I take it now, the knockers will be angry."

"Good sir, your hospitality knows no bounds, but now that we are rested we are eager to be on our way. We can stay no longer," said the Dainnan.

Diarmid said, "Since I heard of the recruiting for the Dainnan at Isenhammer, all my thought is there."

Imrhien merely nodded.

"Then," Trenowyn said, "good speed, and the fruit of errantry and valor to you in the mouths of poets forever."

"And to you," returned Thorn.

Morning mists still lay upon the hilltops, and dew sparkled on the grass. Leaves, dark and glossy, dripped liquid silver. Glittering cobwebs laced the garden-hedge.

By the gate in the lane they took their leave of Silken Janet and her father. Their breath turned to vapor on the biting air. Overhead, the goshawk swooped and gave a piercing cry that startled all the magpies. They rose out of the trees like smoke. In reply, the cock crowed defiantly from behind the cottage. The sound rang between the hills. Over Woody Hill a Windship sailed, an alabaster leaf in a wide, cloud-daubed sky tinted lilac and mauve.

The lane became a track that took them winding up the hill and over it. They stopped on the brow for one last look back at the two small figures waving by the gate, then stepped forward. Briar Cottage disappeared from view.

Like fish's scales, mosaics of cloud rippled across a turquoise sky. The last of Autumn's leaves rained like shreds of opalescent silk to become part of the mold underfoot, for it was the first day of Nethilmis, the cloud-month, and Winter had already begun to settle her chilly mantle over the land. Through undulating, lightly wooded country, the travelers followed the track; over little wooden bridges and around the skirts of hills, with Errantry following above, Thorn singing, and Diarmid whistling like a blackbird. The Ertishman's wounds had healed with remarkable speed—all that remained were the lightning marks on his hands and a small white scar on his brow.

They went with good speed and spent the night in a deserted shepherd's hut, made cozy with beds of dry fern and a blaze in the fireplace. Thorn's cloak remained buried somewhere in the mines along with his other gear that had been lost, but Janet had provided other cloaks, thick and tightly woven, which proved almost as warm. A shang wind passed through the region during the dark hours. Imrhien half woke to its tingling spell.

On the following day the track met the Road, but it was not the Road as they had left it. Last seen, it had been overshadowed by trees, hemmed in by wight-haunted forest. Now it was open and clear, rolling away over gentle slopes under a fleecy sky. No traffic could be seen in either direction. They struck out, Thorn setting a cracking pace, impatient to make up for lost time. Late in the day, they found shelter in a shallow cave under a hill and made camp.

In the afternoon of the third day, with the sun a bonfire in a smoky haze, they came to the King's Cross. Here the Road swept around a central square, from which it branched in four directions. In the middle of this square squatted a massive plinth from which a stone column thrust skyward. It was topped by a statue of a horseman wearing a crowned helm, facing west to Caermelor. His chiseled tabard was emblazoned with the crowned lion device of the Royal House of D'Armancourt. On the pillar's base were engraved the distances to towns and cities in all four directions.

The Crown and Lyon Inn stood at the northeast corner of the crossroads. Its half-timbered upper stories, high pinnacled gables, and numerous chimneys commanded a good view of the countryside and the junction. On the topmost gable, a weather-cock swung to the west. As darkness fell, lamplight streamed out between the windows' mullions.

"In Gilvaris Tarv the mercenaries speak of this establishment," said Diarmid. "It has long been haunted by a buttery wight, one of those creatures that has power over all ill-gotten gains and dishonestly prepared food. Years ago the wight was thriving. Word got about. Folk started to talk about the old taverner's deceitful ways and how he watered the ale and served dog-pie. The wight grew fat and bloated. Patronage declined, until at last the old taverner departed. The new landlord now keeps a good, clean table, and the Crown and Lyon's reputation is restored. Here we should break our journey one last time before we part."

"I would not tarry, but for the sake of friendship," replied the Dainnan. At these words, great desolation overcame Imrhien, but resolutely she set her shoulders, pulled her taltry well forward, and entered the common room of the inn with her companions.

It was not crowded, but such occupants as it possessed were milling around a table where a speaker was holding forth at length, captivating his audience. It was impossible to see him through the press. The three newcomers sat at an unoccupied table near the window and ordered ale. Imrhien kept her face in shadow. At the next table, two rustics were involved in an eccentric exchange; a yokel was stubbornly trying to impress his sweetheart's father.

"Sir, might I buy ye a double john-barleycorn?"

"Nay, thank ye. Naught for me."

"What about a single?"

"No, gramercie—naught."

"Ale? Dandelion wine? Lemon-water?"

"No, I'd as fain not."

"What about a posset?"

"Nay, for certain."

"Ptisan? Gruel?"

A shake of the head.

"Well then, a triple grape-brandy?"

"Oh, aye, that I will."

When the serving-girl returned, Diarmid said, "They say these premises are troubled by a buttery wight."

For the first time, the girl noticed the Dainnan, lit by the smoky lamplight. She gasped, almost dropping her laden tray. Her hands trembled as she set frothing tankards on the table. Their lids were missing, the hinges broken; they had been well used over the years. Recovering her composure, she answered proudly, "Good gentlemen, the Crown and Lyon has the leanest, most hollow-bellied buttery wight of any tavern in the five kingdoms—too weak to lift even an empty cup." She was about to elaborate further when Diarmid interrupted:

"Your customer over there has an attentive audience. Pray, what draws them so?"

"Why, sir," she said with a polite bob, a dimpled smile, and a sidelong glance at the Dainnan from beneath her lashes, "he and a party of other folk have just come in today. Survivors of an attack on a road-caravan some while back—they had been given up for lost—"

With a crash, Diarmid's bench toppled backward as he jumped up. White-faced, he sprang toward the crowds, elbowing them apart. The serving-girl stood openmouthed. Curses flew from the disturbed knot of patrons, then a stream of Ertish from Diarmid, and suddenly he was calling out Muirne's name over and over, laughing and weeping and clasping his sister in his arms, she shrieking and crying as she clung to him. Imrhien tried to push through to join them, but there were too many broad backs and hefty shoulders in the way. She returned to the table.

Thorn remained calmly seated, his elbow resting on the rough planks of the table. He signed, <<A happy meeting.>>

When the chaos had died down somewhat, Diarmid extricated Muirne from the melee and introduced her to Thorn. Next, all gentlemanly reserve cast to the winds, the Ertishman felt driven to introduce himself to all and sundry, in great excitement, and to call for ale to be served to everyone in the house. Now that the Dainnan's presence had been discovered, Thorn became the focus of attention. Dainnan uniform commanded the respect and admiration of all citizens, and they looked upon him as though he had stepped out of legend. The unexpected presence of such an honorable personage in such comely form had disconcerted the serving-girl exceedingly, and she was not alone in her awe.

Muirne beckoned Imrhien away. She was glad to follow. Many folk had commented on her looks, in case she was unaware of them, and she had withdrawn deeper into her taltry.

"I am so glad to see you, *chehrna,*" Muirne said as the two embraced. "I thought you were lost."

<<Muirne>>—the sign for Muirne's name was the sign for a sparrow—<<my dear friend. How came you here?>>

"After the attack, when we were all separated, I could not find you and Diarmid, but I came upon a band of stalwarts from our caravan and some other women, and then a few more caravaners found us. Fifteen we were, in all. We salvaged a wagon and caught some of the strayed horses to pull it, and—oh, we had many adventures along the Road, too many to tell in one sitting, but we got through, and only today we came here. I still cannot believe it! But come—join the revelry, dear Imrhien."

Imrhien shook her head—it was not pleasant to be among staring strangers. Thorn, surrounded by awed onlookers competing to buy ale for him, was regaling them with tales of adventure. Diarmid had already ordered a second round and, tankard in hand, was talking earnestly with other men who had got safely through from Chambord's Caravan. When asked about the terrible scenes they had witnessed after the attack, some looked grim, others turned their faces away. They would not speak of it and were glad enough of pleasant diversion. When Diarmid began his own heroic tales, they all clapped him on the shoulder and told him what a good fellow he was, especially when he called for their tankards to be filled a third time. Some more travelers came in, and there ensued a general party, which looked as though it would last well into the night. In the wide hearth, a fire bristled.

<<I will retire early to my chamber—I am told it is ready.>>

"Oh, but you will come with us in the morning won't you? Diarmid is accompanying us on the wagon. We are going to Isenhammer together. I am going to enlist in the King-Emperor's army as an archer, and Diarmid shall try for the Dainnan. Most of the other survivors came here to enlist, too—those that did not will be going to Caermelor on foot. Where is the Dainnan who was with you?" asked Muirne. "The one introduced to me as Thorn? Diarmid speaks of him highly. There he is, I would like to thank him. *Obban tesh,* but he is handsome—" She broke off at the sound of her name being shouted across the room.

"I must go. Diarmid calls. Sleep well, dear friend, since that is your wish—I shall greet you again in the morning." A knot of people opened up to receive Muirne and closed behind her again. Thorn was by now seated on a table, the center of a sea of attentive faces. They hung on his every word. The tavern-girls blushed each time they glanced in his direction.

Guided by the girl who had first served them, Imrhien stole upstairs and went to bed. She lay for hours staring at the warped rafters, wondering about White Down Rory and listening to the songs and laughter and hubbub from below. She could clearly hear what was going on in the common room. A customer had produced a puzzle-cup in the form of a double vessel, one bowl forming the inverted base of the other, which swiveled between brackets. Several uninitiated applicants were invited to drink from it and predictably drenched themselves, to the entertainment of the onlookers. The jollity increased when someone else brought out a three-merry-boys fuddling cup, a trio of mugs whose bodies were joined and whose handles were interlinked so that they had to be emptied simultaneously to prevent spillage. With the roistering in full swing, the patrons were ordering ale and cider in measures: pottles, noggins, tappit hens, mutchkins, and thirdendales. Rowdy song arose.

Later, oddly, the talk quietened. More sobering tidings were discussed. Hordes of unseelie things had been passing through in the night, and these days the inn's doors were always heavily barred with iron at sunset.

As Imrhien listened, half dozing in her bed, ever and anon a tall, lithe shadow moved across her thoughts. The shutters of her window blew open in the breeze. A big black bird flapped out of the night, landed on the sill, and flew away again. When she went to fasten the shutters properly, there was no sign of it.

In the morning, the wagon stood ready and packed on the cobblestones of the inn-yard. Muirne's companions were climbing aboard. A stableboy went running, an ostler called out orders. Sparrows perched on posts, watching for crumbs. A green-varnished saurian crouched atop a rain-butt, its spiny tail curling down like a hook. Behind a pile of bags and barrels, someone was whistling. The yard was busy with preparations for travel.

Thorn stood by a side-door. The innkeeper, rotund, rubicund, and balding—as seemed almost obligatory for those who followed his trade—and swathed in a large smirched apron, stood before him, bowing repeatedly. The man's voice carried across the yard.

"'Tis an honor, sir, an honor, I assure you, sir. Please accept the night's lodging and all expenses on the house, sir, if it please you, and all the very best to you and those of your fellowship. We don't see many of Roxburgh's knights here, no indeed, sir, even being as we are so close to the Royal City, so to speak—but they're always welcome at any time, at the Crown and Lyon." He pressed gifts of food on the Dainnan, who waved most of them away, laughing. Many a covert glance was being cast his way from the inn-staff and the few guests moving about. They watched him with awe, not openly but from a respectful distance, feigning preoccupation with their business.

Imrhien had paid Diarmid's bill. To his consternation, he had recalled too late that his money-pouch lay submerged somewhere in the meres of Mirrinor, and in the heat of the moment he had landed himself badly in debt. Imrhien still retained her own pouch with its three jewels concealed under Janet's clothes, but she paid the innkeeper with one of the sovereigns that had remained secure in the linings of her old, ruined traveling outfit—for which she received seven shillings and sixpence change. The Ertishman's discomfiture knew no bounds—to be indebted to a girl was more than he could bear—but Muirne's money too was scarce, and there was nothing else for it.

"To you I owe my life and now my purse," he said awkwardly to Imrhien. "I shall repay you, I promise, just as soon as I receive my first wages."

<<It was nothing. You have been a staunch friend and ally. I am in your debt.>>

"Will you not accompany us to Isenhammer?" Muirne pleaded.

<<I go to the carlin.>>

"I will escort you, then," Diarmid said heavily. "It is not safe to travel alone, especially for a woman."

"Go your way to Isenhammer, Captain Bruadair," interrupted a musical voice. "The road to White Down Rory is fair in all seasons, and I would fain take a stroll along it." Thorn had crossed the yard to where they stood.

Diarmid's halfhearted protestations were overruled. He looked constantly toward his sister and the loaded wagon bound for Isenhammer. Plainly he was relieved to be absolved of his perceived duty toward Imrhien.

"Then, I shall go with Muirne," he said at last. "My lady, prithee send word to let us know where you are staying, and I shall have repayment delivered to you with all speed." Now that he was taking his leave, he spoke with painful courtesy, unable to meet Imrhien's eyes. "I . . . you have been kind . . ." His words trailed away. Turning to the Dainnan, the Ertishman lifted his head.

"My lord," Diarmid said, clearly moved, "if I am successful in assaying for the Brotherhood, then I would have only one boon in the world left to wish for—that I might do my duty under your command."

"That may yet come to pass," said Thorn. Abruptly, Diarmid dropped down on one knee and bent his head. After a moment, as if bestowing on him some title of honor, Thorn touched him on the shoulder.

"Rise, brave captain, and good speed. Fare well."

Diarmid stood up. "Fare well, both my companions on the Road," he said. "May we meet soon."

He bowed deeply to them both, then, as an afterthought, suddenly enveloped Imrhien in a swift embrace and jumped up onto the wagon. Imrhien's hands danced urgently.

<<Good speed, Diarmid; good speed, Muirne. Our meeting is short-lived—may we meet again soon, and for longer!>>

Diarmid reached down and helped his sister climb aboard. Then Imrhien tossed up a wrapped package to them. It contained the fire-red ruby. If her friends should not find success in Isenhammmer, at the least they would not have to beg on the streets. Before they had a chance to find out what the parcel contained or even call out their thanks, the driver gave a shout. With the crack of a whip, a clatter of hooves, and a rattle of iron wheels, the wagon moved out through the archway, turned into the road, and bowled away.

It had rained during the night. Thorn's and Imrhien's boots swished through wet leaves. Lacking polish, Imrhien's allowed water in. Soon her feet were drenched. The grasses by the verge, tall and cream-colored amid new blades of pale wine-green, bowed their heads in obeisance to the faintest caress of air. Thrushes trilled. Errantry soared overhead, scattering the songbirds, then swooped to alight on the Dainnan's shoulder. He raised his feathers, shook them into place, opened his hooked beak in silent commentary, and snapped it shut.

Sunlight brushed Imrhien's skin with warm flakes, although the breeze was knife-sharp and bitter. Stamped against a blue enamel sky, the first wattle-blooms of Winter bubbled in bright, soft gilt on the trees and powdered the distance with gold-dust. Oak-leaves yet clung to ancient groves by the wayside, in masses of bronze and saffron that could not outshine the wattles' glory. But Imrhien might as well have been walking in a black tunnel under Doundelding, being blind to all save the path before her feet and deaf to all save the voice of he who walked beside her.

The road to White Down Rory ran up and down, through trees that parted occasionally to allow glimpses of rolling meadows and wooded slopes beyond and secret, misty dells threaded by streams glimmering like electrum. The way rolled down into one of these dells and ran beside a willow-lined beck that widened into a pool. Dragonflies flickered across its surface—at least, they appeared to be dragonflies until one looked closely. In fact, the forms between those shimmering double vanes were tiny folk, much smaller than siofra. Toadlike waterleapers scattered into the reeds at the approach of the intruders, flapping their fans of wings. When fully grown they would be huge and quite terrible, if they survived to adulthood.

There the travelers stopped to rest, and from a wallet given him by the innkeeper Thorn produced great doorsteps of bread and thick slices of ham. Her heart sickened by the imminence of parting, Imrhien could not bring herself to eat. Presently he put the food away without sampling it himself.

All the way, as they walked side by side, he had laughed and sung and they had made jokes in handspeak, and she had taught him the sign for "shang." Travelers coming the other way on horseback had hailed them blithely, without pausing, and he had called a greeting in answer. Now he fell quiet, meditative, watching the still pool with its reflections of bare willow-withes and dormant cloudlets. The goshawk perched on a branch and closed his mad orange eyes.

Where the stream entered the pool, Imrhien found smooth, water-worn stones, flat ones, and skipped one across the water to break Thorn's reverie. He looked up with his flash of a smile like a piercing blow to the heart and came, surefooted as a lynx, to the stream.

"How many times can you skip a stone?"

Having practiced with Sianadh at Waterstair, she had almost perfected the subtle flick of the wrist. After a few tries, she achieved an eight. Thorn spun a few pebbles that bounded high, then sank.

<<You must do better!>>

He nodded and gathered another handful.

Sianadh had been a great stone-skipper at Waterstair—the champion (so he said) of his village in Finvarna—but she had never seen him skip one more than a dozen times. Thorn's missiles now jumped twice seven, thrice seven, thrice nine times, and though she tried she could not match that and flung away her last pebble, half-vexed, half-admiring. A haggard hand shot up out of the water, caught it, and slowly withdrew. The pool was inhabited.

Thorn juggled pebbles and made them vanish and reappear.

<<Teach me!>>

He let the stones fall. They rolled on the turf.

<<I would, but there is no time. The day wears away. We must go on.>>

The road was rutted and strewn with fallen leaves. The wheel-ruts were many, and the leaves looked as though they had been disturbed recently, as if many travelers had passed to and from White Down Rory. They met a wagonload of folk coming from the village, then others on foot, staves in hand.

The sun wheeled its way to a low Winter apogee behind the clouds, which thinned and drifted toward the north, leaving only the white scuff-marks of their passing. Now light sharpened each feature of the landscape, imbuing them with every tint of green, every shade of somber gold. Near at hand, the leaves were etched by their own shadows; far off, pastel chalk-dust overlaid the dozing hills.

Long shadows were stretching to the east when at last the travelers came over the crest of a hill and saw below, down among the folds of the hills, the roofs of a village. The road ran swiftly down. Thorn turned his compelling eyes on Imrhien.

"To which house are you bound?"

Ethlinn had given clear directions.

<<A track leads to the right, at the bottom of this hill. It skirts the village proper, passing over a bridge.>>

Imrhien guessed the Dainnan was impatient to be on the road to Caermelor. He had accompanied her this far out of courtesy—one of the precepts of the Dainnan code was respect for women. But now, within sight of the village, there was no need for her to delay him any longer. Besides, if he continued by her side, there would come a time when her growing distress would well up and show itself.

The road entered a thick clump of trees at the bottom of the hill. It was here that the track branched off. Just past the intersection, it turned suddenly and vanished from sight behind the grove.

<<Leave me here. Turn back for Caermelor. I have not far to travel now. I shall be safe enough.>>

"As you wish."

Imrhien turned away from Thorn and strove to master her thoughts. Her hands were shaking violently. She heard him step close beside her shoulder, felt his heavy cloak blow against her skirts.

"Change your path. There is yet time."

He was a dark flame. His nearness was too near—she must die of it.

"Come with me to the court."

But she started, as if stung. Go with him among the courtiers? To be made a laughingstock or, worse, to see him made one? To have to bear the pitying glances and the whispered asides? Yet there was that in the intense gaze he bent upon her that might have melted quartz-crystal to milk. Avoiding it, fixing her eyes on the ground, she shook her head.

<<No.>>

"Are you sure of this, in your heart?"

A nod.

Imrhien noticed a small thistle was growing between two stones in the road, just beside the toe of her boot. Its leaves were dagged like the sleeves of aristocrats. She forced her thoughts to dwell on that thistle.

"Then we must part," she heard Thorn say, "for my path lies to the west. Yet methinks it may be long ere we meet again, *caileagh faoileag*."

Silence. She dared not raise her head, for he would not fail to observe that she stared with the eyes of madness. Dimly, from far above, the plangent cry of the goshawk was borne down the breeze.

"I must needs ask you—a matter has been troubling me." On the brink of a question, he hesitated, sighed. "No. It is not possible. But there is something about you, I thought . . ."

He extricated something from beneath his tunic. "This, a gift for you."

It was the red crystal phial of Dragon's Blood that he dropped into her palm. Tears pricked behind her eye sockets. What had she to give him in return? To gift him with one of her jewels seemed paltry and somehow discourteous.

"May I have something of yours?"

<<Anything.>>

Three sudden, sharp pains. Her hand flew to her head. A trio of golden hairs lay in Thorn's palm. "These I shall take as a token," he said, twisting the fine filaments together and rolling them into a circle. "Safely I shall keep them." He placed the ring on a finger of his left hand. "And now, since the phial was nothing, what would you truly ask of me?"

The thought flashed into Imrhien's head, unbidden: *A kiss*. She hoped he had not read it on her countenance. In her confusion, her hands faltered, bungling the signs.

<<I would like to tell you with my voice that I wish for your blessing on my enterprise. I go now to the carlin who dwells here in the hope that she might heal my face—restore something of what I was—I ask your good wishes for this undertaking.>>

He nodded and stood a moment as if pondering. Then swiftly, before she understood what was happening, he stepped forward, placed one hand gently under her chin and the other behind her head, and kissed her full on the mouth.

Only twice before had there been direct contact between them. Now, bolts like the Beithir's, only sweet as ecstasy, went through and through from head to toe, over and over, until she thought she must die; then he released her quickly and strode away up the hill, and she fled, stumbling, weeping, through the trees.

Salt tears coursed down Imrhien's face, stinging. The footpath in its ribbed tunnel became blurred, swimming in grief and loss. She ran faster, to outstrip sorrow, to leave it behind, but always it followed close at her heels. Away and around and down, over the bridge and up and around again, now slicing between high hedges or under stone walls, now passing across open turf, now through an oak coppice, now beneath the spreading boughs of chestnuts, black in the fading light. Eerie, slitted eyes glared from among tree-roots and winked out. Sudden laughter rattled in outlandish throats. Things scurried suddenly, unseen. A white hare bounded across the path. Something hooted.

Ahead, warm yellow lamplight spilled from two windows and filtered through the trees, growing stronger as she neared it. Her face drenched with salt water, she found herself at a cottage door. The tears would not stop, nor did she care anymore, although they made her flesh itch intolerably. Distraught, she thumped her fists on the portal and slumped against it, dragging in breath with hoarse gasps.

When the door opened she half fell inside, was caught by strong arms, and looked into the face of an old woman. The beldame held her shoulders in an iron grip for a few moments. Her left eye bestowed on the unexpected visitor a searching stare. There was a hollow where her right eye had been. The eyelids were crudely stitched shut. Above the eyes, a painted blue disk on the forehead.

"Great ganders, what's all this?" exclaimed the woman. "Govern yourself, colleen!"

Shudders racked Imrhien's body. The crone led her to a straw pallet and bade her lie down.

"It will be a cure for the paradox you're wanting, no doubt. That much I can see. I shall do what can be done. But first, drink this. 'Twill calm you."

Imrhien gulped the liquid. The flavor was unusual but not unpleasant, reminiscent of riverside herbs nodding in the rain—cool and fragrant. Tranquillity flowed along her veins. She lay quiescent. Only her face still itched, and she tore at it idly with her fingernails.

"Stop that. It is for me to see to." The carlin drew Imrhien's hand away, firmly. Placing her own sinewy hands on her patient's face, she hesitated, then drew a sharp breath.

The girl cared little. An irresistible desire to sleep had surged over her, and she abandoned herself to it, closing her eyes and drifting. The carlin's voice seemed to issue from far away:

"Very well, sleep now. That will give me time to mix up the mud."

Then sleep's dark current carried her away under the green herbs that overgrew its banks, in a ceaseless rain.

* * *

*There was a face, once. It had been the first one. But it was more than a face—it was comfort to assuage yearning, satiation to defeat hunger, warmth to drive out chill, cool to calm heat, movement instead of stillness, company against loneliness, sweet sounds to alleviate silence, peace to replace distress. Two eyes, a nose, a mouth—there was nothing else about it—no characteristics of age or gender, yet it was the one face to be recognized above all. It meant the source of life.*

*Its disappearance had precipitated a void that sucked the light out of that part of existence.*

*The second face had begun like the first, as beloved, yet differently. It had evolved, over time, and become the countenance of a man of wisdom and kindness, the corners of his eyes crinkled with good humor. Always he had been there, smiling down from a great height: solid, dependable.*

*The third face had altered, too. It had made its appearance on the edges of the lacuna left by the first, beginning as no more than a blur, an irritation to be dismissed, but evolving to be the sweet visage of a little child: precious, cherished, a friend and companion, a marigold. Apple-blossoms reached over the child's head. Petals drifted like snow. Small green fruits swelled and ripened on the boughs, like red lamps, and were gathered . . .*

*Woman, man, child. A dream?*

*A churning of thoughts, released by sleep, or, at last, some memory?*

For as long as she could remember, the rain had been drumming its impatient fingers. Seemingly it had done so since time itself had begun—but no, it had been raining only during the night, and now the night was over.

Imrhien was lying on a straw pallet among blankets of white wool. There were bunches of herbs hanging from the rafters, a mortar and pestle on a low table, and a boy kneeling, building up the fire. He finished his task, glanced at her, and moved away. She raised herself on one elbow and saw, through narrow slits, Maeve One-Eye sitting in a chair, watching her. The beldame's shaggy bush of hair stuck out in all directions like spikes of frost.

Imrhien's face felt odd—very peculiar indeed. It still itched, but not unbearably, and it tingled. Her cheeks were numb to the touch, and stiff; her eyes would not open properly.

"You will not feel a thing under all that mud," observed the carlin. "I put it on you while you slept. That way, I knew you would, at least, not wriggle about. It is caked on thickly, and it has dried—do not try to smile—you will find it impossible. All the way from Mount Baelfire it is, the blue mud—that's the only place in Erith you can get the really good stuff. You look a terrible sight, I can tell you. Once it has soaked right into the poisoned areas, the mud will flake off of its own accord and take some of the bad flesh with it. How long *that* will take, I cannot say—it varies with each case. It might be one day or three, or ten, but you will not be able to eat while it is on, so I hope you are not hungry. Look in the glass, over there by the window."

Light-headed, Imrhien stood up. Immediately the itching returned with redoubled force. The carlin's long mirror stood by the window. It was made of glass and silver, the frame wrought in the shapes of twining lilies and watermaidens with flowing hair. The surface gleamed like watersheen—an eldritch-seeming looking-glass.

Imrhien viewed in it her reflection, tall and slender, dressed in the country garb of Rosedale. Her long hair cascaded free of the wimple, in ringlets and straight tresses, like skeins of tangled silk, framing a mask with two slits for eyeholes. But the irritation of salt tears under the hardened mud was too much to bear, and she raised her hands to her face. Somehow she must find relief. Her fingers worried at the mud-mask, and it came off in her hands.

It lifted off in one entire piece.

Beneath it, the face.

Ah, the face. The lips formed such a perfect, rosy bow, as though painted upon the smooth, creamy peach of the skin. Clean-molded lines, high cheekbones, a softly rounded chin and small, neat nose, the soft curve of the cheek, arched eyebrows, the great jewels of eyes, fringed with their sweeping lashes—this was the face looking back at Imrhien from the glass.

Scarcely knowing what was happening, not daring to believe,

she touched that face with her fingertips, explored it all over, gently, and it did not disappear; only, color like roses flooded it, and the light of morning sprang into the eyes. The lump that had been sticking in her throat ever since she awoke expanded painfully now.

Was it beauty or homeliness that gazed out of the mirror's frame? She could not tell, for aesthetic perception is subjective, and she habitually assumed the source of her own reflection was repugnant. Only, she knew that it was symmetrical and thus more acceptable than before. More acceptable—that was all she had hoped for.

By her side, Maeve One-Eye gently took the hollow mask of mud from the girl's frozen hand. The carlin had been gazing in silence. She squinted, as if she perceived a bright light that hurt her eye or a sight she would rather not have seen.

Now she spoke.

"Well. This has worked a wonder. See you, lass? See you?"

The lump broke apart. A force welled up and gushed forth.

"Yes. I see," softly Imrhien said.

# Some Ertish Words and Phrases

*alainn capall dubh:* beautiful black horse
*Ambarcaim!:* Look there!
*chebrna:* dear damsel
*clabmor:* terrible, tragic.
*cova donni:* blind shotman
*darubshie:* self-destructive fool
*doch:* damned
*hreorig:* ruinous
*inna shai tithen elion:* we have lived the days
*lorraly:* in the natural order
*manscatba:* wicked ravager
*mo:* my
*mo gaidair:* my friend
*mo reigh:* my pretty
*mor scathach:* an unseelie rider that sticks to the shoulders of its prey, becoming as heavy as stone, and rides the life out of it
*obban tesh:* an expletive
*oghi ban Callanan:* Callanan's eyes
*pishogue:* glamour; a spell of illusion
*samrin:* milksop
*Sciobtha!:* Hasten!
*scothy:* mad, crazy
*sgorrama:* stupid (noun or adjective)
*shera sethge:* poor, unfortunate
*skeerda:* bad/devious person
*Ta ocras orm! Tu faighim moran bia!:* I am hungry! I need a lot of food!
*tambalai:* beloved

*tien eun:* little one
*uhta:* the hour before sunrise
*uraguhne:* despicable scum

**A Short Pronunciation Guide**

Baobansith: *baavan shee*
Buggane: *bug airn*
Cuachag: *cooachack*
Each Uisge: *ech-ooshkya*
Fuath: *foo-a*
Gwragedd Annwn: *gwrageth anoon*

# Acknowledgments

Much research has gone into portraying wights as "accurately" as possible—that is, true to their traditional folk origins. It has been a joy to rescue the early written records of these traditions from the cobwebby darkness of out-of-printness. By weaving them into my tale, I hope to bring them into the light of the twenty-first century, as they deserve.

**The Each Uisge and the Water-Bull:** Inspired by *Popular Tales of the West Highlands,* by J. F. Campbell. Alexander, Gardner, Paisley and London, 1890–93.

**The Duergar:** Inspired by *Folk-Tales of the North Country,* by F. Grice. Nelson, London and Edinburgh, 1944.

**The Beulach Beast:** Inspired by "The Biasd Bheulach" in *Witchcraft and the Second Sight in the Highlands and Islands of Scotland,* by J. G. Campbell. MacLehose, Glasgow, 1902.

**The Buggane:** Inspired by *A Manx Scrapbook,* by Walter Gill. Arrowsmith, London, 1929.

**The Trathley Kow:** Inspired by "The Hedley Kow" in *Folk-Lore of the Northern Counties,* by William Henderson. Folk-Lore Society, London, 1879.

**Cobie Will and the Sleepers:** Inspired by *The Denham Tracts,* edited by James Hardy. Folk-Lore Society, London, 1892.

**The Lake Cow:**

*Come thou, Einion's Yellow One,*
*Stray-horns, The Parti-coloured Lake Cow,*
*And the hornless Dodin,*
*Arise, come home.*

Sourced from *The Four Ancient Books of Wales,* by W. F. Skene. Edmonston & Douglas, Edinburgh, 1868.

**The Pipes Leantainn:** Inspired by "The Friar and the Boy," by W. Carew Hazlitt, in *National Tales and Legends,* London, 1899.

**The Trow-Wives and the Swatts:** Inspired by "The Trows' Revenge" in *County Folk-Lore III: Orkney and Shetland,* edited by G. F. Black. Folk-Lore Society, London, 1903.

**The Trows and the Trow-Stock:** Inspired by "Da Trow's Bundle" in *County Folk-Lore III: Orkney and Shetland,* edited by G. F. Black. Folk-Lore Society, London, 1903.

**The Spinner with the Long Lip:** Inspired by *Folk-Lore of the Northern Counties,* by William Henderson. Folk-Lore Society, London, 1879.

**The Trow-Boy Who Stole Silver:** Inspired by *Shetland Traditional Lore,* by Jessie M. E. Saxby, Norwich, London, 1888. The trow-boy's lament, ". . . when I be allowed to veesit Trowland for a peerie start—but a' I gets is eggshells tae crack atween me teeth followed by a lunder upon me lugs and a wallop ower me back. So I wanders *wanless,* poor object!" is quoted from this source.

**The Trow-Wife's Song:**

*Hey! co Cuttie an' ho! co Cuttie,*
*An' wha'ill dance wi' me? co Cuttie.*

*She luked aboot an' saw naebody,*
*Sae I'll henk awa' mesel', co Cuttie.*

Quoted from page 39 of *Shetland Folk Lore,* by John Spence. Johnson & Grieg, Lerwick, 1899.